P9-DDD-825

MEET ME AT MIDNIGHT

ALSO BY JESSICA PENNINGTON

Love Songs & Other Lies
When Summer Ends

MEET ME
AT
Midnight

Jessica Pennington

TOR TEEN

A TOM DOHERTY ASSOCIATES BOOK

New York

MEET ME AT MIDNIGHT

Copyright © 2020 by Jessica Pennington

A Tor Teen Book
Published by Tom Doherty Associates
120 Broadway
New York, NY 10271

www.tor-forge.com

Tor® is a registered trademark of Macmillan Publishing Group, LLC.

The Library of Congress Cataloging-in-Publication Data is available
upon request.

ISBN 978–1–250–18766–6 (hardcover)
ISBN 978–1–250–18765–9 (ebook)

Our books may be purchased in bulk for promotional,
educational, or business use. Please contact your local bookseller
or the Macmillan Corporate and Premium Sales Department
at 1–800–221–7945, extension 5442, or by email at
MacmillanSpecialMarkets@macmillan.com.

First Edition: April 2020

Printed in the United States of America

0 9 8 7 6 5 4 3 2 1

To Platte Lake and the twenty-some years (and counting) of summer memories that made this book possible

MEET ME AT MIDNIGHT

DAY 1

Sidney

Here's the problem with knowing someone since you were ten and vacationing with them since you were thirteen: they know way too much. They've seen things. The neurotic things you only did once. The embarrassing things you wish you could forget. Usually it's people we love who know these seemingly harmless things. But when it's someone you hate . . . those tiny bits of your past become the ultimate ammunition. And with the right arsenal, it's war. The war I call summer lasts exactly fifty-six days. It doesn't end, and it has only two sides: mine and *his*.

Asher Marin doesn't let me live anything down, and he doesn't let me forget. I don't let him, either. It's why we're both darting out of our cabins at 8:37 a.m. on the first full day of summer vacation. Why I sat by the window, barely able to make out the shadow of him at his, as I ate my bowl of cereal this morning, twitching out of my seat with every flutter of activity from the kitchen window that mirrors mine. It's our sixth year vacationing together in twin houses that sit atop a little hill overlooking a sprawling inland lake. And saying that we know each other doesn't even begin to describe the two of us. To survive summer, I don't just have to *know* Asher, I have to get *in his brain*.

"Your hair looks pretty today," he says. I'm walking out of my door as he walks out of his, my cereal bowl discarded so quickly I'm not positive it isn't in shards in the old metal sink. We're mirror images starting our days, as we each make a hard turn onto the concrete sidewalks that run alongside our houses—toward the deck that juts out from the hill rising up from the shoreline. He's lazily smiling, and someone who didn't know him—didn't know *us*—would think he was being sweet. Complimenting me. But he's not smiling, he's smirking. I don't have to look at his face to know; I can hear it in his voice. In the way the word *hair* comes out on the whisper of a laugh he didn't allow himself to let loose.

Because Asher's in *my* brain, too. He knows I hate when my curls get like this, wild and untamable in the summer humidity. When I was younger I'd try to straighten them every morning, like I did for school, and as the day went on and the Michigan air took its toll, the curls would rise up around my face, consuming me like my very own auburn wildfire. When I was sixteen, I finally decided it wasn't worth the effort. Wasn't worth the snickers throughout the day, the sideways glances from him as my hair revealed its true form after a day of swimming. Who was I trying to impress, anyway? I like how easy it's made my daily routine for two months out of the year.

My hand is going to my hair without thinking, but I catch myself, twisting a few pieces in my fingers and squinting my eyes at him, still coming down the little sidewalk, keeping pace with me. I speed up, and he matches me.

"I love that shirt," I say, my voice level and innocent as I eye the vintage green T-shirt that stretches across his chest. "Did Jordan pick that out?" I say *Jordan* the way he says *hair*. Like it's a weapon shooting off of my tongue.

"Jordan and I broke up." His voice matches mine, friendly and light. We're maybe thirty feet from where our paths will merge into one, and I squeeze the towel rolled tight under my arm. My pulse speeds up, adrenaline pooling in my veins as we partake in the world's slowest two-person sprint. We're just a couple of pumping arms short of looking like old people powering through the mall in their bright-white sneakers. My flip-flops slap against the stone.

"Oh, did you?" My voice drips with mock innocence. Asher and Jordan broke up about a month ago. I overheard my mom talking to his in one of their weekly phone calls leading up to our joint family vacation. *Poor baby, such a sweet girl, blah blah blah.*

"Stalking me?" he says, his voice taking a teasing edge.

It *sounds* a little stalkerish that I know about Jordan. But knowledge is power, and I can't help that my mom insists on updating me about Asher every time she talks to Sylvie. As if *I* didn't have the means to contact Asher a million different ways, if I wanted to. As if we're friends and I need to know what he's doing the ten months out of the year I'm *not* being subjected to his presence. "You wish." I roll my eyes, even though he can't see them. "You must have been distraught, if your mom had to call mine to talk about it."

"Devastated," he says dramatically, not sounding it at all.

"Lucky girl," I say.

"How's . . . oh, what's his name . . . ?" In my periphery I can see his hand slap against his thigh like he's trying to recall some lost bit of information. We try so hard, the two of us. We smile and tease and torture—the kind of animals that like to play with their food before they kill it.

I cringe, knowing what's coming next. I shouldn't have pushed him on Jordan, I should have just left it alone. *But that smug face of his.* I set myself up for this.

"Taylor . . . ? David . . . ? Evan . . . ?" There's a long pause and I inwardly cringe. "Or was it all of them?"

I take in a deep breath and let it out. My face doesn't change, my eyes don't move. They're focused on the deck looming below us, up ahead—the end goal.

His voice is casual. "None of them stuck, huh?"

"*Now* who's stalking?"

"I can't help myself. Apparently your love life is better than an episode of *The Bachelor.* And *you* have a chatty mom, too."

I snicker. "You watch *The Bachelor?*" We've reached the spot at the crest of the hill where our paths converge and lead down into a single walkway of cement stairs. I narrow my eyes as we both squeeze onto them. They're barely wider than one person, but we walk side by side, as fast as two people possibly can without running or tripping or looking like we're purposefully racing. And we *are* racing. I let out a little snort. "That's sad."

"As sad as your two-week boyfriends?"

"Ten days," I correct him with a shrug. "What can I say? I'm easily bored."

It's true, there's something that happens to me after the first week of dating someone. When the glittery newness has worn off, and I start to notice all of the little things that drive me crazy. Taylor constantly chewed with his mouth open. David started calling me *babe.* Like, *You look cute, babe. Good night, babe. Do you want some popcorn, babe?* All I could think about was the old movie I used to watch at my grandma's house with my cousins. That little pink pig. And that my name *isn't* freaking Babe.

And Evan—okay, I'm the least proud of Evan. He was a full inch shorter than me. And it shouldn't have bothered me; I know it shouldn't have. And it didn't . . . for nine full days. But by day ten, all I could think about was our prom pictures. About dancing with him in two-inch heels. If I'd be able to see the top of his head, and if he'd have to stretch up on his toes to kiss me. If I'd have to wear flats to our hypothetical wedding someday. They were all little things—things that didn't matter for ten whole days—things that wouldn't matter anytime soon. But things I couldn't let go of. Things I couldn't imagine overlooking for months or years. And so what was the point? Best to end things before they got too serious; before I screwed it up too badly and it felt like an actual loss.

"They were heartbroken, probably," Asher says as our shoulders bump roughly and my foot slips off of the step and into the lumpy grass, throwing me off balance. He grabs me by the elbow and pulls me straight. I shake him away and he snickers.

"Devastated," I say.

"I imagine." His voice is level, serious. Mocking.

"I would bet you imagine a lot of things about me."

He lets out a little grunt but I can tell he wants to laugh. "This is probably our last summer, Chipmunk."

"Don't call me that." I practically growl the words.

"But it's so cute." I can hear the mock pout in his voice, can see his lake-blue puppy dog eyes, even without looking at him. I will never forgive my father for letting that nickname slip in front of Asher.

"I'm going to *destroy* you," I say with a smile. "You'll be calling me something very different by the end of the summer."

"Sounds dirty," he says, and I let out an irritated grunt. "Looking forward to it . . . Chipmunk." There's a smile in his voice.

As we descend onto the wooden deck, we both abandon our illusion of normalcy and *race* for the chair. It's sitting along the far side of the square deck, its soft, thick cushion the lone pop of color in a string of hard, white plastic lounge chairs. The unicorn chair, as I like to call it. The one comfy, padded lounge chair. A mystical, magical chair amongst a sea of cheap plastic ones. I hip-check Asher and twist toward it, but he lunges from behind me, throwing an arm around my waist.

"Let me go," I grunt, trying to pull away, my feet kicking at his ankles. But he pulls me tight to his chest and twists us. And then I'm falling. I'm free-falling, until I'm in his lap, on top of the lounge chair. I twist this way and that.

"How much do you hate me right now?" The words whisper against my neck and send a shiver up my spine.

"Hard nine," I say through gritted teeth, and his chest shakes against me in unreleased laughter. "Let. Me. Go."

"Gladly," he says, loosening his arm and reclining back onto the plush green pad.

I stand there for a minute, staring down at him, his head tipped back, eyes closed, laid out on the unicorn chair like a summer prince. At his long, tan legs stretched out in front of him, and the messy golden brown hair that skirts across his forehead. Asher has a swimmer's body. Broad shoulders, slim waist. Lean muscles I wish I could look at without scowling. But I can't, because Asher Marin is the absolute worst. And by the end of summer, I'm going to make him regret all of the summers that came before this one. All of the pranks and the snarky comments. It doesn't matter who started this between us so long ago, because this summer I'm going to finish it.

I'm about to lay my towel on one of the hard plastic monstrosities on the opposite side of the little deck, but then stop. Asher may have speed and brute strength to his advantage, but I'm more patient. He's a bomb, but I'm a sniper's bullet.

"Enjoy your chair," I say, a smile on my face. Then I turn and walk back toward the houses. I veer a little once I get to the top of the stairs, letting him wonder which house I'm going to and what I'll do there. He can't see me now; I'm blocked by the hedge of wild bushes that grow along the top of the hill. Let him get used to not knowing where I'm headed—because what I have planned for him this summer? He'll never see it coming.

Asher

There's a one-in-four chance Sidney Walters is going to murder me someday. Except no one will ever suspect her, because she'd be neurotic enough to make a checklist—or ten—and cover all of her bases. Sidney would do research (probably annotated) on how to hide my body. She's been researching it for the last ten months, for all I know. Maybe since we were thirteen and started vacationing together here.

Even though Sidney's favorite part of summer is screwing with me, she *looks* innocent. Like now; she is almost certainly about to soak all of my underwear in sugar water (that attracts ants and other bugs, in case you were wondering) or lace my body wash with something only detectable by dogs. And when the neighborhood Chihuahuas start trailing me through town she won't even bat an eye.

It's also possible she goes after my food—there was the time she used a syringe to put vinegar in the grapefruit I ate every morning. Total serial killer move, right? Sadly, Sidney could walk right into our cabin with a fistful of syringes and a backpack full of hair remover, and my mom wouldn't blink an eye. She'd probably offer her a cup of coffee and ask how her senior year had gone before sending her on her way with a smile. Because Sidney Walters is a proverbial ray of sunshine— with everyone but me. Awesome, very likable (if I do say so myself) me.

I fought for this chair—threw half of my oatmeal away for it—so I'm sure as hell going to sit in it. Leaving now would be admitting fear, which is as good as admitting defeat when it comes to Sidney. I close my eyes, put on my headphones, and try to listen to the beats of my favorite song. But my mind keeps wandering back to my room, and if I remembered to put my things in all of their strategic spots. Summer (for me, at least) is about self-defense and preservation as much as it is about offensive strikes. Minimizing vulnerabilities. Making my attack zone smaller. I'm not sure when I started thinking like a Navy SEAL.

I try to mentally walk through everything on my dresser and remember what I left out, but I can't visualize it. Instead, I focus on what I have lined up for Sidney this summer. I spend more time during the year than I'd like to admit thinking about these eight weeks of vacation. And this year in particular, it was basically all I could think about for the last six months. Senioritis was *strong* with me.

Could I do something more productive with my time this summer? Obviously. I could sit down and write that letter to Mr. Ockler. The one Dad has been on me about for months. A letter, not e-mail, because anything important comes in print, my dad says. *All it takes is one letter, Ash. A quick note to show how passionate you are about financial planning.* One letter, and in Dad's eyes, I'll be set for life. I'll have an apprenticeship to work through college, and the second I graduate I'll be ready to start building my own office. Walking door-to-door, telling people how I can help them enjoy their retirements. Just like Dad. All I have to do is write that letter—but thinking about pranking Sidney is so much more interesting.

I have a whole box of supplies, and to prevent it all from falling into enemy hands—*Sidney's hands*—I have it stashed in the boathouse storage area under *her* cabin. With Sidney, it's all about psychological warfare. She overthinks things more than anyone I've ever met. So when I need something I plan to stroll right into the boathouse in broad daylight, when she's no more than twenty feet away. It's sure to throw her off the scent— she'll never believe I would hide anything that obviously.

Her first instinct will be to check, but then she'll convince herself I'm just trying to distract her, or lure her into something, and she'll decide not to go down there. Plus, it's spider city in the boathouse; I can't imagine her actually digging through the crap in there to get to my box without having a major bug-induced meltdown. And that would be its own kind of victory. A win for me, either way.

Sidney

My room—clad in dark wood paneling—is a little musty when I walk in. Probably it's always a little musty, but I only notice it the day we arrive each summer, before the scent takes up permanent residence in my nose and becomes my new normal. I don't notice it again until I get home and unzip my bag, greeted by the damp earthiness of my vacation clothes. It's not a bad smell; it's almost comforting, the way it reminds me that for the next two months I can forget about test scores and papers, and focus on nothing but what my body can do when it's racing through the water. And this summer, training will be my middle name. Because in ten short weeks I'll be a collegiate swimmer. And I've been promising my mom for years now that I'm going to break her 1,650-yard freestyle record. The record that's held for almost twenty-five years now. I'll never have more time to train than I do this summer. *Watch out, Mom, I'm coming for you.*

I haul up my giant duffel bag, slamming it onto the squeaky bed that bounces like it's a trampoline. The mossy-green comforter is the same one that's been on this bed since I was twelve. Since that first summer we arrived at Five Pines Resort and Lake House A. I shove the wooden window open, letting the mid-June air, hot and wet, drift into my room. At home I'd die without air-conditioning—would murder and maim for it—but the heat isn't the same here. We're four hours north, in a little beach town that feels too small to exist outside of the months of June, July, and August. It's always a little cooler here in Riverton— the breeze slides across the lake, like there's some sort of spell over it, working in our favor as we lie out in the sun, draping ourselves over rafts and plastic chairs.

I abandon my bag—I should have unpacked last night when we got in, but it was late and the drive had zapped all of the energy out of me. But I can unpack later, when the sun is down and the water isn't calling me. I make my way down the little hallway (also covered in brown wood paneling) and into the kitchen. The kitchen in Lake House A is a fraction of the size of our kitchen at home. It's what Mom calls a postage stamp, tucked into a corner across from the little dining room and living room. The kitchen and dining room look out onto the yard and the neighboring house—Lake House B—and the living room has a row of windows that look out over the kidney bean–shaped lake.

Mom is unpacking bags and boxes, setting our toaster and a few pans onto the little counter—apparently all of us were a little lazy when we got in later than usual last night. Two months is too long for garage-sale pots and pans, Mom said the second summer we came here. She swore in the kitchen a lot that year. That summer, it was mostly just her and me. Mom working on her stained glass, and me turning into an almost-literal fish. We came up as soon as school let out and Mom had been set free from her classroom. Dad came up for a few sporadic weeks, and most weekends. That year, Lake House B was occupied by a nice older couple, who sat on their porch and brought freshly baked cookies out to the bonfire at night. The Wortmans.

I'm about to hit the door when Mom's voice stops me. "Hey." I pause, hoping I haven't missed my chance at a clean break from unpacking, but knowing I have. "Can you run out and get me a few things from the store?"

"Big or little?"

"Little," Mom clarifies.

"Sure." Better to get out of here than to get roped into unpacking boxes. Mom packs like we're never leaving here. In reality, I think I could survive with my swimsuit and a towel. And my paints. Maybe a small library of books. Okay, I need a *few* things. But still not as many as Mom.

Dad looks up at me from where he's hunched over a box in the dining room. "Don't forget," he says, giving me a wink. Dad's here for almost two weeks before he has to check in at the office for a few days, and then mostly he'll be here, working remotely, like he has for the last five years or so. I glance out the window to where our little boat is already tied alongside the dock that juts out into the still water. Mom hates driving the boat, but Dad and me, we've always lived out on the water, the wake misting our arms, wind burning our cheeks. Driving it still makes me nervous though, and I usually opt to let someone else do it. Boats steer funny; they're not like cars, which turn exactly when you want them to. Asher says I think too much to drive a boat properly. As if thinking is ever a bad thing.

Down the road from us, there's a tiny convenience store called The Little Store—its actual name, I swear—that also doubles as one of the town's two pizza places. It's dark, like the walls of our house; like the mossy insides and writhing bodies inside the white container of worms my father sends me to retrieve on the first day of vacation every year. When I was twelve, I would ride my pink bike—balancing the plastic container precariously on my handlebars the whole way home.

Now, I steal Dad's car keys from the little nail by the front door, and give a quick "I'll be back" as the screen door slams behind me. Through the open kitchen windows I can still hear the rustle of paper bags as Mom unpacks a week's worth of groceries from the local market twenty minutes away, where she grumbles about everything costing twice as much as at home.

I walk alongside the house, down the little cement sidewalk that runs to the gravel driveway. Straight ahead of me is the monstrosity—as my parents call it—that is Nadine and Charlie's house. They own Lake House A and B, and until two years ago, they also owned four more tiny shoebox rentals, before they tore them down to build their dream house. Technically, this place is called Five Pines *Resort*, but with two houses left to rent it hardly qualifies, if you ask me.

Charlie is quiet and short, light on words but always quick to smile if you happen to see him out and about fixing something, which is rare. He works a full-time corporate job at a bank an hour away. Nadine is the opposite. She's loud and eager to talk to you, though never about anything good. Her blond hair is wild and she always looks like she's about to board a cruise ship to some exotic locale. Her clothes are loose and flowing and bright, and her lips are always hot pink or red. It's hard not to look at her, though I'm well practiced at it, now that she's around entirely too much. It's a little strange, spending your summer vacation in someone's backyard.

While the lake houses are small and plain, the home that looms over them is like Nadine—tall and wide, and strange in a way you can't quite put your finger on. It's the color of a blueberry—not quite blue, not quite purple—with pale green shutters and a white porch that wraps around the front. It looks like something that should be sitting out on a farm, not a lake.

Last summer, when the house seemingly sprouted out of nowhere during the off-season, there were a handful of yard decorations that sprang up with it. A gnome with a red hat at one corner, a whimsical green toadstool by the back stairs leading down into the yard that faces A and B. The strangest was a rooster, almost up to my chin, positioned near the front door. But this year the house seems to have spawned a whole army of tacky ornaments. They're littering the gardens that circle the house, dotting the mulch with dogs, tiny girls in frilly dresses, and geese. I can't catalog them all without staring, and the walk to my dad's car is over before I can appreciate even a fraction of them. What is going on at Nadine and Charlie's house? And how could their daughter—pretty, fashionable, always-put-together Lindsay—let this happen?

My dad's car—a silver SUV with dark windows and shiny chrome—is sitting along the backside of the little house, in front of a massive wall of firewood that lines the driveway. Beyond it, the old metal swing set is bordered by tall grass, which Charlie has clearly given up on trimming. It makes my twelve-year-old heart a little sad to see it neglected. My phone buzzes, pulling me out of my lawn-gnome-and-swing-set-induced haze, and I swipe the screen to life as I open the door and push it with my hip. Not even out of the driveway, and already my mom has texted me three more things she forgot. And I'm not finding them at The Little Store—I'm going to have to drive into town, to the "big" market that is still little by normal standards. Texting my mom a quick *ok*, I drop into the seat and twist the keys in the ignition. Without warning, the car is filled with a deafening jolt of drums and screaming. My hand flies for the volume knob, my heart in my throat. *What the . . .*

"Dammit, Asher," I mutter, just as a messy mop of brown hair pokes up over the back seat. I startle again, not expecting that he'd be *in* the car. He cocks his head to the side and his blue eyes twinkle as a smile spreads across his face.

Like most epic rivalries, it would be impossible to pinpoint the exact reasons I loathe Asher Marin. Maybe it's the way he walks into my family's cabin each summer—the one identical to his next door—and smiles at my mother as if he's thrilled to see us all. As if he hasn't been dreaming of tormenting me for the last ten months, the way I've been dreaming of all the things I'll do to him. It could have been the self-tanner he put in my sunscreen when I was fourteen, or my frozen swimsuits when I was sixteen, or last year's crowning glory, the cayenne pepper he laced my toothpaste with.

But those all came after. And there are so many that it doesn't even matter what started it anymore. All that matters is that this summer, the summer before I go off to college— probably the last summer I'll have to see Asher Marin for eight weeks straight—I'm going to finish it.

"Happy first day of summer, Sidney." He meets my narrowed eyes and laughs, deep in his throat. And just as he clears the door and steps aside, I put the car in drive and peel out of the driveway, a bright red brontosaurus craning its neck around the house as I leave them behind me.

DAY 2

Sidney

Riverton is only four hours from where I live, but it's like another world up here. One with grocery stores that take checks but not credit cards, and close at five o'clock sharp. All of the houses have names, like Blue Thunder, Copper Cove, and Lake House A. Where random businesses crop up out of the woods, and instead of parking lots, everyone just parks on the side of the road for a quarter mile in either direction.

As I pull up to River Depot in my dad's car the next day, cars are everywhere, even on a Monday. I see the swarm of red shirts down by the canoes as I cross the little bridge over the river. It feels like forever before I find a break in the cars and can wedge myself between two with out-of-state plates, and set out for the big brown building. River Depot is a small, brown log building from the street, but beyond its doors it opens into multiple rooms and levels built into the hill that slopes from the road to the river.

This is the third summer Kara has worked the desk at River Depot. Her grandma lives three houses down from Five Pines—a little cabin passed down through Kara's family from back before the lake became a trendy tourist spot. We met my first summer here when I was twelve, and I accidentally stole her inner tube.

And by *stole*, I mean it washed up on our beach one morning after a bad storm, and with no way of knowing where it came from, Kara found me two days later, lying on the hot-pink plastic tube where I had tethered it to the end of our dock.

She dumped me off of it while I lay there with my eyes closed, and when I surged out of the water, completely bewildered, she laughed at me like a wild little water pixie. Which turned out to be a pretty accurate description of Kara. She's tiny—barely four foot nine—and even though she makes me feel like a giant at five foot eight, she's one of my favorite people in the whole world.

We were inseparable that first summer—the only summer Asher's family wasn't with us. Kara brought her float to our dock, and we strapped it next to the yellow version my parents bought me at The Little Store down the road. She crashed dinners when her grandma let her, and the two of us were wild little summer pixies together, covering our toes in glittery polish on the deck and pretending to fish out of a little rowboat, even though neither of us ever caught anything and would have been too freaked out to pull a fish off of a hook even if we did. Some days, we'd be joined by Nadine and Charlie's daughter, Lindsay, who was a year older than us, and would get dropped off to swim and drive around the WaveRunner docked at Five Pines. But by the next summer, Kara had turned fourteen and was working at River Depot in the afternoons, and when Lindsay made an occasional appearance she was more interested in my new neighbor, Asher.

By the time I make it to River Depot I'm sweaty and hot. I find it hard to believe any canoe trip can be worth this kind of dedication, but the massive lines outside the gazebo where they sign people up tells me I must be wrong. I push past the crowds and into the gift shop, which is dead and deserted compared to outside.

"Yesssss," Kara squeals from behind the counter as I round a

rack of postcards and shot glasses, all covered in the iconic images of a Michigan summer—lighthouses and waves and tower-
ing golden sand dunes. "*Now* it's summer!"

She wraps tiny arms around me from across the counter, ignoring someone approaching with a box of graham crackers and
a bottle of lighter fluid. "When did you get in?" she asks.

"Saturday night." I glance at the man next to me, but Kara
isn't fazed.

She gives me a quick up and down, like she's checking me
out. "You're still in one piece," she says, looking amused with
herself. "A whole day in, and no serious damage yet?"

"We're too busy unpacking," I say, wondering what Asher has
planned for me this summer.

"You stocked, or should I dig up some bottles of hot sauce
and hair remover?"

I smile. Deep down, I think Kara lives vicariously through
my ongoing escapades with Asher. She can barely temper her
amusement with the two of us. "I'm good."

"I work all week." She sticks her tongue out like she's going to
gag and makes a desperate sound deep in her throat. "But there's
a party Friday. Promise me you'll come?" Her voice is high and
whiny. "Just *once?*" she begs, her head tipping into a pleading dip
at her shoulder.

On my left, Graham Cracker Guy clears his throat.

"I'll think about it," I say, but we both know I'm not going.
I hate parties. The small talk with strangers, and not knowing
what to wear with a bunch of people I don't know. And one
thing I've learned over the years is that everything in Riverton
happens just a little differently than I expect it to. I hate being
unprepared, and while *one* party would remedy that, I just can't
seem to rip off that bandage.

"I'll text you the address," she says.

"Miss?" Graham Cracker Guy has more patience than I
would have expected. It must be the beginning of his vacation—

I've seen other tourists have total meltdowns for a lot less than being ignored for three whole minutes.

Kara's head snaps to her right as if she just noticed someone was there, and a smile lights up her face. She's all white teeth, blond hair, and sparkle. I notice the tiny pink stone that glitters in her nose, new from the last time I saw her. "Is this going to be all?" she asks the man as I walk out a side door and onto the deck that stretches out toward the river. I stop at one of two windows cut into the wooden wall to my left, THE GRILL painted in white above them. Arriving at the lake is the official start of summer, and nothing says summer like ice cream.

"What can I get you?" a friendly voice says, pulling my attention away from the river and to a pair of brown eyes housed in a very pretty face. An almost *too* pretty face. The kind with cheekbones I could trace with my finger, and a jaw as sharp as the awkwardness stabbing me in the chest right now.

"Ice cream?" I say, suddenly unsure why I even stepped up to the window. Ice cream. It was definitely ice cream I came here for.

"Any particular flavor," he asks with a smile, "or should I surprise you?"

"I like surprises." I hate that I said it. That somehow my filter has been disabled by his brown eyes, and everything is just falling out of my mouth unchecked now. I said it nervously, but it sounded flirty. I give myself a mental pep talk. *You can do this, Sidney. Just keep it up. You're on vacation now; the mysterious, worldly girl from somewhere else. He doesn't know you paint rocks for fun, or that you can't ski for your life. You can be anyone this summer.*

But who I actually am is a girl staring like a weirdo at a guy who is clearing his throat and asking—maybe not for the first time—if she wants a cup or a cone. "Waffle cone." I smile. "Sorry, big decision. Not college-decision big or anything, but, you know . . . big . . . *ish*." Oh good, the nervous rambling has started.

He laughs. I'm not sure if he's laughing at me or with me, but I laugh, too, just to convince myself it's the latter. "Done," he says, taking a step away from the counter, toward a long white freezer that runs along the opposite wall.

I give myself a mental pat on the back for being wild and letting some random hot guy pick out my ice cream. *You're a regular summer wild-child, Sidney Kristine Walters.* When he comes back he has a massive cone topped with three different colors.

"Wow," I say. "That may be more ice cream than I've eaten in my whole life combined."

He points to the scoops one at a time. "Superman." He looks from the colorful swirl of ice cream to me, and I nod my approval. "Strawberry." I give another approving nod. "And brown butter bacon." My face scrunches up without even thinking, because I'm one of the only people in the entire world who doesn't like bacon-flavored things. "Yeah." He shakes his head. "Took a risk with that one."

"It's fine," I say, reaching for the cone with a smile. But before I can grab it, he has a spoon in one hand and knocks the offending scoop into a container.

"I'll give that to Ellis later; he'll eat anything. Let me take another shot at it." He walks back to the freezer and reaches down into it. I'm not sure if he's flirting with me, or he just really loves his job.

"I like anything chocolate," I offer.

He comes back to the window with a swirl of brown and white topping my colorful cone. "S'more," he says, giving me a skeptical look. "Chocolate, marshmallow, and candied graham cracker bits."

I smile. "Perfect."

He smiles at me like he just aced a test.

"I'm Sidney," I say. It bursts out of me almost beyond my control. "I have a friend who works here—" I nod back toward where I can see Kara at the desk, her eyes fixed on us. "So you'll probably see me around. I'm on vacation. I have no life," I offer as an excuse. *Shut up, Sidney.*

"I'm Caleb." He hands me the ice-cream cone as I pass a ten-dollar bill—my mom's grocery store change from yesterday—across the counter. "So I guess I'll see you around, Sidney."

I take my change with a nod and a smile, and head back toward Kara, licking at the dribble of blue ice cream that's now escaping down my cone. Holy hell, this is going to be a giant puddle by the time I make it to my car.

"Yummy, huh?" Kara says as I approach the counter.

I have a feeling she's referring to more than the ice cream, and I have to agree. "Very."

"What if I told you the party was at *his* house?"

"Is it?"

"No." She smiles and I smack her shoulder. "But he'll be there."

"I'll think about it." And as I walk out to my car, I am definitely thinking about it. Because seeing Caleb at the party seems like a better option than making daily ice-cream trips.

Asher

Sometimes I think our parents are in on this whole Ash-and-Sid-prank-each-other-into-fiery-oblivion thing. Or that they have their own game, where they see how long they can go without acknowledging the tension between us. Like, they each get a point for not smiling at something snarky we say to each other. Two points if they keep talking right through it. Money could be passing under the dinner table for all we know. I wonder if they pick a winner each summer, or if the longevity of their game is only surpassed by ours. Sure, we do our best to plaster smiles onto our faces in front of them, and keep our mouths shut, but you'd have to be completely oblivious to not notice the twisted game we've had going on for years.

And yet, our normally capable parents haven't acknowledged our feud since the first summer it started, when we were fourteen. That was the second year my family came up with Sidney's, and back then the pranks didn't feel like the norm. Sometimes I barely remember what things were like before all of this, that first summer when Sidney and I were on the same team, but there *was* a before.

I especially suspect they're using us for their own amusement when they do crap like announce that we're going to start having dinner together every night. Sidney's mom, Kris, claims it makes sense. Why should we sit in our separate homes, eating meals at the same time, when we could sit around and eat with each other?

Because it gives us more time to guard our homes?

Because I'm closer to my room and all of my stuff that Sidney inevitably wants to mess with?

And because she's Kris, she also reminds us that not only will it be fun and practical, but we'll also save electricity and water (and basically everything but our sanity) by having these joint family dinners. *Nightly.* That's *fifty-six* dinners.

Which means Sidney and I have an entire hour that we have to play nice while we're held captive at the dining room table. I'm not sure we even know how to function like normal people anymore. Will we just implode from being in the same area for an hour without tormenting one another? Will the angry little crease in her forehead become permanent being in my presence for fifty-six hours' worth of dinners this summer?

Tonight we're at her house, seated at opposite ends of the long oval table, with our parents coupled up on either side of us. We are the reigning king and queen of mealtime misery, and all we can really hope is that neither of us tries to behead the other and gets blood all over the floor. (Or our grilled chicken, roasted broccoli, and sweet corn, which is delicious.)

These dinners *do* have a few foreseeable perks, though. I

glance toward the hallway that leads to the little bathroom I know Sidney uses. I'm sure there's more than one way I can use this time in enemy territory to my advantage.

At the very least I can have some fun. I catch Sidney's eye and hold her gaze. Even when I spear a piece of broccoli, I keep my eyes on her, daring her to look away. Yes, we can do this. Nothing makes time fly like harassing one another. Sidney's eyes narrow in annoyance, but she doesn't take them off of me. I reach for the salt shaker and blindly shake it over the blurry yellow blob that is my corn cob. Sidney reaches for her water glass, and her fingers tap against the glass as she gets a hold on it. I fumble with a roll when my mom holds the basket out to me, and Sidney clumsily spoons rice onto her plate, a chunk of it falling onto the table. In my mental tally, I give myself a point. She gets one when I pick my spoon up by accident and try to gouge a piece of chicken with it.

When I tip over my glass of water, both of us break our gaze at the same time, looking to our parents, who are all laughing. At my clumsiness or our little game, I'm not sure, but when I crawl under the table with a rag thrown at me by my mom, the game is officially over.

Sidney

As Asher hoists himself off of the floor, I realize for the first time since we started our little staring game that the area around my plate looks like it should be adorned with a paper placemat and crayons. There is a heap of rice that never made it onto my plate, three pieces of broccoli I must have knocked off while blindly cutting my chicken, and a blob of melted butter. *Way to keep it classy, Sid. You'll fit right in on campus in a few months.* Thoughts of school always bring back what I'm really focused on this summer—not food fights with myself, or staring games with Asher. Sitting to my right is the reigning queen of the Division II 1,650-yard freestyle, and if I have anything to say about it, by the end of my freshman season, she'll be abdicating her throne. I've promised her since I was nine and wearing my first team Speedo that I'd do it. Back then it was a pipe dream, the kind of thing you say when you're too young to know what it even means. But now, it's in my sights.

"Set your alarm," I say, and my dad groans. I roll my eyes. *He's* not the one swimming two thousand yards across the lake before breakfast; I'm not sure he has any room to be grumbly and cranky. I, on the other hand, have to sit across from Asher and try not to laugh at him spilling food all over himself while I'm trying to eat a meal.

Asher clears his throat and sets his fork on his plate. "I can spot her," he says, looking at my dad and not me. A whole new kind of staring game is happening, and I will my dad to look at me, but his eyes are fixed on Asher.

I'm not sure if I'm laughing or choking, but there's a strangled noise sliding out of me, making everyone look my way. *As if my dad is going to put my safety in* Asher's *hands?*

"Are you sure?" My dad's voice is hopeful, and it makes my stomach sink.

Please please please, no.

"It's no problem." Asher stabs a piece of chicken with his fork, and meets my eye. "I can't sleep past six thirty anyway." A side effect of the early morning swims Asher probably does all year. I suspect the only person I know who trains harder than me is Asher. He makes the guys on my team look flubby and soft. One more reason I need to stay on track this summer—college will be a whole different level of competition, and half of the team will be female versions of Asher.

Game on. "I leave at six." I don't break eye contact as I smile, and hope Dad doesn't call me on the lie I'm hoping will deter Asher. Even he's not going to give up thirty minutes of sleep just to torment me.

Asher gives me his own smile, and I wonder if anyone else realizes it's more killer than kind. "Not a problem," he says coolly.

Dad claps his hands together. "That's settled." He lets out a relieved breath and shakes his head, like he just woke himself from some sort of nightmare.

"I didn't realize it was so horrible," I say, my voice soft but biting.

Dad gives me a sympathetic glance. "It's not, Chipmunk—"

God, that nickname. I shoot Asher a warning look, and his face is pinched tight, his shoulders lightly shaking.

"It's just"—he lets out a sigh—"it's so early. And . . . boring." His face mirrors the shock in my own, like he can't believe he said it. I can't believe he said it *out loud*. My dad—the guy who prides himself on having shown up to every one of my mom's meets in college—admits that watching his daughter train bores him?

I take a drink of my water, setting my glass down softly. "But we always do the morning swims together."

"I know, but this is Ash's thing, too . . . maybe he can even give you some tips while he's at it."

I snort. Asher as spotter, making sure I'm not hit by a rogue fishing boat? Okay, fine. But my pseudo-coach? No. Hard pass. I give Dad a little smile that I hope says, *Sure, I'll think about it.*

Across the table, Asher is smiling at me. I fight the urge to scowl and stab a piece of broccoli instead.

"I'll meet you at the boat at six," he says, lifting a cob of sweet corn to his mouth and taking a slow, deliberate bite.

"Six fifteen," I correct. "I like to shower and wake up first." I'd *like* to leave at six thirty like usual, but now my lie is out there, and it's going to cost me fifteen minutes of precious sleep.

Asher bites his bright yellow corn cob in a slow, straight line, holding my eyes. There's a smile hidden there, and I try to school my face and the scowl I can feel brewing. He takes the last bite at the end and mouths *ding*.

I almost lose it. *My mother and her stupid stories.* A few years ago my mother just had to tell everyone the "cute story" about how I used to eat my corn on the cob like the old-fashioned electric typewriter my grandma had when I was little. I'd eat it in a straight line, say *ding!* when I reached the end, then start in on the next row. *Chomp, chomp, chomp, chomp, ding! Chomp, chomp, chomp, ding!* Only Asher would remember that stupid story a million years later. Does he take notes somewhere? Record all of these stupid family conversations on his phone?

"Six-fifteen." He smiles behind the cob. "Should be fun."

Fun. I think he and I have different definitions of the word.

"Definitely. Don't forget your suit, you can take the leg back," I say. "I'd be happy to give *you* some pointers as well."

Asher smiles and our parents chat across the table about winery trips and new restaurants to check out, as if we've become invisible again. "Looking forward to it."

DAY 3

Sidney

The next morning, I am nearly unconscious. You would think, since I've been getting up at the crack of dawn every other day of vacation for the last five years, it wouldn't be an issue anymore—that my body would remember what's happening and snap into gear—but when 6 a.m. rolls around it's not familiar, it's painful. So painful. Like my eyelids will need to be surgically separated if they're ever going to function properly again. My room is dark and the hallway is dark, and I think maybe I've seen the light of day for the last time as I stumble toward the bathroom door. My eyelids are permanently closed. This is my life now.

I slink into the bathroom, opting for the dim light above the vanity, rather than the fluorescent box that hangs over the little shower stall. Stripping off my tank and shorts, I step into the shower, ready to be blasted awake by the cold. I could just wait to jump into the frigid lake, but I'd rather shake off the sleepiness before I start training. Especially for my first morning swim with Asher. Gah, even just thinking about it is miserable. He'll probably try to run me down with the boat, so I need to be awake when I get out there, in case I need to go all action-movie mode and swim under the boat or something.

Head limp against the cream-colored tiles, I push the clear

plastic knob up and to the right, mentally preparing for the on-slaught. The strange smell hits me almost as quickly as the cold. It's familiar, but so out of place—tangy, maybe. Almost citrus, but not quite. It smells like my childhood, somehow. Everything in this house has its own unique smell, but this one is a first, and it doesn't fit. The cold sharpness against my skin distracts me, but as the pelting water numbs me and loses its bite, I relax and let my eyes slowly crack open.

What the hell?

Red streams *everywhere*. My first thought is that I'm bleed-ing, that I somehow, unconsciously, sliced my foot open. It looks like something out of a horror movie. Like there should be a bloody red handprint on the shower wall next to me. I'm tired, but I would have remembered severing my toe, I think. My eyes travel from the swirling red drain up my stained legs, and to my blotchy red stomach. *Red*. I'm red all over. My brain is still foggy and I feel a little like I'm in the last dregs of a nightmare.

I look up toward the showerhead, the water lightening in color now, and tentatively stick out my tongue as the smell fi-nally registers. *Cherry*. It smells like my favorite Kool-Aid, the stuff I used to live off of every summer, back before I cared about how much sugar I drank.

"*Asher*." I say his name like a mumbled curse, deep in my throat, my teeth clenched so tight they squeak a little under the pressure.

When I head out, my towel is stained from rubbing, but I still couldn't get all of the red off of my skin. It's concen-trated around my knees and elbows, and in patches across my stomach—thankfully covered by my swimsuit—and my face. My face, which is turned toward the dock, where my new safety buddy is now standing, waiting to trail me across the lake. He's lucky I'm too claustrophobic—and easily bored—to go to prison, or he'd need to be worried about being out on the open water with me.

"Mornin'," he says, his face focused on the can of gas he's dumping into the tank as I approach the little silver boat. My dad brings a small fishing boat to the lake every year, but for lake swims we always use the little silver rowboat that belongs to Five Pines, and ditch the oars for an outboard motor on the back. Asher reaches forward and I can see his suit sticking out from the waistband of his shorts. His phone is in a plastic bag sitting on the floor of the boat. *Clearly he doesn't trust me, either. Good. He shouldn't.*

I sit on the little bench that stretches across the front of the boat, my eyes fixed on the back of his head as he pours the gas. When he turns, he looks me right in the eyes. His travel from my face down to my splotchy wrists and linger on my knees, which are the reddest parts of my body. *Note to self: moisturize your knees once in a while.* I lift my little canteen to my mouth and take a casual sip. "Morning."

The corner of his mouth twitches and I wait for the smile, but it doesn't come. "You smell nice today," he says, still on the brink of that smile. I'm not sure if I remember what Asher looks like smiling anymore. Smirking, yes. But smiling is as good as admitting guilt. And that is one of the three unspoken rules of this war we wage each summer.

1. Never admit guilt
2. No serious injuries
3. No snitching

Rule number one means we don't smile, or laugh, or implic- itly gloat. I'm not sure why—maybe because saying out loud that you filled someone's drink with soy sauce or left earthworms in their bed just sounds mean. Rule number two ensures we never have to break rule number three. We haven't snitched on each other since we were fifteen and Asher put marbles on the floor beside my bed. I'm not sure if he was actively trying to kill me, or just wasn't thinking, but I lost my balance and cracked my head on the nightstand. I wouldn't have ratted him out to my parents, but it was bleeding so much I was sure I was going to die, and I had to get six stitches. All in all it was only a one-inch cut. Asher apologized profusely—the only time either of us has—and maybe the whole thing would have stopped at that point, if I hadn't retaliated a few days later. Head wound or not, I wasn't going to *literally* let him land the winning blow.

Asher starts up the engine and takes a seat across from me. We're not ten feet from the dock when he reaches his silver mug toward me. "Coffee?"

I shake my canteen in front of me. "I'm good."

"Right." I can see that smirk about to break through. "You probably filled up on Kool-Aid this morning, huh?"

Asher

Sidney stands up so quickly, I have to cut the engine so she doesn't topple over the side. Before it has even quieted, she's climbing over, lowering herself into the water.

"What are you *doing*?"

"Swimming," she says, walking through the shallow water that's just up to her thighs. "Arms. Legs. Water." She pulls her T-shirt over her head and tosses it in a crumpled pile into the boat in front of me. "An obnoxious boy following you in a boat. Sound familiar?" She keeps walking, and I keep the boat far enough to the side that I won't bump into her accidentally. She's wearing a plain suit—dark navy—but tight and shiny and cut high on her leg, like a team suit. As the water reaches her chest, she dips down into the water and pushes herself forward, a billowy cloud pluming up around her as her feet leave the sand.

Sidney disappears under the water and comes up about fifteen feet ahead. Her cheek dips down into the water, and then up, and down, as she swims steadily into the light chop of the lake. I start the motor back up and idle the boat to the side of her, giving her a few feet and keeping pace. I have the air horn Tom gave me in one hand, though a quick scan of the lake tells me there's not a boat to be seen anywhere near us. The fishing boats are already settled into their spots for the morning, and the speedboats pulling skiers and tubers won't hit the lake for hours, after the morning chill burns off. The only ones cutting across the lake at this hour are neurotic swimmers and the guys hell-bent enough on annoying them to ruin their own mornings.

I look at the other side of the lake, imagining the little bay I know dips inland there, but it's still too far to make out. This is going to take a while—Sid isn't going for speed, she's building endurance. Open-water swimming is so much harder than in the pool, where there aren't waves and frigid temps and currents to deal with. I can't remember the last time Sidney and I spent an hour straight alone together, unless you count the time we spend lying on the deck chairs in silence every morning, after we vie for that stupid padded lounge chair. The unicorn. I know she calls it that, though she never says it in front of me anymore. I laugh, because her head's underwater and I can. I shake as I think about her diving toward that chair, and standing under a stream of cherry Kool-Aid. *Thank you, family dinners.*

Sidney's head bobs up, and down, and up, and down. It's quiet out here. The motor is barely running; the lake is only slightly choppy, yet to be churned up by a day's worth of skiers, tubers, and Jet Skis. And Tom was right, I'm already bored. I glance at my phone, sitting on the bench next to me. It's been ten whole minutes. Swimming in open water is so much slower than in a pool, even in a lake as calm as this one. And Sidney doesn't seem to be in any rush—maybe this is all part of her plan.

"I'm bored," I say toward Sidney's bobbing head, but of course she doesn't respond. She doesn't even pause to tell me I'm being a baby. *She can't hear you.* The thought frees something inside me.

"I can't believe you do this every other day." That's a lie, though, because it's totally something she would do. "Scratch that. I can totally believe you'd do this every other day. Because you're the most obsessive person I've ever met. You can't do anything halfway. That's why I have to pack my bags for vacation like I'm going off to war." I ramble on, to the open air. "You're a worthy opponent, Sidney Walters. You're neurotic, and have a stick up your ass the size of a small oak tree, but you're worthy. No doubt."

I raise my voice a little and imagine Sidney can hear me. I like the idea that she's forced to listen to whatever I say, each of us captive to the other. "Did I ever tell you about the time I tried pranking my best friend Todd?" I laugh. "Of course I didn't. Well, it was last year, a week after I got home, and I was still wired from the summer. From our . . . whatever this is. The crap we do to each other. Todd had come over to my house and stolen my favorite pair of headphones—he'd wanted them forever, and I forgot to bring them to the lake, so when they were gone, I knew who took them." Just saying this out loud sounds like I'm completely unhinged. Saying it to someone's back is a whole new level. "So I got into his car, and I put glitter in all of his air vents. I had to use a little dropper, to get the glitter to sit on the edge of the plastic vents. Todd's air-conditioning has been broken since he got that car, but he always breaks down at some point and turns on the air. Like he thinks it's magically going to fix itself at some point, or that the air coming in will somehow be cooler than the air outside. So he was good and sweaty by the time he got blasted." I laugh just thinking about it again. "Man, he was pissed. Because it turns out he *had* texted me about grabbing the headphones for a trip he was going on. My mom gave them to him and everything. I missed the text. It took him a million showers to get the glitter off, and I swear it's *still* in his car, wedged into all the little cracks." When I shake my head I'm not sure if it's at myself or at Sidney. Maybe it's at what she does to me. "You mess my head up," I say to the water.

Sidney

Asher goes on and on until we finally reach the little bay on the opposite side of the lake. Telling me about how his friend Todd didn't talk to him for two days. Apparently it's *my* fault that Asher was a jerk to his friend? If he's trying to make me feel guilty, it isn't working. But if he's trying to annoy me, then he's nailing it. Because him talking to me while I swim is a lot like when the dentist has your jaw jacked open and asks you how school's going. *Have you been flossing? Are you still swimming? If bus A leaves Cincinnati on Tuesday and bus B leaves Detroit on Wednesday, what is the square root of pi?* It's a special kind of torture, when you can't respond. But acknowledging that I hear him would just help his cause, so instead I just push myself as hard as I possibly can, until my arms and legs feel like limp noodles.

When the water starts to lighten and I can make out the bottom—he can't claim I didn't make it to the other side, I'm clearly in the bay—I wave Asher over to me. He cuts the engine and lets the boat drift until it's sidling up beside me. Even though it's just one of the little rowboats, I know I can't get in myself. Not unless we let the boat drift in another hundred feet to the *really* shallow water. And I'm too tired for that.

I try anyway. I put both hands on the edge and try to pull myself up, but I can't get any traction when the boat dips. The metal digs against my palms. I haven't done an open-water swim in ten months, and my entire body feels spent. If my dad had come, I would have swum a half today, just to ease myself into it. Asher scoots to the edge of his seat and reaches his arm out with a smirk. And as I grab it, all I can think of is how he called me neurotic, and said I had a stick up my ass. No, a *tree* up my ass. I brace myself against the boat with one arm and give a tug. And when he loses his balance, I give one more, until he splashes into the water.

"Your turn," I say cheerily, still hanging from the side of the boat with one arm.

"Brilliant." Asher shakes his head in the water. "Now neither of us is in the boat."

"You're *swimming* back," I say, giving him the sugary-sweet smile I usually reserve for when our parents are around. There's no hiding my guilt now anyway. Asher is already stripping his T-shirt up over his head, kicking his legs to propel himself up out of the water. The edge of the wet cotton slaps me in the face as he throws it into the boat.

"Gross," I mutter.

"It's lake water. You're covered in it," he says, rolling his eyes. He holds his breath and sinks down into the water, coming up with his shorts in his hands. As the fabric sails over me and into the boat, I'm suddenly aware of the fact that he's now effectively in only his underwear a few feet away from me. I spend at least fifteen hours a week around guys dressed in no more than Asher, so I don't know why I feel heat creeping up my neck now. Maybe because it's weird to be near your nemesis while he's naked. *Almost* naked.

"Well, there you go," he says. "You got what you wanted."

I raise my eyebrows, unsure what he's referring to.

"I'm practically naked over here."

My nemesis is not only naked, but also a mind reader, and I want to scream at him to get out of my head, but all I can manage is: "Ugh."

"Whatever, Sidney. Next time you want me to take my clothes off, you can just ask." He dips down into the water and surfaces a foot away from me. "Quite frankly, I'm tired of you objectifying me like this. I'm not just a pretty guy in a Speedo. I'm a *person*."

"Hardly," I say, but my eyes catch on the sharp angles where his neck meets his shoulders, and suddenly my eyes are drifting lower, to the planes of his chest.

Asher laughs, and it catches me off guard, the way it barrels out of him. And as if he realizes his mistake, he dunks down, cutting the sound off with a torrent of water. When he comes up, it's slow and dramatic, like when a creature emerges in a scary movie. Water drips down his face in shimmering streams. And he's right in front of me, so close that the water churned up by his legs is brushing against mine. I could count the droplets of water clinging to his dark lashes.

Asher slings an arm up over the boat, facing me. His feet graze mine in the water as they lazily flutter there. Hair wet and glistening, the last little rivulets of water drip down his tanned face, sliding from his chin down to his chest. When he braces himself against the boat all of his muscles tighten, and something in my chest does the same.

"What are you doing?" I don't mean it to sound so breathless, so alarmed.

Asher leans forward, his mouth next to my ear, his warm breath a stark contrast to the cold lake. Under the water, his hand rests on my calf, and a little shiver that I hope he doesn't notice runs through me. Every inch of me vibrates at the touch.

"Sidney?" His voice is whisper soft, so close his breath tickles my ear. I should move away, should find some sort of inhuman strength to hurl myself into this boat, but I can't. For the first time in forever, I feel like I've forgotten how to swim.

The water is chilly this far out, but I don't feel the cold at all now—my entire body feels like it's on fire. "Yeah?"

His hand slides down the length of my calf to my foot, and he leaves it there, softly cradling my arch in his palm. "I'm helping you into the boat." There's a hint of a laugh in his voice.

I find that inhuman strength I wished for when I push my foot roughly against his hand and propel myself up and into the boat. Unfortunately, it isn't graceful, sexy, or defiant. I flop into the boat much like my heart is flopping in my chest. And when I take the seat next to the motor and start it up, I think I hear his laugh mixed with the roar of the engine coming to life.

DAY 5

Sidney

My dad has this thing for vacation jerky. We call it that, because literally the only time Dad wants to eat jerky is when we're at the lake. Some vacationers gorge themselves on tropical drinks with little umbrellas, or all-you-can-eat buffets. My dad stuffs himself with teriyaki beef sticks until it starts to feel like his summertime cologne, and everyone in a two-house radius judges.

In his defense, they *are* pretty tasty. They sell them at the big store in town, and Dad doesn't like to put them on Mom's shopping list (because the judgment starts in *our* house) so he usually sends me. *Here's twenty bucks, run to the store and get yourself something fun. Maybe grab something for me while you're there?* As if I'm going to find anything fun at the grocery store. Dad thinks he's being slick, but Mom always snags me before I leave and gives me her own list of things she needs.

I'm just about to pull out of the driveway when Asher comes dashing toward the car. He pulls at the handle just as I slip the car into drive, but I don't unlock it. I swear I still feel a phantom tingle where his hand was on my leg, and it makes me want to floor it. He cocks his head to the side and palms a piece of paper against the window. Two taps on the glass, and I roll it down. "I have to grab some stuff for my mom."

"Ugh." I let out a disgruntled sigh, because while I can say no to Asher all day, Sylvie is a different story. "Fine." It's not the car's fault, but I press the button to unlock the door more aggressively than is necessary anyway. Asher climbs into the passenger side and immediately skips to the next song on my playlist. "You have a car, you know."

"My mom sent me over to see if your mom needed anything. And your mom insisted we didn't need to drive *two* cars. She practically shoved me out the door so I wouldn't miss you."

I can already feel it—Mom's current obsession with her carbon footprint is going to be the death of my sanity this summer. I turn out of the driveway, and we're halfway to the store before either of us breaks the silence.

"Jerky run?" Asher asks, sounding almost sympathetic.

"You know it."

We park the car and silently head into the store, both of us turning toward the deli. Asher grabs my list, and I'm trying to get it back from him, my hands reaching around and behind him, when I hear my name.

"Sidney?" It comes from behind me, an aisle or so down. Standing next to a display of marshmallows, his red River Depot shirt now swapped for a soft gray T-shirt, is the dreamy ice cream guy. Right here in my grocery store.

I grab the list from Asher, who is momentarily stunned motionless, and compose myself, straightening a little. "Hey, Caleb."

He closes the gap between us and sticks his hand out to Asher. I take a deep breath and let it out loudly. "This is Asher." I introduce them as they shake hands next to the little case of jerky sticks that got me here. I grab a pack and put them in my basket.

"Your . . ." His eyes swing from Asher to me. ". . . brother?"

Asher and I say no at the same time. He sounds absolutely disgusted by the prospect of having to be related to me.

"Our families vacation together," I say, realizing too late that it sounds sort of weird. "Our moms were college roommates, and we come up here every year. We have houses next to each other over at Five Pines." I point to the doors like an idiot, as if the houses are right outside. "Almost identical houses, actually. It's a—"

Asher puts his hand on my shoulder. "I don't think he needs our family histories." I shrug his hand away, but at least he shut me up.

"I actually have to go find some apples," I say, taking a step away, toward Caleb.

He smiles. "What a coincidence. I love apples." I head toward the far corner of the store and he falls into step beside me. I don't look at Asher, but I hear his footsteps behind us, getting softer, not louder, thankfully.

"I bet there's a name for this," I say, when we've rounded the aisles that separate the fresh food from everything else.

He looks at me questioningly. "Shopping?"

"No." I laugh and it feels good to be able to. "The phenomenon where you've never seen someone before, and then suddenly they're everywhere."

He smiles. "I don't know that I'm *everywhere*."

"I'm just glad I was here first," I say, a teasing lilt to my voice. "*You're* following *me*."

He smiles and shrugs. "Fair enough."

I walk toward the little fruit section and he follows me. "I'm just picking up some stuff for my mom." I pull a plastic bag off of the carousel and grab two apples from the edge of the shelf.

I'm not sure why I feel the need to explain why I'm at the grocery store—I suppose I don't want him thinking this is what I do for fun. I *did* make it sound like I was lonely and pathetic, and would be lurking around River Depot whenever possible.

Caleb reaches into my bag and takes the apples out. "Take these," he says, handing me two of the same apples, but from a different row.

"O-kay." I'm not sure what just happened. It felt like the shopping version of mansplaining. Was I just produce-judged? I don't know how to pick out apples? I may not be a culinary wizard, but had it mushed into applesauce in my hand I would have put it back myself.

I make my way through the produce section and Caleb picks out a watermelon for me, switches out three of the four peaches I picked up, and advises me not to buy the raspberries that are on sale, because they won't last more than a day. I know he's really spooked me with his produce pickiness when I find myself peering behind me, wondering where Asher is, in a desperate way I don't know how to feel about.

I must be looking at Caleb with as much apprehension as I'm feeling, because he finally stops touching my food, like it's been electrified. I'm not sure it shouldn't be—maybe that would teach him to keep his hands out of someone else's basket.

"I'm sorry," he says, putting his hands up in surrender. "My dad owns this grocery store."

I let out a long whoosh of air and my shoulders feel like they drop about three feet. "Thank god." Suddenly my personal-shopper experience is making a lot more sense. "I was starting to worry you were just overly aggressive about produce."

"Guilty," he says with a smile. "Sorry, I can see how that was probably weird. Apparently I get aggressively helpful when I'm nervous."

And *I* ramble.

He *sounds* nervous now, and it makes something flutter in

my stomach, so I try to switch the subject. "How have I never seen you around here before? Sometimes I feel like my family's designated grocery-getter."

He shoves his hands into the pockets of his shorts and looks over at me. "Maybe you weren't looking?"

I've been to this grocery store a million times. "Maybe," I say, my voice skeptical.

Caleb smiles and his eyes crinkle in amusement. He's smiling at *me*. "I usually spend summers with my mom in Tennessee."

"Ah. It's not nice to make people feel crazy."

"Noted," he says, taking a loaf of bread out of my basket and replacing it with another heavier loaf as we pass the bakery area. He holds his hands up like I have a gun pointed at him. "Last time, I swear."

I'm still staring at his hands, which are now on my shopping basket—the only thing separating us—when Asher comes around the corner. "Hey, *Sid*—" Caleb looks at the same moment I do, and I can tell just from the obnoxious tone of Asher's voice that this isn't going to be good. "Are these the right ones?" Asher holds up a bright blue box of tampons, and looks past Caleb to me.

I bite my lip to keep from screaming, but if he thinks he's embarrassing me with *tampons*, he's seriously delusional. "Yeah, I think those are going to work for you, *Ash*. Though you should get a bigger box, because I hear they work great for nosebleeds. You know, in case someone were to punch you in the face at some point." I pause dramatically. "Or something."

I give him a sugary-sweet smile and Caleb chokes back a laugh. "Not unless provoked," I say in my most demure tone, looking at him as innocently as I can muster, "of course."

"Got it, Slugger," Asher says, and I can tell he wants to smile, but he turns his face from mine to Caleb's, and *then* he lets it loose—a toothy, blindingly white smile. "Careful with this one," he says, and if I could growl, I would. Not that I would ever actually hit Asher, but right now I'm seriously considering if I could leave him here, or make him chase my car.

Asher retreats back into the aisle he came from, and Caleb shakes his head, like he's been in an Asher-induced fog, and can't quite break out of it. He raises his eyebrows like he wants me to explain, and I just shrug. There is no explaining me and Asher.

"Kara said you're coming to the party tomorrow night," he says.

"Did she?" I'm still flustered, and I feel like I've lost some of my flirting mojo. *Asher strikes again.*

"You don't sound convinced."

"I'm . . . debating." I walk toward the checkouts, hoping he follows. When he does, that flutter is back, tickling my ribs.

"*I'll* be there," he says, as he grabs a plastic bag from my basket and sets it on the black conveyor belt we're now standing beside. I do the same, and piece by piece we unload the basket together. "You know, if you need something to throw into the pro column of your list."

"How do you know I have a list?" I smile and he shrugs. There's a moment of silence as the cashier hands me my bags and I take a step toward the doors. I give him a quick glance back. "I guess I'll see you tomorrow, then."

Asher

When we got back from our shopping trip, my dad and Tom drove to the marina to get a new sensor for Tom's boat, so I'm sitting on my deck, avoiding the girls-only rock-painting party that's happening on the deck next door.

Sidney paints rocks. Literally, rocks you find on the ground. She collects them at the beach—I've never figured out a rhyme or reason to which ones she picks out, because they're all different—but she sifts through the sand like she knows exactly what she's looking for. And then she spends hours sitting on the deck or a blanket in the grass, painting them with little designs. Again, no rhyme or reason I can decipher. There are rocks with words on them, some with colorful flowers. One had a skull on it. It's the only art I've ever seen Sidney do, and it's so random I can't help but be intrigued.

She can easily paint four or five in a day. Ten if they're really simple and she's committed to avoiding me the entire day. By the end of each summer she has to have painted at least a hundred, if not more. My mom always leaves with some, but are there just buckets and buckets of these things sitting in her room somewhere? Does she give them to her friends at home? I shouldn't care about something so stupid, but I can't help but wonder: *What is she doing with all of these rocks?*

Last summer, her mom started painting them sometimes, too, which means my mom also got involved, and now it's like a little rock-painting sweatshop when the three of them go at it, like they are right now. My phone buzzes with a text and my eyes dart from the painting party next door to where my phone is lying on top of my book on the railing of our deck.

Lindsay: You home?

Yes. That's the truth, but it's not what I start to type. Because even though Sidney's known Lindsay even longer than I have, she's always sort of weird when she comes around. Lindsay is Nadine's daughter, but I haven't seen her around much the last few years. The first summer I was here, Lindsay seemed to be an almost permanent fixture on the beach. Her mom or dad would drop her off and she'd spend the day lying on the dock or on a towel spread across the grass on the hill. But after that first summer she didn't come around as much. And last summer I didn't see her once, despite the fact that her family built a house right behind ours. But still, radio silence. I'm debating what to say when I hear footsteps behind me, and turn to find Lindsay standing on my deck.

"Hey." I try not to sound startled, but I'm pretty sure I do. Because I am.

"I'm sorry, is it totally weird that I just showed up?" She looks embarrassed. "I was in the house and I saw you right after I texted, so I just . . ."

"No, it's fine." I stand up and give her a hug, and the smile returns to her face. I nod toward the white plastic chair next to mine. "You wanna hang out?"

"Yeah. Cool." She sits and kicks her feet up on the wooden railing of the deck. Lindsay looks like a stereotypical lake girl . . . deeply tanned skin, long hair down the middle of her back that looks like she just spent a day at the beach, and shorts that look like she lives in them. There's a light outline in the denim where her phone is stuck into her pocket.

We sit and talk about my senior year and her first year of college. I tell her about going to Oakwood in the fall, and she tells me about the sorority she pledged. How she's moving into the house in the fall. She's soft and sweet, and the longer we talk, the harder it is to think of a single thing that could make Sidney dislike her. But when she leaves—giving me another hug before she hops off of the deck, and promising to see me around—Sidney is most definitely watching her walk away. I want to ask her what the deal is, but we aren't those people. We aren't friends.

DAY 6

Sidney

After dinner Friday night I immediately launch into get-ready mode. In the shower, I linger longer than I do in the mornings, letting the water run hot and relax me. I scrub at my knees and elbows, until they're red from the friction and not Kool-Aid. I mentally run through my wardrobe as I feel my muscles go soft and limp. Caleb has already seen my hair in all of its wild, summer glory, so I don't bother straightening it. But I do put three different products in it, and silently applaud myself for giving it plenty of time to air-dry into smooth, shiny curls. It's possible I won't be at the party long enough for my hair to rebel. Fingers crossed.

In movies there's always a long montage of a girl putting on outfit after outfit, flinging things onto the floor and frantically pulling items off of hangers before finding the perfect outfit. That's what I look like, except for that last part. I never find the perfect outfit, but I settle on a short white skirt with a rough hem and a sheer, soft pink shirt that flutters just above my waist. It's the most flattering outfit I own—it shows off my long, toned legs and softens my broad shoulders. The dip of the neckline makes my chest look like there's more there.

But it's dressier than I'd like. Probably too dressy for drinking with people like Kara or Lindsay. Kara, who is always casual—she's T-shirts and shorts and nondescript tank tops. And Lindsay, who is Lindsay. There's a chance I stick out like the out-of-place tourist that I am. Which is basically my personal nightmare.

Maybe it only feels dressy because I've been living in my swimsuit for a week straight now. That can definitely warp your sense of style. When I get home in August it usually feels weird to wear clothes every day. Pants are like a straightjacket for my legs. I wonder if I should put a swimsuit on under my outfit, but tell myself that Kara would have warned me if I should have. Most locals don't live on the water, so it's more likely we'll be in a house or a backyard than on the lake.

When I walk into the kitchen, Mom is sitting at the table running her little metal scoring wheel across a piece of red glass. During the year she teaches middle school English, but in the summer she makes stained glass pieces to sell at craft shows and online. She tries to get as much work done in the evening or sitting outside as possible, so she can enjoy the days on the lake. Days on the lake that she likes to remind us are partially funded by her summer glass business. There's a crack of glass just as I pass through the dining room into the kitchen.

"Are you and Ash going to the same place?" Mom asks. She doesn't say *party* because I didn't say it. I told her I was going to hang out with Kara and some of her friends, which is the truth. She can fill in the blanks, but I'm not voluntarily serving up motherly anxiety on a silver platter for her. I already know where this line of questioning is going, though.

"He'll probably want to stay longer than me," I answer, trying to route her brain away from gas savings. "And I'm not drinking."

"But what if Ash needs a ride home?" She's using her mom-voice now. "I'd feel better about it if you rode together, just in case."

"Mom . . . in a few months I'm going to be going to parties and you won't even know it. Asher, too."

"Maybe you can drive each other to those parties, too?" she says in a teasing tone.

"Maybe not," I say, my level of disgust matching her tease.

"For now, I *do* know about it, and it would make me feel better if you'd just—"

"Fine." I give in, because there's no winning with her. Another five minutes, and she'd be googling drunk driving statistics and making me watch some video narrated by a sobbing mother who wishes she could see her daughter just one more time. My mom has a knack for finding that stuff in record time. I'm not entirely sure she doesn't have it sitting on her computer and phone in little folders neatly labeled with each cautionary activity. DRUNK DRIVING, DRUGS, SEX. When I turned sixteen there was a whole texting-while-driving marathon presented to me, and to this day I barely even text when I'm a *passenger*. I'm thoroughly traumatized. She should teach classes, because she has this whole mom thing down.

With a quick kiss on my head she walks past me, toward her bedroom. "You look nice."

"Thanks." Her words help unwind the little ball of tension still spooled in my stomach, but also, she's my mom, so it hardly counts. She's genetically programmed to love me and think I'm beautiful.

I text Asher to let him know we're riding together and tell him I'll be ready in five minutes. The party starts in fifteen. I've had Asher's number for years, but I'm not sure I've ever used it before. I've only seen it on my screen once. An obvious one-ring pocket dial earlier this year.

Alone in the kitchen, I lean against the counter, nervously eating a trail bar. I pull at the hem of my skirt and consider for the nine hundredth time if I'm overdressed. Or underdressed. Either way, I'm 100 percent positive I'm overthinking it, and there's zero chance I'm going to stop until I get there. I tip my head back, my neck hanging loose, and take a deep breath.

The screen door slams and my head snaps down. Asher is in the doorway, in the same shorts he was in earlier, and a dark gray SWIMMERS DO IT BETTER T-shirt that looks so soft I'd want to touch it, if it wasn't on Asher. *Casual.* The word buzzes over his head like an old neon sign. He looks so much more casual than me. Even more casual than what he usually wears. Is he *trying* to torture me?

He looks at me a second too long, and I take another quick glance at my white skirt and pink gossamer shirt before pushing off of the counter. "I'm going to change really quick." I'm about to cross into the living room when Asher grabs my wrist. Something sparks across my skin, reminding me of his hand on my foot, my leg. I pull my arm free to make it stop.

"You look—fine." *Fine.* He looks pained to have said the word. It hurts worse to hear it.

"A ringing endorsement," I say. I'm not sure what I expected from him, but *fine* doesn't make me feel great about my go-to outfit. Have I looked *fine* every time I've gone out *thinking* I was absolutely killing it? Even though it's Asher—who lives to torment me—it still leaves a little dent in my self-confidence.

He shoves his hands down into the pockets of his shorts. "I wouldn't lie—I have to walk in with you."

"And I have to walk in with *you*," I say, glancing down at his T-shirt and raising my brows dramatically.

"Oh, come on, this is hilarious." He looks down at the shirt again, as if he forgot what was there. "And think how good you'll look next to *this*." He waves a hand across his shirt, top to bottom.

That makes me smile against my will. *Stupid, traitorous smile.* I wish he really did look bad; that he wasn't the kind of guy who looks good in everything.

"Do you want *me* to change? Because that would be quicker. If you go in that room"—he glances down the hallway that leads to my bedroom—"we might never get out of here." He crosses his arms over his chest and his face is smug. "I bet you started getting ready right after dinner."

I *hate* these freaking co-family dinners. "Stalker," I mutter, because I hate how predictable I am even if he's not. "Fine," I say.

"Fine, you're not going to change?"

"Fine, I won't change . . . if you do." I give him a *take that* look.

Asher rolls his eyes.

"You offered," I point out, my voice innocent and sweet.

"I'll meet you at the car in five," he says over his shoulder as he walks out the door.

I'm sitting in Dad's car, blasting the AC, when Asher comes out of his house. It's dusk, almost dark, but I can still make him out in the light cast from the porch light. And suddenly, my clothes offer a whole new kind of problem. I mutter his name like a curse.

Asher

The entire drive is a struggle to keep my smile in check. Sidney's face is a mask of simmering, barely concealed rage. Like maybe she'll run us off the road just to take me out.

Because we match.

I didn't plan to do it. Well, okay, I did. But not until I was in my room, looking at the pink shirt in my drawer. It was meant to be.

As we walk up to the house I can't control myself any longer. "How much do you hate me right now?"

Sidney jabs her elbow into my side and her mouth twists into a scowl while mine breaks into a grin.

"You *asked* me to change," I say, pushing the rolled-up sleeves of the shirt to above my elbow. "Demanded it, really." My voice is laced with mock annoyance.

She grunts. Only Sidney could make a grunt sound dainty. "I was just being helpful."

"You're never being helpful," she counters, and when we get to the door she pauses, like she's not sure what to do. Maybe she's going to bolt.

"You're overthinking this. It's just a party. With people you'll probably never see again." I push the door open so she can go ahead of me. "And I was helpful just yesterday, when I picked up your tampons."

Her head snaps toward me, her eyes narrowing into slits. Sidney's going to punch me one of these days, I'm sure of it. I'm not entirely convinced I won't have it coming. Good thing I have that box of tampons she refused to pay me back for, so I'll be able to stop the bleeding. It's also a good thing Mom isn't the type to ask for a receipt and change, or I'd have some explaining to do. As it is, I just have a giant box of tampons under my bed. *My summers are so freaking weird.*

"You mean *your* tampons?" she says as we step into a living room filled with people. This house isn't like the rental houses right on the lake. It's a normal house that people live in all year, with family pictures on the walls and furniture that matches. And it doesn't smell like it's closed up for six months out of the year as the Michigan winters blow through. But it doesn't have the lake or the river. It's on a side street in the country, outside of Riverton's little downtown area.

We're only two feet into the house before Kara is on us. "Wow," she says, and I'm already regretting that I didn't run on sight. "You guys look like a matching pair."

Sidney puts her hands on her hips and makes a little strangled noise.

"Like prom dates or something," Kara continues, giving my pink button-up a once-over from top to bottom.

I roll my eyes.

"Why are you so dressed up?" Kara looks from me to Sidney,

a can of Diet Coke in her hand. She's in a Riverton Football T-shirt that's tied tight at her back, and a pair of worn jean shorts. She looks like she just threw clothes on, but she has about ten times more makeup on than Sidney.

"Am I?" Sidney says with a groan, running her hands down her skirt again. "I should have texted you."

Kara's voice is soft and soothing. "No, you look great." She glances over at me with a smile. "You, too, Ash."

"Thanks, Kara." I give her a one-arm hug and walk toward the kitchen, looking back to see Sidney's bewildered eyes fixed on me. She's looking at me like I'm standing in the middle of the room naked, not like I just hugged someone I've known for five years. Someone who *does* go to parties. "Getting drinks, you want anything?"

Kara pouts. "Not me. I have to get up ridiculously early tomorrow."

Sidney just shakes her head.

Sidney

I scan the room, letting my eyes wander over all of the people I don't recognize.

"He's not here yet," Kara offers with a smile that tells me she knows who I'm looking for. "He mentioned at work he might be late. They moved him from the The Grill to livery crew."

"Livery crew?"

"The guys who pick up all of the canoes at the end of the line. They had some equipment to track down from people who got out at the wrong spot and just abandoned their canoes."

"Ah."

Kara tips her head toward the kitchen. "You wanna go see what's up over there?"

"Sure, I'm up for whatever."

Kara laughs. "Yeah, that sounds like you."

I pull on the little nubbin of fabric at the back of her shirt and she squeaks out a little *hey*. In the kitchen, the countertops are covered in plastic glasses and various partially empty bottles of alcohol. There's a giant case of cheap beer at one end of the counter, and a clear glass bottle filled with a greenish-brown liquid that just says NOT YOURS on it, in black marker. Beyond the kitchen, there's a little dining room area where a long wooden table fills most of the space. A big blue tarp is spread under it, and the top is littered with more red cups.

Near the table, Asher is throwing back a shot of something with two guys. I've never seen them before, and I wonder if he even knows them, or if he's just being Asher: friend to all. He tips the glass back, and when his head comes down, his eyes meet mine.

"You wanna play?" Kara says, grabbing my hand and pulling me toward the table.

Asher is at one end, standing with another guy. Kara and I take our places at the opposite end.

"Can we play?" Kara says. "Wilson, you think you can handle double-fisting? I'm not drinking tonight."

The guy smiles and snorts, like Kara's being ridiculous. "For sure," he says, leaving his side of the table to join ours.

"All three of us?" I say.

Asher laughs. "You're with me, Chipmunk."

I growl and Asher laughs again. Is this an alternate dimension I've fallen into? Does Party Asher have no self-control? "Why can't Kara and I be a team?"

"Because neither of us is drinking." She shoves a hand against my back. "Get over there."

Asher hands me the Ping-Pong ball. "Try not to suck, okay?"

I stick my tongue out at him and he pretends to grab at it. "What the hell?" I can't help but laugh, because it's such a goofy, un-Asher-like thing to do. "Get a grip on yourself, Marin."

Asher smiles and waves a hand toward the table as if to say *it's all yours*.

Unfortunately for Asher, I really do suck at this game. It takes me three shots to not over-throw and even make contact with the cups.

Asher doesn't tease me again. He shouts "so close" and "next time" whenever I miss, and high-fives me like I just won the Olympics when I finally sink my first shot. He's dramatic about each glass of beer he has to drink, throwing his head back and chugging loudly, even though the glasses are only half-filled since the guys are doubling up. It's utterly surreal to hang out with Asher like this—maybe it's all the beer he's had to drink because of my horrible hand-eye coordination.

When we finish—not win, because Kara and Wilson absolutely annihilate us—Asher tries to pitch a cup into the trash and I slap it out of the air. "Hey! Those can get washed or recycled."

Asher lets out a booming laugh. "Okay, Little Kris." Asher pats me on the head. "Your mom is really rubbing off on you."

I narrow my eyes and turn back to the table.

Asher comes up beside me and whispers in my ear. "I'm just kidding. I love your mom. Please don't tell her I said that." I smile, and we're standing like that, Asher's lips by my ear, when Caleb walks into the kitchen.

Asher looks from me to Caleb, and says he's going to go get something from the kitchen. Kara trots over to my side of the table and gives me a high five.

Caleb looks nervous but happy when he makes his way through the kitchen to us.

"You came," he says, like he's both surprised and glad that I'm here. He sidles up next to me and puts an arm out. I carefully try to give him a hug while avoiding the red cup he has in his hand. It's awkward but not horrible.

"I did." I wish I could think of something flirty or clever to say, but I just feel caught off guard. Something about Asher being nice to me has made me feel less like myself.

Kara has a little smile pulling her lips tight, and she looks like she's about to explode with happiness that the two of us are standing next to each other.

Caleb takes a sip from his cup. "Anyone stalked you around the grocery store lately?" His voice is light and teasing. "You know that's my job."

I smile back at him. "No one picks out apples like you do."

Kara looks between us like she's confused why this is funny.

"Caleb is a produce expert, did you not know?" I explain.

"Guilty," Caleb says, lifting his cup a little.

Kara and Caleb are talking about a disgruntled customer at River Depot, explaining who everyone is to me, when I feel someone next to me. Kara's eyes drift to my side nervously, and I look to see Asher there. He holds a cup out in front of me, and I look at the cup and then him. "*Still* driving us," I say, eyeing the shot glass he has in his other hand. "*Still* not drinking."

"It's Diet Coke," he says, leaving it there in front of me.

"Oh." I take the cup hesitantly, and turn back toward Caleb. I sniff it, just to make sure it isn't a giant cup of soy sauce that I'm going to spit all over myself.

There's a soft tickle against my ear and the smell of alcohol. "You're welcome," Asher whispers, and it sends a little shiver up my spine. He needs to *stop* doing that. I don't turn to look at him until I know he's walked away, because I'm afraid of how close he was to me.

I take a long drink from the cup. Kara is looking at me like my hair is on fire.

Caleb shifts from foot to foot, like he's not sure if he's going or staying. Or like he's got something in his shoe. "Are you guys . . . a thing?" he blurts out.

"Definitely not," I say, at the same time that Kara says, "They hate each other." She says it in a very matter-of-fact way, but looks at me questioningly, her brows knitting together, as if I need to confirm this. I nod, my eyes wide. What is *wrong* with people? You accidentally show up in matching shirts and suddenly the world is spinning in *reverse*?

"Okay, it's just that you match, and he seems—"

"*Deranged?*" I look from Kara back to Caleb. "We *live* to mess with each other," I say. "I was being weird about what I was wearing, and he had this stupid swimming shirt on, because he thinks he's *hilarious*, and I told him to change, and he said he would, but *then* he put that matching shirt on, just to be an ass . . ." I'm rambling, and I'm not sure how to stop myself. Kara mumbles something I can't make out but her eyes cut to Asher across the room.

"Got it." Caleb smiles and sets his cup down. "You wanna sit down somewhere?"

Do I want to sit down in the shortest skirt I own? No. Do I want to talk to Caleb somewhere that isn't the grocery store produce section, or in the middle of the next beer-pong game? Yes. Kara gives my arm a squeeze and says she's going to find some friends that are supposed to be here. Sometimes it's easy to forget that Kara lives here. She has a million friends, a job. She's the only friend I have here, but for her, I'm just one tiny piece of her life during the summer.

Caleb and I sit on a blue love seat pushed against one wall of the living room. Like Kara said, he had some trouble at work, and he spends most of the night telling me about how ridiculous the tourists are that come to River Depot. The kids from the city who have never held a paddle before, and the moms and dads who think they're going to need Mace to fend off wild creatures as they canoe through the woods. "As if Mace would help them," Caleb says, laughing. I wonder if he's forgotten that *I'm* technically a tourist. Though I don't feel like one—Riverton is my second home.

Every once in a while I hear Asher's voice boom across the room and it startles me. It isn't angry, it's just loud. Louder than I've ever heard him. I can't make it out, but I can't help trying. I spend the rest of the night with 60 percent of my attention on Caleb, and the other 40 listening for Asher. Toward the end of the party it sounds like his voice is being muffled by something, like maybe he's outside or in the basement. He seems off tonight.

An hour later, Caleb looks at his phone and frowns. "I have to go. We have a training thing in the morning." The same thing Kara has to go to.

"Okay. Well . . . I'm glad we got to hang out." Smooth, Sidney. Smooth.

"Me, too." Caleb runs a hand over his short blond hair. "You wanna go out tomorrow night?"

Something tightens in my chest. "Yeah. Definitely." I hand him my phone. "Text me."

Caleb smiles and gets up, reaching his hand down to pull me up from the couch. It's the first time we've touched all night—even on the little couch, we were at opposite ends. I'm not sure if I should just shake his hand while I've got it, or hug him, or . . .

He pulls me by my hand and wraps his arms around me, making the decision for me. "Night, Sidney."

"Good night."

When Caleb is gone, I wander through the house. Kara is long gone; she sent me a text an hour ago saying she was leaving. But I still have to find Asher. I weave through the kitchen, to the little room that looks like an office. I poke my head out into the yard, but don't see him. Finally, on my second pass through the living room, I see him coming out of the stairwell. He *was* in the basement.

"You ready to go?"

He looks past me, eyeing the kitchen. "Nope."

"Come on, I'm over this."

"So go home."

"You know I can't. I'm driving you home."

He just looks at me blankly, and I can't tell if he's about to say something, or if he's just going to fall asleep.

I spend fifteen minutes trying to coax Asher out to the car. I promise him food when we get home. Threaten to call his parents. Tell him that if we stay for a single minute more, I'm going to pass out from exhaustion. We've both been up since 6 a.m. That seems to convince him—maybe he forgot how tired he was. He lowers himself into my passenger seat in a slow crumple, and when we pull into our driveway he bolts from the car before I can even cut the engine. But he doesn't go to his house, he takes the walkway straight to the lake.

Crap.

I find him sitting on the hill, just on the other side of the row of flowering bushes that divides our yards from the fire pit area on the edge of the downward slope to the lake. I thrust a bottle of water at him, and ask him if he needs something to eat. He tells me to leave, but I won't.

"Why are you being nice to me?"

"Because I don't think you're going to remember this in the morning. And I'm not being nice. I'm making sure you don't die. That's not being nice, that's just being a decent human who doesn't want someone else to die."

"Right," he says. "Human."

I cross my arms over my chest. "Your parents will kill me if they find you dead in a puddle of your own vomit tomorrow morning." I'm trying to be patient with him, but I'm cold and so tired I feel a little drunk myself.

"You're not, though."

I shake my head, unsure what he's talking about. "Not what?"

"Human," he mumbles.

"Go to bed, Asher."

"Make me," he says, smiling.

God, he's impossible. I think about what could get Asher to leave, and decide talking to him may be my best bet. Maybe I can drive him back to his house with my presence alone. I sit down on the concrete walkway next to him. "You know, you weirded out Caleb tonight. You just *had* to mess with me and wear that stupid matching shirt." I take a swig of my own bottle of water. "At least I get a do-over tomorrow night."

Asher groans, like he's heard this a million times.

"You know, if you don't want to listen to me talk, you could just go to bed." I give him my best *I can be as obnoxious as you can* smile. "Problem solved."

"This is the only nice shirt I have with me." He pinches some fabric at his chest. "I don't know why you have so many nice clothes with you, but I don't." His words are all slurring together. "So I wore the pink shirt, because it was my only nice one. And you looked nice. Too nice." He grabs at the bottom of his shirt, and gets it halfway up his chest before he thinks better of it. He starts working at a button and he has half his shirt undone when he starts up again. "So then we *both* looked too nice. And yeah, we also matched. Sorry."

He dressed up so I wouldn't be the only one? My overtired brain can't even process it. Asher being *nice?* But I saw his face, he was thrilled that we matched. I would bet that was the whole appeal. Looking nice and taking the spotlight off of me was just a side effect of torturing me. He's got all of the buttons undone, and is sliding one arm out of his shirt. "What are you *doing?*"

"I'm hot," he says, tossing his shirt to the side.

I look out at the lake because it's weird to look at him shirtless, even though that's how he looks all day. But he was just clothed, and *I'm* clothed, and that's different somehow. "Seriously, will you go inside, please?" He doesn't move and I stand up. "I can go wake up your parents."

"Fine, fine." He throws his hands in the air. "I'm *going*."

But he isn't. He's just sitting there, his head turned up to the sky, like he's investigating something there.

"Do you remember that first summer?" he says.

It's actually what I was thinking of when I saw him sitting here. The way we used to sit out on this hill for hours past when our parents had given up on the evening. When the night air got colder, and no one wanted to refuel the fire, because firewood is at a premium up here, and Nadine hoards her personal stash— ironically lined up right outside Lake House A—like the greedy little troll she is. That first summer together feels like a lifetime ago.

"Ouch." I smack at a bug that's feasting on my thigh. I nudge Asher in the side with my toe and nod toward the houses. "Please?"

"Just go."

"I can't leave you here."

"I'm not going to die in a puddle of my own vomit, Sid." Apparently when Asher's drunk, he calls me Sid. It's highly unnerving. "What if I promise not to lie on my back?" He rolls over so the last few words are muffled in the grass, and I can't help but laugh.

"Come on, Asher." I poke him once more with my toe and walk away.

"Where are you going?"

"Shh," I whisper-scream behind me. "I'll be right back." I hike up the concrete stairs. "Don't die," I yell back at him in an angry whisper. He's rolled onto his back again, but I don't think anything's going to happen in the two minutes it's going to take me to get to the house and back.

I return with a giant orange pitcher of water—the one my mom used to make my cherry Kool-Aid in—and a box of toasted sesame crackers.

Asher looks at the pitcher as I set it down next to him, and takes the box out of my hands, looking at it like he's not sure what to make of it.

"The kitchen is right next to my parents' room. I had to be stealthy. Drink the water."

"And the world's grossest crackers were the *stealthiest* thing you could find?"

"For your information, I love these." I grab the box away from him and open it, sticking my hand inside.

He takes the pitcher with one hand. "I'm definitely going to puke if I drink all of this."

"Let's take that risk, okay?" I don't expect him to drink *all* of the water, I just didn't want to make multiple trips and risk waking my parents.

He lifts the pitcher up to his mouth, holding it by the handle, and takes giant gulps, his neck bobbing with each swallow. Maybe he *is* going to make himself throw up, just to spite me. To drive me to leave, maybe. I grab the handle and pull it away from his face, and a little rush of water spills down his face and onto his bare chest.

"Sorry," I say, my eyes snapping back to his face.

His eyes go wide in feigned shock at the word.

"Whatever," I mumble, lowering myself onto the grass beside him and stretching onto my back.

"Settling in?"

"Seems like you're never leaving. I might as well."

We lay in silence, looking up at the sky, and my eyes get heavier by the minute.

I'm not sure how long I'm asleep, but when I jolt awake, Asher's face is right next to me, slightly angled into the grass. He's so still I have a momentary panic that he's dead. I roll onto my side to face him. "Asher." I whisper it harshly, because I won't let myself really commit to the idea that something could be wrong. He doesn't move. "Asher." I can hear the panic in my voice. I grip his shoulder, and he startles with a soft jerk. I pull back like I've just been electrocuted. But Asher wakes slowly, his eyes fluttering, mouth parting. His eyes open, and close, open and close, as if he's reorienting himself, unsure of where he is.

He shifts a little, onto his side, and I think maybe he's finally going to get up, but instead he reaches one hand toward my face. And I realize—for the first time since I thought he was dying here on the grass—how close we are. There are only inches between our faces, and I can feel every one of them sliding away as his hand meets my cheek. He brushes a piece of hair behind my ear, letting his palm brush my cheek, before stroking two soft fingers lazily down to my chin, like he's in no hurry. Like we lie on the grass touching each other all the time. Voice whisper soft, Asher says, "How much do you hate me right now?" His eyes close. He's going to pass out again, and it's hard to decipher whether I'm hopeful or worried.

I don't know if I've been holding my breath, but my chest feels like it's going to explode in the two seconds it takes his eyes to open again. And when they do, he leans forward, and with no hesitation, presses his lips to mine. I'm not sure if it's seconds or minutes that the heat of his lips caresses the chill of mine, but when he pulls away, it's with what sounds like a little sigh. Then he rests his palm on top of mine between us, closes his eyes, and like nothing absolutely ridiculous just happened here, he falls back asleep.

I don't.

THE FIRST SUMMER

Sidney

Being here with the Marins is so much different than last year, when it was just the three of us. I spent a lot of time by myself—mostly because otherwise it meant spending a lot of time with my parents. And they're not bad, but I'm going to be fourteen next month; space is my middle name. I had Kara once in a while, when she'd come over to swim, or lounge on the dock in the chairs we'd drag down the hill from the deck. But mostly it was just me, hanging out during the day, swimming and lying in the sun, and just being. Things were chill. Quiet. Like me and my parents.

This year, the whole atmosphere at Five Pines is different. There are tiki torches running along one side of the sidewalk that leads to the water. A string of twinkly lights haphazardly strung in a tree near the Marins' deck. Music plays from a speaker propped up on the wooden railing, pouring music out over the yard. The adults spend most of the day bouncing from drinks on their deck, to card games on ours, to lying on the lounge chairs. And it's not that I feel unwelcome, it's just . . . too much. Too many parents, too much giggling. Too many re-counted college stories I just don't need to hear.

We're almost a week into vacation, and Asher and I aren't strangers anymore, but we're not friends yet. I think that's my fault. Because Asher is probably the cutest guy I've ever met. He's funny, and nice, and the kind of guy that wouldn't give me two minutes at my school. He's even a swimmer. On paper, Asher Marin is pretty much my dream guy. Which means that when he comes within five feet of me alone, I forget what words are.

A few days into vacation I bought a paint set at the dollar store in town, and I've started painting rocks. At least if we talk, I have something to do with my hands now. Something to fill the nervous quiet spots. It hasn't happened yet, but I'd rather be prepared.

I'm painting a rock on the deck when Mom sits down in the chair across from me. She tilts her head to the side, and I know we're about to have a Kris Walters heart-to-heart. Mom picks up a rock and toys with it in her fingers. "This is cute, Sid."

"Thanks."

"So, listen . . ." Mom rubs her thumb over the smooth surface of the gray rock. "Is everything okay with you and Asher?"

My hands still. "How could they not be okay, we haven't really even hung out."

"I know. And I just thought . . . well, it's just that Sylvie was thinking . . . do you not like him? Did something happen?"

Other than me being a class-A jerk, no. Nothing has happened. "No, nothing happened. I'm just being my hermity self."

Mom smiles and rubs her hand over my shoulder. "Hermits are awesome. People wouldn't keep them as pets if they weren't."

I smile. "Those are crabs, Mom."

"Either way." Mom tucks a piece of my hair behind my ear. "Asher's nice. You're nice. I just don't want you to be bored this summer. Maybe . . . make a little effort? If you hate him, you can paint rocks twenty-four/seven, okay?"

"Okay." I put my hand out and my mom deposits the rock into my palm. "I think I can do that."

As Mom walks back across the lawn toward the deck and the other parents, she throws back a "Love you, Sid" over her shoulder.

I haven't really spent time with Asher since our parents had a mini-reunion at an alumni night swim meet three years ago, when we were ten. We shared his tablet and played games, and we haven't been in a confined space together since. Until tonight. Because *I can do this.* After dinner, I see Asher from my kitchen window, making his way down to the hill at the edge of the yard, where the fire pit is situated just beyond a row of tall bushes covered in big red berries that look like miniature apples. I wash the last dish, setting it on a towel on the counter to dry. The sink is still full of silverware, but Mom will do those, because *yuck.*

Last summer I helped Dad make fires every night, but this summer Asher has unofficially claimed the job. I grab a stack of newspapers from the little screened-in porch, take a deep breath, and head toward my demise. I mean, the fire pit. Hopefully the only thing to crash and burn tonight will be some logs. Fingers crossed. Asher is throwing logs into a haphazard pile within the metal ring when I set the papers down on one of the three wooden benches.

"Hey." Asher smiles at me, and I smile back without thinking, because lips . . . teeth . . . blue eyes.

"Hey," I finally squeak out. "Do you want some help?"

Asher puts his hands on his hips and looks from the sandy circle to me. "Yeah. I suck at this." I laugh and he looks at me. "What?"

I don't say anything, because the fact that he admitted that means we are so different. I'm afraid to talk to him, and he's confident enough to admit he sucks at something; he doesn't care if I know.

"I'm actually awesome at this," I say, picking the papers up and handing them to Asher. "I'll fix the wood. You start twisting these." I take a piece of paper in my hands and twist it.

Asher sits on the bench across from me and works on the paper, making a little pile on the ground in front of him while I pull all of the wood out of the circle.

"You don't like my stack?"

"It's more like a pile." I find a thick, straight log and stand it on its end in the middle of the ashy circle. "Fires need air, you can't just dump the wood in there." That's what my dad always said. I stack another piece of wood at an angle against my first. "I mean, unless you want to douse it with lighter fluid, but I consider that cheating."

"I didn't realize there were rules." He's smiling at me like he thinks I'm funny.

I shrug. "There aren't, sometimes I just make them up."

Asher watches me as I stack pieces against my first, creating a cone. Before I put on the last piece, I wave at Asher. "Stick a handful of paper here." I use my log to point to the gap and Asher squats down, shoving paper into the open space there. "Do the same thing on the other side," I say, and he does, carefully removing a log before shoving in more paper.

Asher is standing next to the fire pit, hands on his hips, looking pleased. "Nice."

"We're not done yet." I pick up another handful of twisted papers and start sticking them into the cracks between the logs, leaving short pieces exposed. Asher grabs paper and does the same on the other side. "These are like a bunch of tiny fuses."

Asher nods but doesn't say anything. I pick up the long lighter on the bench next to me and hold it out to him. He shakes his head. "You should probably do the honors."

I circle around our creation, lighting all of the little paper tails on fire. The center begins to glow, growing brighter and brighter, until the flames break through the cone of wood. I sit down on the bench behind me, right next to Asher. I didn't even think about it, but now that I'm here, it would be weird to move.

"Where'd you learn that?" he asks.

"Lots of trial and error last year. But mostly my dad taught me."

"That's cool."

We sit in silence for a few minutes before Asher finally breaks it. "My mom said you swim a four-hundred-yard IM. That's one of my favorites."

"Yeah?" I love individual medleys because unlike the team events, you don't have to worry about whether you're screwing something up for someone else. It's just you, good or bad. IMs are a love-them-or-hate-them kind of thing, and something about knowing Asher and I are in the same camp relaxes something inside of me. It's a very tiny, very specific thing we have in common.

Our parents join us at the fire, and while they talk, Asher and I roast marshmallows, make double-decker s'mores (his idea) and throw the tiny little apples into the fire to see if they'll explode (also his idea). Eventually the adults announce that they're going back to the Marins' cabin to play cards, and tell us to douse the embers when we leave.

Once we're alone, we get quiet. We sit for a few minutes, staring at the fire and poking at glowing logs with our metal roasting sticks, before Asher breaks the silence. "There's a meteor shower this week. It doesn't peak for a few days, but we can probably see some tonight." Asher stands up and walks behind his bench, sitting down on the grass. He lies back on the ground, and I stay on my bench, watching him. Asher looks prettier in the dark somehow. Maybe it's the last of the fire, casting his skin in a soft warm glow. Maybe it's the way he smiles while he's talking to me, and light glistens off of his white teeth. Everything in my chest tightens as I look at the empty space next to him on the grass and force myself to stand up and walk over.

Only a few inches separate us. We're wedged between the bench and the cement walkway that leads down to the dock. Maybe I should have moved the bench over so we weren't so close, but now I'm here, and it would be weird to get up and move it just so I don't have to be so close to him. *Don't be a nervous jerk, Sidney.*

I'm prepared for how awkward it's going to be to lie in the silence together, but Asher doesn't let it last more than a few seconds. As soon as my head hits the grass he's pointing toward the sky. "Meteor showers usually originate around a certain constellation, so if we find it, then it'll be easier to see the meteors. Especially this early in the shower. And into the night."

"It's close to midnight."

"Most meteor showers actually peak closer to four or five a.m." He points up into the sky. "We're looking for Perseus."

"Which one is that?"

"He's a god." Asher's fingers trace across the sky like he's mapping it out with his fingertip. "But honestly, he looks more like a one-legged stick figure. Like something my three-year-old cousin would draw."

I laugh. "They all look weird to me."

Asher taps at the sky. "There." He traces his finger in a pattern I can't follow. "Do you see it?"

"Mhm." I stare in the general direction of Asher's hand, hoping it will magically come into focus for me.

"Really?"

"No."

Asher pulls his phone out of his pocket and his fingers fly across the screen. He holds it out to me. "They're pretty hard to find if you don't know what you're looking for." The screen is filled with stars and lines, and he's right, this hardly looks like a person, let alone a god. Someone had a *very* vivid imagination back in the day. I turn my eyes back to the sky and keep searching.

"Anything?" he says.

I don't say anything, just shake my head. But as I'm staring up into the sky, wondering if my brain just isn't wired to see constellations, I see the tiniest little spray of light. "There!" I thrust my finger at the sky and Asher laughs. "I saw one!"

"Is it your first?"

"Yeah."

"Well, there should probably be eight or ten an hour right now. Not that we'll catch them all, but . . ." His voice trails off into silence.

We lie on our backs and stare up at the sky until I'm woken up by Asher patting my hand with his. "Sid, it's really late. I didn't know you fell asleep."

We make our way back to our houses, but the next night we're in the same spot. "How do you know so much about constellations?"

I can feel Asher's shoulders shrug next to me, ruffling the grass. "We learned about them in fourth grade, and I just always thought they were cool. I guess I was kind of a nerd about it afterward."

I nod. "Can you show me Cancer?"

"Is that your sign?"

"Yeah."

"So you have a birthday soon." It's not a question, just a statement.

"You know all of the zodiacs, too?"

"I know generally when they are." Asher points a finger at the sky. "Cancer is one of the faintest." He traces his finger along the sky like he always does when he's trying to find something. Then he taps at the night sky, like it's a framed map overhead. "Okay, there."

I stare and stare as Asher traces a shape across the sky, but honestly, I don't see anything but a mass of tiny lights.

"I'm a lost cause for constellations," I say.

Asher laughs, and we go back to looking for meteors, counting twenty that night. We lie on our backs every night that week watching for meteors, tallying them up like stones dropped in our beach buckets. Even after the shower ends, we spend most nights on the grass, staring up at the sky, our fingertips so close we could touch.

And the next month, when it's my birthday, I find a surprise on my bedroom ceiling. A constellation of my very own, mapped out with glow-in-the-dark stars. Cancer—my very own crab—one I love enough to keep as a pet all summer long.

DAY 7

Asher

I don't remember getting into bed, but that's where I wake up the next morning. In a cold puddle.

Holy crap, did I actually pee the freaking bed?

I'm still in the fog of sleep as I let my brain work through how I'm going to break it to my mother that her eighteen-year-old wet his bed. What a proud mom moment that will be. Could I get everything bagged up and thrown away, without being caught? I don't even know where someone would buy new sheets around here. There's one little strip of stores that includes the grocery store, a dollar store, a hobby shop, and a salon. It's a forty-five-minute drive to an actual mall.

I am never drinking again.

The clock says 9:20. I hear voices in the kitchen and spring out of bed, feeling my head revolt against my body being upright. My stomach lurches and I give myself to the count of five before walking, to make sure I don't puke. Two long strides from the bed and my door is locked with a click. I'm about ten minutes away from my mom barging in, insisting I get up and enjoy the day. I strip my clothes off and throw them on my bed, rolling my sheets into a pile and wrapping them in the crinkly plastic mattress pad underneath. How much would it cost to replace all of this? These aren't even my sheets, they're Nadine's, so can I really just toss them?

I dig clothes out of my drawer and pull on a pair of basketball shorts. I haven't figured out what to do with everything yet—how I can get it all to a Laundromat undetected—but making an appearance will buy me time. When I get into the kitchen my parents are sitting at the table. There's a plate of cinnamon rolls in the center, and Sidney is in the chair to the right of my mom, wide-eyed and smiling.

"Good morning." Her tone is so chipper it almost hurts.

"Morning," I mutter. "My alarm didn't go off."

"I hate when that happens," Sidney says. Her voice drips with mock sympathy.

"Sidney brought us extra cinnamon rolls," Mom says, just before biting into one.

"I love them, but Dad doesn't," Sidney says. "We had way too many." Sidney bites into one of the gooey circles. "Plus I wanted to see if you wanted to take a run with me. I was going to drive down to the trails that run by the river."

"That's a great idea," Mom says. "You two will be teammates soon."

Sidney's eyes dart from my mom to me, but if she's surprised that the two of us will both be swimming at our parents' alma mater in a few months she doesn't show it. I suppose even without talking we have our moms to keep us both flush with intel. I'm about to tell my future teammate there's no way I'm running this morning, when I realize that this is my chance. My ticket out of the house for a few hours, no questions asked.

"Awesome." I sound unintentionally ecstatic. Sidney's surprised face makes the sharp pang my own voice just shot into my head almost worth it. She never expected me to say yes. "Give me a few minutes."

Sidney turns back to my mother, who is peppering her with questions. Glancing at everyone at the table with their attention focused on gooey rolls—and Sidney—I make my way to the sink. I've never been so glad to have her in my house. Quietly, I open the cabinet underneath and pull out a black trash bag. I don't look back at the table. I clench it in my fist, close to my side, and walk as fast as I can toward the hallway without running. When I'm back in my room I stuff my pile of bedding into the black bag, pull on socks, shoes, and a T-shirt, and shove my bag of shame out the window. It lands on the gravel driveway that runs behind the house, wedged between it and Dad's car. From the corner of the yard I see a flash of movement. Nadine is standing in the yard, looking between my head hanging out of the window and the giant bag now lying on the ground. I give her a tentative wave, trying to look casual—*nothing to see here!*—and retreat back into my bedroom.

"You ready?" I say as I walk back into the kitchen, grabbing a napkin and a cinnamon roll before bolting toward the door.

Sidney follows after me, keys in one hand and a bottle of water in the other. "Feeling good this morning?" she says, her voice more annoyed than sympathetic.

"Fantastic," I say.

"You *look* fantastic."

I haven't looked at myself at all this morning. I didn't even stop in the bathroom. For all I know she covered my face in Sharpie last night.

"Do I have a dick on my face or something?"

"What?" She looks legitimately shocked. "No." She shakes her head, her face twisted in disgust. "What am I, a ten-year-old boy? Give me some freaking credit."

Sidney turns toward the car and I jog to the right. I pick up the garbage bag and haul it toward her car on the other side of the driveway.

"What are you doing?" Sidney says.

"Pop the trunk."

She leans her hip against the car and crosses her arms. "Not until you tell me what's in the bag."

"I'll tell you in the car," I say, and hear the trunk click and pop.

"Well?" We're a mile down the road when Sidney finally presses me on the contraband in her trunk. "Am I helping you hide a body or something?"

"Why, do you have experience in that? Have a checklist you need to go back for?"

She gives a little grunt of annoyance. "Please, as if I'd keep any evidence of that," she says softly.

"I need you to drop me off at the Laundromat."

"Why?"

"Because I hear they have the best breakfast in town." I roll my eyes. "What do people *usually* do at Laundromats?"

"Doesn't your dad do laundry on Tuesdays?"

"Just drop me off, Sidney."

She drums her fingers softly against the steering wheel. "Did you . . . have an *accident* or something?" Sidney is barely controlling herself. She sounds like she's about to break into laughter at any moment. Her shoulders are shaking gently.

"What did you *do*? Put my hand in warm water or something? Jesus, Sidney."

"Settle down." She sounds defensive. "You seriously thought you *peed* the bed?"

"What the hell was I supposed to think when I woke up in a wet bed?"

Sidney shakes her head and rolls her eyes. I think she mutters *boys*. "You *obviously* never babysat. Pee has a . . . very distinct smell."

"Well excuse me for not sniffing the sheets I thought I peed on. I was a little distracted by the fact that I thought I *peed the bed*!"

"Wow, you are a drama llama this morning," Sidney mutters. I had fully expected drama today, but this isn't what I had in mind at all. We drive the rest of the way in silence. When we pull into the parking lot in front of the Laundromat, Sidney unlocks the doors.

"What are you doing?"

"Dropping you off," she says matter-of-factly.

"Sounds like I don't need to be here," I say, annoyed. Not that I want to run with her, but at least I could just sit somewhere for an hour.

"You still need to wash them," she says. "They're going to be sticky."

"From?" I practically growl it at her. I am so not in the mood this morning.

"Lemonade," she says, trying her best to contain the smile working at the corners of her mouth. "*Your* favorite, if I remember correctly."

I slam the door and yank my bag out of the trunk. Apparently I'm spending my hour at the Laundromat.

"How much do you hate me right now?" she yells out the open window as she pulls away.

Sidney

Asher probably kisses anyone when he's drunk. Maybe everyone. I bet his standards are super low under regular circumstances, so what can I expect from him when he's trashed? Obviously I *can't* expect him not to kiss his arch enemy. Though that seems like the least you could expect of any guy who isn't currently starring in a Bond movie. So what's *my* excuse? Shock? Retaliation for that stunt he pulled in the lake? I *had* just woken up. Maybe I thought it was a dream.

I'm looking out the kitchen window, thinking about our drunken kiss and obvious mutual lack of standards, when my date—a guy who *actually* seems to like me—pulls into the driveway.

"Mom, I'm going out, I'll be back in a few hours." The door is half-open when I shout it behind me. Mom is sitting on our little screened-in porch, at her table covered in glass.

"With Asher?" The question shouldn't sound like an accusation, but it does, so I practically screech *no* as I let the door slam behind me.

And then, as if my mother just chanted his name into a mirror three times in the dark, Asher appears. Standing in the yard, halfway between our houses. He looks from me to the old black car sitting in the driveway, and as I pivot right toward Caleb, he pivots left, and heads toward the lake.

Caleb must catch the look on my face as we step out of his car five minutes later, because he looks apologetic when he meets me at my door. As I stare at the stone-covered restaurant that looks like a hobbit house built into the side of a hill, Caleb stares at me.

"You were so dressed up at the party." He shoves his hands into his khaki shorts. "I just sort of figured that was your norm."

He's not wrong, my first instinct would have been to wear the white skirt from the party. But it's still in a pile on my floor, light grass stains up one side from last night. *That kiss.* Instead, I'm wearing a cute blue tank top that hangs loose but is far from dressy. It could be, if I had paired it with a skirt, but I'm not wearing one. I'm wearing cut-off shorts. Because I was determined to show Caleb that I wasn't some stuck-up tourist who doesn't know how to relax. I didn't expect that he'd bring me to the *one* fancy restaurant in all of Riverton.

"You wanna go somewhere else?" Caleb runs a hand over his short hair, and his face is scrunched up in a way that tells me *this* was his plan. He doesn't want me to say yes. And so I don't. I shake my head, force a smile, and tell him it's fine. The only thing calming my nerves at all is the fact that Caleb isn't much more dressed up than I am. He's wearing a button-up shirt, but it's short-sleeved, and we're both wearing sandals. Not the cute, dressy kind; the beach kind. Flip-flops. And as mine smack against the tiled entryway, I tell myself to breathe. That no one is looking at me, or noticing what I'm wearing.

You'll never see any of these people again. The words remind me of Asher, of what he said to me as we stood outside the doors of that house just last night. Before I can stop myself I'm thinking about the kiss. As Caleb and I are led to our table, tucked away in a dark corner, I can feel Asher's lips, warm and slow. The weight of his hand laid on top of mine. The scrape of the grass against my bare legs as I twisted myself toward him. I have a menu in my hands by the time I shake myself free from the thoughts.

"This is really nice," I say, looking across the room at the small wooden tables topped with candles and white china. The long row of windows overlooking the lake in the distance. The light fixtures all glow amber, and everything about this place feels warm.

"It was my mom's idea." Caleb grimaces, as if he brought her with us. "I made the reservation myself."

He smiles and when I laugh he does, too. And it feels like something inside me snaps, because I'm not nervous anymore. The waiter offers us a wine list, and looks nervous that we might actually take it. Caleb asks me if the fritters sound good as an appetizer, and when I nod he orders them. While we wait, he tells me about how his dad brought his mom here on their first date, and it's both sweet and weird. Sweet that he tells me, weird to think that this could be the start of something. Weirder because he also adds that they're divorced.

When the appetizer arrives, he awkwardly puts a few pieces on his plate with the little silver tongs they brought us. In my opinion, anything that is stick-shaped and fried is finger food. This isn't what I had in mind when I thought of a first date with

Caleb. I figured we'd be riding the little water bumper boats at the tiny amusement park on the edge of town, or going on a dune-buggy ride. Silver tongs and sea bass were not on my radar.

My sea bass *is* delicious, though. And as I pick pieces off with my fork, and Caleb saws at his steak, I realize we haven't had to talk about anything real yet. We've had witty banter, and fun flirting, and quirky produce shopping, but we don't actually know *anything* about each other yet. Except that his parents went on a first date in this very restaurant. So technically, I know more about his parents than I do about Caleb.

When my fish is gone I break the silence. "Do you play any sports?"

He shakes his head. "Not since seventh grade. It turns out it takes more than being tall to be any good at basketball."

I smile and nod. "Yeah, I was the tallest girl in my class in seventh grade, and I was the absolute worst at basketball."

"You swim, right?" He must catch the surprise on my face because he immediately offers, "Kara mentioned it."

My heart swells a little at the thought of him asking about me. *Good sign.*

"Yeah, I'm swimming at Oakwood in the fall." It still feels weird to say it. Weird that after all of these years of dreaming it, it's actually happening. I always hoped it would happen, but maybe deep down I prepared myself, just a little, for my dream to end after high school.

"Cool," he says, sticking another bite of red meat into his mouth. There's a long stretch of silence and with every second that ticks by I deflate a little more. There's something really shitty about someone not realizing when something is a big deal to you. That you spent thousands of hours of your life working toward something, and you're in a small fraction of people that actually made it. It's not that I need everyone to ooh and ahh about it, but he's obviously not interested. At all.

"Yeah," I say, sticking a forkful of rice into my mouth. I kind of want to ask him if he has any beloved pets, and then give a dismissive shrug when he mentions them. I totally wouldn't do something that mean to anyone but Asher though, and the thought makes my lips quirk up just a little.

"What?" Caleb asks, eyeing me quizzically.

"Hm?"

"You were smiling."

Was I? I just shake my head because words are hard right now. And maybe going on a date the day after that kiss wasn't such a good idea. Or maybe, that was the *whole* idea. Could Asher have known? Last night is such a blur; did I tell him? I'm stabbing a piece of fish ten times more aggressively than is necessary when Caleb's voice cuts through the quiet. "What are you going to major in?"

"I don't know, actually."

"Really?" The surprise on his face unsettles me.

"Really. Why does that surprise you?" *You hardly know me,* I silently add.

"Kara just mentioned that you're . . . well, she didn't use these words exactly . . . but she said you're super organized. That you like plans." He makes a slashing motion with his hand like he's karate chopping the air.

I push some rice around on my plate. "I do like a good list. You'll have to stop talking to Kara or she'll give away all my secrets."

"I'm sure you have more exciting secrets." His lips turn up in a smile and mine do, too. We're back to the flirting, the witty banter, and when he drops me off at my house, he doesn't kiss me, but I can tell he wants to. But he's a nice guy, the kind that tries to impress you on a first date, and doesn't steal kisses. And as I'm sitting at the kitchen table eating one of my mom's famous chocolate chip cookies, a text chimes on my phone.

Caleb: I had fun tonight.

Sidney: Me too.

It's true—almost. Tonight was a perfectly adequate night, but I'm not sure that when Kara grills me about it, I'll call it fun. Caleb is nice enough, but there's definitely something missing there. And for the first time in a long time, I don't feel like waiting ten days to find out what exactly that thing is.

Caleb: Beach day soon?

Sidney: I was thinking

Caleb: Uh-oh

Sidney: We start school soon, and we'll be on opposite sides of the state. I was just thinking, maybe it's better if we keep things casual.

Oh god. Did I seriously just type *casual?*

Sidney: Friends casual! Not late-night texts casual!

Caleb: I get it. Text me if you ever want to hang out.

Sidney: Sounds good.

I'm just tucking my phone into my pocket when I open the door to my bedroom and my bare feet come into contact with something wet and cold. A breath later they slip out from under me. I crash onto my back, and my hands slip and slide as I struggle to grab hold of anything in the darkness of my room. Something thick and oily coats my hands and my feet, and as my eyes adjust, I see that the floor is shining with a white slickness. While I was out with Caleb, being completely traumatized by last night's kiss, Asher was continuing to torment me. He was rolling out what must be hundreds of feet of Saran Wrap. It's thick under me, taut over the thin, worn carpet, running in every direction, like a second floor under my feet. I raise a hesitant finger to my nose. *Mayonnaise. I hate* mayonnaise.

In my brain there are a million perfectly orchestrated pranks prepared for this summer. But as the light of the little fish-cleaning house glares into my room, throwing slashes of light over my floor that now glistens with the world's most disgusting condiment . . . a new idea overshadows all of them.

It's on.

DAY 8

Asher

When I leave for a run around ten, I'm not nervous that Sidney is sitting on the deck staring daggers at me. Because Sidney doesn't do anything on a whim. *She'd* never decide at 8:05 p.m. to go to the store and buy twenty rolls of Saran Wrap. To her credit, she would have worked out the square footage and known that she didn't need twenty rolls. That it was total overkill, and she could get by with twelve.

After two hours of watching a movie with our parents, I snuck away to the bathroom, opened her bedroom window, and then told everyone I was going to bed. I felt like crap so I'm sure I looked it. Totally believable. Twenty minutes later, when everyone moved down to the fire pit with giant margarita mugs in hand, I slipped in through the window and went to work.

Sometimes the beauty of a prank is in the spontaneity of it. The thrill of being caught, the last-minute problem-solving. It took me an hour just to tape the Saran Wrap to the baseboards and stretch it in a giant haphazard weave across the room, making sure I covered every square inch. Of course, if I had planned things out like Sidney, I would have realized I should start the mayo at the far end of the room, and work my way back to the window. Sidney wouldn't have had mayonnaise-covered shoes sitting in her room all night. But even if those sneakers smell like mayo for the rest of my life, it will be worth it to think about Sidney sliding across the room when she got back from her date.

It's a sweltering hot day, and I spend it on the lake, swimming the shoreline after lunch and lying on the dock through the afternoon.

"Ash!" I'm sitting on our deck reading a book when my mom's voice rings out of the kitchen. It's close to dinnertime, and I take my book with me, knowing I'm about to be enlisted for some sort of food prep. But Mom isn't working on dinner, she's purging or something. The table is covered with the contents of our fridge as my mom holds a package of some sort of meat up to her nose.

She thrusts the package at me. "Smell this."

"Um. Okay?" I sniff the package she's holding out toward me. "It . . . smells like meat, I think."

"Like good meat?"

"Yes?" I don't know if I've actually smelled raw meat before. "It sort of smells like nothing?"

She nods at me, like I've just confirmed she's not losing her mind, and turns away from me, pulling another white Styrofoam package out of the refrigerator and giving it an appraising glance before sniffing it. I'm about to ask her what she's doing when I smell it. I can't pinpoint exactly what it is, just that it's wrong and out of place, and *bad*.

"Go smell the drains in the bathroom," Mom says with a sigh. "Maybe something's backing up?"

I don't know if that's how plumbing works, but Mom looks so frustrated sitting on the floor of our kitchen sniffing all of our food that I'm not going to question it.

"Where's Dad?"

"I sent him to the store for baking soda boxes."

I nod, even though the longer I stand here, the less I believe baking soda is going to fix this problem.

In the bathroom I smell the sink drain, and the tub, and then the toilet, just to cover all of my bases. But now that this odor has invaded my nose, it's all I smell.

Smells are weird. On one hand, they're unmistakable. The smell of pancakes on the griddle can take me back to Saturday mornings at my grandma's house the second I smell it. I can tell if a pool has too much chlorine without ever getting in the water. But right now, the smell overtaking our house is like a word stuck on the tip of my tongue. Every time I think I can name it, it's just out of reach.

I go from room to room, pulling up blinds and opening windows as far as they'll go. First the living room, then my parents' room, the bathroom next to it, and then my room. I might throw up. There's nothing different about my room, except for the overwhelming smell. Whatever is in this house, my room is ground zero.

"Mom?" I shout toward my doorway as I start to pull things away from the wall, looking for vents. The only explanation for a smell this bad is that something has died somewhere.

My mom stops a few feet back from the door. "Oh god," she mutters.

"I think something died in here. Maybe we should have Nadine call somebody?"

"I'll go up to the house."

This isn't going to be fixed quickly, but Mom still sprints out of the house, as if every second she wastes will count.

I'm headed across the room toward the last small window when I see the pile of mayonnaise-coated socks and shorts from last night. There's a towel, too. But without even smelling it, I know it can't be the cause of this.

Oh crap.

Out the window I can see Mom crossing Nadine's yard, closing in on the back porch. I throw myself at the window and yell her name. She stops in her tracks.

"Has Sidney been here?" I'm trying to keep my voice in check, but I can hear the annoyance.

Mom is far enough away that she's almost yelling for her voice to carry far enough. "What? Why?"

"Mom. Yes or no? Has Sidney been in the house today? While I was gone?"

She nods, and takes a few more steps toward Nadine's house. I'm out of my room and through the house in a heartbeat, and before I know it, I'm across the yard and practically sprinting down the sidewalk toward the deck. Sidney's sitting at the little plastic table, rocks spread in front of her, and when my feet pound on the wood planks, her head snaps up. The look on her face when she sees the annoyance on mine is enough to confirm my suspicions.

"What did you *do*?"

She narrows her eyes at me and turns back to her rocks, swiping her brush across a shiny black one. "You can dish it out but you can't take it?"

Sidney

"You started it." When it comes out of my mouth I regret how much I sound like a bratty eight-year-old, but I don't regret saying it. I'm not sure why I even have to explain it to him. This is what we do, it's who we are.

"In what delusional world did I start *any* of this?"

"Pffsh." It sounds like a wild animal is stuck in my throat. "I still smell like mayo, Asher."

"And before that?"

"Hey, you *deserved* to wake up and regret you ever drank that much. I was covered in bug bites from babysitting you, just so you wouldn't die in a puddle of—

"—my own vomit." Asher rolls his eyes. "I know, I know. I wasn't *that* drunk, Sidney. You could have left anytime you wanted."

That sounds like an accusation and I don't appreciate it. *Wasn't that drunk?* He was drunk enough to kiss me. "And before *that?*" Before that, he kissed me. And I regret asking, because I don't actually want him to say it out loud.

"Before that, I put Kool-Aid in your shower. *You* smelled like cherry. *My* whole house smells like something died. My mom is losing her shit in there." He nods up at the house and my eyes follow.

Crap. Crapcrapcrap. "I didn't mean—"

"Just come fix whatever you did. We've searched the whole house. What did you do, stick something in the vents? Put some sort of slow-release capsules into our drains?"

I wish I'd thought ahead enough to do any of those things. "I put a fish under your bed." I don't meet his eyes. "Well, not a whole fish, more like fish . . . parts, I guess. But they were wrapped in paper, like at the grocery store and—"

"Caleb teach you that trick?" He shakes his head. "*Paper*, Sid?"

"I didn't realize. I mean, it was all frozen, and I just thought . . ."

"Our houses are a million degrees; you obviously *weren't* thinking."

There's nothing I can say, so I just shake my head. He's right. I was so mad last night, so worked up after my mediocre date, after finding my room like that when I was already mad at him about the kiss. I wasn't thinking, wasn't acting like myself at all.

He's already walking away from me. "Just fix it."

If Asher weren't in front of me, I would sprint to the house to tell Sylvie how sorry I am. But instead I leave a healthy distance between us, so it doesn't feel so much like I'm being summoned. Asher can be a real drama llama when he wants to be, but when I step into the kitchen and see the counters covered with food and the fridge swung open, completely bare, I know this isn't one of those times. And the smell . . . oh man. I am in so much trouble right now.

My skin prickles at the thought of facing Sylvie and Greg, and my parents, when they hear about this. "Where's your mom?"

Asher is standing at the edge of the living room, where the little hallway branches off toward his room on one side and his parents' on the other. "I told her to hang out at your house and take a breather." He shoves his hands into his shorts pockets. "She doesn't need to see this."

I wonder if it's him he's worried about looking bad, or me. Either way, I'm thankful I don't have to see Sylvie right now, while I'm the reason her house smells like *this*. Asher walks toward his room and I follow.

He doesn't look at me, and I don't say anything. When his bedroom door opens, I'm hit by a second, stronger wave of stench. *Crap crap crap.* "Fix it," is all Asher says as he closes the door behind him, entombing us in the smell.

"This isn't what I thought it would smell like," I mutter as I get down on my hands and knees in front of his bed.

"What did you *think* it would smell like?"

I grope a hand around under his bed. "Like the seafood section at the supermarket?" It's not actually a question, it's the truth. I thought it would smell like the little space around the lobster tank. But the truer answer is that I *didn't* think.

Asher shakes his head. My hand fumbles on something wet and soft, and I almost hurl right on the side of his bed, but I make myself hold on to it and pull it out. The newspaper is soaked through, disintegrating in my hands. All around it, the carpet is wet.

"Sidney . . ." Asher's voice is a perfect balance of disgust, disappointment, and sadness. I don't know if I've ever been so shamed by the use of my name. "What were you thinking?"

His eyes go from the mushy pile in my hands to his bed. Being sure to avoid me, he pushes his mattress up against the wall, exposing the metal frame underneath. There's a dark wet spot, and just as Asher steps into the rectangular frame, a muffled voice comes from the house. "Hello?"

"Back here." The words slip past my lips without thinking.

The look of horror on Asher's face registers before my mistake does. And before either of us can move, the bedroom door is opening, and Nadine is stepping in.

She gags as she takes a step toward me, sounding like she's about to dry heave. Asher is crouched down in his bed frame, one hand holding his mattress up to the wall. The soggy pile of papers is in my hands, no doubt dripping onto my shoes. I'll have to burn them. At this rate, we might have to burn the whole house down. Nadine jabs her chin at the soggy pile in my hands. "What is that?"

I have never wanted to drop something so badly before, but I hold on, trying to remain calm. I look to Asher, and swallow about nineteen times before the words finally come. "Fish," is all I say.

Nadine's bracelets jangle as her hands settle on her hips. "*What* is it doing in here?" She looks to the dark spot on the floor. "Besides soaking into the carpet pad and floor." She shakes her head.

Behind me there's a soft crash and then Asher is standing at my side. "It was an accident. A joke." His voice is light, the friendliest I've heard it all day. He nudges his elbow gently into my side and says softly, "Take it into the kitchen, Sid." Then his voice is strong and confident when he says, "We're cleaning it up right now. We'll take care of it."

I'm still standing at the edge of the kitchen, listening for her response, when she walks past me and out the door without a word.

Asher

Dinner should be at our house tonight, but for obvious reasons it's been moved next door. It's late for dinner, almost eight o'clock, because we had to get fans stuck in all of the windows, and Sidney drove to four different places trying to find a carpet-cleaning machine to rent. I disassembled my bed for her and moved my mattress into the hallway, but we didn't speak. The parents have hardly said a word to us, either, but disappointment practically radiates off of them.

"I'll do the dishes tonight," Sidney offers, and I almost feel bad for how shitty she must feel right now. She's not the kind of person who takes parental disappointment well. My guess is that Sidney is making herself feel ten times worse than her parents ever could.

"Obviously," her mom says, just as my mom says, "Asher will help." We didn't go into details about what happened—maybe the parents don't want details about who to be mad at when it's easier to just be mad at us equally. They're not completely wrong.

Sidney's poking at a piece of garlic bread when there's a knock on the door so loud the metal frame of the screen door vibrates against it.

Tom is up out of his chair, a step away from the door, when it swings open. Nadine steps into the kitchen, one of her usual brightly colored dress-shirt things hanging off of her. It's like a giant rainbow fabric-bag. Her blond hair is twisted up into a swirl on the top of her head, and her red lipstick is uneven at the edges, bleeding into the pale white of her skin. I will never understand how someone can live on a lake and be so pale. Or cranky. Isn't lake life supposed to be for easygoing people who love margaritas and cold beer and putting their toes in the sand? Or has country music been lying my whole life?

"Nad—" Tom's confused voice is cut off.

Nadine slams a piece of paper onto the table between the dads. "I want you all out in forty-eight hours."

"Nadine—"

"It's something every year. A mysterious stain." I think of the Kool-Aid shower, wonder if there are stains, and if she knows it somehow. "A broken piece of furniture." The deck chair we broke two summers ago. The one Nadine replaced with *the unicorn*. "I find pots in the wrong houses, and cabinets stocked with the wrong things."

"We share," Mom says, her voice soft and shocked.

"Because you are too comfortable." Nadine's face is cold. "This isn't your house. It's mine."

Kris looks like she might throw up. I know what she's thinking: for two months out of the summer, these are *our* houses. We don't think about the other people who stay here after us. These houses wait for us all year. They're *ours*. Our houses on *our* lake.

"Nadine, we've always paid for any issues," Dad says. That makes my face heat red. I didn't realize they were paying for issues that Sidney and I likely caused. Why haven't they said anything to us? Have they been skimming the money out of my college fund or something?

"Yes, but *I* have to fix them. *I* have to worry about the state of things for the next renters." She glances out the window toward my house. "*I* have to wonder what is happening in these houses."

Tom rolls his eyes but she can't see it. "This is awfully extreme, I'm sure we can—"

Nadine shakes her head briskly. "Forty-eight hours and I want you out. You'll get a full refund for the next seven weeks."

Dad's face pales and Mom looks like she might cry. *I* might cry. Or scream. Sidney is sitting, still and quiet, just like my mom. They both look like they may burst into tears at any moment.

"Where are we supposed to go? It's peak season, we'll never find rentals." Tom's voice is still calm, his face a mask of cool fury.

"Nadine, please," Kris says. "We've been coming here for years, this is a second home to us."

Nadine's eyes look at Kris sympathetically, and for a moment I think she's going to cave. But then her chin lifts just slightly and her face is hard again. And I may be imagining it but I think her eyes settle on Sidney for just a second too long to be comfortable, before she turns back to the four adults now muttering obscenities under their breath. "Forty-eight hours."

Sidney

After dinner, Mom, Dad, Sylvie, and Greg convene in our living room, and Asher and I are out on the deck after washing dishes in silence. We sit in white plastic lounge chairs, both of us avoiding the unicorn. Probably because it's a reminder of how our neurotic feuding has led to this. I came out here thinking it would be a good spot to eavesdrop without being obvious, but once the angry voices died down it turned out I couldn't hear anything at all.

"This is *our* fault." I've been thinking it since Nadine barged into our house, and I can't help but say it out loud.

"*Ours?*" Asher mutters, and it's the first time he's really spoken to me since Nadine walked in on us.

Defensiveness wells up inside me, guilt scraping at my throat.

"I'm gonna cruise around the lake and look for rental signs."

"Can I come with?" I hate how desperate, almost panicked my voice sounds.

There's a long stretch of silence, and I'm expecting more annoyance from him. More anger. Because no matter what I say out loud, this *is* my fault. There should be smoke coming out of Asher's ears, for how hard he's thinking about this simple question. As if he's just been asked to go on a boat ride with a serial killer. I don't even know why I want to go. Maybe I just don't want to be alone out here when our parents finally emerge. The guilt is so much easier when it's directed at us, and not just me.

The silence is killing me, so I finally break it. "I want to hit something."

"Not it." His eyes finally swing from the imaginary spot on the lake where they've been fixed and land on me. The lightness in his voice surprises me.

I roll my eyes. "And ruin that pretty face of yours? I would never."

Asher smirks. "You think I'm pretty." The familiar snark in his voice relaxes something inside me just a fraction.

"*You* think you're pretty." I hear the whir of a blender and look back at the cabin. It's not fair that they get to drown their sorrows in peach daiquiris and we just have to suffer. With each other. But sitting here is just making me anxious. I'd rather be doing something, helping somehow.

Maybe my inner monologue has come out, because Asher shifts in his chair and says, "Fine, let's go."

He stands and holds a hand out to me. A normal person would probably take it without thinking, but I just stare at it. As if I'm not sure what to do with such a strange appendage. He rolls his eyes and grabs my hand, pulling me up out of the chair. Then he walks away, headed toward the boat. I don't know why I'm so unnerved, but I am. I feel like I'm about to walk into an ambush. An animal fed treats before being led to the slaughter. *Not* that Asher touching my hand was a treat. *Obviously.* I think about the other night, the way he touched my face, laid his hand on mine, put his lips on mine, and a little shiver runs through me. I don't know if it's pleasure or fear. Maybe the two feel too similar when it comes to Asher. He walks toward the boat, and

I let myself wait a few seconds, watching him cross the grass and step onto the dock.

He stops and turns toward me. "Are you coming?"

The lake is calm, smooth like glass as we skip across it in Dad's little fishing boat. Asher is in the back, sitting behind the steering column, and I'm on the bench seat that stretches in front of it. The air is blowing his hair into what looks like a mohawk and it's such a funny look for him, I'm having trouble taking my eyes off of it. With his hair off of his face it's easier to notice the bright blue eyes, and the way his cheeks are red from the sun. He *is* pretty. Obnoxious and arrogant, but pretty. I'll give him that.

"You look like a dog with its head out the window," I say, my eyes drifting past him to the shoreline.

"I feel like one."

I want to bite back with something snappy, but all I can think about is that there aren't many rental signs out on the lake. I've spotted three so far. Two of them were tiny little cabins that looked smaller than my bedroom, and none of them were next to each other.

"What do you think happens if we don't find houses?" I sound nervous. A kind of nervous I don't usually let Asher see.

He shrugs. Maybe it's the wind that's making his cheeks so red—his whole face is starting to pink up. "We all go home, I guess."

We sit in silence as we make our way around the long oval lake. Usually we're boating *across* the lake—slowly—and it's surprising how quickly we boat around the entire perimeter when we're going at a normal speed. It's half an hour later when Asher cuts the engine in the deep water in front of our houses. *Our* houses. That's what I wanted to scream at Nadine while she stood in *our* kitchen. We're still hundreds of feet out from the dock, much too far to just let ourselves drift in.

"What are you doing?" I ask Asher.

He doesn't speak, just opens a compartment next to him and starts digging around.

"Are you going to kill me out here?"

Asher pulls out a tangle of silver metal and rope and shakes his head at me. "Stop it." He starts pulling on the rope until he has it bundled in one hand. He tosses the anchor out toward the deeper water and pulls on the rope until it's taut, and the stern of the boat swings toward the shore. Then he slumps back into his seat. "I don't feel like going back yet."

"We're just going to sit here?"

"Yeah, do you think we can manage that?" He sounds angry, and I'm not sure what to make of it. Our usual banter is teasing and snarky, but it's really never felt mean or angry. I'm not sure what I did. It's not like this was *all* my fault. Our pranks are tit for tat, and he's done just as many of them as I have.

I don't say anything, just look at him from under my lashes, and shrug with a muttered *whatever*. I look at the shoreline. At the two little white houses sitting like mirror images above the water, Nadine's house looming twice as high behind them. And it finally sinks in that whether we find new houses or not, we're never coming back *here*. My chest tightens and I can feel the tears threatening. It's too much—too many things ending. High school, and friendships, and summer vacations. These two stupid, tacky little houses.

The tear escapes before I can stop it, trailing down my cheek like a silent good-bye. I keep my eyes focused on the shoreline, avoiding the boy whose eyes I can feel on me.

"I kind of thought we'd come here forever." Asher's voice sounds as sad as I feel.

"Forever?"

He shrugs. "Forever-*adjacent*, I guess."

"Yeah, me, too." And I mean it. I had told myself that this was going to be the last year, that once I was in college I'd be too busy to go on family vacations, too old to hang out with my parents. But deep down, I think I knew I'd be back here. Maybe not for two months, but for a week or two, at least. Escaping summer classes or a demanding job. Taking a break before swim practices start each fall. The sadness is welling up again, and another tear falls and splashes against my bare leg. This time I wipe it away; there's no way Asher didn't see it.

"Mom said you made the team at Oakwood."

I take a deep breath to steady my voice. "Yeah." I can't help but smile. "I found out a few months ago."

"Weird that we'll be on the same team for once, huh?"

I shouldn't be surprised we'll be teammates, because Oakwood has a great Division II swim program and it's where our parents went, where our moms swam. It's been at the top of both of our lists for a long time. But I am surprised, because I always thought Asher would go Division I. "Your mom never said anything until yesterday morning. I had no idea," I admit.

Asher shrugs. "Maybe she thought it would be funny if we just ran into each other in the pool."

He looks as nervous as I feel when he says, "On the bright side, you'll have easy access to terrorize me."

"Ditto."

"We can go in now if you want." Asher stands up and puts a hand on the anchor's rope.

"Maybe just a little longer."

He smiles, and I can't remember the last time I saw him smile at me. But then the memory of our kiss hits me like a wave—the curve of his mouth before he kissed me, the softness of his lips, the look in his eyes. His smile now doesn't hold the promise it did that night; it's small, inconsequential, but I return it. "We can stay as long as you want," he says. But we both know it isn't true.

DAY 9

Asher

The parents spend the next day feverishly house hunting. They sit around the kitchen table in the morning, huddled together like some sort of war council, and we don't see them again until midafternoon when they come home during a gap in their showings.

"How's it going?" I ask my dad anxiously. He's sitting on our deck with a bottle of beer. The way he's looking out at the lake longingly, like he might be saying good-bye soon, isn't making me very optimistic.

"It's . . . going," he says, taking a drink and setting his bottle on the white plastic table beside him.

"I'm sorry," I say, because I feel like I need to. "You guys must know the shit me and Sid do every summer, and I don't know what happened this time. Things just . . ." He's still looking out at the lake. "I'm sorry we screwed this all up."

"Not that I want to condone this weird feud you and Sidney have going on"—Dad takes a sip and puts his bottle back down—"but I don't think that's what this was really about."

"But Nadine said—"

"I know what she said, but this is the first time she's ever said anything to us. I think she's got some sort of agenda of her own." He points to the giant house looming behind us. "Ever since they built that house, things have been tense around here. Maybe she's finally over having renters in her backyard."

"Then why build your house behind rental houses?"

Dad doesn't say anything, just points his beer at me and raises his brows, as if to say *exactly*.

It doesn't change the situation at all, but it makes me feel a tiny bit better to think that this isn't entirely about Sidney and me.

Dad swallows and licks his lips. "Listen, I know things are . . . weird . . . with you and Sidney. But you need to figure it out. Fix things with her. We've always let the two of you hash things out, because you're both good kids." Dad sets his empty bottle on the railing. "But it's starting to affect everyone."

I nod.

"How's the letter going?" Dad's voice is brighter, like he's flipped a switch from the sad Sidney situation to the bright and happy topic of my future as a financial planning wizard. Or maybe since he's a wizard, that would make me an apprentice. Or me being a wizard would make him a mage?

I don't know anything about wizards or mages, so I suppose I'm just avoiding *The Letter*. It sounds so ominous and important. It *is* important. And maybe a tiny bit ominous, too, though it's hard to pinpoint why just the thought of it puts a knot in my stomach. "I'm working on it."

"Can I read what you have so far?"

Dear Mr. Ockler . . .

I have a feeling Dad wouldn't be impressed by my current progress. "Maybe next week?"

Dad nods, and looks back out toward the lake.

"You think there's any chance we'll find houses?"

Dad pushes himself up out of his chair and turns back toward the house. "No idea, but we'll do what we can." He takes a few steps toward the kitchen door, where I see Mom standing.

"We have a few showings left today, and a bunch of properties we still need to hear back from. We've called everyone locally we can, trying to find houses that might not normally be available." He puts a hand on my shoulder. "It's not looking great, though. And you should know, Mom and I agreed that the Walters get first dibs if it comes down to it. This whole thing started with them."

My stomach sinks. Sidney could stay, and I could leave? How is *that* fair? I glance over at the deck by the lake where Sidney is laid out on the unicorn, her hair fanned out behind her. She looks peaceful from this distance; soft and gentle. I can almost imagine she's that girl I met my first summer here, and not the competitive psycho she actually is. Her sunscreen and water bottle are on the deck beside her. As I look at her I think about a very important question: if this is the end, what will my final farewell to Sidney Walters be?

Sidney

"Wanna see the new house?" I hear Mom's voice before I see her. The door slams and she comes bounding into the kitchen, practically yelling into the living room, where I'm curled up on the couch with a book. "You're inside?" she says, clearly disappointed that I'm not fully embracing the day I've been given at the lake. It feels like she just walked in on me shaving my head or something.

"Too much sun this morning," I say, turning so she can see my red chest, framed by the white straps of my tank top. "I loaded up on aloe, so hopefully I'll be back out there tomorrow."

Mom nods in approval.

I set my book down on the couch and follow her out to the car where Dad is waiting for us with the engine running. Across the yard I can see Asher in his kitchen, talking to his parents.

Did they find a house, too? We follow the road that wraps around the lake for at least fifteen minutes, until we're in a tangle of little side roads I don't recognize.

"Where are we?" I ask, looking out the window at the water, trying to place our location on the perimeter of the lake. I'm disoriented by the faraway strip of trees and houses I can see past the homes in front of us.

"Pretty much the opposite side of the lake," Dad says.

"In that little bay that dips in," Mom adds approvingly. "The water is always calmer over here."

My mother, always finding the silver lining.

I don't say anything, because I don't really have any opinions about the different areas of the lake, and I'm not sure why I even asked. All I know is *my* side of the lake. The side where the bottom is sandy, and the shallow waters stretch out farther than seems possible. We turn off of the main road and onto a dirt path that leads into heavy pine trees. I assume it's a road until it finally empties out into a grassy yard. There's a gray house ahead. Unlike Lake House A or B, this one looks more like an actual house and less like a cabin. It's bigger, and newer. We pull up behind it, right next to a FOR SALE sign.

"Are we buying it?" I ask, before I can stop myself.

"We talked them into renting it while it's on the market," Dad says. "A Realtor may have to bring someone through once in a while."

Mom cuts in. "But it's a vacation home, and it's been on the market for over a year, so chances are good we won't be bothered too often."

Dad nods. "Fingers crossed."

"Cool." I don't know what else to say. I don't plan on having a problem with any house they pick. It is, after all, my fault that we're being kicked out of *our* house.

I follow Mom and Dad to the side of the house where a

beautiful dark wood door leads into a little tiled entryway that dumps into a long room. To the right is the kitchen, and to the left is a round wooden table and white chairs. Behind it, a row of three windows looks out toward the lake.

The kitchen is twice the size of our old kitchen, with a little peninsula that juts out and three bright red metal stools. Beyond it is a large living room with skylights, and a three-season room to the left that leads out to a large two-tiered deck. Like Lake House A, this house is set on a hill, but we're right on the edge of it, practically hanging over the water, set alongside a little jut of trees. To the left of the deck, a small beach area stretches out, and a dock cuts into the water.

On the opposite end of the house there is a master bedroom with bathroom on one side of the hallway, and a large bedroom on the other side. Beyond them are a laundry room and a large bathroom. At the end of the hallway are two more bedrooms. Everything in this house is in shades of white, blue, and gray, with pops of yellow here and there. Compared to the dark paneling and garage-sale furniture of Lake House A, it's like looking into the sun, being surrounded by so many pale colors.

"This is ridiculous," I say as I join my parents out on the deck. The sun is setting and the trees that stretch up across the hills on the opposite side of the lake look like they're on fire. The house isn't that fancy, but it's a million times nicer than what I'm used to at the lake. There's an attention to detail here that Nadine obviously never bothered with. This feels like a house someone might live in all year. It almost feels too nice for a vacation house. There's something comfortable and low-stress about worn-in furniture and mismatched lamps. "We can afford this?"

I regret saying it. My parents don't ever bring up money. I have no idea how much our usual cabin costs, but this one is at least twice as big and ten times as nice, so I can only assume.

"It would be a bit of an adjustment," Mom says, leaning on the railing next to me, her eyes fixed on the lake. Her voice sounds cautious. Maybe this isn't a done deal. Maybe I shouldn't get my hopes up. I look out across the water, trying to make out where our old house would be on the horizon, but everything looks like a mass of green and blue from this distance.

Behind us a door slams, and I hear voices inside the house. I hear Sylvie first.

"Did they find a house, too?" I say in Mom's direction, before they reach the deck and it becomes rude to ask.

"They did," Mom says, her voice full of relief.

I smile, glad that Asher and I didn't ruin everyone's summer. Maybe this can all still be salvaged after all.

"Where?" I ask as Sylvie steps out onto the deck, followed by Greg and Asher.

Mom pushes her hair back from her face and looks to my dad, who takes a step toward my mom, like they need to be a united front. But a united front for what?

Asher pushes through the door from the three-season room and his lips are tipped up in the faintest hint of a smirk. He looks like he's about to sneak off to find my purse and fill it with earthworms. But he stays right where he is, just outside of the door, and greets me with a tip of his head. "Hey, roomie."

My heart sinks. Drops to my feet and rolls right off of the deck and into the lake. "Excuse me?" I'm talking to Asher, but I'm looking at my mother, who is giving Asher a sideways scowl.

"We were getting to that," she says, a smidge more irritated than I've ever heard her with him.

Asher looks appropriately scolded, and shoves his hands into his pockets. "Sorry, Ms. Walters." *Ms. Walters?* What a little suck-up.

"Seriously?" It's the only thing that will come out of my mouth—I can't even form a full sentence. All of the words have left my head.

"Obviously you're not sharing an actual room." She shakes her head at me, like I'm being ridiculous, even though I've only said one word. "This is the best-case scenario. We can't find anything else on short notice and together we can afford this."

I look back out at the lake and let it settle over me. Seven weeks in the same house as Asher Marin. Not just dinners together, but probably breakfasts and lunches, too. A shared television, and deck, and yard. A shared bathroom, maybe. Access to my . . . *everything.* I'll have to buy padlocks for my dresser drawers. Maybe something industrial to lock up my unmentionables.

"My room is off-limits," I say, fixing Asher with a stare.

"Of course," Dad says, a little more aggressively than I was expecting. I think he and I have different concerns regarding what Asher could do in my bedroom. Behind my mother, Sylvie is nodding her agreement.

Asher has wandered over to the side of the deck closest to the yard, and I sneak a glance at him. He's already looking at me, his face emotionless. "Of course." He shoves his hands into his pockets and raises his brows at me. "Same goes for you."

I cut him a glare and my eyes dart over to my parents. This is the most we've ever let on about our . . . *issues* . . . in front of them. "Of course."

Mom squeals and Sylvie does a giddy little jump in place. Dad and Greg nod in approval, clearly proud of themselves for finding a solution to what could have been a disastrous end to everyone's vacation.

"This place is going to be like a freakish college reunion soon," Asher mutters as he walks past me. "Let's go pick bedrooms." He says it so casually that I'm waiting to hear what teasing comment comes next, but nothing does.

I follow him off of the deck and back into the house, which, even at dusk, is luminescent. We're halfway down the long white hallway when Asher finally speaks again. "I don't care which one I get, so you pick." He stops in front of the two rooms at the end of the hallway, one on the left and one on the right.

"We're *sharing* a bathroom? What kind of fresh hell *is* this?"

"The kind where we don't have to go home and sit in our normal houses for the summer." He nods toward the bedroom door to my left. "Don't be a baby."

I fight the pout I was about to give him and I can see the smirk forming as I twist my mouth into what I'm sure is an absolutely demented-looking smile.

"You can lock your bathroom door from the inside," he says. "Not that I plan to creep into your room."

I let out a little snort as we walk into the first bedroom. It's a pale blue-gray with yellow-and-white-striped bedding and little lamps with shades wrapped in lace. There's a huge painting of daffodils on one wall and a mirror trimmed in shimmering white shells. At the foot of the bed is a long wooden box with a wicker lid. I run my hand over one of the dark blue pillows scattered on the bed. "I'll take this one."

"Sure you don't want to look at the other one?" Asher asks, glancing toward the open bathroom door.

"Why, did you do something to it?"

"Maybe I did something to this one." His brows hitch, and he shoves his hands into his pockets. "You've never seen this room before." He smiles. "You wouldn't even know what was wrong." He looks around the room. "It could take you days to figure it out. Weeks, maybe."

I shake my head at him. "I'm good. I like this one." I sit down on the bed and bounce a little. "This window faces the lake."

Asher shoves his hands into his pockets again. He looks like he's about to say something, but then he turns and walks through my bathroom door, closing it behind him.

I lay back on the bed and watch the fan spin in slow circles over the bed. This room smells so fresh and clean it's unnerving. I take a deep breath and try to find any of the musty lake smell I'm used to, but all I smell is the fresh linen candle on the bright white nightstand, and the lingering smell of Asher. I walk over to the bathroom door and twist the lock roughly. This is the last time he's going to be in this room, even if I have to barricade my door.

DAY 10

Sidney

When I see the piece of paper lying on my bed, my first thought is that we didn't even make it twenty-four hours in this house without Asher invading my room. My second thought is that I need to do a full sweep to figure out what he's done. Everything on my dresser looks normal. Usually if Asher messes with my room, the telltale sign is him messing around with all of the crap I keep neatly organized on my dresser. He finds some sort of sick pleasure in leaving things in complete disarray. I think of my bathroom items and know I'll need to check that out, too. But first, the paper.

It's a postcard-size piece of white paper with Five Pines written across the top in dark blue—from one of the little notepads Nadine puts in every room of her houses. I collected them all when we left and shoved them in my bag—the most ineffective, passive-aggressive *screw you* of all time. Though it did make my vindictive little heart happy to put them in the kitchen drawer of our new house. *Ha. In your face, Nadine—I stole your stationery.*

I grab the paper off of the bed and read the words written in neat blue pen.

Meet me at midnight
on the dock.

Asher. I mentally add the signature, because while his name isn't there, the list of people who could have left the note is short. Cryptic notes aren't really Sylvie's or Greg's style, and if Mom and Dad wanted to talk to me they'd just do it. No need for midnight meet-ups and mysterious notes. Plus, even if there was a full roster of suspects, I've gotten enough ransom-style notes from Asher to recognize his handwriting. Between dinner and then our first campfire here, I wonder when he had time to sneak in here. But just as quickly as I think it, I remind myself that we live in the same house now and he's just one room away. I locked the bathroom door, but I had never expected him to be bold enough to just come right into my bedroom from the hallway. It's a whole new ball game now. One where we have a frightening amount of access to each other. I suppose I should be thankful that we're sharing a shower, so there'll be no more Kool-Aid in my future. *Note to self: never shower first.*

By eleven thirty I have the rest of my room unpacked. Kara texted me and convinced me to go to another party next weekend, since I tanked our last plans by forcing us into a last-minute move. I *should* just go to bed. Avoid Asher's mysterious meeting, and crash. After a full day of packing and unpacking two families' worth of stuff, I'm exhausted.

Don't go. It buzzes in my brain like a dying lightbulb, warning me this absolutely can't be good. *Don't go, don't go, don't go.*

But at 11:59 I'm not lying in bed, I'm slipping on my shoes and traversing the wooden stairs down to the dock. There's one light pole by the walkway, but we haven't figured out where the switch is yet, so it's pitch black beyond the small halo of light that surrounds our deck. On the set of wooden stairs leading to the dock I stub my toe on an uneven step and barely catch myself from falling. Maybe *this* is Asher's secret plan—let me tumble down the stairs and roll to his feet. Possibly unconscious.

I don't see him on the dock until I'm about to kick him with my foot. I let out a little squeak when I realize the dark spot is his body. He's sitting on the edge about halfway down, his feet dangling into the water.

"You scared me," I mumble, standing awkwardly next to him as he drags his feet through the water like a little kid seeing the lake for the first time. He doesn't get up, so I slip my shoes off and squat down next to him, sitting down carefully on the old wooden dock.

"You rang?" I say quietly, because my voice feels riotous in the dark stillness of the night.

"I wrote, actually."

I spread my hands out in front of me. "And here I am."

There's a long beat of silence as we both fidget our feet in the water, our eyes firmly fixed on where they're submerged. My eyes have finally adjusted to the dark, and I sneak a glance up at Asher, who sucks in a long breath, like he's about to confess to something horrible. After all we've done to each other, it has to be truly awful to have him this nervous.

"I want to call a cease-fire."

I don't say anything. I'm not sure I heard him correctly. Maybe I did stumble down the stairs, and this is me, in an unconscious otherworld where Asher isn't Asher. Maybe I'm dead. Or this is a dream.

"A truce," he clarifies.

"I know what a cease-fire is. I'm not an idiot."

"I would never call you an idiot." Asher sounds annoyed. Maybe he's as tired as I am.

"Why?"

"Because we could be doing better things with our evil-genius-style skills, Sid."

Asher never calls me Sid. Unless you count the night he was drunk—the night he kissed me. It sends a warm fuzzy ball into my stomach that makes me uncomfortable and a little nauseous. "What do you propose?"

"I propose we combine forces against a common enemy."

The only other people around are our parents, and I don't see it going over well if we turn our attention to them. "I can't sabotage my mom's shampoo, I still need my parents to help pay for college. And *my* shampoo," I say. "That crap's expensive." I hold a lock of hair in my fingers. "I have to buy sulfate-free shampoo, and special conditioner, and these special extra-soft towels, just to keep this hair in check," I say matter-of-factly, stopping myself from the nervous ramble that is waiting just behind my lips.

"Nadine," Asher murmurs, and I turn to look at him, not sure I heard him correctly. "We call a truce on all of our crap with each other. And we focus on making Nadine's summer without us so much worse than it ever was with us there."

"That's . . ." I think about it for a minute—let it marinate in my brain a little. It's immature. So childish. ". . . super spiteful," I scold, and his face drops a little. I turn my eyes to the water and then back at him. "I like it."

He smiles and I can't help but do the same. "So you're in?" His voice is hopeful and surprised.

"I'm in."

Asher

"Should we talk details?" Sidney asks. "Is this a permanent cease-fire? Or for certain hours? Or just when we're together on a mission?"

I snort at the word *mission*. I guess I'm not the only one in my own imaginary one-person army around here.

"And are we talking all summer, or just until Nadine is thoroughly punished?" I'm not sure Sidney has taken a breath yet.

Or blinked. "And what *is* the goal with her, anyway? Do you think we should—"

Here we go. "Sidney?"

"Asher?"

My name holds the same amount of disdain as usual, except it's coming from right next to me, as opposed to our usual sparring distance, so it stings a little more.

"It's been ten seconds since I suggested this. We don't need a detailed strategy just yet. Can you calm your control-freak brain for two seconds?"

She narrows her eyes at me, but it seems like she's having to try a lot harder than usual to look annoyed with me. Maybe it's all in my head. "You'll appreciate my attention to detail now that we're on the same side."

I hold my crossed fingers up in the air between us and she rolls her eyes. "I'm counting on it. Otherwise, what else can you really offer?"

"Whatever," she mutters. "You'll be sor—"

I laugh as she stumbles on the last word. "Go ahead," I challenge. "Finish it."

"Sorry."

"Sorry you said it?"

She shrugs. "Sorry I forgot already. Being on the same side might take some getting used to." She looks at me with a truly puzzled look on her face. "What am I supposed to do with all of the extra time I'd usually spend"—she looks around like she's searching the night air for the word she needs—"plotting?"

I was going to say torturing. "I don't know, I guess we just plot *together*? And we do normal summer stuff? Like we used to?" My eyes have fully adjusted to the dark and I can see the pained expression on her face. "I'm not saying we have to do it together," I add, just to make sure we're on the same page. "I mean, the plotting, yes. But the other stuff . . ."

She doesn't let me finish. "Plan."

DAY 11

Sidney

I'm not a mean person. I'm really not. And while I don't love parties and huge groups of strangers, I'm not straight-up antisocial, either. So it probably shouldn't be this hard to force myself out of bed. Why does the thought of sitting at our kitchen table with him make me feel like my bed is the only place I could ever be truly happy? Any normal person would think that not being in a feud with someone would make life so much easier.

Except that when someone has been your nemesis for long enough, it's not easy to switch off that little voice in your head. The one that says you have to be alert. Watch for traps, be prepared for retaliation. Set your own traps before he catches you in one of his. Do. Not. Trust. Because what if this truce is the longest prank ever? Asher seemed genuine when he suggested the truce—and I *do* want to make Nadine's life miserable—but that voice is still screaming in my head, telling me that now is not the time to let down my guard and trust him.

I glance at the clock; it's 6:02. I've already listened to the soundtrack of Asher's morning. The open and close of his door, the bathroom faucet turning on. Does he brush his teeth *before* he gets in the shower? Weirdo. He took a short shower—barely long enough to have washed everything—and then there was the click of the door again. Listening to it all felt a little bit like being in the bathroom with him; my room even faintly smells like his body wash now. *As if this whole situation could get any more disturbing.*

I'm running out of time—if I procrastinate much longer he's going to give me crap about forcing *him* to get up early when I'm not even going to show up on time. Or maybe he won't. Does our truce require us to be civil at all times? More than that, are we going to be friendly now? Or are we simply stopping the pranks? I really wish we'd outlined more specifics on how this whole thing works. It's not that I can't be nice to Asher—I'm not a monster, I think I could be nice to anyone. I just want *expectations.*

When I finally walk into the kitchen at 6:32, Asher is sitting at one of the red stools at the breakfast bar, shoveling oatmeal into his mouth from a little glass jar. The kind my grandma makes strawberry jam in. He meets my eyes and nods toward the mug sitting in front of the chair next to him. I press my lips together. I mean for it to be a smile, but it's like my face doesn't know how to do that when looking at Asher. I'm pretty sure it looks more like a grimace, or like I'm constipated or something. It's not great, is what I'm saying. Trying again would be even weirder, so I don't.

Shake it off, Sidney. Just treat him like a normal person. A normal person who filled your yogurt cups with sour cream last summer, and froze your bathing suit once, but is now making you coffee.

I go to the refrigerator to dig for fruit and yogurt—that is hopefully *not* sour cream—and notice the top shelf is lined with pretty little jars like the one Asher is eating. They're stuffed with oatmeal. Some of them have strawberries, and others have swirls of gold and brown—honey and maple syrup, probably—and nuts. "Your mom makes these for you?" I say, picking up one of the little jars and examining it more closely.

"Am I twelve?" He shakes his head, and it reminds me of his

dad. Like he's scolding himself. "Sorry. No, I make them. Feel free," he says, jerking his chin toward me and my little glass jar. *Apparently I'm not the only one struggling to adjust.*

I put the jar back, then hesitate and pick it up again. *It's just oatmeal.*

This kitchen has four times as many drawers as our last one, and after I make three unsuccessful attempts at locating the silverware, Asher silently points his spoon at the one directly behind him. I open it and grab a spoon, wondering when breakfast became such a stressful time for me. I try again for a smile, and this time my mouth makes what I'm pretty sure is a C+ effort. There's no teeth, but definitely a clear improvement in my performance.

I sit down at my mug of coffee, thankful that we're sitting side by side and not across from each other. We're eating in complete silence, our awkwardness accompanied by the scrape of spoons, the soft setting down of our mugs, the squeak of our stools as we fidget and shift.

Our walk to the boat is as quiet as our breakfast, and by the time we reach it I feel like screaming just to crack the silence. Is this his way of messing with me, without actually messing with me? Seeing how long he can go before I crack and say something first? No, surely not. The truce was *his* idea, after all. But I think of his silence at breakfast, how he didn't say anything until I did. We're always quiet, though. I'm not sure if I *want* a change, or if I'm just expecting one.

At the boat, Asher steps on and holds out a hand for me. I look at it like it's covered in acid, and my eyes dart to him. He's holding back a smile, and when I finally take his hand, whatever hold he had on himself snaps. While I sit in my usual seat at the bow, he sits in front of the little engine, shaking with laughter. His face is pinked with the exertion of trying to hold it back.

What is wrong *with him?* Apparently this truce is driving us *both* a little mad.

He's barely composed himself when he tells me, "Tomorrow night we're going to scout at Five Pines." We finish our swim, walk silently back to the house, and carefully avoid each other the rest of the day.

DAY 12

Asher

You'd think a truce would mean Sidney and I could just act like normal people. The kind who can sit around and talk about normal things, like how to prank their former landlord. You would be wrong. Less than forty-eight hours into our truce, it's become very clear that we don't *know* how to act like normal people. We know how to annoy and avoid. And how to ride in a car in total silence. So I guess we're going to wing our first night at Nadine's.

We've only been out of the Five Pines houses for a few days, but already it feels like we don't belong here. Lake House A and B are dark—lights off, blinds drawn. There are no cars at either house. Even the air smells different—like it's missing the soft tang of fish that usually wafts out of the little hut next to Nadine's house, where the dads clean their catch. After Sidney weaponized that smell, I can't say I miss it.

"Creepy," Sidney says from behind me. Her eyes are fixed on the tall blue elf that peers at us from beside a little bush, with a red hat slumped on his head. I've always thought Nadine's statue collection was the weirdest thing ever. I swear their eyes follow you, like creepy little concrete Mona Lisas. And it's not just gnomes, it's frogs and dragons, and there's even a red brontosaurus statue. A *brontosaurus*. There were a few here when I first came, tucked in around the tiny cabins that used to sit in a row here, but since the house went up last summer they seem to be multiplying exponentially.

Sidney shakes her head in mock disgust, and I want to laugh, but I don't. We're behind Nadine's house, in the strip of trees that runs along the driveway and separates her property from the next. It isn't the time or place to be amused by Sidney, truce or not. We parked down the road, at The Little Store, which had been closed for hours by the time we arrived, and then we walked the half-mile to Five Pines.

"What do we do now?" Sidney whispers.

"We scout."

"Okay . . ." Her voice is sarcastic. "And what exactly does that entail? You know, for those of us who aren't expert-level lurkers."

"As if *you'd* qualify," I scoff. "All hail Sidney, Queen of the Lurkers," I mutter. Why can't she just talk to me like a normal person?

"Whatever." She takes a step ahead of me and I grab her arm, but she shakes away roughly.

"Sidney," I whisper-yell as her dark form struts off ahead of me, moving from the cover of the trees to the driveway. She bends down next to the house, and plucks a gray—almost blue—elephant statue out of the red mulch. It has yellow swirls painted across its bulging stomach, and ruby-red gems forming a little triangle that dips from the top of its head down its trunk. It's one of the most normal *things* in Nadine's collection, co-zied up next to what looks like a praying mantis statue. Sidney smiles triumphantly as she hoists it into her arms and cradles it—just as a light flicks on overhead, bathing her in bright white light. Motion lights. *That's* the kind of thing we're supposed to be scouting.

Shit.

Sidney

When I was a kid, I was a big believer in the T-Rex method of hiding. You know, the whole *Don't move and they won't see you* approach. My mom loves to tell stories about how she'd catch four-year-old me doing something, and I'd freeze in place, convinced that I was invisible if I could just stay still. Apparently my parents thought it was so hilarious that they played along, and I was eight before I fully grasped that this was actually the worst method of hiding ever. But ten years later it's still my first instinct when the light flashes on. I'm as still as the stone statue in my hands as the halo of light floods down around me.

Asher whispers my name so loudly he might as well just be talking. "Move." Then louder. "Sidney, *move*." And louder. "*Run*."

The word snaps me out of it and I start sprinting across the yard like someone's just fired a starting pistol. Asher takes off after me, and I can hear his feet padding on the grass behind me. The elephant is cradled under my arm like a football as we hit the sidewalk next to Lake House B, both of us on the same side for once, and it's not until I hit the stairs and am barreling downward, toward the water, that I realize this probably wasn't what Asher had in mind. I should have run *toward* the car, not away from it.

Where the stairs descend past the row of dense bushes, I come to a stop, practically throwing myself onto the ground beside them. Asher is two seconds behind me, and we're lying on our stomachs behind the bushes, in a row: Asher, me, and the elephant—I'm going to call her Edith—next to me. If we had rifles we'd look like something straight out of a WWII movie. Well, except for the elephant.

Asher looks over at me, to where I have one arm draped over

Edith. "What were you *doing?*" His face is so close to mine I can feel his breath.

I scrunch up my nose in mock disgust. "Brush your teeth next time there's potential that we're trapped next to each other."

"We wouldn't be trapped"—he rolls his eyes as he says the word—"if *you* would have just waited to hear the plan."

"Because you're the leader?"

"You *asked* me what to do!"

He's right, but I can't give him the satisfaction. Across the yard a door slams, and we both freeze. Through the gaps of the bush I can make out a silhouette in front of the house.

"We have to leave," Asher mutters.

Obviously. I get up slowly, hunched over so I stay below the tall bushes.

"This way," Asher says, jerking his head at the water.

"You want to *swim?*" I shake my head at him. "That's how people die, Asher. You don't swim across a lake in the dark, are you nuts? We should at least take a canoe or rowboat and go that way."

He shakes his head, looking at me like I've completely lost it. Maybe I have. I'm feeling very Bonnie and Clyde right now, like we're standing on the edge of a cliff, being closed in on by the police. *I think that's what happened.* Except the police are Nadine and the sirens are her yippy little dog circling the yard on its leash. The cliff is this lake I love so much, and I'm so worked up right now, I'd swan-dive off the edge for drama's sake if I wasn't sure I'd break my neck in the eighteen inches of water along the shore.

"We're not swimming. And we're not stealing a boat." He mutters what sounds like, *Are you kidding me?* "We're going to walk down a few houses"—he says it slowly, like if he talks too fast I won't comprehend any of it—"and then we'll circle back up to the road."

"Oh." That's a much better idea. A much simpler and safer idea. He doesn't need to know that.

"Follow me."

"So you can run ahead and leave me to get snatched?"

"*Snatched?* By *what* exactly?" His eyes are wild. "We're not going to jail tonight, Sidney. I mean, unless you decide to go rogue again."

"Fine, let's go. Lead the way, Oh Wise One."

Asher looks down at my feet. "We can't just leave it here." He's eyeing the squatty little statue still lying on the grass.

"I can't *steal* it."

"Oh, so jacking a boat for your big escape is fine, but tacky yard sculptures is where you draw the line?" He rolls his eyes. "Can you just stop arguing with me for ten seconds?"

I start mouthing *one . . . two . . . three . . .*

"We're not stealing it. We'll bring it back when we can actually put it where it goes." He waves his hand toward the house. "It was sort of hidden behind that bush, I doubt she'll even notice it's gone."

I squat down and secure Edith under my arm again. "Fine. Let's go."

Asher

Along the lake, everyone has a dense crop of trees that divides their property from the next. They're great for privacy and crap for walking through. My legs are getting torn up as we make our way through the long patch of trees and undergrowth a few houses down from Nadine, cutting our way back to the road.

Maybe it's the branch that cuts a thin slice along my knee that finally pushes me over the edge. "Just pretend I'm someone else." I can hear Sidney behind me, swearing under her breath as she probably gets her own cuts and scrapes, but I don't look at her. I'm tired of the scowl she's had permanently plastered on her face all night.

"Excuse me?" she says, her voice aimed at my back like an arrow.

"I've seen you talk to people like a normal human being. I've seen you be nice to Kara, to Caleb, to a random person who checks out your groceries." My voice is level. "I know you've got it in you, somewhere deep down. So when we get back to the house, just pretend I'm not me . . ." I hold a branch up to pass under it, and let Sidney go ahead of me. She gives me a skeptical side-eye glance as she passes under it. As if I'd snap her with a freaking tree branch. The look on her face makes me want to. ". . . if that's what you need, to make this truce work."

"Is that what *you're* doing?"

"I don't need to."

"What's *that* supposed to mean?"

"Sidney . . . just keep walking." I let her get a few steps ahead of me. It's not like we're getting lost in this twenty-foot stretch of trees. "And stop thinking about it."

DAY 13

Sidney

Kara sits down on our blanket while I strip off my tank top and shorts. "You couldn't make Asher do this with you? I thought he was your new swimming buddy."

We're at the beach, where the river cuts through the sand and empties into Lake Michigan. Some professional swimmers have those tiny training pools with a fake current that keeps them from going anywhere. I have this. And Kara, because my mom said, "If you're going to try to strip me of my record, at least don't drown while doing it." Not that I'm going to drown, but when currents are involved it's better safe than sorry.

I don't want to talk about why I couldn't ask Asher to come with me. Instead, I tell Kara he was busy, with as much indifference as I can muster, and I jog into the water. Into my happy place. I kick my legs harder, lengthen my strokes, thinking about the movements. If I can overcome the current and push myself forward, maybe I can overcome other things.

When I'm swimming, it's easy to let my brain go on autopilot. I think about what Asher said. *Just pretend I'm someone else.* I think back to the first summer, and try to let that Asher into my brain again. The Asher who showed me stars and left me birthday surprises, and built fires with me. I try to convince myself that all the summers since never happened. As the current beats against me, I think about everything we did that summer—all of the boat rides and trail hikes and beach trips. The nights by the bonfire. The newness of having just met each other.

Asher told me to stop thinking about it, but maybe what I really need to do is stop *remembering*. I need to go back to the first day of that first summer together, and start over. Or maybe it's the last week of that first summer that I need to redo.

And I will. The water is getting colder, and I stroke and kick, and kick and stroke, feeling the burn in my muscles. I'll give Asher one chance. *One*. And if he turns the tables on me—*when* he turns the tables on me—I'll strike even harder. But for now, I'll show Asher just how wrong he is about me. *I can be so much nicer than he could ever hope to be.*

Asher

I'm not sure why being pissed at Sidney finally motivates me to start my letter to Mr. Ockler, but it does. Maybe because I need something to take my mind off of how horribly this whole truce is going. Why is it so difficult for Sidney to just treat me like a normal person? My phone is lying on the bed in front of me, and I stare at the blank note screen. From the bathroom door, I can hear Sidney getting ready. The faucet going on and off, and things clinking against the counter. I'd love to know what takes her so long in there. Maybe she just really likes spending time in the bathroom.

I tap the yellow screen and think of all of the things my dad told me to tell Mr. Ockler. How excited I am about this opportunity (that my dad got for me), and why I'd be great as a financial planner (because people like me). You would think being a financial planner had more to do with being great with numbers, but the hardest part of it is actually sales. Building up a client base, going door-to-door meeting people and letting them know your services are available, getting people to give you control of their money. Dad loves to talk about how he spent the first eighteen months of his career walking door-to-door—*scorching heat, pelting rain, the coldest snow in all of Michigan*—building up a client base before his company would let him open a new office. How the first five years, he worked nonstop. The funny thing is that he thinks he doesn't anymore, because he can work remotely, but he's always on his phone or his laptop. He doesn't let a notification go unnoticed. Same job, different office, if you ask me.

Dear Mr. Ockler,
  I'm really excited to work with you. I'd be a great finan-cial advisor because, while I have zero interest in money or numbers or the stock market, people always like me. They probably wouldn't mind me standing on their porch and try-ing to sell them something. My dad says if I don't write this letter he's going to stop feeding me.

I laugh at my own joke, and the noise coming from the bath-room stops. I must sound like a lunatic. The thought of it makes me laugh again. Let Sidney be freaked out and think she's shar-ing a bathroom with some sort of weirdo. If she's going to treat me like one, I might as well lean into it.

Dear Mr. Ockler,
  I'm beyond thrilled to work with you. I'd be a great finan-cial advisor because I've had a ton of experience planning and plotting. Not with money, mostly with condiments, and sugary beverages, and things that smell funny. But still. I've seen movies and I know every good business has a rival. You'll be glad you have me on the team when it's time to fill a lobby water cooler with fish, or draw something inappropri-ate on an office window with shaving cream.

I imagine old Mr. Ockler dressed in black, spraying shaving cream on office windows, and laugh so hard my head finally slumps against the bed, muffling it. And I swear I hear a soft chuckle come from the bathroom. But maybe it was just my imagination.

DAY 14

Asher

There's exactly twenty-six hours of radio silence between Sidney and me after we make our harrowing escape from Nadine's yard. Not a word as she got into my car at The Little Store. A silent drive back to the house. Yesterday, she was gone all morning, and then painted her rocks through the afternoon. Before dinner she disappeared with what looked to be a tote bag of those same rocks, telling her mom she'd be out with Kara and not to set a spot for her at dinner. I spent my meal looking at an empty chair, and by the time I heard her bedroom door close that evening, I was debating if I should apologize. I'm not even sure why or what for, but this quiet and calm Sidney freaks me out just as much as the Sidney who swapped my cologne out for bug spray.

I was prepared for our swim this morning to be a no-go, but when I hear Sidney shower at exactly six, I figure I'll be optimistic and at least show up, totally expecting to find a hostile Sidney on my hands. But what I actually find is a message on the bathroom mirror. It's written in bloodred lipstick and if it weren't for the actual words, it would look like something straight out of a horror movie, the way the red slashes almost seem to drip down the glass.

Meet me at 6:30
in the kitchen
—S

Curious doesn't begin to describe me. I might be walking right into something horrible, but I skip everything but pulling on my suit and shorts anyway. I'm tugging a shirt over my head as I walk into the kitchen. Sidney is zipping around like an old-school pinball game, opening cabinets and closing drawers, stepping in front of the oven, and dumping something into the sink. It smells like butter and sweetness. There are two plates sitting on the breakfast bar in our normal spots. A cup of coffee and a bowl of fruit sit between the plates, and on mine, there are five tiny little pancakes.

"Um." I'm not sure what to say. I stare at the plate like it's the first time I've ever seen food. Like I'm an alien visiting from another planet. Which is pretty close to how I feel, because it's definitely the first time Sidney has made me food. Unless it was laced with something. She must see the look on my face, because she smiles. A big, gleaming smile, like I haven't seen on her in years. Not directed at me, at least.

She points the spatula at me and waves it around. "It's fine. Truce-certified and all that. Eat yours while I finish mine."

I sit down tentatively and grab the containers of butter and syrup next to me. I cut the first pancake into four mini bites, trying to stall until Sidney sits down and starts eating. Is it possible that she's actually making me *non*-disgusting food? Maybe I'm as jaded and traumatized as she is, but I decide to risk it and stick the first bite in my mouth. She's flipping pancakes as I let out a little moan. They're not just pancakes, they're *chocolate-chip* pancakes, and they practically dissolve on my tongue.

"These are my favorite," I say as I spear three more bites onto one giant forkful.

Sidney nods. "I know." She flips the last of the pancakes in the pan. "See, I'm perfectly capable of not being a paranoid, tree-up-my-ass bitch." She's smiling, but I can hear the hurt in her voice. I didn't realize she'd heard me while she was swimming that morning.

"I'm—" I look down at the plate of tiny pancakes. "I'm sorry, I was an ass the other night. And before that, too, I guess." I shove another bite into my mouth and talk around it. "Also, why are these pancakes so tiny?"

Sidney shrugs. "Hey, it's sort of true. But, as long as you keep yourself in check, I'll do the same." She scoops a pancake out of the pan and drops it onto a paper plate next to the oven. "Plus, I can't let you be the nicer one. That's just unacceptable." She points her spatula at my plate of tiny pancakes. "I haven't made pancakes in a while, so if the first batch sucked I didn't want to throw out half of the batter. Plus, tiny things are just better."

I laugh. Leave it to Sidney to think through a plan B for her breakfast. And to turn even *this*—not being jerks to each other—into a competition. "Well, so far you're kicking my butt in the niceness department. How are you even managing this?"

She flips another pancake onto her plate and smiles. "I'm taking your advice and pretending you're Logan Hart."

"The singer who grew up around here?"

"I'm practicing for when he randomly stops by, and I need to wow him. I heard he has a house on the lake."

"I bet that's a rumor. Something they tell tourists to get them to pay more for houses or something." I stuff another bite of pancake into my mouth.

"You're such a buzzkill." She has the same biting tone in her voice that I'm so used to, but her face is bright, cheerful. It makes me wonder if all she was missing before was the smile. *Does her voice just sound like that? No, surely not.*

"You're right." I stuff the last bit of pancake into my mouth and mourn the loss of it. "You never know what could happen.

I mean, you're making me pancakes, so I suppose it's official: anything is possible now."

I won't lie, the pancakes were delicious. But I can't shake the feeling that maybe Sidney took the time to chop one of those chocolate laxative bars into tiny chocolate chips. That halfway through the lake I'll buckle over in the boat and beg her to put me out of my misery. Because no matter what I said about trusting each other and the truce . . . we're still us. And I'm not sure she wouldn't grant me my wish to die—tiny, delicious pancakes or not.

DAY 19

Sidney

I was joking when I asked Asher what I was going to do with all of the time I'd spent plotting, but almost a week has passed since we met at the dock and I'm surprised by how true it actually is. Without pranks to think about and plan for, and recover from, I don't just have more time—I feel lighter. And even if it's not going to last all summer, I'm not ready to jeopardize it. So when Asher gives me a tiny wave as he walks past the deck—where I'm lying out on one of the lounge chairs—I wave back.

There's a towel tucked under his arm, and he's heading down the steps, toward the dock. Despite our breakfasts together the last week, our new normal has been to hang out in our own little areas. Me on the deck, sometimes with the moms or Kara, and Asher out on the dock. I feel a little bad about it. It's pretty out on the dock, surrounded by water, but it is not comfortable out on the uneven wood planks. Even with the two towels Asher lays down. Yesterday I considered that maybe I should buy him one of those cheap plastic floats to lie on. But now, I'm realizing there is a much easier solution.

"Hey." The word is out of my mouth before I can stop myself. Asher stops in his tracks. "You can chill up here. I mean, if you want to. It's not my private area or anything. We're sharing the house, you know. *Mi* deck *es su* deck. Or something like that . . ." *I'm rambling. Why am I rambling?*

He steps up onto the wooden deck and spreads his towel on the chair next to me without a word. We sit there, side by side, reading our books for at least an hour before we say anything. Every little sound we make seems to echo in the air, the soft brushing of the papers under our fingers, the squeak of our chairs as we shift around.

I've abandoned my book and am lying with my eyes closed, almost asleep, when Asher's voice breaks the noisy silence around us.

"Do you want to ride together to that party tomorrow night?"

I forgot the party was tomorrow.

It's hard to keep the days straight up here. There's no school, no jobs, we hardly even watch TV. Somehow three weeks of vacation have flown past. And there's nothing to separate the weekend from every other day. I told Kara I'd go to this party, since I survived the first one. Since it seems to be the only time I can see her this summer. The party Kara assured me Caleb isn't going to, because he's visiting a friend a few hours away.

"I sort of owe you one."

I turn to look at him, startled when I open my eyes to find his too close to me. We're in mirror positions on our chairs, our faces a foot apart. I don't understand how a foot can feel so close, or why he thinks he'd owe me anything. It was my mom who forced us to drive together to the last party.

He raises his brows like I'm missing the obvious. "You probably barely remember, because I'm such a graceful, charming drunk." A giant smile spreads across his face, the kind of self-amused smile I used to see as he was saying, *How much do you hate me right now?* "But there *was* that whole thing after the last party."

I close my eyes for just a second, but it's long enough to remember everything that happened that night. It sends a tight knot of unease into my stomach. *Drunk. He was drunk, Sidney. He only did it to screw you up for your date.* I have to look away from him. "Oh right, when you almost died in your own vomit." I say it because I know how much it annoys him.

"I would never."

I look at him and there's that smile again.

"I'm way too pretty for that."

"Mmhmm."

"Did you just admit I'm pretty?"

"No."

"You did."

"I'm just not arguing with you anymore." I turn to him with my own self-amused smile. "I'm the nicer one now. I plan on keeping it that way."

"Excuse me?" He looks at me with complete confusion, and I throw my hand to my chest in mock horror.

"One word," I say, holding up a single finger, just inches from his face. "Pancakes." The word is almost a whisper on my lips.

"Oh, so now we're keeping score?"

"I didn't say that."

"Mmhmm."

Asher closes his eyes, and I close mine, and we lie in our deck chairs in peaceful silence until Sylvie announces lunch with a yell from the kitchen window, and we spring out of our chairs like we were just caught. What's the punishment for conspiring with enemy forces?

DAY 20

Sidney

I'm not sure how I turned into this girl, but it's my third weekend in Riverton, and my second at a party. Asher and I drove together as planned—no matching outfits this time—but as soon as we stepped through the front door we split off in separate directions. My phone buzzes in my pocket, and it's a text from Kara.

> Kara: Running late. Sorry! Be there in an hour.

My stomach sinks. *An hour?* I'm in the middle of the living room, standing by myself, and suddenly I feel like there's a giant spotlight shining on me. *Attention partygoers, we have a lonely loner out-of-towner over here!* Yes, my aloneness is on full display. Making my way to the kitchen, I scan the room for anyone I know. Anyone I've said even two words to in the past, or recognize from The Little Store or River Depot. But all of the faces look new tonight. They don't look unfriendly, or unwelcoming, just new. And new looks like work—more work than I'm willing to put in tonight.

I stop in the kitchen and snag a red cup. There's no way I'm passing an hour without one. And if I have to—even though Asher promised he wouldn't drink tonight—I'll call my parents to pick me up. *No questions asked* is their motto, and while I've never tested it, I believe them. Mom doesn't want me to be featured in a viral video she'll compulsively share on social media.

There's a big blue cooler on the counter, and I put my glass under the spigot, letting a reddish brown juice fill it close to the brim. I take a sip—wow, it's strong—and walk toward the sliding glass door that leads into the backyard. There's a fire burning in one corner of the yard, but no one is sitting on the benches around it yet. *Freedom.*

The fire is glowing bright, and all that's separating me from its flickering solitude is a small set of wooden stairs. I'm about to step down when the sound of my name stops me.

"Sid?" It's Asher. Correction: it's *drunk* Asher. I think. Only drunk Asher calls me Sid. Except we haven't been here long enough for Asher to be drunk.

I turn slowly to find him standing a few feet behind me. He closes the small gap between us in just a few long steps, and I take a sip from my cup, trying to look natural.

"Where are you going?" He looks around me, like he's looking for something. "Where's Kara?" Not something . . . some*one.*

I let out a disgruntled sigh, blowing any chance I had of pulling off the relaxed-and-mingling look. "She's late." I glance back toward the yard. "I was going to sit by the fire."

Asher's face pinches up as his eyes dart from the fire to me. "By yourself?"

"No, with my invisible friend Roger, here." I swing my arms out to my side, like I'm presenting someone to Asher. Though they're down by my hips, so apparently my imaginary friend is tiny. Which is fine. Tiny things are awesome.

Asher smiles and rolls his eyes. "You're such a little hermit." He grabs my hand and pulls me along with him toward the house.

"What are you doing? Where are we going?"

"You're coming with me." His voice is firm, like he's letting me know I don't have a choice. We're crossing through the sliding door into the house. Into the throngs of people, the little clusters of friends. All of the strangers I was trying to avoid. Asher isn't like me, though. He gravitates toward people and they flock to him. He's the kind of person who can talk to anyone, without knowing a single thing about them.

I try to pull my hand away, but he holds it tight. "I don't want to talk to people." It sounds sort of pathetic when I hear it out loud, but it's also true.

"Then just talk to me," Asher says, not looking back at me. I stop pulling against him, and his hand loosens around mine as we enter the kitchen. He stops at the counter where bottles and cups are sitting in a jumbled mess, and looks down at my cup. "You gonna keep drinking that?"

I take a sip. "Sure. It's actually pretty good."

Asher eyes the cup and smiles. "I bet it is." He pulls a red cup from a stack of them and sets it on the counter.

I eye the cup warily. "Should I stop drinking? I mean, I can call my parents, I guess, if I need to."

"Relax." Asher rolls his eyes. "I said I wasn't drinking. And despite what you saw last time, I'm not a raging alcoholic."

"You're a midlevel alcoholic?" I try to school my smile but the punch is pushing it to the surface.

"I'm entry-level at best." He picks up a bottle of Coke and fills his cup. "But I'm thirsty." With his cup in his left hand, he grabs my hand with his right, and we're back into the mess of people.

"You're very pushy, you know," I say, tugging on his hand.

He laughs. "I know, but if I don't drag you somewhere better, you'll just sit in the backyard like a mosquito buffet." We're pushing through the living room and Asher is smiling and nodding at people as we pass. "I'd have to help Kara identify your remains by the time she got here."

It's true, mosquitoes love me. "It's because I'm so sweet," I say mockingly. That's what my mother always said, anyway, while I was slathering myself with cortisone cream, trying to soothe the welts after a hike or a particularly rough bonfire.

"You're mocking *yourself*? How much of that punch have you had?"

"Just trying to pick up the slack."

Asher stops and looks at me. "I don't mock you."

I put my one free hand on my hip, my other still trapped in his.

"When?" His voice is incredulous. "When have I mocked you?"

"How about every morning?" He looks at me blankly and I grab a piece of hair between my fingers. "'Your hair looks really pretty today.'" I do my best impression of his mocking, singsong voice, and roll my eyes.

"I *do* think your hair looks pretty."

"Whatever."

"Okay, I *did* say it to annoy you. But that's because I know *you* don't like it. I think it's really pretty." He shrugs, like this is a totally normal thing to say to me. "I'm glad you're not flattening it anymore."

I can't help but smile. "Straightening it."

"Whatever."

I don't say anything, because life makes no sense anymore. My brain might be broken by how little sense it all makes. But while I'm contemplating the weirdness that is now my life as Asher's ally, he continues to pull me across the room, until we hit a carpeted stairwell leading to a basement. He lets go of me and we make our way down, single-file, barely squeezing past people making their way up.

The basement is one big long room with light green walls and a floor full of retro brown tiles. At the bottom of the stairs there's a cluster of chairs and couches to our left. And beyond that, there's a big round table in the corner. It's a game table, the kind that has a wooden lid, and usually hides a poker board inside. As we approach I can make out a guy and two girls sitting in metal folding chairs around it. Three more chairs sit empty, and Asher tugs me by the hand until we're standing behind two of them.

"Hey," Asher says, and the guy nods. The girl to his right smiles, and the girl on his left is . . . Nadine's daughter, Lindsay. A little wave of guilt washes over me when I think about the fact that we were lurking around in her yard not too long ago. She's smiling especially wide at Asher until her eyes meet mine, and then travel down to our hands. I free my hand of Asher's, having forgotten it was still there. I suppose being dragged from room to room will do that to you. Like Stockholm syndrome for your hands.

I wave my previously captive hand at the group in front of us, trying to prove that I am not, in fact, a hermit.

"This is Sidney," Asher says as he pulls a chair out for me. I look at him, shocked by the gesture, and he winks at me. "Pancakes," he whispers, before turning back to the table. "This is Trevor, Hannah, and you know Lindsay."

"Hi." I sit down in the chair Asher still has a hand on, and he sits down next to me.

Asher looks past me to Lindsay. "I thought you were up at school for the summer."

Lindsay sets a handful of cards on the table in front of her. "I am, but I'm home most weekends. Not many freshmen stay for the summer, so it's pretty dead."

I take another sip of my drink and remind myself that being at a table full of strangers and Lindsay is still better than wandering around in the house or sitting alone at the bonfire until Kara gets here. I take another big gulp of my punch.

In front of us, the table isn't covered in the cards or other cliché drinking games I was expecting. It's a giant game board. An intricate map with mountains and lakes and rivers. Little dotted lines to show borders. There are silver, gold, black, and bronze pieces scattered around the board, but I don't know what any of them are. I have no idea what game they're playing, but anyone could tell what *kind* of game this is. It's a war game. I look at Asher and smile. Game on.

Asher

"Is it cool if we play as a team, since she's new?" I ask, knowing no one is going to argue. Everyone at the table has played before, and also everyone is drinking, so it's not the best time to introduce a virgin to the mix.

Sidney's elbow pokes me in the side. Her voice is soft. "We're going to start in the middle of the game? It looks like they already started."

"Last weekend," Trevor says, beating me to it. "We probably could have finished if this one"—he jabs a finger at me—"hadn't decided to get trashed."

"One time." I shake my head at him. "I said I was sorry."

He smiles. Trevor loves giving me crap. "I know, I know, you were having a rough night. You were having g—" I cough and pull Trevor out of his drunken ramble. He looks at Sidney and then me and finishes clumsily with, "We forgive you."

I met Trevor two summers ago at a party, and that's mostly where we hang out. Once in a while his folks take us out on the big lake in their boat, so we can wakeboard. He knows just enough about me to be awkward around someone like Sidney, who would kill for incriminating information about me.

Sidney sets down the little figurine she was examining in front of her and looks at me curiously. "Why were you having a rough night?" It's such a normal question, but it sounds utterly foreign coming out of her mouth. It makes me glance down at her cup to see how far gone she is. It's still half full.

"I don't think I actually said that."

"Oh, you did," Trevor says, taking another sip from his cup.

I take the gold piece from in front of Sidney and put it back in its spot. "You can't move these, everything is in play right now." I pick up her hands from the table and set them in her lap, suddenly aware of the fact that I just touched her thigh. "No touching," I say, pretending to scold her, but also reminding myself.

She gets quiet, and maybe we're done talking about my drunken night. "This isn't what I imagined you doing at parties," Sidney says. She starts to pick up her hands, then sets them back down, as if she suddenly remembered she wasn't allowed to move them. I want to laugh but I don't, because if Sidney thinks she can "out nice" me, she's so wrong. Instead, I look at the small stack of cards Trevor has placed in front of me.

"But you *were* thinking about me at parties, huh?" I hold the cards between us.

Sidney looks at me, and I can tell she's biting her cheeks, the way they pull in on the sides, making her cheekbones look sharper. Her hands flinch in her lap and she makes a disgusted little growl deep in her throat. "Mostly I was imagining you being drunk and obnoxious," she says, raising an eyebrow. "From what I saw at the last party, I wasn't too far off." She smirks at me, then flicks one of the cards with her finger. "Tell me what these mean."

While everyone takes their turns I explain the story cards to Sidney, and show her which pieces are mine and how to move around the map. It takes me longer than it should, because she's super into it and starts suggesting moves while I'm still explaining the different territories.

"So everything with the blue coin is currently mine."

"Ours," she corrects, taking a sip from her cup. It's close to empty, and I wonder how much that has to do with her willingness to be teammates. Or the way she's smiling at me right now, as Trevor makes a bad move into one of our neighboring territories.

I pick up our cards and she leans into me, her hand cupping my ear. "We should start moving toward the river," she says, but she's waving her finger toward an entirely different area of the board. Even tipsy, she's thinking two steps ahead. "The lower half of that territory to the north is basically wide open. We could take that smaller one and then work north. We'd have him surrounded before he can finish his beer."

"What are you majoring in?" I interrupt her, and she looks confused.

"English, I think. Why? What are you majoring in?"

"Finance." I shake my head. "You have the brain of a criminal mastermind."

She looks at me blankly. "Um. Thanks? I think." Her finger pulls a card toward us on the table. "I don't think they have majors for that, though."

"Seriously. I suddenly feel like I should be thankful you haven't done *much* worse things to me over the years." I tap a finger on the edge of the table. "You didn't put some sort of slow-metabolizing poison in those pancakes, did you?"

She smiles and shakes her head. "I do take it easy on you, Marin. I appreciate you acknowledging that, finally."

"Consider it acknowledged."

There's a long stretch of silence before she says, "Finance? Really?"

"Really."

"Hm."

"What did you think I'd major in?"

She shrugs. "I don't know. I just have a hard time imagining you working at a desk. I could see you as a teacher, or something like that, though. You're good with people."

"You work with people in finance, too."

She shrugs. "I guess so."

"Maybe your true calling is as a guidance counselor."

Sidney tips her head to the side and smiles devilishly. "I shouldn't be counseling anyone on how to make good life choices." Her eyes dart to where Lindsay sits and then back to me. "My track record has been less than stellar lately." She turns toward me, her nose grazing my shoulder, and I still. She makes the tiniest noise, and when she lifts her head I can feel her breath against my cheek. "I'm surprised you don't *still* smell like fish." She smiles and turns back to the board.

When Kara finally arrives, Sidney's second cup of punch is almost empty. We've already taken most of Hannah's treasure, and we're deep in an invasion of Trevor's northern territories.

Sidney's sitting with her legs tucked under her, and we're shoulder to shoulder as she reaches for another of our battle pieces. I roll the dice, and as two sixes appear, Sidney lets out a little whoop. She marches our piece forward into the territory, knocking another piece out of the way with a little slap of her tiny bronze figurine.

"Point awarded!" she yells as she slides the blue chip into its place, stretching so far across the table, she can barely reach.

"No, no, no," Trevor mutters, trying to find a way out of what just happened.

"Yes, yes, yes," Sidney whispers, a strange combination of sweetness and utter annihilation.

She throws her palm into mine as she sits back down on her heels. Kara is behind her, frozen in place, like the two of us are sitting in this basement naked or something.

"What are you guys doing?" she says, her voice mirroring the confusion on her face. I watch her eyes dart from me to Lindsay, and back to Sid.

"We're winning!" Sidney says—practically yelling—at the same time that I say, "Playing a game."

"I can *see* it's a game, Ash." Kara rolls her eyes, and then opens them wider as she tips her head toward us. "What are you *doing*?"

I look at Sidney—so close she's touching my entire right side—and back to Kara, seeing for the first time what she's seeing. How strange this must look. Probably as strange as it felt when we sat down. But after an hour of playing together—smiling and laughing and pillaging castles—it doesn't feel that strange anymore. Before I can say anything, Sidney's voice—slightly higher than usual (a side effect of her second drink?)—cuts through the basement.

"We've called a truce," she says, very matter-of-factly, her body twisted in her chair toward Kara, who is now standing beside her. "He wrote me a note, and we had a midnight meeting, and rules weren't really discussed, but we'll get to that at some point, I suppose. But either way—" She nods at Kara, like she's confirming this. "We agreed on it. We're not enemies," she says, and then turns to me with a mischievous smile. "For now."

"Why?" Kara sounds perturbed.

"Top-secret reasons," Sidney says as she twists an imaginary key at her closed lips. Apparently drunk Sidney is even more paranoid and neurotic than sober Sidney. But she's also a lot nicer and kind of adorable. She's first-summer Sidney again, the one who didn't constantly scowl at me, or assume I was mocking her. "I'll tell you later, though," she says in a conspiring whisper to Kara.

"Interesting," is all that Kara says, but she looks to me like she's expecting more information.

I shrug. "Sid pretty much covered it."

"Sid?" Kara looks like her brain is about to explode.

"Also, we're kicking butt," Sidney adds, her eyes on Trevor, who is taking his turn again and moving troops closer to our most valuable piece of land. Hannah lost the last of her territories twenty minutes ago and left the table. "Trevor's about to see just how much butt we kick if he puts a single troop in our capitol."

Trevor mutters, "Next time, you don't get a partner."

Sidney's eyes light up. "Next time?" But she looks to me, not Trevor, for an answer.

I'm not sure how I feel about Sidney becoming a permanent fixture at the game table. Especially as an opponent. As an ally—a tipsy ally—this is fun. But I don't know that we need another way to compete. We're just barely pulling ourselves out of the awkwardness of this fragile truce. And who knows if we're even capable of continuing that when we're *both* sober. Are there enough chocolate-chip pancakes and conquerable territories in the world to make that happen?

"What are you thinking?" Sidney asks, her brows furrowed.

"I'm thinking about your pancakes," I say, and Sidney breaks into uncontrollable laughter.

"Sooo . . ." Kara's eyes move from Sidney, to me, to the table full of cards and metal trinkets, and settle back on Sidney. "Are you coming with me, or . . ." Her eyes are back on me.

Sidney pulls one leg off of her chair, and then stops. She rubs the blue chip between her thumb and forefinger, and lets it roll into her palm. "Actually . . . do you care if I just finish here?"

"We'll play all night, but you don't have to stay if you don't want to. I can go solo." I don't want her to feel like she's stuck with me after I basically dragged her down here. Especially if Kara is going to hang around all night looking at us like we're some sort of science experiment gone wrong.

She looks to Kara and raises an apologetic brow. "Do you care? I sort of got sucked into this."

Kara smiles, but it looks more nervous than happy. "Sure, no big deal. I'll be upstairs if things get to be . . ." She looks from Sidney to me again. "Too much, down here."

Sidney gives her a thumbs-up, and turns back to the table. "Let's do this, Marin."

"Wow. You are a total nerd." Sidney drops into the car way later than we planned and pins me with a serious (and seriously drunk) look. "You know that, right?"

She's smiling at me, and something in my chest tightens at the idea that this could be our new normal. "Says the girl who paints rocks."

"Point awarded," she says, and we both laugh. She shakes her head as she fastens her seat belt, missing the slot a few times before she gets it in. "But my rocks are awesome. Don't forget that."

I put the car in drive and try to keep my voice as casual and uninterested as possible. "What do you do with them all anyway?"

Sidney rests her head back, turns to look at me, and whispers, "Don't you wish you knew."

She's onto me, because I don't know why, but I do. I really, really do.

DAY 21

Asher

I don't get pancakes every morning, because—as Sidney keeps telling me—she isn't my personal chef. But I do get a smile. This morning, I also get a bottle of water and a protein bar. They go along with the note I scrawled on the mirror this morning—our primary means of communication—asking her to go on a morning run. We both run every other day, so it just seemed logical that we could do it together. But it also means that we now spend every single morning together, swimming or running. Swimming is easier, though—one of us always has our head in the water. There isn't any expectation for small talk other than the few minutes we spend getting in and out of the boat.

Our very first run was silent, and for two miles I was pretty convinced that I had made a horrible mistake. At every turn we veered in different directions, finding that our normal running routes—and apparently our instincts—were completely opposite. Sidney likes to keep to the street—the busy ones where cars are blasting past us—and I have a tendency to veer off-road whenever I have the chance.

Our second run, I let Sidney lead. That morning we ran a mixture of her usual road route, and a few adventures onto trails and dirt side roads. On our half-mile cool down, we decided we'd take our first real crack at Nadine soon. I asked Sidney about Edith the elephant, who I now know is living on her dresser.

So now, as we run, we plot.

"Have you ever heard of potato-ing someone's yard?" I ask her, my voice far too normal for the strangeness of the words. We're a mile into our run, turning off of the main road and onto a long dirt road that curves into a stretch of national forest.

"Um. No." She looks at me like maybe I'm just teasing her.

"Basically you spread powdered mashed potatoes all over someone's yard. You know, the kind that come in the cardboard boxes?"

"Okay . . ."

"So the next time it rains, the yard fills with mashed potatoes."

Sidney laughs so hard she has to stop running. "Wow, that's . . . that's sort of disgusting."

"And I was thinking . . . maybe we could write out some sort of message, or weird picture, with the potatoes?" She's giving me the strangest look. "What?"

"That's just . . . it's awesome."

We take off running again. "Thanks."

"Only one problem."

I groan, long and loud and dramatic, because Sidney has been a total buzzkill about all of my ideas so far. Yes, we have to be careful, but we're not throwing bottle bombs into her yard or something. So while I've been coming up with all of the devious ideas, Sidney has been considering all of the possible repercussions.

"Do you think mashed potatoes could kill the grass?" she asks.

"It's not like they're acid. They're potatoes. They come *out* of the ground, right?" The thing about Sidney is that she doesn't just come up with some pretty weird and elaborate ideas—she can also think through every little detail. She needs an answer to every tiny question that comes up. It makes me wonder how long she spent thinking about all of the pranks she pulled on me before she actually went through with them. And what provoked her to go off-script with the fish? She clearly hadn't thought that one through, even a little.

"True, I guess potatoes *are* vegetables," she says, her voice so thoughtful it makes me laugh.

"You *guess?*"

She smacks my arm as we run, and I speed up so she has to push herself harder to do it again. "We'd have to spend a lot of time in the yard to put the potatoes on the grass. It's not exactly sneaky."

"We can go in the middle of the night. Like *really* late. Three a.m. or something?" I slow down so we're side by side again. "I bet it wouldn't take that long . . . we can get all of the potatoes ready beforehand, so all we have to do is spread them. Even if we do something cool, we could probably be in and out in twenty minutes?" I ram my shoulder into her like we're bumper cars. "We'd have to buy a million boxes of potatoes, though."

"And hope that it rains sometime soon, before the dog eats them all," she says. "Damn dog." We run another ten feet before she speaks again. "We could buy the potatoes this afternoon . . . might need to hit a few stores to get enough. Maybe go to Nadine's tomorrow night or the night after, once we can think through all the details?"

Crap. This is the perfect time to ask Sidney what I've been trying to work myself up to for days now. Even though we're acting like normal people who don't hate each other anymore, it's still hard to talk to her in person. We're doing things together now, but only because of the lipstick notes. When we're together, we mostly talk about our plans for Nadine. *Or* how weird it is that our parents are experiencing a second-coming of their college years. I'm not sure how to break us out of that. Sometimes I'm not sure why I still want to. But I do.

We're running on a side road that stretches into the woods

when I clear my throat and come to a stop along the side of the road. It's a service road of some kind, and it's unpaved. But it's also shaded, which makes it perfect for running, despite having to sporadically dodge a tree root cutting through our path. Something rustles in the undergrowth beside me, and Sidney's eyes snap past me. "I was going to go to the drive-in tomorrow night. They're showing that new movie, the one with the woman who disappears on the train."

She nods with a smile and lets out a long breath. "Yeah, that looks really good." She shakes her head. "That's cool, we can do it another night."

"Yeah." I stub my toe into the ground. "I was just thinking, if you wanted to go with me, we could check it out." The regret is heavy as the words hang between us. This was such a horrible idea. "Just . . . it's kind of pathetic to go to the movies by yourself, you know?"

I can see her entire jaw tense as she swallows. "Um."

"Don't feel like you have to. I just wanted to see it, but seriously, no pressure." *Crap, this is awkward.* If we were on the main road at least I could wish that a car would accidentally swipe me and make this end. But no, I decided the dead quiet of the woods was the best place to do this. *I'm a genius.*

Sidney bites her lip and doesn't smile, but her face looks even now. Not interested, but not disgusted. "Yeah. No. I mean, you're right. It looks really good." She bites her lip again. "I'll go."

She starts running again without a word, and I follow a step behind, then pull up alongside her. I feel like we're running in a weird bubble of awkward tension, and I have to pop it before we both suffocate in here. "You know what the perfect movie snack is?" I say, my voice teasing.

"Popcorn?" Her voice drips with sarcasm.

"I mean, popcorn is great, but . . ."

"Gummy bears."

"Yuck."

"What?" She sounds personally offended. "No, gummies are the best, come on."

"Try again."

She laughs. "I'm not making you pancakes."

I let out a huff. "Oh, come on."

"Nope." Sidney shakes her head as we make a U-turn at the end of the dirt path. "You're all strung out on the 'cakes, Marin." She's right. I've managed to talk her into making them twice this week. The first time by mentioning them to my dad, who asked her, and the second time by agreeing to do two of our dinner dish shifts solo. The only thing Sidney wants to be less than my personal chef is the post-dinner dishwasher.

"Puh-leasssse?" I clap my hands together as if I'm praying to the goddess that is Sidney, Queen of the Pancakes.

"We're not taking pancakes to a movie." She's shaking her head at me like I'm an idiot, but she's smiling. And the nervous energy is long gone. "I'll make us chocolate-chip muffins."

"Yes!" I throw my fist up into the air. "Deal!"

"But you're buying my ticket," she says.

"For muffins? Obviously."

"I need to save my money for mashed potatoes." She laughs and rolls her eyes—at herself, which is a nice change from them being directed at me. "As one does."

I laugh. "As one does."

We don't talk the rest of the way home, but it's a different kind of silence from what has become our normal the last few years. Let's hope spending four hours in a car together doesn't ruin it.

DAY 22

Asher

The next night, we're pulling into the Cherry Bowl Drive-In in my parents' small black SUV. It's dusk, and the lot is just starting to fill up with cars. The Cherry Bowl is on the edge of town, and it looks like something straight out of a fifties sitcom. The property is circled by wavy sheets of metal that would look like something from a junkyard if they weren't painted a pretty pale aqua. Inside, there's nothing more than a big open field that is 60 percent half-dead grass and 40 percent dirt patches. To one side a little painted brick building houses the concessions and bathrooms, and at the far end a giant white screen stretches into the sky.

In the passenger seat Sidney has a plastic container (which I assume/pray is full of muffins) on her lap. She brought two bottles of water that are now sitting in the console between us. We've been quiet the entire drive and I'm hoping this wasn't the worst idea ever, because this is exactly what I was hoping to fix.

I back into the first available space, and Sidney unbuckles her seat belt, but doesn't get out. She twists in her seat and looks quizzically out the back of the car, where the giant screen is.

I open my door. "Come on," I say, closing the door behind me and making my way to the back of the car. Sidney meets me as the trunk door is slowly rising above us. And I'm not sure if the look on her face means I'm getting any of those muffins she's got gripped in her hands, or if I'm out of luck.

Sidney

I'm trying to ignore how much this feels like a date, because that's just ridiculous. Asher and I don't do dates. A few weeks ago we didn't do civil conversation. But the back of the car is covered in a soft plaid blanket—the one Sylvie usually packs for the beach—and there are pillows piled up along the back of the seat. I set my container of muffins on the bumper and stare into the comfy yet intimidating space, reminding myself that the only reason Asher bought my ticket is the baked goods I came with. *You* told *him to buy it.* One hundred percent *not* a date.

"This is—" *Weird. Intimidating. Slightly horrifying.* "—nice," I say, my voice more tentative than I'd intended. I climb up into the trunk and wiggle myself into the passenger-side corner. Best to claim my space first. My toes nervously push the blanket back into place where I pulled it up climbing in. Asher climbs in after me and sits on the opposite side, leaning back onto the pillows with his hands crossed behind his head. His feet hang over the bumper.

There's a half-foot of space between our outstretched legs, and the trunk is normal size, but it feels claustrophobically small. The smell of Asher's body wash dances in the air around us, as if it's taunting me with the fact that I can't escape it. I would endure torture before I'd admit it to him, but I love the smell of Asher's body wash. It's warm and spicy, and it reminds me of summer. Maybe because *he* reminds me of summer. It's a chicken and egg thing, I guess. But right now, it reminds me of being in our bathroom in the morning, and the way the smell seems to permeate the entire room, even if it's been hours since he showered. The way it seems to soak into my skin as *I* shower.

And the thought of being naked in that room sends a shiver down my spine. *You're in a car, Sidney. Definitely* not *in the shower. Fully clothed. Shake it off, Walters.*

"I just figured if we're going to be sitting in the car for the next four hours, we didn't have to be wedged in the front seats." *Four hours.* I forgot the Cherry Bowl showed double features. I haven't been here since my parents took me our very first summer. Asher pries the lid off of the container of muffins, but leaves it where it was, between our knees. He pops one of the tiny muffins into his mouth and moans. "Plus, there's less pressure not to get food on my dad's seats now. He's weird about that."

Ah. So this isn't special, it's practical. It's oddly comforting to think that—that this wasn't some special thing Asher did for me. But that feeling is quickly followed by a strange pang of disappointment that twists in my belly and climbs into my chest. The feeling confuses me, and I tell myself it's just because of the nice things I've done for him. The pancakes multiple times these last few weeks; the runs we're going on together. That of course I'd want him to do nice things for me, when I'm doing them for him.

But the pancakes are fun to make. And the runs aren't any kind of punishment. It's nice not to go alone. Nicer to have someone there to push me, which Asher and his long legs do, every single time. And I really like running off-road. I'd never do it by myself, because even though I have a right to run anywhere I want, all I can think about is someone leaping out of the woods and dragging me to some creepy cabin, where I'm never heard from again. At least with Asher there I have a 50 percent chance of not being the one snatched.

But Asher has done nice things for me, too. He saved me at the party by dragging me to that game. Which is dramatic but also an understatement, because I can't wait to play again. Every morning, swimming or not, there is a cup of coffee waiting for me. It's all so strange in comparison to before. So is this all just about outdoing each other? I suppose it's not hurting anything if it is. I pop a muffin into my mouth and nestle back into the pillows behind me. It looks like Asher stole every spare pillow in the house—bed pillows from his room, two square blue pillows with birds embroidered on them from the porch, a few of the colorful throw pillows off of the living room couches. It's like sitting on one of those really luxurious hotel beds that has way more pillows than seems reasonable for one bed.

"Thanks. This is definitely better."

And Asher really did outdo himself with this setup. I'm noticing the candy now. There's a giant box of gummy bears shoved into a little black compartment to my side, and boxes of Junior Mints and Starburst on his side. I bet he's a really sweet boyfriend. The thought makes me *literally* choke on my muffin. I try to swallow back the cough, and that just makes it worse. One giant cough escapes me, and then a second, and by the third Asher is reaching over and patting me on the back, like I'm a toddler who hasn't quite mastered chewing.

Thump. Thump. "You okay?"

I cough one last time, take a long swig of water, and decide I'm going to survive. The choking, at least. Whether I survive this night and my twisted thoughts is still up for debate. I turn to Asher to explain that I'm fine, and he won't be needing to Heimlich me, when I realize that he's now right beside me. Our calves are still separated by the muffin container, but our hips are just inches apart, and our shoulders are grazing. There isn't even room to put my hand down. *Hands, meet lap. Your new home for the evening. You'll like it here. It's safe, and you can't get into trouble.*

"I've actually always wanted to Heimlich someone." He looks over at me suddenly. "And yeah, I know that sounds horrible. I mean . . . I don't *want* anyone to choke. I'm just saying *if* it happens, and I'm the only one who knows the Heimlich . . ."

He shakes his head like he's getting off track. Like most swimmers, Asher and I both lifeguard at our pools. Apparently his CPR and emergency training really made an impression on him. "But you know, in a restaurant or something. A stranger. Definitely not a friend." He pops another muffin into his mouth. "Too much responsibility."

A friend. When the hell did *that* happen? But it has—that's why there are pillows, and my favorite candy, and why he doesn't want me, of all people, to choke. It's why I'm sitting in this car with Asher at all.

"It *does* sound horrible." I decapitate a green gummy bear and let the silence settle around us, because I have a real mean streak. "But also . . . I totally get what you're saying." I still have a muffin sitting in my lap, forgotten during my near-death experience, and I take a bite. Hopefully this isn't the one that makes Asher's weird dream come true. "You'd be like a hero sweeping in."

Asher smacks his leg, and his pinkie grazes my thigh. If he notices, he doesn't say anything, doesn't apologize. "Exactly! It's basically the closest I could ever get to being some sort of superhero."

"'Asher Marin . . .'" I use a deep voice like a movie voice-over. "'Saving diners from their food . . . one blocked esophagus at a time.'" I grimace. "The tagline could use some work."

Asher laughs. "Yeah, that doesn't sound very sexy. Superheroes are supposed to be sexy."

"You'd have to make up for it with a killer costume."

"You just want to see me in spandex," Asher quips, and it's my turn to laugh.

"Am I that transparent?" I say mockingly. We're back in familiar territory, him teasing me.

"Only when it comes to the way you lust over my body." Asher throws his arm behind me, and even though it isn't touching me, I know it's right there on the pillows. "I feel like I should apologize . . ." He turns to me, and our eyes lock.

"For what?" I say, so soft it's barely a whisper. The list of things either of us could apologize for is long. Way too long to hash out before the movie starts, maybe even before the summer ends.

"My overwhelming sexual presence." His mouth quirks up in a half smile, and he winks. Pressed up against me, his shoulders shake with unreleased laughter.

And suddenly, it feels like we're playing a whole new kind of game. I really wish I knew the rules.

Asher

It's true that I didn't want to come to a movie alone. But I would have. I don't know that many people around here, so if people think I'm a weirdo, well, I'll survive. And I could have asked Trevor, if all I really needed was a body in the car. But it was Sidney I really wanted to see this movie with. Because she notices everything, and this is one of those mind-screw movies where you have to watch it four times to catch all of the little hints and extras they're giving you.

"I think she can secretly understand everything," Sidney says in the middle of a dramatic scene.

"What? No way. She doesn't speak English."

"Think about it . . . the only reason he thinks that is because someone else told him that. But did you see that shot earlier where her eyes cut to him when he said something about the body they found in that sleeper car?"

"Shit," I mutter.

"Sorry, I'm ruining it for you."

"No, I didn't even notice that. I wonder what else I missed." And I really do, because I catch so many more clues after she says that. When the movie ends we spend intermission raging over the big twist that neither of us saw coming, and which ultimately ruined a great movie for both of us. When the next movie starts—a rom-com about identical twins who fall for the same boy while at summer camp—we spend the movie pointing out all of the implausible bits, and we talk through the awkward make-out scenes.

During a particularly steamy scene, Sidney cuts in with a confession.

"If you ever tell anyone, I'll deny it, but I've always wanted a hurricane named after me."

It comes so out of the blue, I wonder how long she's been sitting next to me, contemplating if she could admit that to me after my Heimlich confession. And I don't know what it means that she did. Maybe just that it's awkward as hell to watch people make out on a fifty-foot screen while sitting next to someone you don't make out with. "You're a monster."

She slaps my leg but laughs. "I know, right? Sort of like you, though . . . I don't want it to be a devastating category five or anything, just something that sweeps off the shore"—her arm sweeps out in front of her—"and is super scary, but then magically dissipates before it ever gets close to actually hurting anyone."

"Tropical Storm Sidney." I pop another Junior Mint into my mouth, trying to ignore that it feels like she branded my leg by touching it. Telling myself I shouldn't try to make another joke just to get her to do it again. "I like it."

She smiles, and fidgets her hands on her thighs before casually plucking the box of mints out of my hand and holding them in her lap. Hurricane Sidney makes it official: Operation Movie Night is a definite success.

DAY 23

Sidney

> Caleb: Hey! Want to hang out tonight?

I stare at the text on my screen, trying to decide if he's asking me out on a date again, or just being friendly. Hanging out *definitely isn't the same as* going out, *Sidney. It's 3 p.m.*

I should say yes. I should get out of this house, and remind myself what it feels like to be a person who doesn't spend all of her time with her nemesis. We eat breakfasts together, swim and run together, do dishes every night. Less than twenty-four hours ago, I willingly sat in a trunk with him for close to five hours. It's very possible that my brain is being subjected to something like Stockholm syndrome. A million years from now I'll be telling my grandkids about this: *And then, I made my captor pancakes. With chocolate chips, because that was his favorite.* And they'll say, *Grammi, what was wrong with you?* I don't even know how I'd answer that. What *is* wrong with me?

Captive or not, the idea of hanging out with Caleb doesn't interest me after last night. I do feel like seeing someone who isn't Asher, but it's not Caleb. I shoot him a quick, *Sorry, I'm busy* text.

> **Sidney: What are you doing after work tonight?**

> **Kara: You?**

> **Sidney: LOL. Yes, please.**

> **Kara: Yay!**

I meet Kara at River Depot at eight o'clock, after her shift. They have the best ice cream in a twenty-minute drive, and she's assured me that Caleb isn't working. A boy-free ice cream trip is exactly what I need right now.

"So about the party," Kara says, her eyes looking up from the giant cup of ice cream we're hunched over. It's her dinner, but I have my own spoon, and I'm dedicated to excavating every piece of cookie out of this cup. Kara lets me because she's the best.

"The party you begged me to go to and then basically bailed on?"

"The party you went to with Asher."

"The party I *drove to* with Asher. I was going with *you*." I stab the spoon back into the quickly disappearing mountain of cookies 'n' cream.

Kara holds on to the wooden bench and leans back, like she's trying to stretch. I don't know how she stands around all day on the concrete and doesn't want to cut her feet off. She tips her head back up and angles her head at me. "Okay." One corner of her mouth tips up into the faintest hint of a smile.

"Okay, what?"

She shrugs. "Okay, it sounds like you're not ready to talk about it."

"There's nothing to talk about."

"Okay."

I point my spoon at her face. There's something weird about it, like she wants to smile but won't let herself. "I don't like your attitude."

She finally smiles. "I don't have one."

There's a long stretch of silence as we finish the ice cream, scraping at the sides with our spoons as the trickle of the river fills the air. River Depot is quiet at night, once the docks are closed for the day. It's just us and a few other groups and families eating ice cream on the dock overlooking the river. A few kids are sitting by the gas fireplace on the deck one level up.

Kara flicks my arm with her pink-nailed finger and bites her lip. Words come out of her in a rush. "But things *were* weird with you and Ash at the party, right? You know, if you two are . . ." She waves her spoon in the air and her eyebrows will blend right into her hairline if they stretch up much farther.

"Are *what?*"

"I don't know. Who can know anything with the two of you." She looks at me like I'm a puzzle she'll solve if she gets me at just the right angle. Like she has too many middle pieces, and if she could just find a corner piece, she'd be happy. "You hate each other, you obsess over each other. And now you're being *freakishly* nice to each other?"

We go to the movies together. I keep the words in my head, where they belong. "Asher and I aren't . . . anything."

"Okay, it's just that at the party, it seemed like—"

I cut her off with my spoon pointed at her like I'll stab her with it at any moment. I haven't completely ruled it out. "There's no *thing* with me and Asher. I can be nice to someone without it being a *thing.*"

"Even Asher?"

"*Especially* Asher." I hate how high and defensive my voice has gotten.

"And you're . . . sure he feels the same?" She chews on her lip for a second. "Because I've always suspected that *underneath* all the pranks and asshat-ery . . . he's actually kind of in love with you." The last words are barely audible over the sound of the river.

I drop the spoon into the empty bowl. A tiny, maniacal laugh escapes my throat. "What would ever make you *think* that?" If I didn't know she'd just been at work for eight hours, I'd think she was drunk. Or maybe she is. Maybe she keeps a tiny flask on her key chain or something. There is just no other excuse for saying something so ridiculous.

Kara shakes her head. "I don't know. Forget I said anything. It was stupid. You two are making me stupid."

It's maybe the stupidest thing I've ever heard.

"So you're positive there's nothing going on there."

"So positive." I pick up the spoon nervously and drop it back into the little white puddle. "I seriously can't believe you're making me say this."

"Okay." Kara raises her hands in surrender. "But for the record, if there *was* something there . . ." She catches my eye and words race out of her. "Which there isn't. But if there was . . . that would be okay."

All I can do is nod.

DAY 24

Sidney

We drove the extra thirty minutes to get to the cheap grocery store yesterday. The one where you have to deposit a coin to take a shopping cart, all of the bags and boxes are store-brand green, and the powdered mashed potatoes we're going to dump in the grass cost exactly what they're worth to us: $1.29 a box.

I clap my hands together and watch the white flakes disintegrate. "I had no idea a trunk full of dehydrated vegetables could make me feel like such a delinquent."

Asher laughs. It's quiet, like he's worried someone will hear us, even though we're still two houses away from Nadine's and it's just before 3 a.m. There's definitely no one around to hear. We're parked at Kara's grandma's house, in the heavy trees at the end of her driveway. The wagon we usually use to haul all our crap down to the beach is already half-filled with opened boxes.

"As if this is anywhere close to the most delinquent thing you've ever done," Asher says.

I tear one end of a box open before placing it in the blue canvas basket of the wagon. We need to spend as little time as possible in Nadine's yard, so we're taking Asher's suggestion to prep everything ahead of time. I wanted to do it at our house, but when he pointed out that our parents might wonder why we're suddenly hoarding mashed potatoes, I talked to Kara and hooked us up with our base of operations for the night.

"Don't forget Edith." Asher jerks his head toward the backseat, and I let out a little moan.

"Aw. Do I have to?" I open the back door and pull Edith out of the seat, where I have her strapped in. I bring her to the back of the car, cradled under my arm. "I'm sort of attached to her. She's the elephant in my room." I smile at my own joke, waiting for my pun to sink in.

Asher just shakes his head, a smile on his face. He puts a gentle hand on my shoulder, and his voice matches it. "It's time to send her home, Sid. Time to set her free." I wedge her into one end of the wagon, surrounded by boxes, and then pull her back out.

"I'll carry her." I'm not trying to be dramatic, I just don't want her to fall out and get broken. I won't lie, I'm half-expecting a sign in Nadine's garden where Edith usually sits. Something like, I KNOW WHAT YOU DID, right next to a grainy black-and-white security cam photo of me running away with her. But when we get to the edge of the house, wagon in tow, there's nothing behind the bush but a little patch of dirt, dug out of the red mulch. I pat Edith on the head like she's my good little elephant, and shimmy her down into the mulch, twisting her a little so she doesn't tip over. This time, I'm careful not to step into the path of the motion-sensor light.

I blow her a kiss as I turn around, and Asher gives her a little salute. And I don't feel like he's mocking me, he's just playing around, having fun with it like I am. Asher doesn't take anything too seriously—especially himself—and I'm really starting to appreciate how much fun it is to have someone go along with my weirdness. Because it doesn't feel so weird anymore.

Asher leaves the wagon of potatoes in the trees alongside the driveway, where it's dark with shadows, and both of us take a box in each hand. Now that I'm actually here, in Nadine's yard, with all of the grass sprawling out around me, I'm not sure where to start. Yesterday we plotted over our pancakes and agreed that doing some sort of design was too much pressure. We'd just go to town on the yard with as many potatoes as humanly possible, and call it good.

On the opposite side of the yard, Asher is silently shaking potatoes over the grass, walking backward as he empties one box and then two. It feels like watching a movie on mute as he silently moves through the yard, nothing but a faint chuh, chuh, chuh as the powder is liberated from its box.

I walk around the yard, laying the potatoes down in lines across the grass. When something moves in the tree line, my attention snaps to the noise, and a cascade of potatoes rushes out of the box, making a white arc in the air. I swap my empty boxes for full, and with a box in each hand I twirl in the center of the yard, my arms outstretched. White powder spirals out into the air. I start moving around the yard in little circles, spraying the potatoes around me like a cyclone of white dust. It's 3 a.m., I'm exhausted, and it's possible I've totally lost it.

Five minutes in, we've each emptied ten boxes, and still the yard looks green. The grass is a little long, hiding our efforts. Which reminds me that Nadine has a sprinkler system keeping her yard so long and luscious. We don't have to cross our fingers and hope that it rains—our potato masterpiece could be ready as early as this morning. The thought spurs me on, and I grab two more boxes.

A flash of movement in the corner of the yard closest to Lake House A catches my eye, and I hear the faintest squeak as Asher pushes himself forward on the little swing set there. It's old and covered in weathered green paint with peeling white stripes. The sand that used to surround it has been almost completely overtaken by weeds.

When Asher waves me over, there's an almost magnetic pull

urging me to approach the old green monstrosity. Those swings hold a lot of memories for us. The first summer Asher was here, we spent time on them—late nights talking, swaying gently as we shared the kinds of things teenagers divulge with someone new—our favorite songs, the coolest things we'd done that year, everything that annoyed us about our best friends. But we never swung on them. Thirteen-year-old Sidney was way too cool for that. She didn't know Asher well enough, hadn't wanted to look like a dork in front of this cute boy she was still figuring out. If only I'd known then what a game-playing little nerd he would become. The thought makes me almost laugh out loud.

By the time I reach the swings, Asher is already in the air. I follow, pushing myself up, higher and higher. I can't remember the last time I was on swings like this, and I wonder why, because it's sort of awesome. And a little disorienting in the dark, when I'm drunk from no sleep. We've both ditched our green boxes, and are soaring higher and higher, the squeaking of the chains crescendoing through the night air.

Asher jumps, and in the silence it's beautiful, the way he arcs soundlessly through the air, landing in a graceful crouch on the grass ten feet in front of me. Just as he stands, a door slams. It's the familiar, clanging metal of Nadine's side door. There's a little yip and the faint scratch of paws on stones.

Asher's head snaps to me, and he motions with his hand for me to jump. I let go, my hand holding on a second too long, and land much less gracefully than he did. As I topple to the side, sharp pain lances through my ankle. My gasp is muffled by the last squeaks of the swings we've abandoned.

"Are you okay?" Asher whispers so quietly, I'm almost not sure he actually said it. He reaches a hand down for me and I take it. My first two steps have me wincing, and we need to run, not walk. Maybe I can hop. God, what a nightmare. All of our careful planning, and we're going to get caught because I can't do something most eight-year-olds have mastered. Kill me now, I'll never hear the end of this.

Asher steps in front of me, and it takes me a second to realize what he's doing. Even when he crouches down a little, I'm still looking at him, confused. "Get on," he whispers over his shoulder, and the scuffing of gravel draws my eyes to Nadine's house again. She usually takes the dog in the trees along the driveway, but she could hear us and be around that corner in seconds.

Then, I don't think. I jump. The second I'm on his back, we're tearing through the yard, my legs pinned under his arms. We cut along the far left edge of the yard, near the trees, where it's dark. I'm smacked by a low branch as we push through the narrow area between the trees and Lake House A, where everything is overgrown. A mumbled apology floats over Asher's shoulder as I squeak at the hit and dip my face into his neck to shield myself from anything else I don't see. We make it to the front of the house, and turn sharply to the right. We're outside the doors to the boathouse that sits under it, its entrance hidden by the deck looming overhead.

Asher pushes on the old wooden door, and it opens just as he leans back, letting me know to get off. We can't make it in together—not if I want to keep my forehead intact. He pushes the door open and I hobble in behind him, holding his arm for support. When we're inside, he closes the door behind us.

He flicks his finger across his phone, places it on a little shelf, and the rafters above us are lit up, the whole space bathed in dim light. The boathouse is a weird place; it's filled with randomness. On the left wall are long wooden pegs that hold old orange life jackets, speckled with mildew. Along the back wall are random beach toys, paddles, lawn chairs, and a few of Nadine's rejected yard sculptures. There's a cartoonish frog with a cracked head, and a gnome that's missing a foot. *I feel your pain, pal.* I see an old five-gallon bucket and flip it over before sitting on it.

"Shit," I mutter just as Asher squats down next to me. His elbows rest on his thighs, and he's now eye-level with me. He takes his cell phone from the shelf and places it on the ground in front of him. It washes his face in harsh shadow. "I think I just rolled it," I say softly. "It'll be fine in a few hours." I wince. "Probably."

He moves silently to where my leg is extended, and puts a hand on either side of my ankle. "We're not staying here a few hours." His eyes meet mine, and his brows rise. I nod, letting him know it's okay if he touches my injured foot. His fingers push gently above my ankle, and in the cool dampness of the boathouse, his skin feels like it's on fire. *My* skin feels ablaze under his touch. He cradles the ball of my foot in his palm, and tips my foot one way and then the other. I should be worried about all of the spiders that are undoubtedly setting up their underground fortress in this room, but all I can think about is the way Asher has one hand on my lower calf, and the other on my ankle. And how no one has ever been this gentle with me. *Also, how long has it been since I got a pedicure? Am I sandpapering his hand right now?* This night is falling apart in so many ways.

A slight twist has me hissing, and Asher stops, his hands stilling against my skin. He whispers a very sincere apology as he rests my foot back on the floor. The smell is back again. Even against the mustiness, the smell of Asher is winning out over everything. I stand up, and Asher's hand is on my arm. "Sit back down," he says quietly, but I don't listen.

"We have to get out of here. I'll be fine with some help. We'll go out the same way we did last time, along the water. Then you can come back and get the wagon." I look up at him, wondering if he'll take that as me throwing him under the bus. "If that's okay with you. I would, but you know . . ." I glance down at my offending foot.

Asher slips an arm around my waist, gripping me above my hip. I put my arm over his shoulder and he softly pushes the door open. Outside, it's quiet. We creep to the edge of Lake House A, poking our heads out in tandem to see if anyone is in the yard. I half expect to see Nadine come tearing through the yard, but the coast is clear, and we make our way past Lake House B and into the line of trees that separates the yard from the neighbor's. After twenty minutes of walking through the trees very ungracefully, we're slipping back into the car, letting out twin sighs of relief as we reach safety within the SUV.

By the time we get home, my ankle is already feeling less tight, but Asher still insists on helping me walk until he dumps me on my bed. With a crash and a huff, I sink into the softness of my yellow comforter. Asher moves for the door, and I expect him to leave, but instead he quietly shuts it.

"That didn't exactly go as expected." My voice is little more than a whisper. The last thing we need is our parents wondering why we're awake—and in the same room—at four in the morning.

Asher squats down next to the bed. He catches my good foot in his hands and slips my shoe off, setting it on the floor by my nightstand. Then he gently holds the other, and slips that one off, too. I turn on the bed, swinging my feet onto the mattress, trying not to think about how easily Asher has helped me tonight, or how weird it is to have him in my room for the first time since it became mine.

All of those strange thoughts from movie night are back again, milling around in my brain, forcing me to think about weird things like why anyone would ever break up with someone so sweet. The only light is the little lamp next to my bed, and it washes us in a soft yellow light. "Sorry," I say, shifting my hips until I'm no longer on the edge of the bed. I reach behind me to stack my pillows so I can lean back against the headboard.

"For what?" Asher is standing now, and reaches over me for

one of the extra pillows on my bed. He puts it under my foot. Holy hell, the sweetness just keeps coming. I'm going to have to undo all of this work when I change into my pajamas, but I can't make myself stop him when he's being like this. "I'm pretty sure you didn't intentionally twist your ankle."

"Still."

Asher squats down next to me again, his head cocking to the side. "You know you *can* make it up to me, if you feel bad. I mean, you *did* jeopardize the mission."

I turn my head to face him, ready to tell him I know *exactly* what he wants. And I'm not getting up to make breakfast for anyone tomorrow. It will probably be lunch before I wake up. But when my eyes meet his, I don't say anything. Because he's not looking at me like he wants pancakes.

I should move—every reasonable cell in my body says that I should—but I don't want to. And before another breath can pass between us, his lips are on mine. Maybe I'm in shock, or just nearing exhaustion, but all I can think is that Asher Marin is kissing me. Again. Totally *not* drunk. And I'm just . . . frozen. My lips are still.

What are we doing? Do I want this? For the last few weeks I haven't been sure what I want. I missed the pranks at first. The teasing and the attention. But so quickly, that was replaced by a different kind of attention. New, exciting, scary. Now I'm not sure what I want.

When Asher pulls back, there's a worried look etched across his face. The loss of his lips definitely doesn't make me happy. I don't know *what* I want, but that isn't it. And before I can even process it, or tell myself what an idiot I am, my hand is sliding behind his neck. My lips are on his again, and we're kissing.

Like everything we do, this kiss feels like a battle. His was soft; mine is harder. He brushes my lip with his tongue, and I bite his. He's still beside the bed with me twisted toward him, and as he pushes himself up, closer to me, one arm snakes behind my back. The other plants alongside me on the mattress. I shift a little, making room for him. My shirt has shifted up, and his hand is on the bare skin of my back, his fingertips pressing into my skin there.

As one knee pushes into the mattress beside me, a loud squeak cuts through the silence so thoroughly, I'm sure my parents have heard it two rooms down. It's a bucket of ice water spilling over me, and I still. Over me, Asher is frozen as well, but he doesn't take his eyes off of me; they're roaming over me like he's never seen me before. Or like he's about to dive in for a second round.

What the hell are we doing? We are in my bedroom, at four o'clock in the morning, making out just a few doors down from our parents. *On my bed.* This is the most un-Sidney-like thing I have ever done, and my face flushes thinking of how ridiculous I am. *Right place, right time.* That's all I am, convenient summer fun in an adjoining room. I try to push the thought away, but it keeps popping back up.

Asher pushes himself off of the bed with another soft squeak, and squats beside me again. He opens his mouth like he's going to say something, but instead he stands up, looming over me at his full height. "Good night, Sid." He turns to the bathroom door—his escape back to his own room—and he's halfway there when my voice finally breaks free.

"I . . ." I'm dying to cut the tension in the room, the heaviness. "I thought you were going to ask for pancakes," I admit, wishing I had something more eloquent to say, or that I had just kept my mouth shut and let him leave. Wishing I had the headspace to determine if I was giddy, or confused, or mad. But all I can let myself think about right now is pancakes. One kiss, and his lips have completely warped my mind.

Asher's mouth tips up into a smile. "I was." He's walking backward toward the door, not taking his eyes off of me for a single second. He shrugs as he says, "But then you kissed me."

A defiant little huff of air escapes me.

"I'm still open to pancakes, though." He grins.

I can't remember the last time I was lacking a witty comeback for Asher. What do I want to say? *You shouldn't have kissed me? I shouldn't have kissed you? Come back here, so I can kiss you again?* I fear it would be the last one. Only seconds pass before he's slipping through the bathroom door, a whispered "good night" gliding into my room as he glides out.

What the hell happened tonight?

DAY 25

Sidney

It's one o'clock before I finally decide that starving in my room would not be a great life choice. Even if it would teach Asher a lesson. I bet most girls don't complain about being kissed by Asher; letting myself starve would be some next-level payback. But I don't have the dedication to starve myself, or the luxury of avoiding Asher indefinitely, when we live in the same house. Controlling when I see him is probably the best scenario I can ask for.

Asher is always sticking his clothes into random loads of laundry, so there's always a pile of his miscellaneous clean clothing sitting in the little laundry room between his room and Sylvie and Greg's. Maybe he does his laundry like that on purpose—if each of us thinks it's a mistake, we just fold the few pieces, and by the end of the week Asher has a full load of clean laundry. I wouldn't put it past him, it's sort of brilliant. So I'm not surprised to see a little stack of his T-shirts when I open the laundry room doors.

I suppose I don't need an excuse to talk to Asher—kissing me with no warning last night seems like excuse enough—but it wouldn't hurt to have one. Just in case he has no intention of addressing the elephant in the room. Sigh. I still miss Edith. If I have to, I'm not above throwing his laundry at him and claiming that's the only reason I came. As I make the harrowing six-foot journey to his bedroom, I hope I won't have to resort to the drive-by laundry-bomb method. Laundry flinging seems immature, even for us.

I knock at Asher's door, but it's quiet. Probably I should just take his clothes back to the laundry room. But something makes me twist the knob and go inside. *Dump them and run*, my brain screams. The rest of me has different ideas, though, because my heart knows I'm not here for laundry. If my brain was in control, I wouldn't have stayed in my room half the day, thinking about all of the reasons kissing Asher is a train wreck waiting to happen.

Mainly, the fact that Asher's only looking for summer fun. And there's nothing about me that would make me think I could handle a friends-with-benefits kind of situation. We're barely friends, for one. As far as I can tell, Asher goes from one girlfriend to the other, every school year. Every summer he seems to be fresh off a breakup. That's months of dating. I mean, sure, I have a horrible track record with guys, but I don't keep them around long enough to smash their hearts. *Months* is heartbreak territory. It's crying-in-your-room-wondering-what-you-did-wrong territory. How-am-I-going-to-face-him-every-day-or-see-him-with-someone-else territory. My pulse is thrumming in my ears just standing in his room, thinking through all of this again. Asher Marin isn't just some guy who wanted to kiss me. *Twice.* He's the guy who has been finding ways to get into my head, and get back at me for years. There's no way there isn't something else going on here. *You were so so stupid, Sidney.*

I walk into Asher's room, past his bed—rumpled and torn apart, like a wild animal slept in it—and set his clothes on the chair next to his dresser. It's clean and white and tall. And covered in his things.

I poke around the cluttered surface—at the little bottle of cologne I can't help but lift to my nose, at the brown leather wallet that he never carries because he hates the way it feels in his pocket. I open his top drawer and the left side is stuffed with wads of gray and black and red, the black elastic waistbands stopping my hand from reaching down. On the right is his toothbrush, a black comb, and two bottles of shampoo and conditioner. Are the bottles in the shower just decoys? Apparently Asher doesn't 100 percent trust the truce, either. *Smart boy.* Maybe he knows how addicted I am to his body wash, and that I'd never tamper with it, and that's why it has no decoy. I'm pretty sure I'd protect that body wash with my life.

I'm not sure what I'm looking for—maybe I'm just in snooping withdrawal—but just before I close the drawer, I notice the little box. I trace my finger over delicate veins of gold foil that run across the blue box, and I know I shouldn't, but I pluck it out and pop the lid off. There's a necklace inside—a pretty one, with charms and beads and a long dangling chain—and I suddenly wish I hadn't opened the box or this drawer, or his bedroom door. Because I came in here looking for answers, and now all I have is more questions. Just one question, really: Does Asher have a girlfriend? He and Jordan broke up, but that was months ago—plenty of time for a new girl to come into the picture. I think about all of the sweet things Asher does—why *wouldn't* he have a girlfriend? And what else don't I know about him? But more importantly, why do I even care? And why did he kiss me?

My phone buzzes in my pocket and I close the dresser drawer before pulling it out. It's just my mom reminding me that the parents will be gone for dinner tonight and we're on our own. Below my mom's text is one from Kara, and then, as if written in neon, I see Caleb's name. My fingers move faster than my brain when I start typing.

> Sidney: Want to hang out
> tonight?

It's at least a minute before the shimmering three dots appear, letting me know he's replying. My stomach clenches. I'm not sure if I'm worried he'll say no, or that he'll say yes.

> Caleb: Absolutely. Cherry
> Bowl?

Ugh. This is the problem with being in a small town. Our options are limited. And I suppose I shouldn't be picky when I haven't talked to Caleb since I told him I just wanted to be friends. But this is what friends do, right? Friends hang out. They swoop in when you need a rescue. And right now I really need to get out of this house.

> Sidney: Sounds good.

I text him my new address. As I shove my phone back in my pocket, I realize I'm still standing in Asher's room. And I don't know why it feels like I just did something wrong when he's hoarding jewelry (and maybe girlfriends), but suddenly I feel like I might break out in hives if I stand in this room for one more second. And when I pass through the bathroom to my room, I can't help but glance at the mirror. The lipstick is sitting on the counter, but the mirror is empty. The last three weeks feel like a quickly fading dream.

I'm laying clothes out on my bed when there's a knock on the bathroom door. It isn't locked, though in retrospect maybe that was stupid of me. "Come in."

Asher walks in slowly, with his hands shoved into his pockets. His face is almost blank, unreadable. My brain wants to scream, *Why did you kiss me? Do you have a girlfriend? Is this all a giant joke to you?* But all my mouth says is, "Hey." I'm surprised by how normal my voice sounds. My hands keep grabbing at pieces of clothing, picking up and putting them down, moving things around on my bed just to keep from being still.

His eyes roam over the clothes strewn about my bed, and then to me, in the ratty shorts and tank top I always wear straight from the shower. He looks me up quickly from my toes to my eyes before saying, "Going somewhere?"

I toss aside the shirt I was holding. "Just the Cherry Bowl."

"The movies haven't changed yet, they're the same all week."

I know this; it's why I wasn't thrilled Caleb suggested it. Well, part of the reason. "I know, it's not a big deal."

"You really want to see the same movies twice in a week?" He tips his head to the side, like he's examining me. "Tell Kara to find someone else. Come with me to Trevor's house. Game Night 2.0, you can have your own game piece and everything."

"I'm not going with Kara." There's a long stretch of silence, and I know I should fill it with the information the look on his face is telling me he wants, but I can't make myself do it. Things feel too weird. There's a tangible sense of aggression radiating from him as he looks over the clothes strewn around my room, and I have to fight to push away the guilty feeling rising up in me. It's completely irrational. *I* have nothing to be sorry for.

"You're going with Caleb?" Asher's brows are twisted in annoyance, and he says his name like it's something sticky he found on his shoe. His hands move from his pockets to his head, gripping the back of his neck like he has a headache. "Since when?"

"Since this afternoon?" My voice is rough and harsh, and it matches the scowl on Asher's face. *Why does this feel like an interrogation?*

"Okay, well, you have fun." Despite the kindness of the words themselves, his voice is still rough and sounds more like, *I hope*

*you choke on your popcorn. I'm glad I won't be there to Heimlich
you, even though it's my lifelong dream.*

"So what, you're mad?" It sounds like a joke when it comes
out of my mouth, but I'm not amused. "I mean, are you even
available, Asher?" I fidget with the hem of my tank top and suddenly I wish I hadn't brought it up. I have just as little right to
be jealous as he does. "Whatever, I don't blame you if you're still
hung up on Jordan, or Lindsay, or . . . whoever . . . it's just that
maybe you shouldn't kiss people if—"

"What?" To his credit, he looks surprised when he says it.
"Why would you even bring up Lindsay?"

So it's Jordan, then. I have to decide if I want to admit that
I broke the truce and was lurking around in his bedroom. He's
sure to be irritated with me, but he doesn't look like he's getting
out of here without an explanation. And he's at max levels of
irritation anyway. Might as well just lean into it. "I was putting
some stuff in your room earlier and—"

He folds his arms over his chest and narrows his eyes on me.
It's the look *Before* Asher would have given me. "What stuff?"

"It doesn't matter." I hesitate, suddenly unsure of how committed I am to dying on this hill. He cocks his head to the side
and pins me with a hard stare. "I had laundry for you, okay?"

Asher raises his eyebrows and I know I'm caught—there's no
reasonable reality where I would bring him his laundry without
ulterior motives—but he doesn't say anything.

"It doesn't matter why I was there." I shake my head, hoping
I can shake away the feeling that I'm the one who did something
wrong. *He's* the one trying to lure me into the meanest prank of
all time. "I saw the necklace."

He smiles, and shakes his head like I just said something ridiculous. It's the kind of smile that tells me there's something
coming. That I'll wake up to my flip-flops glued to the floor or
self-tanner smeared in my swimsuit. It's a menacing smile, a
predator's smile. It's the only kind of smile I used to see on his

face, but it feels strange and wrong, now that I've seen his face look so many other ways.

"Come here," he says, pulling me by my hand before I can stop him. I follow him through the bathroom and into his bedroom. With the focus of a heat-seeking missile, he goes right to his dresser and pulls the little box out of his drawer. The lid tumbles to the ground as he flicks it off with his thumb and holds the box out to me. His look is a command and a warning.

I shake my head, bewildered, and cross my arms over my chest. "That's it." I'm not sure what he wants me to say.

He rolls his eyes. "You don't recognize it?"

"Why would I?" But then I look at it again—the strange purple-blue color of the little stones that hang from it. At the delicate silver chain and charm of entangled fish that dangles next to the biggest stone. I hadn't noticed the charm before. It catches the light and sparkles, and my stomach slowly plummets to my feet as recognition hits me.

"Yeah." He smiles but he's not happy. "You should recognize it, because two summers ago, *you* were basically obsessed with it."

I pull my eyes away from the necklace and look at Asher, whose face has gone from angry to sad.

"My mom wouldn't buy it for me. She was on that kick about limiting our material possessions and focusing on experiences, and I had already spent all my money on that stupid wakeboard I never used." The words trail off as I reach a hand out toward the box.

Asher moves it back just a hair, and I retreat. "Right," he says.

"I don't . . ." I shake my head at the little box, at the way he's looking at me while he holds it. "Why do you have it?"

"I have it because I was on that miserable shopping trip with you, and I saw how much you wanted it." He looks away from me, his eyes fixed on something to my left, and then sweeping across the ceiling to land on the other side of me. "So I bought it." There's a pause, a long stretch of dead air where I think about bolting for the door. "And every year I told myself I was going to give it to you." He swallows and his throat bobs. "But every year it was the same, with the pranks and . . . all of it."

His eyes meet mine again, and I don't know what to do. I just stare at him, feeling like I'm seeing him for the first time. Wondering how I've spent so many years pretending he was my enemy. Wondering just how long ago he stopped feeling like I was his. I bought that stupid wakeboard because I had secretly hoped that he'd take pity on me and show me how to use it. *Holy hell, we're a hopeless pair.*

Asher walks around me, and I can feel him step up behind me. His arm brushes my shoulder, and his hands stretch in front of me, the silver chain hanging there. I'm frozen in place, but it feels like my whole body is lightly buzzing. Asher's fingers brush my neck as he clasps it and pulls my hair out from beneath the tangle of metal. The necklace is cold on my skin where it falls low on my chest, and it feels heavy, even though it's dainty and delicate. But I can feel it—the necklace and his words—hanging there, around my neck, pressing in on me and making it hard to breathe.

We stand there, both of us silent, his front so close to my back that I'm not positive we aren't still touching. Even breathing feels too loud. Asher sets his hands on my shoulders, and then his breath is at my ear. "Sometimes I think you've forgotten how to say anything nice to me."

There's an angry edge to his voice, and the words sting. He's right, I've spent so much time poking at him, convincing myself that he's nothing but the enemy, that I've forgotten what he really is. What I had once hoped he could be. *We* could be.

His voice is still a whisper, the hard edge still there as it brushes against my ear. "This is where you say thank you." His tone is all off. It's hard again, so different from what I've become used to these last few weeks. I hadn't realized how much it had changed until I heard the old Asher again tonight. No, something so much harder than the old Asher.

"Thank you." The words are so soft, I'm not sure I even said them out loud. His hands fall away from me, as if those two words have released him from some kind of spell, but I can't move. Even as he closes the door, and I hear his footsteps move down the hallway and the screen door slam behind him in the kitchen. I'm still frozen in place in the middle of his bedroom when he walks past the window. There's a soft rumble of an engine and the crunch of gravel. By the time I reach the window the taillights are just two bright spots in the shadow of the trees. *Gone*.

I sit on the bed and lie back, letting the smell of Asher's sheets wash over me. It's strangely comforting. I love this smell, how it's just as much a part of my summer as all of the other smells of the house, and the lake. The necklace is long, and I hold the chain away from my chest, running my finger over the details of the two fish tangled together there. A tear slips down the side of my cheek, and then another, and it would be so much easier if it were Asher and not me who was the absolute worst right now.

Asher

When I get home that night, the house is dark and quiet. Dad's SUV is gone, so the parents must be out, reliving their glory days once again. They all seem to be taking this impending empty-nest situation *really* well. I grab a can of beer from the refrigerator, since no one's going to miss it tonight. Sidney's door is closed, and no light seeps from the gap, but she'll probably be home from her date soon. *Or maybe she won't.* It's the second date. The second time she's gone out on a date with another guy after I've kissed her. She's basically screaming what she wants at me; I don't know why I can't just listen.

Sidney out on a date shouldn't irritate me as much as it does. It's not like kissing someone gives you any sort of claim to them. There's not some binding contract of exclusivity that goes along with a kiss. It doesn't even mean she likes me, just that she was bored enough, or lonely enough, or mean enough to put her lips on mine. I think about all of the girls I've kissed just once. One time, no expectations. Maybe it's the fact that she *kissed me back* last night that's really irritating me. That second kiss was all her.

As I walk into my room, I pull my T-shirt off, flinging it onto the floor. Like all of the bedrooms, my room only has a fan—that I leave on all the time—and several little lamps scattered throughout. By the time I reach the bathroom door, my shorts are around my ankles, sent flying with a gentle kick. I flick on the light, and I'm about to close the door when I notice something illuminated by the crack of light streaming from the bathroom. It's Sidney. In my room. *In my bed.*

I whisper her name from the open door, but she doesn't move. So I close the door and use the bathroom, trying to figure out why she's here. As I brush my teeth I come up with four possible explanations:

1. It only looks like Sidney. It's actually an elaborate pile of pillows, or a strategically placed mannequin or something equally creepy.
2. It's some stranger she paid to lay in my bed, who will undoubtedly murder me.
3. I'm hallucinating. Or drunk. I haven't cracked the beer sitting on my counter yet, so the first is more likely at this point.
4. *She's* drunk, and wandered into the wrong bed. Maybe I should pour some lemonade on her and even the score in the morning?

I look at the unopened can of beer sitting on my bathroom counter and shake my head. I sort of wish I was drunk right now, because any of these things seems more likely than the idea that Sidney Kristine Walters could actually be sleeping in my bed right now. *Willingly.* I'm tempted to open her bedroom door, just to confirm nothing horrible has happened in there.

I pull on a pair of gray pajama pants, because I don't think talking to her in my underwear is going to help matters at all.

She's sleeping right on the edge, which seems like a very Sidney thing to do. I don't even know why, it just does. I squat down next to the bed and just look at her for a second. My annoyance over Caleb and the necklace, and the fact that she thinks I'm a total douchebag, has melted away. I set my hand on her shoulder and rub my thumb on her bare skin, trying not to startle her. She makes a little purring sound, and the crack of light slashing down onto the carpet illuminates the way her nose scrunches up. I want to laugh, but that feels like the absolute rudest way I could wake her up. "Hey, Sid?" My hand is still on her arm when her eyes slowly open.

She looks startled for a second, but she doesn't make any noise. With a shake of her head she blinks up at me, scans her eyes around the room, and then opens her mouth in something between a yawn and a deep breath.

"Shouldn't you be at the movies?" I whisper, and all of the anger from before has seeped out of my voice, leeched away by the shock of her in my bed. She's still in the old T-shirt and cotton shorts she was wearing when I brought her into my room earlier. *Has she been here the whole time?*

Sidney doesn't say anything; she just shakes her head. Honestly, it seems rude to show up in someone's room and then refuse to answer their questions, or to even speak. But then she rolls onto her back, and then over again, until she's facing me, but this time from the other side of the bed. I look down at the empty space where her body used to be, and then at her. *I am so freaking confused right now.* When she doesn't move, I lie down next to her, hoping my bed isn't as squeaky as hers.

Her voice is soft. "I didn't go to the movies." I can feel her breath on my cheek as my eyes focus on the ceiling.

"I see that."

"Do you know why?"

I turn my head toward her. "Because you knew Caleb wouldn't create a movie-watching experience half as awesome as I did?" I smile at her, and realize our faces are only inches apart. "Because you wanted to hide in my bed like a creeper and wait for me?" She scrunches her nose up like I've offended her, but a smile is pulling at her lips, so I keep going. "You were sitting on my bed, thinking about how awesome I am, and you suffered a narcoleptic episode. Am I getting warm?"

"You've had this necklace for *years* now." She puts her fingers to her chest where the necklace rests. "Two summers ago."

"That's the basic math of it, yes."

"You suck at this." Her voice is annoyed, but amused.

"What?"

"Talking about serious stuff."

"Yeah, pretty much." I don't think it's that I'm nervous to talk to Sidney about this stuff, it's just that my head is spinning, and the room is dark, and she's in my bed wearing way too little. It's a lot to think about.

"I kind of like that you suck at this." She smiles and rolls onto her back, and I'm relieved by the extra few inches it puts between us. "So if you've had that necklace for two years . . ."

"Do you have a question you want to ask?" I'm still looking at her, but she's looking at the ceiling.

"Do you have anything you want to tell me?"

I roll my eyes and wish she could see it. "You suck at this, too."

"Yeah. But you should have told me. I thought you hated me, and we could have had . . . we could have had less of us being dysfunctional and horrible."

"Maybe I liked us dysfunctional and horrible." She levels me with a stare and I let out a long breath. "What should I have told you?"

She doesn't say anything, she just stares up at the ceiling. And after a minute, she closes her eyes, and I wonder if she's just going to go back to sleep in my bed and hope she wakes up to find out this entire day was just a bad dream.

I take a deep breath, and decide that I don't have much to lose; this is a game of chicken that Sidney is never going to willingly let me win. "Hey, Sid . . ."

She tips her head back toward me, her voice soft. "Yeah?"

"Ask me how much I hate you right now."

She closes her eyes for just a second. "How much do you hate me right now?" It doesn't have the teasing edge it usually does; her voice is nervous, almost shaky.

"I don't." It's such a cop-out. I should have told her the whole truth—*I like you. I've* always *liked you*—but I can't bring myself to do it without knowing if she's going to lose her shit and stop talking to me the rest of the summer. So, baby steps.

"I . . ." She looks back to the ceiling. "Don't hate you, either."

"I'm sorry I didn't tell you sooner."

She looks at me and smiles, but it's a little sad. "Me, too."

Sidney is like the stray cat we had at our house one summer. We fed her for a few weeks, and she purred and acted like she'd stay forever, but then suddenly she was gone. So before Sidney decides to bolt, I turn and press my lips to hers. She shifts, so she's facing me, and props herself up on her elbow so we're level. My hand rests on her waist, and hers wraps behind my back.

We're still pressed together when a door slams and voices filter into the house. All four of our parents are home. Footsteps enter the hallway, and Sidney bolts up. I whisper in her ear, "My door is locked. Just be quiet." And just to see what I can get away with, I kiss her behind her ear.

"Mine isn't," she says frantically, and launches herself off of the bed. In two long steps that are almost leaps, she's in the bathroom, the door softly shutting behind her. A faucet turns on, the crack of light under the door goes dark, and just as strangely as Sidney appeared in my bedroom, she's gone.

DAY 26

Asher

Today should feel different. At least I thought it would. But mostly it just feels the same. And not in a good way. In a really weird, déjà vu kind of way that is making my skin crawl like it used to when I was waiting for one of Sid's pranks. When she jumped—literally—out of my bed last night, I didn't expect to wake up this morning and make out at breakfast or anything. I didn't even expect pancakes. That would have been sort of weird, too.

But I also didn't expect that the kitchen would be empty when I walked in at six thirty. I'm not sure at what point it became our thing, but not having breakfast with Sidney feels wrong. And not just because I had to eat cereal and not pancakes.

"Ash?" I'm still sitting at the table at seven thirty, scrolling through my phone, when my mom files into the kitchen followed by my dad. "You're up early." *You have no idea.*

I tell her I couldn't sleep, instead of telling her the truth: that I show up at six thirty every morning, hoping Sidney hasn't decided to start taking it easy this summer. I wonder what my mom would say if I told her that after all these years of dragging me out of bed, I basically lie awake in my bed at 6 a.m. every day. That I can hardly make myself wait some mornings.

Thinking it, I'm positive that saying I couldn't sleep was the right choice.

Fifteen minutes later Kris and Tom filter out of the hallway, and Sid is a few steps behind, still in the shorts and tank she was wearing last night. *In my bed.* It's almost eight o'clock, and I literally can't remember the last time I saw her get up this late. Except for yesterday. The morning after the kiss. The day she decided that kissing me made her want to stay in her room the entire day, and then go out with another guy. Cue the ominous foreboding. Will that kiss forever be a before and after for me and Sidney? At the table, over my mom's scrambled eggs and her dad's coffee—which I know for a fact is not nearly as good as what I usually make her—we are silent. With each other, at least.

Sidney tells my mom she's excited when she asks her about college starting in a month. She tells my dad she already got her dorm assignment. McLandry House, right across from one of the dining spots. Of course she already looked up her dorm on the map. My assignment still says PENDING and I'm starting to wonder if I'm going to be sleeping on a sidewalk somewhere.

Everyone eats, and I shove bacon and eggs into my mouth, not because I'm hungry, but because I don't want to leave the table. I'm glad we don't have to swim this morning, because watching her cross the lake not knowing where we stand would be pure torture. But deep in my gut I know it: I've royally screwed this all up. The kiss, the necklace, the second kiss in my bed—obviously it's all too much. Not to mention that first kiss, the night of the party. There's a good chance I'll go to my grave without admitting that—drunk or not—I remember every second of that kiss in the grass.

I spend most of the morning in my room, trying to convince myself I'm not panicking. Or hiding from Sidney. But I'm totally hiding from Sidney. Or maybe I'm waiting for her. Right. Maybe she'll just show up in my bedroom again. Yes, I'm a delusional idiot. I text my best friend Todd and tell him the whole gruesome story of the last few days.

Todd P: Wow you finally did it

Asher: Whatever. It's all screwed.

Todd P: That's the state-ranked superstar I know and love! Good to see you haven't lost your competitive spirit, bruh!

Asher: I hate you sometimes.

Todd P: You don't. You love me. I'm the brother you never hoped for but still ended up with. I'm the lime to your beer, bruh.

Asher: I told you to never call me that again. It's not even funny in an ironic way.

Todd P: We're gonna bring it back, bruh. It's a throwback.

Asher: Throw it back where it came from. Are you trying to annoy me into doing anything but texting you?

Todd P: Is it working?

Todd P: Hello?

Todd P: I can see the bubble, I know you're there.

Asher: I'm going to go find her. Thanks, bruh.

Todd P: Bringing it backkkkkkk!

Sidney's lying in the water, stretched out on her inner tube, her neck arched back, hair billowing in the water behind her. There's a rope tethering her raft to the dock, like she's our very own buoy. If she had a warning painted across her, I suspect it would say STAY AWAY rather than the usual SWIM ZONE.

Seeing her out there reminds me of the first summer we met, and there's nothing perilous in those memories. Except for that summer being its own kind of ending. Though I'll never be able to explain how something that never started could be snuffed out so abruptly. I could walk to the end of the dock, but I don't. Because she's probably fallen asleep out there, and if I scare the crap out of her that won't help my case. Or maybe because I'm a coward. And if this is another ending instead of a beginning, I'm not really in a rush to get there.

At dinner Sidney is quiet. Not when my mother comments about all of her running, or when hers asks about her future roommate—a girl from the other side of the state named Ellie. But when I finally will myself to say something—to bring up the fact that our meet schedule has gone up and two of our first three meets are at home—I get a two-word answer as she jabs a chicken breast with her fork: *that's exciting.* I wonder if our parents notice the quiet between us, or if it's just me.

It's probably just me.

Sidney

I haven't been actively avoiding Asher all day, but I wasn't going out of my way to be near him, either. Which made me realize that for a while now, I was. I was putting myself in his way, making excuses to be where he was. I hadn't realized how much of our time was spent together until today, when we spent almost none of it together. It felt . . . wrong. And that realization feels wrong in my head. It's like a misshapen puzzle piece that doesn't fit with everything I've always thought about Asher. About what the two of us have always added up to. But I can't avoid him forever, and if we're going to talk, I'd rather it be alone. So when I see him sitting on the couch, watching TV after everyone else has gone to bed (even though he has a TV in his room) I wonder if he feels the same.

He's sitting on the small sofa, leaning to one side, his elbow propped up on the arm. Our parents all went to bed over an hour ago. Too many late nights, I guess. I sit on the armchair across the room from him, curling my legs under me and shoving a pillow under my side. I lean onto the arm like he does. We sit in silence, the sound of the TV filling the room, though it seems to float right past my ears. I'm not paying attention to anything but the fact that I'm in the same room as Asher, alone in the dark, for the first time since he told me he didn't hate me. Since we were in his bed together. My cheeks flush at the thought of it. It was less than twenty-four hours ago, but it's already starting to feel like a long-gone memory. Or a dream. I was in bed, maybe it *was* a dream.

"You could sit, you know." Asher smiles at me, and I'm

completely unnerved by it. At how casually he does it now, and directed at me.

"I *am* sitting." I glance down at my chair, offering it as evidence.

"You could sit by *me*."

I don't move and Asher laughs. "You can't see the TV over there. I know you can't."

I can see the TV just fine, actually. Not that I'm watching—I'm way too preoccupied to even process what's flashing across the screen. But maybe he knew what I needed. An excuse. A reason to make myself walk the ten feet from my chair to his couch.

I get up and deposit myself on the couch next to him. Not too close, like someone who thinks they're going to be kissed again, but not so far that it looks like I think he has something contagious. I am a very normal, not-enemies distance from him on the couch. *Do I want him to kiss me again?* It's the question that's been going through my head all day. The short answer is yes. A million times yes. No one has kissed me like Asher kissed me, or made me feel the electric jolt that zips up my body when we touch. But kissing Asher isn't that simple. Kissing Asher is, in one word, complicated.

Asher pushes himself up off of the couch and pauses. "I'm getting a drink, do you want something?"

"Can I trust you with my beverage?"

Asher looks down at me like I'm being ridiculous. As if last year he didn't fill my Sprite with salt, and gleefully offer it to me right before a dinner with our parents, only to stare at me in shock as I sputtered and gagged.

"I'm good." I swallow down the panic rising up in my throat. *Sometimes I think you've forgotten how to say anything nice to me.* "Thanks."

The room is dark and it feels like we're trapped in a tiny, suffocating little box, not the biggest room in the house. Now that he's gone, the empty space next to me doesn't look big enough for Asher anymore; it looks more fitting for a toddler. A toddler I'm going to be on top of when he returns from the kitchen. *Oh god.*

Asher returns and sets his can on the little wooden end table. And when he sits, he fits, but the space between us is diminished even further.

"I'm not sure how to do this." The words are almost a whisper, but I wonder if he hears them for what they really are: a scream for help.

He looks over at me, his brows pulled tight. "Do what?"

"This," I say, waving my finger between us frantically. "*Us.*" I say the word a little too harshly, a little bit too much like it's something dirty and unnatural. I'm still not sure that it isn't.

"You're overthinking this, Sid." Asher lifts his arm up onto the back of the couch, and it takes me a minute to register the action. The invitation that lays there, under his arm. It would only take a few inches to close the gap between us, yet it feels like a monumental movement.

"I overthink everything," I say, looking him right in the eyes, even though it makes me a little nauseous. "That's what I do."

He smiles. "I know. It's why you're so good at tormenting me. I bet you've got lists and shit."

I laugh and it comes out more like a snort, and I'm ready to just die. Right here on this crowded little couch. Just kill me now.

I look back at the TV, and then to Asher, before leaning into him and settling against his shoulder. I don't think I'm breathing. My neck feels stiff as I debate whether to rest my cheek against him. It feels like too much, but I'm in it now, and I can't sit with my head cocked up for the rest of this movie, or TV show, or whatever it is we're going to sit here and watch. Or can I? Maybe my neck muscles are stronger than I'm giving them credit for.

I let my head relax against him, and it's done; there's no going back now. *I am snuggling with Asher Marin*. And not in an undercover-agent-getting-close-to-her-mark kind of way. In a really sweet, comforting, *normal* kind of way. Like two people who haven't spent eight weeks every summer tormenting each other. Like two people who *like* each other. Is that who we are now? Or is this just how Asher is with people he's not being horrible to? I don't know Asher outside of summer vacation and this little town we both inhabit for two months—it's totally possible that he's the kind of guy who snuggles with all of his female friends.

"Stop thinking about it," he says softly, his voice teasing but sweet.

Asher rests his hand on my arm, and as we watch the movie and then the next, his fingers trace an idle, mindless path on my skin. I can't breathe.

And I don't hate it.

Asher

It's almost 2 a.m. and Sidney is still lying on me. My hand is numb, but if I'm the first to move from this position there's a definite possibility that it will be the last time we're ever in it. We haven't said anything all night, but there's a tangible current of anxiety rolling off of Sidney. We need to talk, so we don't have another day like today, where she avoids me.

"On a scale of one to ten, how much are you panicking right now?"

The shoulder pressed against my ribs rises and falls as she takes a deep breath. "Something like a twelve." I smile at her voice, because it sounds nervous but it doesn't sound anything like a twelve. And she hasn't moved away from me yet.

"I think we should go somewhere." I sit up, and Sidney's head slides down my chest a few inches before she catches herself.

"Now?"

"Now or never," I say, standing up and pulling her to her feet. I need to show Sidney that we could be so much better together than we are apart.

It's hard to believe only forty-eight hours have passed since the last time we stood here. I know technically each day holds exactly twenty-four hours, but in reality some days just take up so much more space in our lives. Jumping off of that swing feels like a lifetime ago. And standing next to Sidney now in the darkness of the trees, Nadine's yard just beyond us, the minutes that pass in silence feel just as long.

"We're a good team." My words aren't much more than a whisper. Silence stretches out as we stand side by side marveling at the white disaster that is Nadine's yard. It's not the mountains of fluffy potatoes I'd imagined in my mind, but it's pretty gross looking; a white sludgy mess. There are dark spots criss-crossing the yard showing everywhere Nadine has walked. "I get the panic. I swear I do," I say.

"But?"

I bump my arm into hers. "See, you get me."

She smiles, and it feels like my chance to turn this panic-fest into something else. Something that doesn't set us back to what we've always been. Because I'm sure Sidney's already decided that this is all going to end in ruin. She's already convinced herself that the only way to avoid hurting each other is to avoid liking each other. I wonder if this is how Taylor and David and Evan all met their fates. Sidney, alone in the dark, with too much time to think. Too much time to panic. "Just give me three dates."

She looks straight ahead as she says, "March seventh, June twelfth . . . and October twenty-third."

"Smart ass." I poke her playfully in the side and she jumps.

"Guilty," she says, but she doesn't sound it. She sounds proud of herself. And like she's starting to loosen up again. She sounds like drive-in movie Sidney. Like chocolate-chip pancake Sidney, covered in flour that first morning and dripping with newfound optimism.

"Three dates," I continue, and I wish we were still on that couch where I was touching her, and not standing here, inches apart. "And then you decide."

"And you?" she whispers, her face still turned toward the yard. "When do *you* decide?"

I'm about to answer when she suddenly turns to me. "Four dates," she says. "Two for you and two for me." She smiles and turns away from me again, but her voice sounds lighter. "I'm not sitting around waiting for you and your dates," she says, and I laugh.

"That seems . . . fair," I say, not at all upset that she seems as interested in this proposition as I am. That *she* wants to go out with *me*.

"Okay, so four dates before we decide this is a complete train wreck." The tone of her voice—the defeat it's already laced with—confirms how she sees this all ending.

"Or four dates before we decide it isn't."

"So this is date number one?" I can't tell if her voice is hopeful or disappointed.

"We live together." I drape my arm over her shoulders and turn her around, to where our car is waiting two driveways down. "We can't call it a date every time we end up in the same place. Unless you want to use this as one of yours?"

"No way." She looks up at me with mischief in her eyes. "My dates will be awesome."

I look behind us, the white grass still visible in the moonlight. "I expect nothing less."

DAY 27

Sidney

Today felt a lot like the last few weeks, but it also felt entirely different. And not in any kind of obvious, over-the-top way. It was more like a change of context. Like I saw everything Asher did in a different light. He made me pancakes this morning. Technically, he made all of us pancakes, but I knew they were really for me. And not just because mine were the only ones with chocolate chips. It was like everything he said was directed at me, as if we were having a private conversation, even while surrounded by our parents.

"Did everyone have fun last night?" Asher says as we're all sitting around the table, cutting into our pancakes. I'm not sure why he's been begging *me* for pancakes, when his are just as good. Our parents tell us about the wine tasting room they went to after dinner, about the dessert wine that put them all in bed early.

I wonder if anyone noticed that Asher and I barely had anything separating us this morning. That his knee was touching mine under the table. I'm not sure if it was the first time, but it certainly *felt* like it.

When I ask Asher if we should tell our parents about us, he says no, and I agree. No sense in getting their hopes up when we're only four dates away from ruin. But when Asher asks me to go with him to Trevor's house, I say yes. *Maybe* a little too quickly.

Asher

I met Trevor a few summers ago, at a party at his mom's house. His sister was throwing it, and I found Trevor in their dining room, setting up this elaborate game, even as a party began to rise up around him.

Trev's house is tall and white, and sits on one of the country roads outside of the main downtown area. When we pull into the driveway, Sidney seems nervous, her hands twisting in her lap, then pulling at strands of her hair. They've been moving in a constant loop—lap, hair, twist, pull, lap—since we got in the car.

"Are you nervous to be going to this, or nervous to be going with *me*?"

"Yes," she says, and we both laugh. She pushes her door open and steps out before I have to threaten to drag her, which seemed like a possibility. As we step up to the front door, we're standing side by side. Sidney stops short at the door and looks at me. "This is the same house."

I nod.

She looks down at my shirt and laughs. "Are you sentimental or something?"

I shrug. "It's possible."

She turns away, but her cheeks are burning red as I turn the doorknob and push her in with a hand on her lower back. My shirt is right, swimmers *absolutely* do it better.

We're in the corner of the basement again, except now it's quiet instead of buzzing with people. Everyone is in the same chairs, but the game board is completely different. It's clean, a brand-new game ready to go.

"We're playing the same game again?" Sidney asks.

"Yeah, but it won't be the same. All it takes is one changed decision, and the whole game is different. You can play this game over and over, and it won't ever turn out the same."

An hour into our game, Sidney is crushing it. We were forbidden from playing together, but her chair is pulled up close to mine anyway. She's perched up on her chair again, her legs tucked under her. Every time I strike one of her territories she softly punches my leg. But after she does it, her hand stays there. Her palm is pressed into my thigh, and at first, it feels sort of rigid against me like she didn't realize she did it, but soon she uses it to leverage herself up as she stretches to look across the board. Her hand relaxes, her fingers begin to tap and flutter against me. At one point, I swear she's tracing a message against my leg. I keep trying to make it out, but all I accomplish is Trevor mocking me when I space out and don't realize my turn has come.

"Do we need a hand check?" Trevor teases. Sid lifts her hands, and I expect they'll go back to her lap, but her left hand returns to its spot on my leg. Knowing Sidney, it's probably there to spite Trevor. I keep waiting for her to move it, but I think maybe she's committed to playing tonight's game one-handed. And that's a challenge I am fully on board with.

Sidney

The last time I played a board game with Lindsay I was drunk. It's different being sober, and I'm quiet. With her, at least. I don't know what to talk about. Unlike Trevor and Hannah, Lindsay knows me. She knows Asher and me together, what we've been all these years. Without the alcohol to loosen me up, I'm thinking way too hard about what I can say to her that won't be weird. Thankfully, watching Trevor and Hannah has distracted me.

"Are those two—" I wave a casual finger toward Trevor and Hannah, who are angled toward each other, talking about something that probably isn't game-related if the look on Trevor's face is any indication. Hannah's thick bangs cover one eye, and she pushes them back behind her ear. "—together?" I whisper the last word like it's dirty.

Asher is turning his head to my ear as Trevor says, "Yeah. Why, you interested?" His face is serious, and Hannah looks like she might hit him. I don't know what to say. But then Trevor laughs, and Hannah follows. Asher warned me in the car that mellow drunk Trevor is not the norm, and I guess he's right. Trevor seems like a total goofball.

"I think you traumatized her." Hannah pokes him in the arm with her elbow. "Say sorry."

"Sorry I traumatized you." Trevor rubs the spot on his arm as if Hannah jabbed him with a hot poker, not her dainty elbow. "I would have thought Asher had done that years ago."

At this, I laugh. Trevor is funny. And clearly he's not clueless about my history with Asher. I'm curious just how close the two of them are, so I ask, "Did you know this is our first date?" I see the surprise register not just on Trevor's face, but on everyone's. "He brought me to your basement."

The girls look personally affronted, and Trevor is just shaking his head, like maybe he's going to get to see the *Sidney and Asher Show* he's heard so much about. Hannah is muttering "Oh come on, Ash" when he throws his hands up in the air. Lindsay looks surprised, but in a different way somehow, and I'm not sure what to make of it.

"Hey now." Asher's voice is amused, not angry. "I did *not* bring Sidney on a basement-date." The surprise on my face seems to be mirrored on his. "You thought I brought you on a basement-date?"

I let my eyes wander around the room as if to say, *Look where we are. We're in a basement. We're on a date. This is a basement-*

date. But I don't, because I was just joking, and I have no problem with Asher bringing me here. More like I was nervous talking to his friends for the first time (sober) and picking on Asher is my go-to stress reliever.

Asher sets his hand on my knee, and it's a lot like when a kitten jumps on your lap. You're really excited they want to play, but also, you know they have tiny, needle-like nails ready to stab you at any moment, and you can't fully relax. Everything inside me goes taut. Is this what it felt like when I did it to him? He tips his head toward me as he says, "This isn't a date, Sid. When I take you on a date, you'll know it." He glances over at Trevor. "And this nerd definitely won't be there."

Not a date. I was only teasing Asher, I don't actually want to get into the details of our situation at a table full of his friends, so I just smile at him and say, "If you say so."

He gives me a smug smile right back. "I do say so."

Asher and I are still looking at each other when Lindsay clears her throat. "Honestly, I can't believe it took this long." The words aren't unkind, but she immediately picks up a game piece. Our little chat is over. She's been quiet most of the night, too, but now her eyes dart to me. Lindsay insisted no partners when we started tonight. I can't help but wonder if she has a problem with anyone being partners, or just me. With Asher. I think of the way she looked at me at the party. Even tipsy I could register the jealousy there. Or maybe it was just shock. I'm not sure which is worse. Was she irritated that he was holding my hand or just surprised that he would? We weren't even together then. We're not together *now*, my brain says. But my brain isn't the one in control when I take my hand off of Asher's leg and put it up on his shoulder, right where she can see it.

We've been playing for hours, and it feels weird that I might leave here soon without having said a word to Lindsay. Probably no one else notices, but I won't let myself be that girl. I finally work up the nerve to ask her something I've always wondered about. "So what's up with the yard sculptures?" I flick a card across my fingertips, over and over, trying to rein in my nervous energy.

Lindsay shrugs. "My mom's nuts about those things. She knows where each and every one of them is." I think about the time Edith spent in my bedroom and wonder if Nadine really did notice her missing. "When people come over for the first time she always takes them around the yard like it's a tour." She rolls her eyes. "They're like her adopted children."

That seems like an exaggeration, and my face must say the same because Lindsay looks at me and raises her brows. "Seriously. I broke one when I was a kid, back when they were at our old house, and she lost it. I was grounded for a week. Total accident."

"Sidney's always been low-key obsessed with those things," Asher says, his voice teasing.

"More like I'm fascinated with the way they've multiplied. They're like a yard sculpture army. The sheer number is what fascinates me." I poke my elbow into his ribs.

"Wasn't there a show when we were kids, where yard gnomes came to life?" Trevor says.

Asher laughs. "Can you imagine?"

"I'd like to think that if they could leave, they would. They deserve a less grumpy owner." I look at Lindsay apologetically. "No offense."

Lindsay shrugs. "She's not the easiest person." She looks from me to Asher. "Sorry about what happened with getting kicked out and everything. I didn't hear about it 'til you guys were gone." She looks to Asher. "You should have called me, I would have talked her down."

Asher shakes his head. "It all happened really fast, I didn't even think about it." He puts a hand on my knee and squeezes, as if he's trying to remind me that it all worked out okay. And I guess it did. When Asher's hand stays on my knee, I try to remind myself to breathe. It's almost enough to distract me from thinking about the fact that Lindsay sounded so casual about Asher calling her. She didn't give him her number, so he already has it.

Before my brain can go down a dark road, I let it run away in a different direction. "I don't think yard sculptures are very loyal. I bet they make a break for it someday. Maybe they'll pile on the pontoon and come to our new house."

Asher tips his head back and laughs. "If anyone could lead that army, it's you, Sid." The lightness of his voice is enough to wash all the other thoughts from my head. Basement date or not—*Lindsay or not*—this is a pretty great night.

I knock on Asher's bathroom door, but it pops open as I do. It's not even closed, let alone locked. Next to his bed, Asher is pulling his T-shirt off, over his head. It's the SWIMMERS DO IT BETTER shirt—the one I made him change out of the first time we went to Trevor's house. The fact that he wore it tonight makes me smile. He picks a gray T-shirt off of his bed and pulls it over his head. I'm a little sad as it slides over his chest and obscures the view I had of him.

"Did you wear it that night just to annoy me?" I ask, suddenly curious.

Asher smiles. "I plead the fifth."

"And what about that pink shirt? You wore *that* to annoy me, right?"

"I told you why I wore it."

"Hm."

He looks at me expectantly, and for a second I forget why I even came into his room.

"I had fun tonight."

He smiles, and lifts the hem of his T-shirt to tie his pajama pants. "Me, too."

I've seen Asher in his pajamas a million times, but never in his room. Alone. They're just clothes. I'm in my regular clothes, because I couldn't bring myself to walk in here in my threadbare T-shirt. It didn't offer nearly enough barrier between us.

I tear my eyes away from Asher's waist, and focus on why I came in here. Which was not to creep on Asher. Definitely not. "You know, you'll have to use one eventually." He looks at me blankly, and I smile. "A date. We said four *dates*."

He smiles, and it's smug and cocky, the smile I saw on rare occasions after a prank—or when one was coming.

"I don't like that look."

He feigns innocence. "What?"

I tip my head to the side and don't offer anything.

"I like that you're begging me to take you on a date."

My mouth opens and snaps shut. "I didn't . . . I mean . . . I just . . ." I shake my head. "You are *so* annoying." This only makes him smile wider, more genuinely, like I've made him truly happy.

"*Am* I, though?" Mischief glints in his eye.

He steps toward me, his eyes burning into mine, and I take a step back, like we're dancers, our limbs giving and taking from one another. We both take another step and my legs hit his bed. The soft impact with the place he sleeps—the place I laid just days ago—makes my breath catch in my throat. He leaves the space between us, and his hand reaches out, smoothing a piece of my hair between his finger and thumb, before pushing it behind my shoulder. Warm fingers rest on my shoulder, then trail to the back of my neck, but he isn't moving any closer to me. Everything about the way Asher touches me is so confident, like it's not just the first time he's touched a girl like this, but that it isn't the first time he's touched *me* like this. Even though every single touch feels like it's the first for me.

I should do something—speak, or blink, or breathe. He isn't kissing me, but he wants to; I can feel it in the way his fingers softly cradle my neck, see it in the tenseness of his arm, as if it's a snake, coiled and ready. It's in his eyes, in the way they're running over my face, as if searching for something. But I can't find the words, so I make myself move. I take the smallest step forward. And again we are like dancers, like the most skilled of partners, as I rise up on my toes, and his mouth lowers to meet mine.

Our first kiss in the grass was all him. *This one* is all mine. It's clumsy to start, even though it's now our third kiss—or maybe our fourth, even—and I wonder if it's because the dynamic has changed. We're *dating* now. Our hands fidget, and our heads fight to find the right angle. When he tries to run his fingers through my hair and catches his finger on a spot that pulls, I laugh, and so does he. It's awkward, but not uncomfortable. Maybe because we've been so ridiculous in front of each other. We have been weird, and childish, and frequently embarrassed. We've seen all the worst parts of each other, and nothing we do now can even come close to that.

As the minutes go by, we find our rhythm against each other's lips again. Neither of us is a quitter, and both of us are perfectionists. I am wrapped in his arms, our bodies pressed together, our hands wrapped around each other's waists. Our fingers explore exposed skin—I thread my fingers into his hair, and he traces the line where my tank top meets my shorts. Goose bumps rise up everywhere his skin meets mine.

We may never stop kissing. My toes are cramping up from the few inches I'm raising myself up, but I won't be the first to pull away. I push up higher, and then all the way down, trying to stretch my stiffening toes. Asher's lips follow as I dip and rise. I smile against his lips and he laughs, but his lips are back on mine before the sound has faded around us. He twines his arms tightly around my waist and pulls me up, like he's giving me the world's tightest hug. I think he's giving my toes a break, until he turns us and pulls me with him onto the bed.

We crash into the comforter clumsily, our bodies still pressed together, and a surge of panic rises up in me as his body settles on top of mine. A few weeks ago, Asher was the one person in the world I would have called my nemesis. *And now he's on top of me, on his bed.* Beds and bodies and our parents down the hall. My breath hitches, but before I can let the full potential of our situation wash over me in a smothering wave, Asher rolls to his back and tilts his head to look at me.

"So a date, huh?" He smiles, and my eyes take in the current state of him. His kiss-reddened lips, the pink cheeks, little tufts of hair pulled this way and that from my fingers.

"A date." I can barely get the words past my kiss-swollen lips.

He smiles back up at the ceiling. "Sidney, will you go out with me tomorrow night?"

"I'll think about it," I say, just as his elbow meets my side and I let out a squeak. I turn my face to meet his, and my voice is as serious as it is nervous. "I wouldn't hate that."

DAY 28

Sidney

The same way our parents never commented on our feuding, they don't say anything about us running together, or spending the day on the dock, or going places together. When we leave the house we get a little wave from my mom, and a disinterested nod from Asher's dad.

"Where are we going?" I ask from the passenger side of Greg's car.

"It's a surprise."

"Wow, and no blindfold or anything? Taking a pretty big risk that I won't figure it out."

"Do you *want* to be blindfolded?" He looks over at me and smiles. "Or is it just instinctual to antagonize me?"

"The second one." I smile back, watching the scorched wheat fields roll by in the window behind him. "Sorry." I shrug. "Antagonizing you is just my natural state. It's woven into the very fiber of my being." I'm tempted to say, *I don't even know why I do it*. But I don't, because then I'd have to think about how much of a lie it is. And I don't want to think about where my distrust of Asher really started. Not when I'm sitting next to him, looking forward to our date. Our *first* date. The goose bumps are back; the ones I get every time I think about him touching me. There is sure to be touching on our date—and after. It's the after that covers my whole body in tiny bumps.

I sort of expect him to scowl, or tell me that I need to stop being horrible, but he just looks back at the road and smiles. Asher is really chill. I guess I always knew that, but I never let myself experience it or really appreciate it. Before, he was always scheming and planning. Always on the defensive or the offensive. But now, he just *is*. He's the bringer of coffee, and the early morning boat talker. He tells me stories while I swim. I know so much more about him than he does about me. I wonder if he notices the imbalance like I do.

In the afternoons, he slumps down next to me on the deck in the sun, or sits at the table while I paint rocks. When Sylvie or Greg asks him to run out to get something, he doesn't groan and complain about how they interrupted his book (which is with him at almost all times). Nothing seems to faze him. Except for me.

I wonder if I seem different to him, too, or if I'm just the same old neurotic Sidney I've always been. But then why would he even like me, if I was? I try to push that question away but it always seems to be there, right on the edge of my thoughts. Because I don't feel any different. I still feel like me, just with one less enemy. And I suppose I'm not on the defensive or offensive, either. I'm not trying to think five steps ahead, unless you count right now, on this date.

Date. Oh god, the word makes me feel like I'm living in someone else's skin. It's not that I don't want to be with Asher right now; I totally do. It's just that when I think about dates, I think about what comes next, and then my mind *is* five steps ahead, and before I can stop myself, I'm thinking way too far down the line. *No*. I mentally slap myself. We aren't even a couple yet. We're dating. Barely dating. On our first date. It's hardly time to start panicking about all of the repercussions of this little experiment not working out. I push the thoughts down as quickly as they surfaced.

I realize I've been panicking in silence for long enough that when my eyes refocus on the world outside this car, I don't recognize where we are. Apparently there's no blindfold needed when Asher has my brain to do all of the work for him.

I love mini-golf way more than any person should. Which is why I basically squeal when we pull into The Grove. It's the strangest mini-golf course I've ever seen, and I've basically lusted after it since my parents took me here once the first summer we came up here. Dad was totally irritated by all of the weird traps in the holes, and Mom just hates miniature golf on principle, so we never came back. Plus, once Sylvie, Greg, and Asher joined us the next year, we didn't need to find so many ways to entertain ourselves. Everyone had someone to keep them occupied.

"Do you have a notebook?"

Asher looks confused as we walk across the parking lot. My eyes are fixed on the giant windmill that's fashioned out of twisted branches. Moss and vines twine over it. "You know, where you keep track of these things . . . my corn-eating habits, necklaces I'm lusting after. The fact that I'm basically obsessed with this place."

"No notebook." Asher puts his hands in the air as if I'm going to search for it on him. "I just remember things."

"It's freaky."

He shrugs. "Not sure what to say, it's just how my brain works."

"Then I guess I like your brain."

"Um. Thanks?" He reaches his hand out as he walks. It's subtle. Casual enough that I could pretend I didn't notice. Maybe I should, but I don't. I take two quick steps to catch up to where

Asher is about to step inside the whitewashed building, and I slip my hand inside of his.

The Grove doesn't have the usual waterfalls and pirate ships. It's agriculturally themed. At one hole, your ball shoots out of a fake cherry tree. That was when my dad had decided he'd never return—when he was almost pelted by his own golf ball. He just doesn't appreciate the challenge of mini-golf like I do. When we take our clubs off of the old wooden counter, I don't need a mirror to know I am basically beaming with excitement. Asher grabs a little clipboard with a score sheet attached, and two stubby yellow pencils.

I reach for a red ball just as Asher does. "Oh, no." I grab a ball and point to the row of others. "I'm calling first-date dibs on this."

Asher picks up a yellow ball and smiles. "First-date dibs, huh?"

We leave the amused desk clerk behind and step through the rickety wooden door and onto the sidewalk. "You asked me on a date. I get to call dibs on things like golf ball colors. And veto things. I also get to claim a bite of your dessert. I don't make the rules."

Asher snorts like I just told a joke. "Technically, you *asked* me to ask you on a date."

"Technicalities are no good on first dates—you have a lot of rules to learn. You've been on a first date, right?"

"Several."

We step onto the faux green grass of the first hole. "First dates are the worst." I drop my ball onto the grass. "But you're starting strong, Marin."

At the little podium next to the sidewalk, Asher has one arm on the miniature clipboard.

"Trevor tried to convince me that I should take you some-

where fancy for our first date. Your comment about his basement really sunk in, apparently." He sounds like he's looking for
confirmation that I wouldn't rather be in a dress at a restaurant
with cloth napkins. That's what Caleb had thought I wanted.
"But clearly this was a great choice. I feel like I brought you back
to your homeland or something." He taps his club against the
strip of green running under our feet and smiles. "Seeing how
excited you are to come here is almost as rewarding as that time
I put coins on you while you were tanning and made the little
solar system on your back."

A sharp laugh escapes me. "I miss the pranks a little." I wince
at the words. "Is that a totally psychotic thing to admit?" I peek
up at Asher and his mouth is tipped up in the promise of another smile, but he doesn't say anything. I shuffle my feet and
try to line up the shot. There's a row of fake corn stalks along
the far end of the hole, and between them, an arched tunnel.
Based on the dark circle at the bottom of the giant bushel basket
on the right side, I'm guessing my ball will shoot out there.

"Just to be clear, first-date rules do not apply to our game."
I shoot him a serious look before returning my eyes to my shot.
"If you let me win, I'll smother you in your sleep."

"You don't care about winning?"

"Oh no, I totally do. But I want to win because I'm awesome. *Or* because you're horrible. Not because you were afraid
I wouldn't make out with you if you beat me."

"You're gonna make out with me?" I can hear the smirk in
his voice.

I keep my eyes on my ball. I couldn't look at him right now if
I wanted to. My stomach is tied in the worst kind of knots and I
wish I hadn't brought up kissing Asher, because now it's all I can
think about. And I don't need him to know that I've thought
several times about pulling him behind the giant windmill and
just calling it quits on this whole game. His ego does *not* need
that boost. But kissing Asher is like eating something amazing

for the first time—I had no idea how much I'd like it, and now it's all I'm thinking about. I want it for *all* of my meals. He can't know that, so I just shrug. "We'll see," I squeak out, my voice not nearly as aloof as I'd been hoping for. "Now stop distracting me so I can kick your butt." I square up my shot.

"And celebrate by making out?" Asher says, just as my club makes contact.

Asher

Sid's ball veers to the right, careening into the wall at what is definitely *not* the angle she was going for, before ricocheting off of the edge of the giant basket and returning back to where she started. She makes a sound that I can really only describe as a growl. *This is where I die; bludgeoned on a mini-golf course.* She turns her eyes on me and I can't help but laugh. Her mouth is squeezed into an angry slash and her eyes are narrowed to slits. But I've seen Sidney pissed, and she looks too cute right now to be as mad as she's going for. I'll live to see another day. I don't bother telling her I wasn't *trying* to distract her, because I know she won't believe me. I'm not sure if *I'd* believe me.

I raise my hands in mock surrender. "Mulligan?"

Sidney uncrosses her arms, and her whole body relaxes. She straightens up a little, and there's a hint of surprise on her face. She thought I was going to put up a fight. Repositioning her ball with the head of her putter, Sidney squares back up to take her shot. And just before she makes contact, her head swivels back to me slowly. Quietly, she says, "Thank you."

DAY 30

> Kara: Hey, birthday girl. Are Kris and Tom taking you out tonight or can I snag you?

My fingers hesitate over the buttons, because I'm not sure how to tell her that I'm spending my birthday with Asher. That I don't even know what we're doing, but I'm insanely excited. Asher hasn't told me anything about what he has planned, except that it's definitely *not* a date. Birthday celebrations don't count. I should tell Kara everything, but the longer I go without telling her, the harder it gets. So instead of telling her the truth, I type back *yes*. I throw in a frowny face, just to show her how much I love her, and then I start looking through my closet for clothes that go along with the one clue Asher has given me so far about my birthday celebration: wear something black.

After dinner Asher and I wash dishes and he tells me he has to leave for a while, but there's another clue in my room. I practically sprint away. In my room everything looks normal, but on the bathroom mirror there's a message scribbled in red:

Trevor will pick you up at 10:00

Trevor? At ten o'clock? I expected something elaborate from Asher, but this is starting to border on weird. I kill an hour playing cards with my mom, tell her I'm spending the evening with friends, and then get ready. At ten o'clock when I open the passenger door of Trevor's car, the look on his face doesn't inspire confidence in my wardrobe choice. Technically, this isn't a date, but we both know it is. My black sundress rides up my thighs as I sit down, and I try to push away the nervousness that is rising up in me as we drive the streets that run along the lake.

"Do you need to blindfold me?"

Trevor laughs so hard I worry he can't actually see the road past his tears. "Asher said you'd say that." He shakes his head. "Literally. Word for word. You guys are the strangest pair."

It should sound like an insult, but it sounds endearing the way Trevor says it, so I don't say anything.

"Your clue was missing a very important word," I say, as I step over limbs and twigs in my shimmery black flip-flops.

Asher is ahead of me, his hand grasping mine. "What?"

"*Casual.*" I mean it to sound annoyed, but I'm so curious I can barely muster any annoyance for the tiny scratches that are accumulating on my legs as we creep through the trees outside of Nadine's yard. "Maybe *wear appropriate footwear?*"

Asher laughs and it's not quiet at all. This doesn't feel anything like the first two times we came here together. He stops me a few feet ahead and twirls a finger between us, asking me to turn around. There's a piece of striped fabric in his hand, and I'm pretty sure it's one of my mom's dish towels.

"*Now* you're going to blindfold me?" I squeak. "I know where we are."

He doesn't say anything, just smiles and twirls his finger again, and I obey. The material covers my eyes, and then my hand is in his again. There's hot breath at my ear. "Slowly," is all he says.

I step carefully, letting Asher direct me over anything in our path. After a few feet he wraps an arm around my waist, moving me more easily alongside him. Then we come to a stop, and he angles me just slightly to the right before letting the fabric drop away from my eyes.

When I turned thirteen my parents had a limo pick me and all of my friends up from school, and take us to this amazing concert a few hours away. I was sure that was the best birthday present possible, never to be outdone . . . until Asher went and brought my dream to life right in Nadine's yard. Seriously, where *does* he keep the notebook full of every weird thing I've ever said?

"When did you do this?" It's maybe ten thirty, barely dusk. I look back to Nadine's house, where all of the windows are dark.

"After dinner. I had some help moving things. And getting Nadine out of the house."

Lindsay. I hate that I have to think of her on my birthday, but for *this*, I will. For this, I will think her name without an ounce of annoyance. Because spread across the yard is Nadine's beloved collection, all posed to make their grand escape. I spot Edith a few feet from her normal hiding spot, walking behind a green frog. In front of it is a line of gnomes—two adults and two children—walking side by side as if they're heading off somewhere together. Through the yard there are animals and strange creatures, all cutting a path to the same place . . . the lake. Little lines of sculptures stream out of garden beds, and like ant trails they all filter into one long line going down the center of the yard between Lake Houses A and B. Asher pulls my hand and leads me farther into the yard. We stand next to the giant brontosaurus, and from here I can see all of the animals lined up along the hill. They stretch all the way to the dock, where two gnomes stand in orange life vests outside of

Nadine's beige pontoon boat. A large penguin sits behind the wheel of the boat, also in a life vest. The seats are covered with frogs and turtles, geese in their tacky little outfits—now with goggles added—and a ferocious-looking lion taking up watch at the back, its head peeking out from the open door. I look behind us, at the herd of animals fleeing Nadine's house, and laugh.

And laugh.

And laugh.

Asher's face may crack from smiling the way he is.

Breathlessly, I say, "Best. Birthday. Ever."

"Better than ceiling stars?"

I nod.

Asher points toward a red balloon floating up behind one of the statues. "*That's* your actual present."

I take a step toward it. "Edith?"

Asher picks up the elephant and holds it between us. Up close, I can see that it's a slightly different color than Edith; darker and more vibrant. "That's actually Edith's baby cousin, Ellen." He smiles.

I look around at all of the strange creatures, each one perfectly placed, some of them obviously too large for one person to move. "This is . . . too much."

Asher shrugs. "It's not a big deal."

But that's exactly what this feels like. And I'm not sure if that should thrill me or terrify me, but it does both. And I wasn't lying when I said this is the best birthday ever.

DAY 32

Sidney

The brochure said this leg of the river takes two hours to float down, but I didn't think about how long that would actually feel like when Asher and I are just staring at each other. I thought it would be hilarious to watch Asher float down the river on this stupid raft I picked out—a giant rainbow-colored unicorn swan. I've never been on one of these floating river trips before, and it seemed like it would be something fun and different, not like sitting in a boring restaurant. But I didn't think about what we'd actually do while we were floating along on this cupcake of a raft. Because all we can really do is talk. Talk and float, and float and talk. Think about kissing. *Not* kiss, because there *are* other people living their lives out on this river, in canoes and kayaks.

"So tell me about Taylor and David and Evan . . ."

We're lying on our backs, arms propped behind us, legs hanging in the water. I wore my two-piece, but I wish I was in one of my Speedos, because honestly, I'm half-tempted to get off of this thing and swim. Especially if Asher wants to spend our time talking about exes.

I fix Asher with a stare that says *I don't think so.* "Tell me about Jordan."

"What do you want to know?" Asher says, his face smug.

I smile. "Why did you break up?"

"Reasons."

"Are you still friends?"

Asher shrugs. "We don't hang out or anything, but yeah, I guess."

It doesn't surprise me that Asher is the kind of guy who gets along with his exes; it would actually shock me if he wasn't. Everyone likes Asher, and that's the way Asher likes it.

"There's not much to say about them," I offer, hoping a simple answer will be enough to get him off of my back. "We didn't date long, and it just didn't work out."

"Are you still friends?"

I wonder if Asher cares, or if he's just asking because I did. I give him the same casual shrug he gave me. "Yeah, I guess. As much as we were before."

I try to change the subject. "Should we hit Nadine again next week? Maybe do something really elaborate? Find a new vegetable to utilize? Maybe bury some frozen fish around her yard, really drive her dog nuts? Though honestly, I don't think anything can beat the yard sculptures." I smile, because just thinking about the gnomes in life jackets cracks me up. "Best birthday present ever."

Asher laughs and I know he's on to me. But I don't care. I will come up with horrible, horrible things, if it means I don't have to sit on this giant swan and spill my guts.

Asher

Sid looks at her phone, which is encased in the plastic bag that's looped to the neck of our swan. I want to laugh at how much she hates talking to me about this stuff, but at least she said something.

"Do you think it's normal that we're going this slowly?" she asks.

"You know it's called a *lazy* river, right?"

"More like a deadbeat river," Sidney mutters and I laugh. "I don't understand how we can be moving *this* slowly. We'll never make it to the beach in time." Sidney hasn't said what lies at the end of this trip, but I assume it's the sunset.

"It's taking exactly how long the brochure *said* it would take."

"Hm." It's really cute how annoyed she is right now.

I don't blame her for being anxious, it's hard to be so close to the water and *not* be in it.

We've missed a few morning swims since game night and our date. *Our date.* Even in my head, where no one else can hear them, the words sound crazy. But Sidney says if we're going to *do this* then we can't get all soft about training. The girl has laser focus. I don't want her to have any excuse to call this off, so now I put extra effort into our morning swims. *Extra effort* sounds like I'm putting myself out somehow, but there's nothing punishing about watching Sidney while she swims. I just have to be sure to focus on her form, while I'm focusing on her *form*. Which is currently just inches away from me, wearing much less than on our morning swims. I need a distraction. "You should hang off of the back and paddle." I'm trying not to smile but it's not working at all, I'm already laughing. "That would be good conditioning."

Sidney leans forward and pushes my shoulder. It's not rough but it's hard enough that it throws our weight all off, and my side of the swan dips under me. I grab for her to stop myself, but the moment has me crashing into the water with Sidney trailing after me, headfirst. We hit the water in a flail of arms and legs.

We surface to snickering from a kayak passing by, the older man pointing his paddle at us. "You all right?"

Sidney's hair is a tangle around her face, and she sweeps it back with her hand. "No worries, we're swimmers. That's why we're so graceful in the water."

The man doesn't seem to know whether she's being serious or not, and just paddles away. I try to stand and can't touch, so I swim downstream to catch our float, which has drifted quickly without our weight. Sidney grabs hold of it just as I do, and I wonder if she was secretly racing me. Probably.

We tread water alongside our raft, contemplating how to get back onto it. I pull on the edge, and it flips over. I try to hoist Sidney up with one hand, but every time her weight hits the edge, it flips. We can't even hang on the same side of it without it flipping over. So she hangs on one side, and I hang on the other, our arms crossed in front of us on the raft.

"I noticed something during your swim this morning." My voice trails off, because I'm nervous to bring this up. Is it rude to critique her stroke while we're on a date? Technically we *are* in the water.

Sidney rests her head on her hands. "I'm listening."

I tell her about her rotation and how she can fix it. She listens and nods, and she doesn't look annoyed with me at all.

"You're good," she says.

"At watching you?"

She squints her eyes and shakes her head, like I'm ridiculous. "At *coaching.*" She smiles. "Which happens to require *watching me*"—she rolls her eyes—"which you're also good at."

"Thanks."

"Are you going to?"

"Watch you?" I can't help but grin. "Probably." She splashes water over the raft, and I run a hand down my wet face.

"Stop it. Are you going to coach?"

I think about it for a few seconds, unsure of how much I want to share with her. "Isn't that what all washed-up swimmers eventually do?"

She laughs and gives me a judgmental glare. "People coach. Professionally. That's not unheard of."

I shrug and think about that stupid letter still sitting in my notes. What would happen if I just didn't send it? If Mr. Ockler found someone else, and my grand four-year plan was completely derailed? Has Dad already secured that position for me? Is the letter really just a formality, something to make me feel like I got it on my own? Sidney is looking at me like she can read my thoughts.

"What?" I ask.

"I don't know, that's just all I can picture you doing." She shrugs. "If I think of you in ten years, it's by a pool."

"You think about me a lot?"

She buries her head into her arm and mumbles. "Whatever."

"Am I always in my suit?"

Sidney laughs and I can feel the vibration through the raft. Her head pops up again. "Hate to break it to you, but coaches don't walk around deck in their Speedos."

"I bet *I* do, in your fantasies."

"So about Nadine." She's looking off into the distance, trying to be casual. "How do you feel about utilizing Saran Wrap on fish, instead of paper?"

She's just trying to change the subject, so I do it for her. "My dad has a college-long apprenticeship set up for me." It feels like the words came out of my mouth against my will, but once they're out it feels right. Like I should have said it a long time ago.

"And you're . . ." Sid spreads one hand out in front of her and I can almost see the invisible line there, waiting to be filled in.

"Indifferent?" I shrug. "Annoyed?"

She nods and looks past me toward the riverbank, like she's searching for something there. "What did you want to be when you were younger? You know, when people asked you what you wanted to be when you grew up? Before you were old enough for them to be all judgy about it."

"A swimmer. Michael Phelps, specifically."

"Even when you were little?"

"As long as I can remember."

She doesn't say anything, just looks at that space over my shoulder again, like she's not sure what to say.

"It's not really a practical career, though." I can almost hear my dad's voice in mine. "It's the kind of thing you do on the side. You know, nights and weekends at some high school or club team."

"I mean, it's not an actual college major, like that's your only option when you graduate. It's just an end goal. You get a degree in something else." She shrugs. "Education, maybe? You'd be a great teacher . . . Or there's business administration . . . *sports* administration. The grad student who helped my high school team was studying sports psychology."

"Are you sure you don't want to be a counselor?" I tease.

"Positive." Sidney is smiling, and it's the new normal. Everything seems to make her smile; it makes me wonder how hard she had to work to keep that from me every summer.

When our feet finally hit the rocky bottom again, we hoist ourselves back onto the rainbow-colored float, our bodies side by side, our feet dangling off the edge. Sidney's head rests on my bicep, and our sides are pressed up against each other.

Just as I'm contemplating whether we could make out as we float, a group of canoes cuts through the water next to us. It feels like we're alone out here, but we're definitely not. So instead, I just think about dead puppy dogs and fish rotting under my bed, and definitely *not* Sidney lying right next to me in her bikini. And when I get back to my room hours later, I lay on my bed and stare at my phone as a list of careers that are *not* what my dad wants fills my screen. There's no harm in just looking.

Sidney

After being so close to Asher for three hours, it feels weird to be a room apart. I look at the bathroom door, imagining him on the other side, then look at my bedroom door, and wonder what's on the other side. Could he be out in the living room, hoping I'll come out, too? It's a long shot that he's as amped up to see me as I am him, but I slide off of my bed in my pajamas and take a chance anyway. I'm careful to open my door quietly, and to not look too eager when I emerge from the hallway, just in case the parents are still up. But the living room is empty and quiet and dark. I look down the hallway, all of the doorways dark.

Inside my room, I open my bathroom door and push through to find that Asher's side is wide open. *Interesting.* I take a deep breath and walk across my room to press the lock on my bedroom door. The confidence I had walking out to the living room disappears as I cross the distance to Asher's door and prop myself against the door frame, trying to look casual. *Oh hey, I'm always strutting into guys' bedrooms at midnight in my pajamas.* Asher is lying in bed, his face illuminated by the soft glow of his phone.

"Hey," he says softly.

"You wanna watch a movie?" I wonder if he sees through me, to the part that desperately just wants to be pressed up against him again, and will take any excuse to crawl into that bed.

He sets his phone down on his nightstand and picks up the little black remote that's sitting there. His bed is pushed up against the wall under the window, so my choices are to crawl on from the end, or crawl over him. I choose the first. Asher props a pillow up behind me, and I settle next to him, our legs and arms pressed up against each other.

He sets his hand on the bare skin above my knee, and it takes every ounce of self-control I have not to close my eyes. Because this feels like a dream, alone in the dark with him. I shift toward him, curling my chest against his arm, and it shifts his hand to my inner thigh, his fingers grazing the sensitive skin there.

He points the remote at the TV. So I guess we're going through with this charade, the one where we watch TV in the dark in his bed. "What do you want to watch?" My cheek is pressed against his arm and I feel the words vibrate through him.

"I don't care."

Asher stops at the first thing that comes on—a sad war movie

I watched with my parents a few years ago—and I drown out the voices as every inch of me focuses on the spot where Asher's hand rests on my thigh, his thumb stroking up and down, so slightly that I'm not entirely sure he knows he's doing it. Maybe I'm the only one not watching this movie. Maybe he doesn't realize that if his fingers keep rubbing in that spot, I will crawl out of my skin and leave it behind like a lizard. Because if I don't run out of here soon, the only other option is to get closer.

As if he can hear me, his thumb strokes wide arches, and his fingers curl and uncurl, and with each stroke against my bare skin, my body feels like it's pleading with me to push myself closer to him. When he moves his hand and puts it back at his side, it feels like a monumental loss, like taking away a birthday present or dessert. But then he twists toward me, and we're chest-to-chest. Then we're mouth-to-mouth.

Asher's hand is back on my thigh, higher than last time, at the edge of my sleep shorts, very close to where none of my ten-day boyfriends ever touched me. He pulls his mouth from mine, the space so tiny our lips are almost touching. "Is this okay?" His fingers slip under the edge of my shorts, and I feel like I should say no, but I don't want to. I kiss him, and nod against his mouth, and his hand moves against me again, a little clumsily, as layers of thin fabric between us are touched and lifted, pushed aside. Soon we are wrapped up together, a mess of kissing lips and searching hands, and twining legs seeking friction against each other.

When we finally fall asleep it's like lying in sunshine, wrapped up in summer.

DAY 33

Sidney

Breakfast was . . . weird. For five minutes—or maybe it was five hours—all I could think about was what we did last night. But then Asher kissed my temple and stole a triangle of toast from my plate, and by the time we left the kitchen for our morning swim, it was hand in hand and normal. As normal as the two of us ever are, at least.

But when we got back, Sylvie and Greg were packing up their car for a trip to the little fish town that Sylvie loves so much. A *family* trip, she told him. It took everything in me not to laugh or even seem interested when Sylvie explained it would just be the three of them, and Asher went into full-on pout mode.

I wonder if telling our parents about us would make things easier or harder. If they'd be more understanding of letting us spend time together, or if they'd go out of their way to make sure we have some space from each other. My parents would probably switch rooms with Asher and become my new roomies. They wouldn't be nearly as much fun.

But Asher being gone is a good excuse to spend some time with Kara. I'm fried from my day on the river, so we're sitting in a shady spot on the deck.

"Still no news?" Kara's voice is even and almost uninterested. "About?"

She raises her eyes and looks toward the house, as if Asher just stands there at all times, like a sentinel at our door.

I shake my head, but the words—the stories—are filling me up, trying to burst out of me like an overfilled balloon. I don't know what's stopping me, but all I can do is shake my head.

Kara and I paint rocks and talk about college—when we'll only be an hour apart instead of four—and around lunchtime my mom sits down with us.

"You want to go to the river this afternoon?" Mom picks up one of my rocks and sets it down next to another one. A large daisy, and a cluster of three little ones. She sets another covered in vines and leaves next to them.

"I swam this morning, but maybe tomorrow?" My mom knows I swam this morning, so it's weird that she would offer to take me to the river.

She nods and digs around in the box I keep my rocks in, pulling out a few more and making her own little rock collage of flowers, leaves, and birds. "I'm going to get my glass and join you out here," she says as she gets up from the table and disappears back into the house.

Five minutes later, she has a small pattern laid out on the table, and pieces of colorful glass cluttered on top of it. Kara and I paint and she fidgets pieces together until they resemble a bird the size of my hand.

"Things seem to be going well with you and Asher."

Mom's words make my stomach jump. What does she know? What has she seen? Does she somehow know what happened last night in Asher's bed? Or on the river? Oh my god, does she own some kind of spy-drone? Everything around me has blurred into a swirl of panic.

Kara's trying hard not to smile.

"I'm glad the two of you are getting along," Mom says.

Getting along. Not kissing, or sneaking into each other's rooms to do who-knows-what. *Getting along.*

"Yep." It's all I can manage in the aftermath of thinking my mother somehow knows all of my dirtiest secrets. The imaginary ants crawl off of me and scatter to the floor.

"Well I'm glad Greg got through to him."

"What do you mean?"

"I know you feel guilty about the fish." Mom pushes a bright red piece of glass into a corner. "You think getting kicked out of the houses is your fault. And don't get me wrong, you're not blameless. Not even close to it." It's been weeks, but her voice sounds irritated again, just talking about it. "But the pranks have never seemed like you." She picks up a piece of glass and moves it to the side. "And I know something happened that night before the fish." At this, Kara's eyes snap from her paints to mine. She knows what happened the night before. My date with Caleb.

"I could hear you in your room doing god knows what . . ." Mom looks to me and raises her brows.

"Mayonnaise." I toss one of my rocks back into the box to keep my hands busy. "That's all you need to know."

"Ugh." Mom shakes her head. "Well, after the fish incident I told Greg he better talk to Asher, tell him to fix things with you. I'm glad it seems to have worked."

Mom is beaming with pride for being the fixer she prides herself on being. I, on the other hand, feel like I may throw up. And it must show on my face, because when Mom excuses herself for another drink it's not two seconds before Kara says, "*Now* do you have anything to tell me?"

I do. I tell her everything. And as the words rush out of me all of our moments click together like puzzle pieces in my mind.

Asher

When we get back from the fish town, Sidney isn't in the house, or on the deck or the dock. The only reason I find her is because I call her and hear her obnoxious ringtone. It's faint, and only rings once, but it's enough to let me know that she's here somewhere.

I walk to the front of the house again and catch a bit of movement in the water, to the far side, out by the little cluster of trees that jut out.

"Are you ignoring me now?" I mean it as a joke, but she doesn't say anything, just squats down and picks up a rock, tossing it into a red sand bucket a few feet away. "Are you mad at me?" I sound amused when I say it, because there's not anything she can actually be mad at me for. She just keeps looking down at her toes, plucking rocks out of the water, like if she ignores me I'll go away. "You can't be, I haven't even been here all day to do anything."

Sidney looks up from her toes and meets my eyes. "Did your dad tell you to *fix things* with me?" She throws up air quotes and she has the angriest fingers I've ever seen.

Crap. "It wasn't like that."

"Wasn't like what?" She stands up and slams her hands onto her hips. "Like you were suddenly nice to me? Suddenly interested in me?"

Crap crap crap. I know exactly how this looks, and I don't even know how to explain this in a way that won't scare Sidney one way or the other. But also, she's blowing this completely out of proportion. "No, it wasn't like that."

"I get why you didn't want to tell our parents now. I doubt your mom would have been on board with you making out with me just to keep the peace this summer."

"I'm not some sort of gigolo over here. My dad told me to

stop the pranks. He didn't tell me to leave my bedroom door open to do it." She's trying to turn this into something sinister, just because she wants to be mad at me and find a way to tell herself this whole thing should be over.

"Well, consider it mission accomplished. I guarantee there will be no more pranks. No dates required."

She's shutting down, shutting me out. It's like I can see the ghost of Old Sidney floating overhead, preparing to reinhabit her body with every word that comes out of her mouth. She decided I was guilty before we even talked. And our next date was going to be a surprise, but I don't have the luxury of springing it on her anymore, not when she's looking at me like she wouldn't get in my car if I paid her.

"I get that you're looking for something horrible about me, but—" She opens her mouth but I cut her off. "Just do one thing for me. *With* me. And then you can pretend like I don't exist for the rest of the summer, if that's what you want. You can go back to terrorizing me. Set all my clothes on fire on the front lawn."

"I wouldn't do that." Her voice is barely a whisper, and it wasn't a smart move to say it, to remind her of what a one-eighty our relationship has taken since the start of summer.

"I know, Sid, I'm just . . ." I don't blame her for being mad, I just want to fix it. I *need* to fix it. "We said four dates. Come with me to Todd's graduation party this weekend." She opens her mouth to argue, and I keep going. "Come to my house. See where I live the other ten months out of the year. Meet my best friend. After that, if you still think that this all happened out of nowhere—that my dad somehow talked me into all of this— you can run away screaming." I shove my hands down into my pockets. "I won't stop you."

"I'm not sure how seeing where you live is going to prove anything."

"It will. Just trust me." But even as I say it, I know that's the problem. She doesn't. Will she ever?

"Maybe I'll see where you live and decide that you're even nerdier than I thought. Maybe your best friend isn't as awesome as you think, and the food will be horrible at the party, and this will all backfire on you . . ." She looks down at her bare feet in the water and I do, too.

"I'll take my chances."

"Fine." Sidney looks out at the water and then back to me. "But it's your last date."

Last. Not second, not next. *Last.* I imagine Sidney will somehow cram *her* second date in before the party, so she can be done with me and cut me loose like every other guy.

"Fine," I say.

"I'll just tell my parents I want to go home that weekend, and you're going to drop me off on your way."

She didn't say it like it's optional, but I try anyway. "Or we could just tell them you're going with me. Your parents won't care that we're going somewhere together for the weekend." I'm testing a theory.

Sid bites her lip, and it's all the answer I need. "You're making it sound like we're taking a romantic weekend trip, and not going to sit in a tent to sneak sips of keg beer out of plastic cups when we're not talking to your friend's sixty-year-old aunts who want to know our life stories."

I can't help shaking my head at the vivid scenario she's conjured up already. "I thought you were mad *I* didn't want to tell them."

"I'm mad about your *motivation* for not telling them. We're not lying, we're just not offering up information on our personal lives. This is not need-to-know information. Our lives aren't in danger. And we have nothing to announce. You're taking me on a last-ditch date to a graduation party . . ." Her voice has lost some of its bite; she's back to sounding like the sarcastic girl who insulted my clothing choices every morning while racing me for a stupid chair.

"That's a lot of explanation for not doing anything wrong."

"We agreed on four dates." She says it firmly, her voice edged with that sharpness again. Before tonight it had been weeks since I'd heard it, and I'm hoping not to hear it anytime in the near future.

"Fine." It's not how I feel at all. I feel like maybe this is all a colossal waste of time. Like I'm playing a game that I can never possibly win, because the winner—or maybe more accurately, the loser—was picked before the race even started. But if I'm going to convince Sidney that I'm really in this, then this is my best chance. Maybe my last chance. "On the plus side, you can snoop in my room and get your lurky-lurker on."

"Your room?"

"Yes. I have one of those. Did you think I slept in a crypt?"

"I wondered." There's the promise of a smile playing at the corner of her lips. This is our happy place—picking on each other. "But why would we be in your room if we're going to a grad party?"

"We have to sleep somewhere?"

"Oh."

"Is . . . that okay? I mean, I guess we could leave early and I don't have to stay for the after-party and the bonfire and stuff. But that's kind of the best part. I mean, I'm only stopping into the boring family part because Todd's mom would kill me if I didn't and—"

Sidney cuts me off. "It's fine. We can stay."

"We have a guest room," I assure her.

"It's a plan then."

"Technically, it's a date." I wait for her scowl, but she smiles. It's weak and tentative, but it's there. Barely.

DAY 35

Sidney

I'm not mad anymore—not really—but the drive is still quiet and awkward. What are we supposed to talk about when we don't know where we even stand with each other? It feels like with that one bit of info—that Asher might not have started things with me for the right reasons—we took ten steps back. And the car ride doesn't help. Because I have three hours to think of all the horrible thoughts that have resurfaced over the last few days. *Why would Asher actually want to date me? Why would he like me after years of going out of my way to make sure he didn't? And if he doesn't like me, then why is he doing all of this? What is the endgame to making me fall for him?* The thoughts marinate and grow and become living, ugly things by the time we get off of the highway and reach the little town where Asher lives.

As we drive he points out everything we pass, like I'm here for a tour. And I don't want to be interested—I try my very best not to be—but I'm dying to see all of these places. The tiny little place where Asher gets coffee in the morning, and the weird little antique shop where he worked after school his junior and senior year. We pass his high school, and even loop through the back parking lot to where the athletic center is. Asher pulls into a spot and cuts the engine, pushing his door open before I can even react. I crane my neck to see him outside his door. "What are you doing?"

"You can't have a tour of my favorite places without seeing my pool."

"*Your* pool?"

"Just get out of the car, Sid. You know you're going to. The chlorine is calling you."

He's right. Of all of the places here, the pool is where I usually imagine Asher. I saw a picture of him once, in a weak moment when I decided I'd look him up online. He was standing on top of a diving block, his arms stretched forward, his legs tensed. That image is burned into my brain, just like the need I've always had to see Asher in the pool, racing through the water.

When I'm outside the car, he grabs my hand and leads me up the sidewalk to the brown brick building. There's something about a pool building that smells like home to me. Every pool is different, but they all smell the same, and the scent nestles into my nose like it's welcoming me. Telling me I belong here.

You usually get to a pool through the locker rooms, so I wonder if he's going to drag me through the men's, until he takes a sharp turn down a hallway and we enter what looks like an office. There are two small rooms connected by a glass window that takes up most of the wall, and beyond that another large window and door lead to the pool area. At the far desk a short round man sits in a white polo and khaki shorts. Beyond the door I can hear the telltale squeals of kids' swim classes.

"Coach!" Ash yells as we step into the little room. I hang a step back and receive a tug forward, propelling me next to him as the man looks up from his desk.

"Ash!" The man's eyes are lit up and he stands more quickly than I would have thought possible. "They toss you out of Oakwood before you even started? I've got a guard spot open if you're looking." He winks and squeezes Ash's shoulder, and then his eyes swing to me.

"This is Sidney, the swimmer from Eastwood I told you about."

My eyes go to Asher but he keeps his on his coach, who is stretching his hand out to me. "Nice to meet you, Sidney. I've heard great things about you. You've got a great coach over there. You and Ash are a big win for Oakwood's program."

I don't know what to say, so I squeak out a thank-you and shake his hand.

"Taking her in to see your pool?" Coach says with a smile.

"That okay? I promise not to traumatize the kids."

Coach laughs and stretches an arm out toward the door. Asher leads and I follow behind him, out into the humid air of the pool area. Just as I cross onto the tile, he pops his head back in. "You mind if we borrow a few training props? I'll get them back before school starts."

"Sure, take what you need," Coach says, as if Asher didn't even need to ask. "You using your vacation to train?"

"Sidney has a record to break." Asher grins.

Coach closes the small gap between us and slaps a hand against Asher's shoulder, giving it a rough squeeze. "Can't ask for a better summer coach," he says, and Asher seems to light up at the praise.

Asher gives the coach another half-hug, and pulls me farther from the door. On the wall to our left, a built-in tile bench stretches across the width of the large space. Asher sits down and motions for me to join him. Ahead of us, six lanes stretch out like watery roads. A row of diving blocks rises up in front of us, and I can't help but think of that picture.

He stretches an arm out toward the far left lane. "That's where I broke the school record for the two-hundred-yard fly my sophomore year." He points to the middle lane. "And that's where I broke the state record."

My whole body twists toward him, shocked by this revelation. "Seriously? You broke a *state* record?"

"Ouch." Asher throws a hand of mock anguish up to his chest as I turn back toward the pool. "*Ouch*, Sid."

I poke him in the ribs with my elbow. "Oh stop, I didn't mean it that way and you know it. How did I not hear about this? My mom tells me the dumbest stuff about you, and she didn't tell me *this*?"

"I made my mom promise she wouldn't tell her."

"You didn't want me to know?" He would have to be deaf not to hear the hurt in my voice.

"I—" He stretches his legs out toward the pool, crossing one foot over the other. "I wanted to tell you myself, I guess." He folds his legs back in and sets his elbows on his knees. This is what he'd look like between races, watching his teammates, waiting for his turn. Less clothes. "Which sounds delusional, because we didn't even talk, and you hated me. But I wanted to tell you." He turns and smiles at me, but there's something new there, something a little guarded. There's a self-consciousness I'm not used to seeing.

"I didn't hate you."

He lets out a little grunt that says, *Sure you didn't.*

Another elbow to his ribs shuts him up. "So tell me all about it. I want to hear everything."

Asher tells me about the meet. About how close the race was and how his lungs burned and he had no idea if he was even in the lead. How the win wasn't as dramatic as he would have thought—how you'd think it would have been deafening or something, like how it is in movies, but the swim meets aren't that popular in a small school. But then his teammates hoisted him up and threw him in the deep end, and everyone went out to celebrate. And then he called me.

That one missed call. The call I was so sure was a pocket dial. It was the biggest day of Asher's life, and he called me. I can't even wrap my brain around that. It's hard to think that this place—somewhere I've never even been before—could have such an impact on us. On who the two of us are. Who we could have been a long time ago if I wasn't the world's pettiest person.

"Do you mind if we swing by my house before we head to the party?" Asher looks a little nervous when he asks, just as we're walking out of the building. "I need to grab Todd's present, and I want to show you something."

Asher

I open the door and let Sidney take two steps into my room as I pray that I didn't leave anything weird lying around. If there's a pair of old underwear shoved somewhere, my chances are probably shot. Suddenly I'm thankful that my mom makes us deep clean the house before we leave. *No one wants to come home to a dirty house* is her motto. Plus, I've been packing for college, purging stuff I don't need, and tossing half of my belongings into boxes for my mom to sell at her garage sale. My room actually looks a little neater than usual. It looks more like Sidney's room at the house than mine.

"This is actually why I wanted you to come with me this weekend." I hold a hand out and encourage Sidney to step into my room. "Well, part of the reason."

"To wow me with your bedroom?" Her sassy tone has me hopeful. Things already felt different after we left the pool, but I still have some lost ground to make up for.

"Not exactly."

Sidney takes two more steps into the room, as if the floor could open up in front of her at any moment, and I stay in the doorway, letting her. It goes against every instinct I have to let Sidney snoop through my room, but I know this is part of winning her trust back. Letting her see the real me—the me she doesn't get to see ten months out of the year. The me that doesn't hide the fact that I've pretty much been in love with her since the first summer we met.

She glances back at me, eyebrows popping up and a smile tugging at her lips, and I nod toward my stuff. "Go for it," I say. "Lurk your little heart out." I try to keep my voice calm, as if I'm not panicking about how this is actually going to unfold. There's a chance she decides that I'm completely unhinged to have had a crush on her for this long. I'm not entirely sure I'm not.

She lets out a melodramatic squeak and her head darts from one side of the room to the other, like she doesn't know where to start—the large dresser along the left wall, my bed and nightstand straight ahead, or the walk-in closet to our right. She veers for my dresser and I swallow down the panic that has started to creep up my throat. It's one thing to say you're going to let someone look through all of your stuff—personal stuff you didn't even curate for them—and it's another thing to watch it happen.

Watching her step up to my dresser is pure torture. My bedroom dresser looks a lot like my dresser at the lake house, except that this one is low and wide. And just like on vacation, I keep most of the stuff I should keep in the bathroom there. My hair gel, my deodorant, the glasses I hardly ever wear. Her hand touches every item gently, picking things up and turning them over in her hands. She smells my deodorant, tries on my glasses, and then glances toward the other end of my dresser.

My dresser goes from everyday essentials to prized possessions. All of my favorite things are huddled on that far end. Tacked on the wall above it are my favorite photos. There's me and Todd dressed up as cheerleaders our junior year, me on the beach the spring break we went to Florida, stubs from concerts and baseball games, a napkin Michael Phelps signed for me when my dad randomly saw him at the airport during a business trip.

I watch Sid's head bounce from photo to photo like a pinball, until it comes to a sudden stop. And I know she's looking at a photo from the lake. Me and Sid, sitting on the dock, our legs pressed together like we'd known each other forever and not for a few weeks. My mom took it from the shore, and the two of us were oblivious, caught up in conversation, our heads tipped toward each other. She puts a finger out to touch it, like she's not quite sure it's real. I had started to think it wasn't. After so many summers at odds, that first summer had started to dim around the edges. Then her fingers trail down, to the dresser, where all of my weird little trinkets are.

My mom calls me the best kind of pack rat, because I hang on to everything that holds any sort of happy memory for me— I've done it since I was a little kid. There was a period, when I was nine, when I refused to take off any of the wristbands I had gotten at concerts and amusement parks and tournaments. They hung on my arm, ratty and faded, until my mother swore she'd cut them off during the night if I didn't do it. I have a drawer with every newspaper article I've ever been in, every swim meet roster, every good moment in my life. But the very best things are sitting on my dresser or tacked to my wall.

"You kept this?" Her voice is soft, and it might just be because she's facing away from me, but I think it's more than that.

I know what she's looking at, but I walk up behind her anyway. Sidney is stroking the smooth rock like it's some sort of magical crystal that may grant her a wish.

"You gave it to me that first summer."

"I remember."

"I wondered if you did. Or if you'd somehow blocked that whole summer out."

"It was a good summer . . . mostly."

"It was a great summer, Sid."

I'm right behind Sidney, so when she slowly turns around, we're practically pressed together. "I thought you had to get Todd's present. Or was this just a trap to get me to realize how sweet and sensitive you are, with your keepsakes and your secret photos?" She sets her hands on my chest. "Because I already knew you were more sensitive and romantic than me." One finger taps just below my collarbone, and all of this touching is a huge relief. We almost feel like the old us again. Well, the *new* old us. "You're nothing but marshmallow fluff in here, Marin."

"I told you I brought you here for a reason."

"And what was that again?"

Proof. "The same reason I do anything. To convince you of how awesome I am." I stroke a finger across her forehead, pushing a loose curl aside. "You haven't figured that out yet?"

"Even that time you put sour cream in my yogurt container and then glued it shut again?"

"Even then."

"And when you tackled me to get to the unicorn chair?"

I grin. "Especially then."

"Hm. I guess I'm just slow sometimes."

"Apparently."

Sidney thumps a hand against my chest and scowls at me. But it's the scowl I love, the one that says she's annoyed, but in a good way. The one that says she's amused. And there's nothing I like more than amusing Sidney. So I lower my head to hers, press our lips together, and wipe that scowl away completely.

Sidney

There's something so weird about being here. It feels like we're storybook characters who just stepped out of their story and into the real world. Like we're watercolor, and we're walking around in stark contrast to all of the normal Technicolor people around us. Asher clasps his hand around mine as we meet at the front of his car, and . . . okay . . . apparently we're doing this. Like, all-in doing this. I wonder what his friends' reactions will be. If they'll think he's crazy for wandering into enemy territory, only to be willingly taken prisoner.

As we walk up the driveway toward the yard, it's easy to tell who Todd is. He feels like the epicenter of the party, with little groups of relatives scattered in his orbit. As we approach, he looks at me like I'm a zoo animal. A really exotic one he can't believe he's actually seeing in person. I half expect him to try to pet my head or something. His face might break in half he's smiling so big. Asher, on the other hand, is trying not to smile and failing.

"Sid!" Todd engulfs me in a hug and it's possible he'll knock me off my feet with his excitement. Asher's hand is still around mine. I can tell Todd and Asher are best friends just by being near them; there's an almost tangible energy between them.

"Okay, okay." Asher's voice is 1 percent annoyed and 99 percent teasing. "Let go of my—"

Todd talks over my shoulder while still holding me in a bear hug. "Your *what*?"

I would be lying if I said I didn't want to hear how that sentence ends.

From behind me, Asher sighs and gives my hand the tiniest tug. "*My* Sid."

Todd gives me one last squeeze and whispers in my ear. "Thanks for coming. It would suck to have my best friend ditch my grad party."

Ditch his grad party? He thinks Asher wouldn't have come because of *me*?

Todd looks at Asher. "You know the drill, the real party starts tonight." He jerks his head behind him, but all I can see is an open field surrounded by trees. "Sid, make sure you check out the video my mom made." The grin is back, filling his face. He turns to Asher. "You're welcome, bruh."

Asher groans, long and low, and shakes his head. "Seriously. Stop."

I laugh, because I can't help it. Asher and Todd are like one of those little old couples who bicker all the time, but are ridiculously cute with how much they love each other. And somehow, meeting Todd makes me like Asher that much more.

There's an older couple approaching us, so we retreat to the food tent as Todd greets more of his guests, tucking an envelope into his pants pocket, where a few more are already sticking out.

Asher pulls me to a table where he introduces me to Todd's mom, Missy. His arm is wrapped around my back, his hand on my waist, as she smiles up at me from her seat. There's no long introduction, no *This is Sidney, our families vacation together,* just . . . "This is Sidney." It's like that with all of his friends I meet. They know who I am.

"It's kind of weird how comfortable you are with me around your friends."

"Why?"

"I don't know." I pick at an invisible piece of dirt on the hem of my shirt as we walk across from the larger tent to a little one that has coolers and a makeshift bar. "I guess I just expected it to be weird. Or for them to think it was strange that you like me now."

"I've always liked you." He squeezes my waist and my whole body electrifies.

Always. I tell myself not to focus on that word, because people don't mean it literally. Like, when I tell someone "I've always loved tacos," I don't mean from birth. I mean from like, the age of nine. Which means I've completely written off half of my life without even thinking about it.

"It's a lot weirder to pretend I haven't had a crush on you for a million years." He kisses my temple and smiles. "But anyone who really knows me knows I've had a thing for you for forever. If I *wasn't* all over you, they'd wonder what was wrong with me."

I stare at him, like if I look long enough I'll be able to see right through his eyes and into his brain. *What the hell is going on in there?*

"Hm," is all I can say. I don't even mean to, it just sort of happens, like my lips have a mind of their own.

"Hm?"

I bump my shoulder into him. "Leave me alone."

"No can do." He slings an arm over my shoulder. "You might run."

I laugh, and lean into him. *Not likely.*

The later it gets in the day, the less I feel the nervous, self-conscious energy from earlier at the pool. It's like there's a direct correlation between how comfortable I am and how relaxed Asher is.

We're in the middle of a field that stretches out behind Todd's property. In the distance I can make out the glow of the white tent, obstructed by a thin line of pine trees that separates their manicured backyard from this wilder, sprawling space beyond it. All around us is open space, ringed by trees to every side. The sky is dark, but flames flicker above our heads, casting us in warm light. The fire dances and crackles, and there's a bouncy song coming out of speakers that are tucked into the tree line somewhere out of view.

There are bodies jumping and swaying behind us as the beat picks up. Drunken bodies. Asher takes my hand and looks down at me with a smile. He has a red cup in his hand, but I'm not sure if he's actually drinking anything. A smile is permanently plastered on his face but nothing else about him seems loose or in any way out of control. He looks like normal, everyday Asher, but with the wattage turned up. I smile back at him before I realize where he's slowly tugging me. Into the bodies. I plant my feet and expect him to try to pull me along, but instead he loosens his grip on me and takes a step toward me, our fingers loosely tangling between us. He's so close to me now, I have no choice but to look up at him. His face gets serious. "I need to ask you something very important."

"What?" I squeak out. "Here? Now?"

He smiles. "Here. Now."

"Are you drunk?"

He shakes his head. "No."

"Are you sure?"

"Yes." He squeezes my hand. "I'm supposed to be asking the question."

I let out a disgruntled grunt. "Ugh. Fine."

I look at him expectantly, and he presses his lips together, like he's trying not to laugh at how much I hate this. I teased him that first time about being horrible at talking about things, but it's me who is really the worst at this.

"Sidney . . ."

There's a long beat of silence and I wonder what could be so horrible that he can't just spit it out. Whatever it is, I wish we didn't have to talk about it now. Not on this night, out here in the dark. Not after *this* day. All I want is to be under the stars with him. To sit on the bench in front of the fire, our bodies pressed together. I want his arm draped over me, like he wants everyone to know we're together. *Together*. A few weeks ago, I could have stood here in silence forever, refusing to let him see me sweat. Refusing to give in. But now, my curiosity and impatience wins out. "Yes, Asher?"

His eyebrows pull together as he dips his head and lowers his lips to my ear. "Will you dance with me?"

A laugh barrels out of him just as I throw my free hand into his chest. "You are the WORST!" I yell, but I'm smiling, relief washing over me. His arm loops around my waist, pulling me close. "How much do you hate me right now?"

"Nine point five," I say, but I can't stop smiling.

"Dance with me anyway?" He sets his red cup on the ground,

and when he pulls me toward the mass of moving bodies, I don't struggle. I throw my hands up in the air, and I don't care how ridiculous I look, because Asher is smiling at me like I'm a present on Christmas morning. And as the fire rages on, so do we. We jump and twist, and when a song gets slower, so do we. As the night fades into early morning we are tangled limbs and warm lips, slow hands and swaying hips. And it's hard to figure out where I end and he begins, but I don't want to anyway.

DAY 36

Sidney

Asher wakes me up with kisses along my shoulder, and fingers running over my back. They loop and curve and slash across my threadbare T-shirt, and they feel purposeful. "What are you doing back there?" My voice is thick with sleep.

"Your voice is different right when you wake up."

"I guess so." I've slept in his bed a few times, but I've never stayed through the night. I always set an alarm and go back to my bed after a few hours. Even with our doors locked, I can't relax enough to really sleep together in the same bed with our parents just down the hallway.

"I like that I know that."

I don't say anything, because "I like that you know, too," seems like too much. So instead I whisper, "That's because you like to collect random facts about me."

"I'm writing secret messages."

"Really?"

"Here, try to guess." His finger dips and trails over my skin, and I try to picture it in my mind, but the word that forms there is probably not right.

Asher's finger stops, and I know I'm wrong but say it anyway. "Potato?"

"Yes, I'm lying in bed with you and writing *potato* on your back." His chin rests on my shoulder, and I can feel his breath on my neck. "I have another question."

The panic doesn't hit me this time. "I'm too tired to dance."

Asher shakes his head. "Why are you fighting this so much?"

"I'm lying in your bed right now. I would hardly call that fighting." I smile sweetly at him and kiss his forehead, only because his lips are out of reach. Covering his mouth would be so much more effective. "You scare me."

"You scare me more."

"Yeah, but I scare you because you think I'm the person you know most likely to be able to hide a body. You scare *me* because you're basically one big heartbreak waiting to happen. You're like all of my relationship fears wrapped up in one pretty package."

"You think I'm pretty."

I could kiss him right now for making a joke. "*You* think you're pretty."

"I'm not sure why it's always *me* breaking *your* heart," Asher says, his eyes pinched in frustration. "The opposite seems *much* more likely here. If it weren't for me, things would have ended three days ago. *And*, if I hadn't asked you to meet me at midnight, you'd still be tormenting me." He jumps when I poke a finger into his side, and grabs my hand with his. "See, you're *still* coming after me."

He shifts to his side and wraps an arm over me, rolling me onto my side with a hand to my back. Now we're face-to-face, in a cocoon of blankets and body heat. "Let's talk worst-case scenario," he says finally. "This whole thing ends in a fiery blaze of heartbreak."

I nod. His tone implies he's having to stretch his imagination right now, but this is the only scenario I can see, currently. We're eighteen, not even in college yet. What are the chances that this lasts a year, or two, or three? What are the chances that we get married? Because that's the only way this whole thing isn't eventually a disaster with our families. And what are the chances?

"We'd be right back where we started, then," he says.

I nod, but I don't think it's anywhere close to the same thing. I think about seeing Asher every day, about actually hating him. Not the play-hate of the last five years, but actual, visceral broken-hearted hate. *Is there any chance that one of us doesn't feel that way in the end?* And beyond that, what about seeing him with someone else after I've loved him? Really loved him?

I can totally see myself falling in love with Asher. I know it's coming, the way I know I'll take another breath. Loving Asher Marin feels like an inescapable inevitability. And to think of seeing him with someone else? I hate the thought of it, even now. Could I actually stomach *weeks* of that? Him treating someone the way he's treated me? Being witness to it? The notes on the mirror, and the temple kisses; the way he's always idly touching me, like it's a reflex for him. The way he winks at me over the kitchen table when he knows I'm the only one looking. I definitely couldn't handle it, which means I'd avoid him. And the thought of not seeing him at all? It's hard to even imagine now.

"You're thinking horrible things, aren't you?" His voice is soft, concerned. He pushes up on an elbow, and as if he could read my thoughts, presses his lips against the soft skin along my hairline.

While his lips tingle against my skin, I try to think about the *best* worst-case scenario. We don't have the houses at Five Pines anymore. This year's house is temporary. And sure, maybe our parents will rent something together in the future, but if everything goes south with me and Asher, who's to say they can't get separate houses again? Surely my parents wouldn't force me to share a house with an ex if they could avoid it. And if we weren't forced together, maybe we would eventually return to something like normal. Something about having that backup plan in my mind loosens the tightest knots of dread inside of me.

A warm finger taps my temple as Asher says, "What's going on up there?"

I can't tell him the truth: *I'm running through all of the possible outcomes of our future demise. But good news! There's at least one worst-case scenario that doesn't make my skin crawl!*

Instead, I say, "I think our parents would flip if they knew we were together."

Together. The word hangs in the air, and neither of us wants to touch it. I said it to lighten the mood, but it's done the absolute opposite. I can feel the tension buzzing between us. The fingers that were idly tracing a circle on my back have stopped.

"Are we—" He sounds genuinely nervous for the first time since we left the pool yesterday. "Together?"

"I . . ." I don't know what to say. I wasn't fishing when I said it. I didn't think it through, didn't weigh the words ahead of time and consider them for three days, like I usually would. This is the verbal version of spontaneously hiding that frozen fish in his room. Being in his bed is doing something to me. Or maybe he's finally gotten me to lighten up. *And look what it's doing to you.*

"I think we could be," Asher says. "Should be," he corrects himself.

"Yeah?" There's a little flutter in my stomach, and I'm not sure if it's telling me to go for it, or warning me that this is the worst idea ever. Right now, everything feels equal parts scary.

"Are you going to make me say it . . . officially, or something?" He says it like he's being tormented, but there's a certain warmth to his eyes that tells me he would. That the idea of it doesn't scare him one bit. He's so much braver than I am. I add it to the long list of things that Asher Marin surpasses me at.

"Like a prom-posal?" I smile thinking about how funny it would be to see Asher plan some sort of elaborate set-up to ask me to be his girlfriend. Like the opposite of all of the pranks we've played over the years. "Did you ever do one of those?"

"Absolutely not."

I squish up my nose in mock disgust. "Prom. Yuck." But I am sort of surprised. Asher totally strikes me as the kind of guy who would do something elaborate and sweet for a girl. I think back to those stars on my ceiling.

Asher smiles. "I will, though, if you really want me to."

I bite my lip to hold back the smile that would give away how incredibly giddy I am about the turn this trip has taken. "I don't think we need to bring any more attention to ourselves while we're still living in the same house."

"Deal," he says, but he looks unsure about it.

We lie in bed for another hour, until Asher leaves for the bathroom, and I contemplate how I went from coming here under duress to leaving with a boyfriend. Asher insists I shower first, and down the hallway, as I groggily stand in front of the sink, *Will you be my girlfriend?* is scrawled across the mirror in what has become *our* color. *Red.* The color of love notes, cherry Kool-Aid, and bleeding, broken hearts. The tube still sits on the counter—a much more expensive brand than our usual tube, obviously stolen from his mom. *Sorry, Sylvie.*

Before I get in the shower I pull the cap off of the tube, and write back one word, three letters. And just for now, I'm going to let myself not think about how badly this all could end.

DAY 41

Asher

I always imagined if Sidney blindfolded me and drove me somewhere, it would mean it was the end of the line. I'd finally pushed her over the edge, and she was driving me into the wilderness to drop me off for dead. I never imagined I'd be excited to be blindfolded. Of course, I never imagined that in this scenario she'd be taking me out on a date. Our fourth, her second. But this is our first date as an actual couple.

"On a scale of one to ten, how weird would you say I am?" Her voice is teasing, but this feels a little like a test, and I can't help but wonder what I'll miss out on if I get this wrong.

"Honestly?"

"Honestly," she says, then quickly adds, "unless it's higher than an eight. You should *definitely* lie to me if it's anything higher than an eight." She laughs and I relax a little—maybe this isn't the serious thing I thought it was.

"A six." I keep my voice serious. "But a hard nine for however long it took you to cover my bed in lemonade while I was drunk and defenseless." She pushes my shoulder roughly just as my smile breaks through. It's not as easy to keep myself in check with Sidney anymore. I feel like everything I'm thinking must be written across my face these days. "And if we're being honest, then you were a straight-up twelve when you were hiding dead fish parts under my bed."

"Well, the only reason I'm even going to show you this is because I know now what a weird little nerd *you* really are. Mr. Board-games-in-the-basement." I wish I could see her face right now. Sidney talks with her face, giving away everything she's actually thinking. It's how I always knew she didn't actually hate me. Or at least, that there was something under all of it that wasn't hate.

She smacks me playfully across my arm and I think I've passed this test. I will live to see another day.

"Are you going to tell me where we're going?"

"No."

"The blindfold was probably a bit much."

"I thought you'd like it." There's teasing in her voice. It sounds like something I'd say to her.

"I'm not saying I hate it." I pull at the fabric across my eyes. "It would be cool if it wasn't covered in flowers, though." I poke at the soft material. "Something a little manlier."

"Sorry, my blindfold stash is surprisingly limited. I figured you had the self-confidence to pull off one of my mom's scarves."

We drive for another five minutes and I try to picture the turns as we make them. The trees passing us, the bridges we cross. In my mind is a map of where we are in town, and when the car comes to a stop and Sidney pulls the fabric away I am . . . not even close. We're in a little parking lot with trees on one side, and a small park on the other. Sidney pushes out of the car without a word and I follow a few steps behind her as we enter the park.

"Are you taking me on a picnic?"

"Cold."

"Frisbee golf?"

"Freezing." She shakes her head at me as she continues to walk ahead of me, as if Frisbee golf is the most ridiculous thing she's ever heard.

"Are you going to tell me?"

"I was going to, but this is kind of fun. Keep guessing."

I run a few steps to catch up to her and grab her hand. She stops us directly in the center of the small park, next to a little fountain with three brass frogs spurting water. Sidney tugs my hand and turns us around, the water dribbling noisily at our backs.

"You asked me what I did with all of the rocks. And where I sneak off to sometimes."

I wait in silence, wondering if she's going to tell me she spends her time sitting in parks. I'm not sure how I'd feel about her thinking that's a better option than having to be around me all these years. "And this is it?"

"Kind of." She fidgets next to me, like even now, in the midst of her confession, she's not sure she wants to make it. "It's stupid."

"I bet it's not."

"You tell me a lot." It's such a weird change of topic that it makes me look at her. But she's right, I've been pouring myself out to Sidney the last few weeks. It's almost embarrassing, how much I want her to know the stupidest stuff about me. "And I sort of suck at that a lot of the time. So . . ." She fidgets with the hem of her shirt and takes a deep breath, like she's psyching herself up for something. "Anyway, this is what I do with my rocks. I hide them here—and at other parks—so people can find them. It's mostly moms and kids."

I think about the skull rock she painted once and imagine it sitting on some six-year-old's dresser.

"You have ten minutes to find as many of my rocks in this park as you can." A smile spreads across her face and melts away the trepidation that was once there.

"You want me to find rocks . . ." I look around me, at the sprawling grass and the benches and the bushes. The little gardens that dip out of the woods and circle around the little sitting areas. ". . . outside." But if I know Sidney, this is a competition, and I'm determined to find at least one. I take a hesitant step forward and she tugs back on my hand.

"For every rock you find, I'll answer one question."

I stop in my tracks, but when she lets go of my hand, I sprint away. Because one rock is definitely not enough.

Sidney

Asher is racing around the park like his life depends on it. Like I just told him there are hundred-dollar bills hidden in the bushes. My heart is a rock in my chest at the thought of what questions would be worth it to him. He starts at a row of bushes, getting down on his knees and brushing away mulch and leaves, running his hand over the area blindly. I look at the stopwatch I've started on my phone. It's been less than a minute as he pulls a shiny black rock covered in little flowers from its mulchy hiding spot. Oh god. This was such a bad idea.

He holds the rock in one hand as he stands and runs his eyes across the park from left to right. His gaze settles on a large tree about twenty feet away from me. It's huge and the base is a tangle of roots that jut above the grass and then plunge back down. Little clusters of flowers are sprouting up out of some of the little crevices. He runs his hands over sections of root, and under little plants, as he works his way around the tree systematically. Asher is usually a frenzy—a haphazard burst of energy in everything he does, but right now he looks like he's done this a million times. Like he's been planning this out for weeks, exactly how he'd search every nook and cranny of this park. He looks like one of those police search parties you see on TV, working in a systematic grid, not missing a single inch. He looks like . . . me.

His hand plucks out another rock and I glance at my phone again. "Three minutes down!" I yell it across the park, and a mom standing by the play set darts a look at me. *Lady, I've got bigger problems than you.* My eyes are back on Asher before I can care. He darts from the tree to one of the black metal benches, and I bite my lip, knowing what he's going to find when he gets to one of the back legs. Three rocks in as many minutes. Holy crap. It's mostly moms and kids who hide rocks and come to public places to find them; there are sites online where you can find locations where rocks have been hidden. I bet they don't get half this excited.

Asher sprints around the park, plucking rocks from what feels like every square inch of the place and shoving them into his pockets. When I call time, his pockets are bulging and my mind is already racing, wondering what he will want to ask me. I should have gone with five minutes. I didn't anticipate Asher's zeal for making me miserable. No, it's not that. I feel traitorous even thinking it. Letting myself slip back into that old mind-set. He's my *boyfriend* now. What is wrong with me that I can still think something like that about him?

He's grinning wider than I've ever seen as he closes the distance between us, and even in my current state of panic it makes me smile to see him look at me like that. He stops in front of me, his eyes practically glowing with delight. And triumph. He looks like a guy who just won a big race. Whose photo will be in the paper tomorrow morning.

I roll my eyes and let out a dramatic breath, trying not to let him see how unnerved I am right now. "Okay, let's see them." I wag a finger at the bulge of his pockets and he turns them out, letting the stones clink against each other as they hit the ground. *Nine.* Apparently I said it out loud, because he laughs before dropping two more rocks he had in his hands.

"Eleven." Maybe he senses the dread in me, because he doesn't taunt me, he just smiles and starts to pick the rocks up. "Should I put these back?" His brows hitch up. "Or are you going to make me turn them in for each question to keep me honest?"

"Did I say one question for each rock, because what I meant was—" Asher cuts me off by grabbing my hand. As he does, I watch him slip a rock into his pocket. I wonder which one it was.

We crisscross the park, putting stones back in all the places they were taken. When we're done, Asher grabs my hand again and kisses me on the cheek as we walk back toward the car.

"Remind me never to challenge you again."

He laughs. "Never underestimate how much I want to pry your brain open, Sidney Walters."

The second part of our date is dinner at The Cherry Pit, because Asher told me once that he's never been there, even though the delightfully tacky cherry-themed restaurant is basically its own kind of tourist destination around here. We're sitting in a booth, sipping on cherry-ade.

"Maybe tonight we can decide what we're putting in Nadine's yard?" We haven't pranked her in weeks. Well, not together, at least. I like to think my birthday yard show was more of a gift—to both of us—than a prank. I doubt Nadine sees it that way, but still.

"My mom wanted to take a picture of all of us flipping her the bird." Asher smiles. "Wants to put it in her mailbox as we leave town."

"Really?" That doesn't sound like Sylvie at all.

"Oh yeah, she can hold a grudge."

Sweet Sylvie? Who knew? "I like it, but it seems like the kind of thing that would end up on the internet and keep us from getting a job someday."

Asher nods but doesn't say anything. I don't say anything.

I'm not sure if it's in my head, or if it's the looming terror of the questions I know will eventually come, but it feels like silence hangs between us. I can't take it for another second, I have to rip off the bandage. "Okay, do your worst." I set my hands on the table, crossing them over the giant red cherry face that serves as the menu. "Let's get this over with."

Asher smiles and takes another sip of his drink. He shifts in his seat a little and his hand pops up, his fingers wrapped around a stone. "How long ago did you paint this?" Asher's fingers peel back and sitting in his palm is a small, pale gray stone, long and thin. I thought he'd start with something a little easier, but no, he's going right in for the kill.

"I picked that rock because it reminded me of the shape of the lake." It's true, I remember holding the delicate boomerang-shaped stone up to the old poster in Lake House A, making sure it wasn't just in my head. "There's even a little divot over here"—I reach a finger out to the rock that Asher has placed between us on the table—"where our bay is." *Our* bay. The word rings between us like I just struck a gong. "The bay where our house is," I clarify, hoping I don't sound as defensive as I feel.

He doesn't say anything, just raises his eyebrows as if to say, *Great, but* when *did you paint this topographically accurate rock?* Asher isn't stupid; that rock is duller than the rest. Its glossy coat is fogged with age and it just looks . . . worn. Like paint that has been subjected to the elements for . . .

"Six years ago." I take a sip of my cherry-ade, willing myself to sound more confident. "That first summer." But nothing about me feels confident right now. I gave Asher the challenge of finding the rocks because I needed something to force me to open up with him. I should be able to just do it, but I can't. And just telling Asher to ask me questions seems ridiculous.

So here I am, luring him into it. I had expected him to ask me about my most embarrassing moments. To pry into my questionable dating past, and make me admit embarrassing things like who my first kiss was with. I didn't expect him to find out that six years ago I was scribbling our initials on rocks like some sort of lovesick psycho. I had completely forgotten about that rock; it should have been scooped up by some little kid years ago.

"I was thirteen, so, you know, keep that in mind." My cheeks redden and I feel a little sick, but Asher distracts me by staring at my chest. Blatantly. Which is not like him at all. And just as I'm about to call him a pig and remind him where my face is, I realize what he's actually looking at. My necklace. His necklace. And it feels like we're on even footing again, me with my love-rock and him with his necklace. And before I can think more deeply about the fact that the L-word just flew through my brain, the waitress arrives with our food. Asher sweeps the stone off of the table and tucks it back into his pocket.

When it's just the two of us, I swallow a chunk of cherry chicken salad before saying, "Okay, hit me with the rest."

Asher talks around a bite of his cherry cheeseburger. "You're not getting off that easy."

"You think that was *easy?*"

"I'm not using them all tonight, Sid. I want to keep you on your toes." He takes a sip of his drink and smiles, but he looks nervous. "I do have one more for you tonight."

"I used to stuff my mouth full of food when I was little. So full I'd panic and spit it all out."

He shakes his head at me, looking completely bewildered. "What?"

"Chipmunk. That stupid nickname you and my dad torment me with. You asked me once where it came from."

"Not it," Asher says.

I shrug. "Okay, well, I'm deducting a question for that anyway, because you would have gotten around to it."

"I want to know why it all started."

I look at him blankly, hoping he doesn't mean what I'm 99 percent sure he means.

"The pranks, the hating me . . ." Asher takes a sip of his drink. "Spill."

THE FIRST SUMMER

Sidney

Once a week or so, Mom and Sylvie like to load us all up and take us to one of the little towns nearby. Quaint, cute, and cozy are words they use to describe the small streets lined with touristy shops. Windows are filled with clothes, and art, and the kind of signs you'd hang in a vacation home, with sayings like HOME IS WHERE THE LAKE IS. It's not usually too bad—the parents don't mind if Asher and I wander off on our own. The last trip, the two of us had lunch at one of the little restaurants where the tables on the patio are made of crisscrossed metal, and everything smells like fish from the river nearby. Asher paid for us, and I told myself it wasn't a date, but it sure felt like one.

But this trip is painful, because Mom didn't invite Sylvie or Greg, or Asher. It's just the two of us, popping in and out of shops. Mom is apparently trying to shove a summer's worth of shopping into her last week. I get a book at the town's little bookstore, and Mom lets me replenish my paints in the craft department of the megastore we pass on our way back to the lake. When we get back to the house I deposit my things on the kitchen table and stop in my room to see what I can do to tame my hair a little. And then I set out to find Asher.

Asher spends most of his time—well, with me. He's usually the one to find me, and that realization sends a little bubble of something warm into my chest. We only have four days of vacation left, but it's not like I can't see Asher again. Our parents usually get together every couple of months, and while we're not usually included, I'm sure they wouldn't mind us hanging out. Maybe they'd get together more often if Asher and I were— were what, dating? Do eighth graders actually long-distance date? It would only be a couple years until one of us could drive, and this isn't exactly a normal situation, seeing how our parents are best friends. I bet Mom and Dad would drive me to his swim meets, and Sylvie and Greg would bring him to mine. We could text and video chat.

I'm lost in my head, thinking about everything, when I come around the corner of Lake House A, and find Asher on the swing set. We've spent a lot of time on the swings. They're tucked away behind Lake House A, with a little hedge of overgrown shrubs next to them. It's a nice escape from our parents during the day. Or at night.

Last week, there was a moment when I was sure Asher was going to kiss me on the swings. There was music playing on his phone—this guitar-heavy ballad about girls and cars—and he wrapped his arm around my chain, so we were right next to each other. But it didn't happen, and I don't know if that was me or him. Maybe we were both just waiting. For what? I don't know.

But right now, Asher isn't waiting for me on the swings. He's not even alone on the swings. Lindsay is on my swing, her seat swaying gently, as she and Asher kiss. I shouldn't watch, but I do. Because I hope that he'll pull away. That he'll scream, "No, I'm saving my swing-kiss for Sidney," and he'll shove her into the dirt. But that's how *my* twisted brain works, not his. Because he doesn't pull away, and he doesn't push her, but inside all I can do is scream.

That night, I don't go down to the fire. I tell my mom I'm not feeling good—which is true, I feel like my insides have been ripped out—and while everyone else is roasting marshmallows and smashing them between graham crackers, I get to work filling Asher's shampoo bottle with mayonnaise, and adding cayenne pepper to his toothpaste tube.

I manage to avoid Asher for a full twenty-four hours, but the next day I fall on my face when my flip-flops are glued to the stairs outside our deck. Asher thinks he can kiss Lindsay *and* knock me on my ass? Anger coils inside me. If he wants war, I'll give it to him.

DAY 49

Sidney

"How are you two liking the house?" Mom is looking at Sylvie and Greg, but it's obvious she's talking to me and Asher. "I know you were skeptical about sharing. The house. The bathroom." She does look at me now. "But it seems like it worked out." Yes. Somehow, against all odds, this has all worked out.

This feels like *the moment*. The one I've been waiting for, where we're presented with footage of our morning breakfasts and late-night couch snuggles. We've gotten a little braver since our overnight at Asher's house. I'm sleeping in his bed more often, sometimes all night. Because there's something really comforting about being in the same space as Asher. And even though the doors are locked and our parents are long asleep, and most nights we start a strategic load of laundry in the little room between his room and his parents', sometimes I can't shake the feeling that they must know there are two people breathing in that room. Bionic parent hearing, or something.

While I'm mentally panicking, Asher says, cool and calm, "Sidney isn't as bad of a housemate as I would have expected."

I smile and roll my eyes. I don't even have to pretend when I say, "Ditto."

Mom takes a bite of her burger and when she puts it down

on her plate I can feel that something is coming. But there's no confrontation. There's just a glance exchanged, from Mom to Dad. An eyebrow raise from Sylvie, and a nod from Greg.

It's Sylvie who speaks first, her shoulders rising a little as she announces, "We're buying the house."

"*This* house," Greg adds, in case Asher and I are feeling extra slow this evening. But there is nothing slow about my brain right now. If anything, it just got a serious adrenaline jolt and is running laps around the room. *Buying this house.* I love this house.

Everyone is talking at the same time, my Dad saying what a good price they're getting, Sylvie suggesting they rent the house out for a few weeks a summer, since "the kids" won't want to hang out with them for an entire summer anymore. "Maybe if we bribe them," Mom says, giving me a soft smile. "Free food all summer," Sylvie says, with a glance at Asher. Greg wants to turn the laundry room into a second master bathroom.

Asher isn't saying anything, he's just eating his burger and sneaking glances at me. And it's like I can see right through him. To the fears that finally have a concrete location in my mind. These are the rooms that it will happen in—when it's all over, this is where Asher and I will be forced to coexist. It won't be a dinner here and there shared at each other's house, it will be all of this. The couch where we crossed out of enemy territory, the bed where he kissed me, the kitchen where I made him pancakes. Someday I won't just have to see him, I'll have to marinate in these memories. And how many new memories— *bigger memories*—will there be by then? Asher smiles at me, and I push it all away. I look at the happy faces that surround the table, and I let mine join in.

Asher

I like to think I couldn't have made it through the last five years without knowing how to read Sidney, but she's not giving anything away tonight. When we leave the dinner table I'm braced for the meltdown. The announcement that our parents are buying this house together seems like the ultimate fuel for Sidney's particular brand of panic. But dinner ends and dishes are washed, and I don't get one. As the silence stretches on into the evening, I can't help but wonder if this is worse than a freakout. If all of this silence means she's thinking up scenarios worse than I could ever imagine. What we need is a distraction. Something to take our minds off of this wonderful—but also horrifying—new development.

"Let's go to Nadine's tonight."

Sidney's face is pressed against my arm, and she pushes herself up off the couch. Last night we were in my bed, but tonight we're back to the couch. "Tonight?"

"We bought everything already. And trash day isn't for two more days, so Dad's got frozen fish guts in the freezer." Sidney's nose scrunches up and I wonder if she's as traumatized by fish as I am. "Let's just do it." It feels like I have to do something, and this is the only thing I can think of. Our war on Nadine is what brought us together. Maybe it can keep us from falling apart.

Sid looks a little groggy, like maybe she had fallen asleep against me. It's hard to tell when she hasn't really talked to me all evening. "I guess." She rubs her eye with her palm and smooths her hand over her hair as she sits up. "We have everything?"

Sidney

An hour later, close to 2 a.m., we're pulling into the driveway a few houses down from Nadine, where Kara's grandmother lives. I like to think we have a standing invitation to park here, since it's too late for me to call Kara so she can give her grandma a heads-up. But it's so late there's no way she's going to even notice us here, unless we're loud. And that's the opposite of what we'll be.

I open the back trunk and start tearing open the white cardboard containers filled with plastic forks. Five boxes later, I dump them into a brown paper bag, and then get to work on the next five. Asher thinks we're going to need at least twenty boxes to finish. Tonight's prank is our last, our pièce de résistance. While I fork the yard, Asher will Saran Wrap Nadine's car with enough layers that it will take her hours to untangle it all. And between the layers, he'll wrap in frozen fish guts, courtesy of our dads' fishing trips. They won't be frozen by the time she has to unwrap it. I can't help thinking—again—how much I wish we had a camera out here, so we could see her reactions. Our imaginations will have to be enough of a reward for this one, though.

With a brown bag of ammo in each of our arms, Asher and I cross through the two yards that separate us from Nadine's.

"I forgot the Saran Wrap." Asher stops where he is and looks back toward the car. "You start, and I'll be right back."

I nod—not wanting to talk any more than we have to—and lay the bags of plastic along the driveway, taking a handful with me onto the grass. I shake the can of orange spray paint—the special kind of bottle used to mark lawns with—and point it down at the ground, spraying it over the grass in long sweeping motions as I walk. Thankfully I remembered to wear my crappy old shoes, because even though I can't see it in the dark, I'm sure a fine spray of paint is dusting the edge of my right foot.

As I shove forks into the lawn, tracing the lines of spray paint first, and then filling in the gaping middle with hundreds of forks, I lose track of time. I'm sticking the forks into the grass with surprising speed, but it still feels like it's taking forever. We should have done a test section at the house, timed it, and figured out how long the entire hand would take us.

My fourth bag of forks is almost gone, and we have a few more in the car, but I haven't even started on the top half of the hand or the finger yet. I'm really glad we didn't attempt something this intricate with potatoes. What a train wreck that would have been.

I'm filling in the lower half of the middle finger when I hear the jangling of metal and the yip of a dog. Before I can react, Nadine's tiny little terrier is at my feet, nipping and barking, and jumping at my knees. I drop the paper bag in my arms and turn toward the house. Nothing. I didn't hear a door, don't hear anything now, but I can't risk it. And I can't risk going back the way I came, along the driveway, where the side door is, so I take off for the lake.

When I'm halfway across the yard, just a few feet from Lake House A, Nadine's voice carries across the yard. "If you run I'll just have the police come to your house," she yells. I take two more long strides and come to a halt. I can see where the car should be, through the trees, in Kara's grandma's driveway. But there's nothing there. I'm not running toward anything, because Asher took the car. *Asher took the car.* He's been gone for almost an hour. It should have taken him less than fifteen minutes to drive to our house and get back. Nadine knows it's me, so what's the sense in running? When I turn to face her, she has her cell phone pressed against her ear. I stand at the edge of the trees, knowing I should do something, but unable to make myself move even an inch. I have never been paralyzed with fear like this before. The plastic forks clenched in my hand dig into my palm as I finally make myself walk back toward the dark yard spotted with white. Toward the ridiculous house and its eccentricities, Nadine, and the police car slowly pulling into the driveway. Alone.

To be fair, I don't think the officer *wanted* to arrest me. Maybe it was the fact that I almost puked, I was so horrified at what was unfolding. Or that I just stood there silently as Nadine recalled the potatoes and the fleeing yard sculptures, and the "horrific" fish incident that got us kicked out in the first place. Or maybe it had something to do with the fact that I was the first person to ever try to open my own police car door, to let myself in.

Officer Jennings is a nice guy. Younger, probably in his mid-twenties. Sitting in the car, he tells me Nadine will have to come to the station tomorrow to file *actual* charges. That until she does, he won't have to take me in.

He drops me at the end of my driveway, and comes around the car to let me out. Why? Because I'm a criminal who sits behind handle-less doors, that's why. Even though I know there's only a 2 percent chance any of the parents would be awake at 4 a.m., I'm not risking it. Not when I haven't even figured out how I'm going to tell my parents that I'm going to potentially face criminal disorderly conduct charges. My stomach twists again at just the thought of it.

I know in my heart that Nadine is going to press charges. She called the police. I think she would have done it then and there if Jennings had made it easier for her. The look in her eyes said she wanted to see me driven away in handcuffs.

And I want to be mad at her, but I'm madder at myself. *What* was I thinking? Lurking around late at night, vandalizing homes? This isn't me. I could be kicked off of the swim team if I have a criminal record. Oh my god. The thought comes to me like a flash of lightning, and right behind it come the tears.

By the time I reach the house, walking past the spot where the Marins' car should be, my face is soaked. I am such an idiot. I risked everything I've worked for since I was nine, and for what? What would possess me to do something so stupid?

Asher.

Asher, who convinced me to turn my *skills* on someone else. Who lured me into the idea that this was all for fun—that we'd be making a better choice this summer not tormenting each other. Asher, who made me feel like he cared. Who wasn't there tonight. Who left me alone exactly when I needed him. *Exactly when I needed him.*

As I open the door to my quiet room, and wipe my hand across my damp face, I know, finally, that everything I feared might actually be true: Asher Marin pulled off the greatest prank yet. He was never my friend, or my boyfriend; he is and has always been my nemesis.

Asher

I've sent Sidney eight texts, and she hasn't answered one of them. But she's read them all. Is it possible that her phone is dead and it's just some sort of glitch? Nadine's yard was empty when I finally got back to the house. I hadn't expected to find my dad sitting at the kitchen table at 3 a.m. It would have been hard to explain why I was coming home that late just to leave with a giant bag of Saran Wrap. Instead I pretended I was just getting in for the night, and then waited until he went to bed to climb out my bedroom window.

I have to admit I never imagined I'd be utilizing windows as much as I have this summer. It was over an hour before I got back to Nadine's, and I expected to find Sidney almost done with our fork mural—a giant hand, middle finger raised—but instead, I found nothing but the forks. I look at my phone again and the string of texts.

> Asher: Heading back now

> Asher: I'm back. Where are you?

> Asher: Are you okay?

Asher: Call me

Asher: Going home. If you're not there, I'm talking to your parents.

And as I pass her bedroom door, a soft light filtering under the crack like her bedside lamp is on, I send one more.

Asher: You okay?

Sidney: Yep

Asher: You didn't answer any of my texts

Sidney: Nope

Asher: What's up? I thought Nadine had murdered you or something.

Sidney: Not that lucky.

Asher: Okay, I'm cashing in Question #4

Sidney: That's not a question

Asher: What's wrong, Sidney??? <--Question

Sidney: Nothing.

> Asher: I know you, and it's not
> nothing. What's up?

> Sidney: Maybe you don't know
> me. Maybe you've been making
> out with a stranger all summer.

It's exactly the kind of thing I expect from Sidney, but it still feels off. I wish we were actually talking so I could figure out if she was being sarcastic or snarky. With her, there's an important difference.

> Asher: I know a lot of things
> about you.

> Sidney: Not a personal
> challenge.

> Asher: No? I have eleven rocks
> that prove I'm ALWAYS up for
> a challenge when it comes to
> you.

When there's no snarky reply, I know deep in my gut something is wrong.

> Asher: I know your favorite
> drink when you were twelve
> was cherry Kool-Aid, and you're
> afraid of spiders.

> Asher: Your dad calls you
> Chipmunk when he forgets you

aren't six anymore, and you secretly love it. You don't love it when I do it.

Asher: It probably has something to do with wanting to make out with me.

Asher: Your favorite meal is that weird cauliflower-crusted chicken your mom makes. Your purple suit is lucky. (I know because it's completely worn-out but you still insist on wearing it. And you have to wear it over another suit so you don't put on a show for lakegoers. But for the record, I am here for that show.)

Asher: Your shampoo smells like strawberries and mint, and your favorite pajama shorts have little stars on them. You don't ever talk about your friends from home, so I'm guessing they suck. If they don't I'd love to hear about them.

Asher: I know you make the best chocolate-chip pancakes ever (but if you tell my mom I said that I'll deny it). You hardly ever drink but when you do, you forget all about how anxious parties make you. I know you're nervous about living with a roommate. And that you think you should get a discount at restaurants that have those make-your-own-waffle stations, because you're doing their job for them.

Asher: I know you're shit at finding constellations and you hate big groups of people you don't know. You love coffee and you think tea tastes like dirt water. When you're really tired you act like you're dying.

Asher: I know that when you sleep your legs make a four and you tuck one hand under your butt. And when you wake up your voice is all rough.

I send message after message, not even sure what I'm hoping to accomplish, but feeling like I'm fixing something.

Sidney: Okay, I think you've proven your point.

Asher: Have I?

Asher: I know you, Sid. And something's wrong.

Sidney: I was almost arrested tonight. I probably will be tomorrow.

Asher: What?? Come in here and talk to me.

Sidney: Talking about this isn't going to fix us.

Fix *us*? Inside the bathroom, I knock on her door, loudly once, then quietly, when I remember it's the middle of the night and we shouldn't be awake.

Asher: Open the door so we can talk.

Sidney: Talking isn't going to change the fact that this summer has been one giant disaster.

Asher: I wouldn't call what's happened this summer a disaster.

Sidney: I would. And if we're smart we'll cut our losses.

Asher: You're not breaking up with me by text from the next room. Dock in 15.

When I reach the dock she's already there, waiting for me. She's bathed in a circle of light from the lamp pole next to the stairs, but otherwise it's dark out here. And silent. I wish it was going to stay that way, because I know the things we're about to say aren't going to be good; I can feel it in the way she's looking at me as I step out onto the dock.

She doesn't say anything, just stands there and looks at me, like she's expecting something from me.

"What happened?"

No one rolls their eyes like Sidney. And this one is A+, it's like her whole head rolls with it. "As if I have to tell you."

"You do, because I wasn't there. And I'm not a mind reader."

There go the eyes again. "How'd you manage it? Did Lindsay help? Has she been in on it the whole time?"

Lindsay? "Excuse me? In on what?"

This time she doesn't bother with her eyes and really does let her whole head do the job, throwing her head back before it comes forward again. "For once, let's own up to what we did, okay? This isn't Kool-Aid or contaminated shampoo, or even rotten fish. This is *disorderly conduct*." She practically screams the last two words. "So you win. You win the whole summer. The last six years. You have trumped *everything*."

I'm having a hard time wrapping my head around what she's accusing me of right now. Of setting her up tonight; potentially getting her arrested. "You honestly think I spent all summer winning you over just so I could get you arrested? *That* was my big finale?"

"What am I supposed to think? *You* sprang tonight on me last minute. *You* conveniently forgot something and had to leave. *You* weren't there when I had to face the music for everything *we've* done this summer."

"And *you* have been looking for any excuse for us not to work right from the start. You're scared of this working, and you're scared of this not working, and you're just . . . scared of everything."

Sidney narrows her eyes at me and her head tips to the right, like she's trying to get a better look at me. "You think you're so brave, but how's that letter going? Don't tell me about being afraid when you can't even talk to your own dad about a decision that affects your whole freaking future."

"Sid, I just need you to try to see this rationally for two seconds, before you ruin everything." And she is. I can feel all of the bricks I chipped away at this summer building back up around her.

"If I'm so irrational, so scared, so horrible—I'm not sure why you'd even want to be with me."

I tug on my hair, because I sort of want to rip it out. I laugh at the absurdity of all this. "Maybe all the compromised food you've fed me over the years has eaten away at my brain."

Sid crosses her arms over her chest and I know this look. Too well. This is her war face. I am the enemy, and she's not backing down until she's the victor. "And maybe all of the suspiciously nice things you've said to me all summer started to convince me you really were nice."

"So I'm *too nice* now?" When I laugh it doesn't sound like me, it sounds slightly deranged. "I can't win. You know, maybe you'll wake up tomorrow and decide this was a horrible idea, but I don't even care. I guess you were right all along. This can only end one way. It's pretty clear that you're not going to let it end the good way. So for *my* sake, let's just forget about this, okay? Because you're right, this isn't the sort of thing we should get into if we're not serious about it. We don't need to screw up our families for a summer fling."

"That's what this was to you."

I hate the conviction in her voice, like she believes it, or at least wants to. "It's the opposite of what this was for me, but you've been convinced this couldn't work right from the start, and I'm tired of trying to convince you you're wrong."

"So we agree."

"No. We don't." I jab my finger at her. "*You* think this can't work because . . . well, for no reason really. You've just decided it won't." I look out at the lake and back to her. "*I* think this won't work, because we've been together for a few weeks, and you still don't trust me. You keep trying to sabotage this. You're looking for problems where there aren't any, and you're already one foot out the door." I pull on the hem of my T-shirt because I feel like I'm boiling over with angry energy. "This is over, because even if I could talk you down from this, I don't know how I can trust that you're not going to do the same thing six months from now. Or two years from now." I take a step back on the dock. "So"—I throw my hands up like Sidney has me at gunpoint, which is how it feels—"I surrender. You win, Sidney. It's over. Just like you knew it would be. So like always, your plan worked."

DAY 50

Sidney

I wait until four o'clock to take the car and drive into town. I'll stop at the store and get some vacation jerky in case I need an alibi. *Another one.* The Riverton Police Department is in a large brick building that is long and low and also houses the city hall, fire department, and community room. The building is quiet and empty, and an older woman sits behind a desk, a pane of glass separating her from me. Maybe she's worried about people sneezing on her, like at a buffet? Oh, right. She's worried about the criminals who come here. Like me. When I step up she pushes open a window to greet me.

I smile. "Could I see Officer Jennings, please?"

She glances up at me but she's mostly looking at her computer. "In regards to?"

"I met him last night." Her eyes snap up to mine and I realize it sounds like I'm some weirdo who met him at a party and is now stalking him at his job. Movement catches my eye and I notice the men in uniforms standing behind her, shifting uncomfortably. "Oh. No. I mean, not like I *met* him. Just that he arrested me. Well, not arrested, but I mean . . ." I rest my fingertips on the edge of the title counter in front of her window. "I was vandalizing someone's yard. Not even vandalizing really, I was just forking it. You know, sticking plastic silverware into it?" I smile at her but she doesn't return it. "Harmless, really." My voice has pitched up nervously. "And yeah, it was going to be in a vulgar shape, but I hadn't finished, so it just looked like a bunch of forks." The woman—Gayle, according to her nameplate—looks from me to the group of men gathered behind her. "So anyway, she called the cops. And he was the cop. Jennings, I mean." *Why can't I just stop talking?* "So that's how I met him. He took me home." Oh no. "To my home! *My* home!"

Gayle's face has gone from concerned to amused, and she pushes her rolling chair away from the desk and walks to a nearby door, turning back to me to say, "Wait here."

The two cops standing by the doorway back to the right have now gained a third person, and they're all trying really hard not to stare at me, but I feel a little like a zoo animal on the other side of this glass. They snicker and mumble something as Jennings walks in through the hallway. He lands a punch to an older guy's arm as he passes. He's in normal clothes—khaki pants and a collared shirt—and I can see just how young he is when he's out of uniform. He stands in the spot where Gayle's chair is. She hasn't returned. Traumatized, probably.

"Miss Walters." He gives me a tiny nod.

"Officer Jennings." I look to the men behind him and try to keep my voice serious and detached, but I'm not entirely sure what I came here to ask or what the formal way to request it is.

Jennings raises a brow at me. "Can I help you with something?"

"I just . . . wanted to check on my arrest."

"To *check* on it?"

I drum my fingers along the countertop. "Yes. To see what I need to do next."

My nerves are absolutely out of control. It's entirely possible that I'm going to throw up right here. I suppose it would make a good case for keeping the glass barrier closed. But Jennings does something I'm not expecting. He laughs. It's loud and long, and barrels out of him. The men behind him smile, like they, too, are amused by my predicament.

What an asshole.

Something on my face must tell him I think so, because he suddenly stops, his face turning apologetic. "I'm sorry. I've just never had anyone so impatient to be arrested."

"Impatient?" I cross my arms over my chest. "I just don't want you showing up at my house. And if I need to make arrangements, I want to do that. I don't want my parents to have to pack up all of my stuff. And I need to talk to my coach and see if criminal charges will get me kicked off of the team before I even start."

"The team?"

"Swim team," I clarify. "I'm swimming at Oakwood this year, if I'm not in jail."

He nods. "Well, the good news is you won't have to call your coach."

I moan. "Oh my god, do you *send* something? Do colleges automatically get notified about this sort of thing? This just keeps getting better, I mean . . ."

Jennings cuts me off. "Sidney." Hearing my first name is comforting somehow—it makes me feel less like the criminal delinquent I've become. "No charges have been pressed."

"She didn't come in yet? I thought she was supposed to do that." A tiny spark of hope lights within me. "Is there a time limit or something? If she doesn't show up by a certain date is it too late?" How long can Nadine legally leave me living in an anxious limbo between normal citizen and official criminal?

"She *did* call this afternoon. She won't be pressing any charges. I was going to call you, but . . ." He looks amused again. "I didn't realize you'd be so anxious."

"That's because you don't know me."

"I think you should give up the pranks, Miss Walters." Officer Jennings smiles at me and shakes his head. "I don't think you're cut out for a life of crime."

I nod. "That won't be a problem."

I'm having a WWMD moment as I pull into Nadine's driveway. Hopefully this isn't one of those situations where I'm not supposed to approach her. Part of me thinks I should just cut my losses, never see her again, and call it a day, but *what would Mom do?* She'd apologize. And if I'm being honest with myself, I'm probably not going to sleep until I do the same. The guilt of knowing what I did and that Nadine *knows* it's me is threatening to eat me alive.

Nadine's front porch faces the road, and I've never actually stood on it. When we needed something—which was rarely—we always went to the back door, the one closest to our houses. I knock twice, and wait. It feels like I've swum a team relay by the time I see Nadine's scowling face through the narrow glass pane that runs down the center of the door. She cracks the door enough to wedge her body into it, but no farther. As if I'm going to burst into her house and set it on fire or something.

"Sidney." She looks behind her and back to me. "Haven't you done enough here?"

"I just wanted to apologize."

Her voice is gruff and annoyed. "Apology accepted." The door is half closed when I put a hand on the knob. She looks from my hand to my face.

"And to say thank you for not pressing charges. I know you could have, and I'm just . . ." I take my hand off of the door and she closes it another inch. "Thank you."

"I'm not the one to thank . . ." She jerks her head to the side, and through the crack of the door I can see Lindsay standing in the doorway to their kitchen. "But you know while you're here, maybe we should talk about how you can fix all of this. You know, those forks aren't going to pull themselves out. And my yard still smells like mashed potatoes when the sprinklers go off . . ." I hear a snort and see Lindsay throw her hand over her mouth.

"Mom, let's just leave it alone." Lindsay pushes past her mom and grabs my elbow. "We'll go pull some forks out, okay?" She pats her mom on the shoulder and pulls the door shut behind her, pulling me along with her toward the side of the house.

We're walking in silence toward the backyard, her hand still on my elbow, when I say, "Why are you home? I thought you were at school during the week."

"Asher called me this morning."

Wow. Heat fills my cheeks. That was . . . quick. I pull my elbow away from her in a swift jerk. "He wastes no time."

"He didn't ask me to come back, he just asked me to talk to my mom. About—" She waves a hand toward the yard, still littered with white plastic. "What went down last night." She shakes her head and there's the hint of a smile on her lips. "It's easier to talk my mom into something in person. I'm sorry she threatened you. It was a bit much for forks and mashed potatoes." She reaches down and pulls a white fork out of the grass.

Lindsay is the reason I'm not going to be a forking criminal. And Asher. Even after everything I said last night, he fixed this.

I bend down and pull a fork out of the ground, and then another. "Thanks. You didn't have to do that. I mean, I really appreciate that you did that. Like, *really* appreciate it."

"It's no big deal." She tosses some forks into a little pile and I follow.

"I've never really been that nice to you."

She smiles and shrugs. "You're not mean, though."

I laugh.

"What?"

"Nothing. I'm just getting a lot of really glowing endorsements this summer." I throw a few more forks on the pile. "I'm sorry about that."

"I'm sorry, too."

"For what?"

"You know what." She gives me a sideways glance. "I know you saw me and Asher."

I don't say anything, just keep pulling forks out of the ground. "It's old news."

"Yeah, but I've always felt weird about it." There's a beat of silence as she grabs another fork. "My boyfriend broke up with me that summer. I was on this medication that made me gain ten pounds and—well, I don't think it was a coincidence. Anyway, Asher was nice to me, and . . ." She shrugs. "I knew he liked you. And I knew it was a crappy thing to do, but not until after . . ."

"You didn't exactly force him."

Lindsay laughs. "What fourteen-year-old guy is going to stop a girl from kissing him?"

Asher. I had thought Asher would. But she's right, how stupid was that? He and I weren't even together.

It's hard to blame Lindsay. She feels bad for kissing Asher because she knew I liked him. She thought he liked me. But I knew she liked him, too. And I wouldn't have felt bad if I had kissed him. I just didn't have the guts to do it like she did. Maybe that's what I've really been mad about all of these years: that she had the guts to do something I didn't. "It's fine."

"I'm sorry my mom kicked you guys out. I know she's a total whack job sometimes but . . ." Lindsay looks to the house like she's checking for Nadine to be lurking at a window. "It's been a rough year or two. My parents split, and my mom's in the house by herself, and honestly, she's never wanted renters here. My dad wanted to rent the houses." She stubs her toe into the grass. "I think kicking you guys out was just a big 'eff you' to my dad." She gives me a sad smile. "Sorry you guys got caught in the middle of it."

"I'm sorry about your parents."

She glances at the house again. "I should probably be more upset, but honestly . . . some people just aren't meant to be together."

Lindsay and I pick forks out of the yard for another hour, making small talk about her first year at college, but none of it can distract me from the words that won't leave my head: *some people just aren't meant to be together.* People like Asher and me. We're not doomed because he's out to get me, we're doomed because he was right last night: down the road I'd screw this up somehow. At least now it's done with, before things go too far, before we hurt our families or each other more than we already have. But if it's the right decision, then why does it still hurt so much?

DAY 52

Asher

I'm probably not in the right mind-set to talk to my dad, but I'm in a *screw it, there's nothing left to lose* kind of mood, so I'm going to run with it. He's by the picnic table in the yard, spreading newspapers and trash bags out so he can clean the fish he caught this morning with Tom. After what has been dubbed *the fish incident*, Mom hasn't let him anywhere near the kitchen with fish this summer.

He's hauling his cooler from the ground up onto the gray bench, when I stand across from him.

"Come to help?"

"Can't. Traumatized." I hold my hands up in the air. "I may never eat fish again. I was hoping we could talk for a minute before you start slicing and dicing?" I take a seat on the long gray bench.

Dad sits down next to his cooler and when he looks at me, his whole face changes. Something like fear and panic wash over him in an instant. "Oh god." He looks up at the house and back to me. "You're not. I mean, Sidney's not. She's not pregnant or something, is she?"

"She's not—*what?*" I try to physically shake away the confusion and shock that has slapped me in the face. "What are you *talking* about?"

Dad is visibly relieved. "I'm sorry, I just—the way that you looked. I thought this was something big. Something bad."

"And your first thought was that I knocked up Sidney?"

Dad winces. "This isn't my finest parenting moment."

"You knew we were together, though?" I wince. "*Dating* together, not accidental-pregnancy together," I clarify.

"I know. We know." Dad glances up at the house again. "Your mom thinks it's adorable you think we don't. Maybe don't tell her about this little freakout, okay? Not unless you want to go back to an open-door policy around the house."

"We broke up last night, so that won't be a problem."

When my dad is disturbed by something—really disturbed—he has a very specific look. His eyebrows collapse into sharp mountains, and his mouth twists up. He shakes his head three times. No more, no less. "I'm sorry to hear that. I really thought this was the year things turned around for good."

"Me, too."

"You want to talk about it?"

I shake my head. "Not now. Maybe some other time." I give him a sideways glance. "Over a beer?"

Dad smiles. "Sure."

"Anyway, that's not what I wanted to talk about. I wanted to talk about the apprenticeship with Mr. Ockler this fall."

At this, Dad is once again his cheery self. "You finally get it squared away?"

"I don't want to do it." I stop him before he can interrupt me. Before I lose my nerve to tell him everything. "Not just the apprenticeship. Everything. I don't want to study finance, and I don't want to manage anyone's retirement fund. It's not what I want to do."

"Since when?"

"Since . . . forever?" I push a hand through my hair. "And I know it's easy money, and I can have this whole business just waiting for me when I graduate, but I know I'll regret it. I want to coach. I've always wanted to coach. And I get that it's a long shot maybe, but"—god, I'm rambling like Sidney now—"I'd rather try for that and fail than go for a sure thing that I'm never going to care about."

Dad looks to the house again, and I finally realize what he's looking for. Mom. His other half, the person he wants to face this hurdle with. I thought I'd face this hurdle—telling my dad—with Sidney. That I'd finally work up the nerve to tell him, and I'd get to tell her, and we'd celebrate. I had imagined pancakes would be involved. Or a late-night make-out session. Maybe both.

But at least she left me with something. "I want to study sports psychology. And I have a plan." I pull out the list I made this morning in my bedroom when I was too afraid to run into Sidney in the kitchen, and I set it on the table. "Do you want to hear it?"

DAY 56

Asher

We take this picture every year on the last day of vacation, after our cars are loaded and we're ready to drive back home. Each family out on the end of the dock. And if someone manages to remember a tripod, *both* families out on the dock. And then it's always me and Sidney at the end of the dock. *The kids.* If photos had names, like famous paintings, that's what our parents would call this one. Usually, we do something funny. Sidney pretends to strangle me, or we pose as if she's about to push me off of the dock. But I know we never actually hated each other before, because those pictures were fun, and now I can't even figure out how to stand next to her. So I walk down the dock and stand behind her.

She's still wearing the necklace—the one I bought her two years ago—the one I probably never should have given to her. Maybe she was right all along, maybe we were doomed from the start, and I ruined everything trying to take us to that place. All the summers to come. But something about seeing that silver chain around her neck just makes me feel worse. That she wants the necklace, but not me. It seems unfair, cruel, and I understand why people want engagement rings back. Sure, it's her necklace, but why does she even *want* it, when she doesn't want me?

I should just stand here and smile, but it seems more appropriate to do something antagonistic. Something that's a throwback to the pictures of summers past. But I don't mock-strangle her, or push her into the lake; I do something that will actually annoy her. I wrap my arms around her shoulders and I smile. Now our photo is just like the others . . . a total lie.

14 DAYS AFTER

Sidney

On the desk in my dorm room, there's a small envelope of photos. They arrived this morning, marking exactly two weeks since the world's most awkward end-of-summer photo. And the last time I saw Asher. While the package says they're from an online printer, I know they're actually from my mom. The combined photographic efforts of my mother and Sylvie. Our summer, distilled into one little cardboard packet of memories. But the memories seared into *my* mind weren't captured on anyone's phone—definitely not by our mothers. It's hard to believe any of them could be in that envelope, but I still can't open it. I'm scared to see what's inside.

The last week of vacation was nothing short of awful. The house had never felt so small, and I had never felt so directionless. Without pranks to play or dates to plan, something was missing. And as much as I didn't want to think it, I knew that thing was Asher. Asher *was* summer vacation. He was my favorite lake, and the best two months of the year. I wanted to be mad at him, to stay angry, but he was right; once a few days had passed, and the shock of my almost-arrest wore off, things didn't seem so dire. It didn't seem so plausible that he had fabricated an entire summer of magical moments just to one-up me. But I also knew it was too late. To fix what I'd broken with him, but also, to forget everything that night reminded me of— that our relationship was a disaster waiting to happen, and that eventually, it would ruin everything with our families. It would ruin *us*.

I painted more rocks that last week than all of summer, trying my best not to paint anything that reminded me of him. Dinners were a throwback to ignoring one another, and it was hard to miss the concerned looks on our parents' faces as they poked and prodded us with questions, trying to draw us into a conversation. By the end of the week I felt invisible. The most words I got from him were forced—hellos and good nights if I was near our parents. An answer if I asked him something casual at the dinner table, just to try to be normal. But all of it was without an ounce of the light I was used to.

And by the time I packed up my room, I wasn't sure what was worse—Asher mad at me, or just being ignored. Treated like I was nothing special. Which I wasn't. I knew that—knew that *I* was the one that ruined it all. But I was sure we still had time to turn things around. I had sparked a controlled burn. Something small and manageable and early—we would overcome it. Eventually. Hopefully. But right now, I still can't open that envelope. I tuck it into a pile of books on the shelf over my desk, and run out of my room.

I was paired with one of my teammates as a roommate. Apparently, it's freshman tradition for all of the swimmers to be paired up together. Every morning, my roommate Ellie and I walk to the main cafeteria, to meet up with other girls from the team. Our dorm is directly across from one of the campus's three dining spots, and it's weird but also comforting to have a built-in group of friends here, who all share something in common. Not that we sit around talking about swimming twenty-four/seven, but it's this strange thread of familiarity that connects us all. In every class but one, I have at least one teammate I can gravitate toward.

After breakfast on Tuesdays and Thursdays, we do core training and weights. While they're preseason captain-led practices that aren't *technically* mandatory, we all know we better have a really good reason for missing one. I haven't yet, even though it's a lot harder to drag myself out of bed now than it was during the summer. I don't like to think about why that is. But today, as I wander through the conditioning room in the college field house, I can't help but notice that Asher isn't here.

When it comes to team activities, I feel like my eyes have a special inventory system that requires me to verify whether Asher and I are in the same room. And currently we are not. I finish my core workout and move to a machine. Ellie spots me at the free weights, and I spot her, and when we're finally leaving for the locker room—hot and sweaty but somehow more energized than when I arrived—Asher finally walks in.

Perfect timing.

24 DAYS AFTER

Sidney

Two weeks into classes, Asher and I have barely spent any time together in the weight room. We are a perfectly choreographed performance of coming and going. But when he's missing altogether, I finally lose my cool. He can't spend *five minutes* in the same room with me? I shouldn't. I really know I shouldn't, but I still stop next to Ryan, Asher's roommate.

"Where's Asher?"

Ryan holds his weight in a curl and smiles at me. "Room."

"Is he coming today?"

"Not likely."

I let out a disgruntled grunt and Ryan laughs. "Chill. He's sick."

A prickle of something goes up my arms. "How sick?"

"I'm-definitely-not-going-back-to-the-room-anytime-soon sick."

Ellie is still standing by the doorway and I wave her away.

"You're going to be late," she says. The only class we share is in thirty minutes, and she's right. We barely have time to shower as it is.

"Take notes for me?" Ellie gives me a tiny salute and walks

away. "Sidney notes, not Ellie notes!" I yell at her back. It's the second week of classes; am I seriously going to skip?

I put my hand out to Ryan. "Room key, please."

"Sidney, seriously." He gives me a serious look. "Now's not the time to give him crap." The way he says it makes me think Ryan knows a thing or two about me and Asher. "You don't want to go in there."

"Key, please." I wiggle my fingers. "You don't need it, you said so yourself."

He pulls his key ring out of his bag and twists a large gold key off, smacking it into my palm. "Don't say I didn't warn you."

Asher

I want to die. Maybe it's the grim reaper knocking on my door, here to drag me off to somewhere my head doesn't spin and my stomach doesn't feel like someone is twisting it into a pretzel.

"Asher?"

I groan and it sounds like maybe I am dying. It's worse than death, or the grim reaper—it's Sidney. Why now? Why? Mentally, I scream but I say nothing. Maybe if I just pretend I'm not here she'll go away. She has to go away.

"I'm coming in."

Wait, what? I lift the bowling ball that is my head off of the pillow to look at the door, then let it crash back down. This isn't the lake house, she can't just barge into my room, or stick a hairpin in the door to wiggle it open. But then I hear a key slide into the lock, a twist of metal, and my room is no longer a Sidney-free space. She's standing just inside the doorway, her face still red from conditioning, her tank top blotched with sweat.

I look her up and down, still trying to process that she's here.

She looks down at herself then back to me. "Sorry, I just came from the gym. I'm gross."

I nod. Blink. And then puke.

"Wow." Sidney shuts the door behind her and walks over to the bed. "Okay, this is not what I expected." She sets a plastic grocery bag down on the desk just beyond my bed and drops her backpack to the floor. Ryan and I have our room set up identically on either side. You could slice it down the middle and it would be a perfect mirror image: a bed against each long wall, desk butted up against the far headboard, and a dresser on the far wall, on either side of our one window. Ryan has a poster of a half-naked girl over his bed, but I haven't gotten around to putting anything on the walls. My dresser, however, is another story.

"What is that?" My upper body is hanging off of the bed, over the plastic trash can I just puked in. I feel too horrible to care that I just puked in front of Sidney.

"I brought you chicken soup from the cafeteria. And some crackers. Ryan didn't say you were . . ." She gestures to the trash can. "Don't eat soup. Please." She looks around the room and her eyes land back on me. "Do you have a cup?"

She doesn't wait for me to answer, just leaves through the little door to her left and disappears into the bathroom. If only our bathroom had two doors like the one she and I used to share, I could hope that she'd just disappear out the other side. But no, she comes back. She's holding the blue plastic cup I keep my toothbrush in, and crosses the room to my bed.

"Drink a little." She holds the glass of water out to me. "Just tiny sips." I take it and pull myself upright enough to take a sip. "Are you good for a few minutes?" She nods at the wastebasket and I nod back.

Without a word, Sid picks it up—wincing just once when she glances down—and disappears into the bathroom again. I hear the slosh of liquid going into the toilet bowl, a flush, and then the shower head turning on. More sloshing and dumping. The whole thing reminds me of listening to her in the bathroom at the lake house, how I could hear her getting ready step by step.

"Do you have dish soap?" Sid's voice is echoing in the bathroom. "Disinfectant of some kind?"

"Why would I have dish soap in my room?"

She pokes her head out of the bathroom door. "In case you needed to *clean* something?" She shakes her head at me. "I'll take that as a no. You and Ryan obviously just planned to wallow in your filth after a few weeks."

"How much do you hate me right now?" I can't help but laugh, even though it makes me a little nauseous.

Sidney doesn't answer. A minute later she emerges with the wastebasket and a handful of toilet paper folded into a thick square. She sets the basket back in its spot beside my bed and stands next to me. Then she gently lays her hand on my forehead. "I'm guessing you don't have a thermometer, either?"

"Must be in the same box as my dish soap."

She smiles and doesn't move her hand. "Funny."

When Sid's hand leaves my forehead, I'm relieved. "Well, Doctor? Do I have a fever?"

"I can't tell. I'm still hot from the gym, so I don't think my measurements are going to be very accurate." She shrugs. "My mom always seemed really confident when she did that, but yeah, I don't know."

Sidney sits on the bed across from me and pulls her phone out of her pocket, holding it up in front of her face.

"You're taking a selfie in my dorm room while I puke."

Sidney is rolling her eyes at me when I hear buzzing and then my mom's voice fills the room.

"Sidney." She sounds happy to hear from her. I can tell she's smiling without even seeing her.

"Hey, Sylvie." She lets out a little sigh. "So I don't want to worry you, but Asher's sick, and I'm not sure what I should do. I figured you're probably the expert on this."

My mom makes a sympathetic awwww sound, and says "Hi, sweetie" really loudly, like I'm farther than five feet away and I might not hear her. "Does he have a fever?"

"He doesn't have a thermometer. I felt with my hand, but I just got out of conditioning, so I'm hot. It's hard to tell. But I think so? He's all sweaty and gross."

"Ditto," I mutter, hoping my mom didn't hear. Sid tries to hide a smile.

"He's still his sassy self though, so I don't think he's on the verge of death or anything."

"All we can really ask for," Mom says. "Does he have any ibuprofen?"

Sidney looks to me, and I shake my head.

"I have some in my room," Sidney says.

"Give him three of those. And again in four hours."

Sid nods like she's sitting in a lecture, taking notes.

"Make sure he doesn't dehydrate. The orange Gatorade is his favorite. Not the melon stuff, the orange," Mom says, very seriously, like melon Gatorade could be my demise.

Sid nods, also very seriously. "Got it."

"You'll stay with him?" My mom's voice sounds nervous.

"Yeah, of course."

"You don't have to," I say, just as my mom says, "Thank you."

"That's pretty much it. If he's still at it tomorrow, make him go to the campus clinic."

"Got it." Sid gives the phone a thumbs-up. "Thanks, Sylvie."

"You, too, sweetie."

Sidney tucks the phone back in her pocket. "I'm going to run to my room for the ibuprofen. And I'll get you some Gatorade; I think they have it at the little convenience store inside the dining hall."

I'm lying on my back, eyes shut, but I push myself up onto one elbow. "You don't have to, Sid. I'm fine."

"I told your mom I would." She turns toward the door, not taking her backpack. "I'll be back."

Most of my day alternates between sleeping and puking. In between, Sidney makes trips to the bathroom (using the soap she brought back along with the ibuprofen and Gatorade). Whenever I wake up, she's sitting on Ryan's bed, a book spread across her lap, thumbing through pages and scribbling in the notebook propped up on one knee.

"Don't you have class?"

"Just one. And Ellie's bringing me notes."

"You're in a class together?"

"Yeah. Cool, huh?" She taps her pen against her notebook and her eyes drop to her book, and back to me, then back to her book. She's staring at a page but I can tell she wants to say something. I'm relieved when she doesn't.

We sit in silence through the afternoon, and when five o'clock rolls around, I ask her to throw me my phone from my desk. I type in ten numbers and leave a message on the voice mail, letting them know I won't be at practice tonight, because I'm sick.

"What practice do you have?"

"I'm doing a stroke clinic with a local club team once a week."

"Really?"

"Yup." I roll onto my back again and look up at the ceiling. I'm not really in the mood to share right now, but she's looking at me like she wants to know more, and it's awkward to be trapped in such a small space with someone and refuse to talk. "I'm majoring in sports psychology. It's part of my long-term plan to coach." I keep going before she can start asking questions. "I'll work with club teams the next few years, then hopefully once I graduate I can get an assistant spot somewhere while I get my master's." I shrug.

"That's awesome." Sidney's voice is soft, and a little sad. "So you told your dad you didn't want to be his mini-me, huh?"

"Yep." I don't want to get into details about this, don't want to tell her that her breaking up with me was the catalyst for making sure I didn't lose the other things I wanted in life.

Doors are slamming down the hallway as guys are coming and going from dinner. "You should go," I say. Sidney has been sitting here all day, occasionally eating one of the crackers she brought me. She must be starving. "I feel a lot better. Thanks for hanging out today."

Sid nods, and tucks her things back into her backpack. She sets the bottle of ibuprofen on my desk where I can reach it, and tells me I should eat my soup once I've gone a few hours without puking.

Her hand is resting on the doorknob when she says, "I'm sorry. About everything."

I don't say anything because I think I know what she's talking about, but I don't want to risk it.

"I know you fixed everything with Nadine." Her voice is soft. "I'm sorry I accused you of setting that all up. I just—I overreacted. And I would have known even if I hadn't talked to Lindsay. I mean, I *know* you wouldn't do that, I never should have implied you would. I just—I'm sorry."

"Okay." It's the only thing I can think to say.

"Okay?"

I nod, and Sidney pulls the door shut behind her.

34 DAYS AFTER

Sidney

Asher jogs past my dorm every morning. I saw him the first time by accident, when Ellie and I were walking to the café across from our building to meet the girls for breakfast. It's not weird or even intentional that he runs by—my building is at a major crossroads where paths from all of the living centers converge at one of the campus's three dining spots.

The second time I saw him, a few days after what I will always think of as *the day of puke*, I waved. Like an idiot. It took a monumental effort to make my arm move, and it's too early to know, but I suspect I'll regret it for the rest of my life. Someday when I'm lying on my deathbed, I'll regret never climbing a mountain or doing something to better humanity, and that one time I waved to Asher Marin on a cold morning in the middle of September my freshman year. Because Asher didn't wave, but some random dude coming out of the café did. And to save face I had to pretend I recognized him from my biology lecture, and I wasn't hopelessly waving at my ex-boyfriend. *Look at me, making friends everywhere I go.* Between team breakfasts and this, I have officially reached social butterfly status. My certificate's obviously lost in the mail.

I get that I did something horrible, but I *did* apologize. And it's been over a month now—weeks of me giving him space and watching him avoid me—and we can't be like this forever. I don't want to lose Asher completely.

Whether he saw me or not, there was no wave. Asher is normally like a distracted dog when he runs, checking out everything going on around him, but when he passes my dorm, he is laser-focused on one thing: not seeing me.

I waved four more different times when I saw him. On the fifth time, I decided I'd be proactive. I sat on a bench along the walkway, clearly in his sightline. And still, nothing.

So now, three weeks into classes, I'm finally fed up. I pull on my running shoes. Usually I run on the track, but today I'm going to make an exception. I'm waiting outside my dorm when Asher passes, and I fall in step beside him. I can't be sure, but it feels like he speeds up, and quickly I fall a step behind, and then two. It takes a near-sprint for my considerably shorter legs to keep up with him. Words come out of me in an explosion. "You're avoiding me."

Asher raises his voice so he doesn't have to turn around. His voice is even. "I'm not."

"You are."

"Okay—" He stops in front of me so quickly I nearly run into him. And when he turns to face me, it makes my heart jump into my throat, because we haven't been this close in months now, not even in his dorm room. I have a ridiculous urge to touch him. "I'm avoiding you." He pulls up the collar of his T-shirt and wipes the sweat from his face, exposing a little of his stomach. *Do not stare, Sidney.* "You're my ex-girlfriend. That's what people do."

It's a lot harder doing this when he's giving me his full attention—I wish we could keep running. "It's not a requirement, is it?" Obviously I know people do this, I just didn't expect that Asher would be one of those people. "You're not friends with any of your ex-girlfriends? You have, what? At least four of them, right?" *Wow, okay, Sid. You've veered down a very unfriendly road.* "I mean—I'm sorry. Just. You're not friends with any of your exes? You said you're still friendly with Jordan. And you called Lindsay, she wouldn't have helped you if you weren't—"

"Lindsay and I were never together." He shoves his hands into his pockets, and I think maybe it's to keep from strangling me, because he looks like he wants to. "And Jordan's different. It's not the same."

"Because she's nicer than me? She wasn't horrible to you for years?" I slam my hands onto my hips. "I watched you puke, I'm not the *worst* person in the world."

Asher's face scrunches up in confusion. "What? No, you're not the worst. And I never thought you were horrible." He shakes his head and the words shouldn't light me up as much as they do. How low are my expectations when I'm excited to hear he doesn't think I'm horrible? "But me and Jordan weren't . . . I mean . . . it's just different."

I nod, but I can't see how it is. I've never been mean to any of my exes. Maybe I avoided them for a few days while the weirdness settled, but after that, I just treated them like people again. I get that lots of exes treat each other like crap, or avoid each other, or whatever, I just didn't think Asher would be one of them. I want to tell him how much worse this is than the pranks or the jabs, but classes start in thirty minutes and the walkway is starting to fill with people scurrying toward food and academic buildings.

"Okay." My tightening throat and the stinging in my eyes won't let me say more.

I'm three steps away when he grabs my wrist, stopping me. The tears have spilled free so I don't turn around. And maybe Asher senses it, maybe he can smell tears—which is a theory I have about boys—because he stays behind me. "I'm sorry, Sid. I'll try, okay?"

I nod, and then my wrist is free, and I don't look, but I know Asher is gone.

49 DAYS AFTER

Asher

Five weeks into classes starting, we finally have our first coach-led practices. And today is our first stroke clinic. Both of our coaches plus all three of our grad assistants are on deck, each one of them positioned at the end of a lane. While we swim pool lengths, they watch our form and bark out corrections. We swim each drill until everyone has it right. It's exactly what I do for my club team, except I have to sound way nicer when I'm yelling out corrections, because they're twelve.

Two lanes down from me, Sidney is swimming her third lap of this drill, struggling to correct her rotation. She's hanging off of the deck looking frustrated as David, one of our grad assistants, crouches in front of her, tapping her shoulder as he tells her whatever it is she needs to correct. She plunges down into the water and takes off with a push again, but David doesn't seem to be pleased. The entire practice, it seems to be nothing but David yelling, Sidney listening, and shoulders being tapped. *Tap tap tap.* By the end of practice I don't know who I'm frustrated with, but I am.

Sidney wants to be friends. I've had a really hard time picturing what that looks like in my head, so mostly I've still been avoiding her. But maybe being friends with Sidney looks a lot like being teammates. And if it had been Ryan struggling today, I know what I'd do. After practice I stand outside my locker room door, waiting for Sidney to come through. After what feels like an eternity, she emerges, her hair twisted into a damp mess of curls on top of her head. For how long she was in there, I didn't expect her to emerge looking like she'd just jumped out of the pool. She sighs when she sees me, running a hand over her hair, like she's smoothing it back.

"What's the deal with your arm?" I say, falling into step with her as she passes.

"Didn't you hear?" She raises her eyebrows at me in annoyance. "It has a mind of its own."

"That's never been a problem for you before. That's your strongest stroke."

"I don't know." She shrugs. "I feel like I was picked up and dropped in a new land." I look at her sideways and she shakes her head like I'm an idiot. "New school, new teammates, new pool. I don't know, I'm just a ball of nerves in the water right now."

I don't say anything, because I don't know what to tell her. Does that make me the worst future sports psychologist ever? I haven't even taken a class yet, I doubt I'm supposed to be doling out psychological advice, but still. I smile at the thought of telling my dad that I'm throwing in the towel and it's all Sidney's fault for wrecking my confidence. We walk together through the double doors and out onto the sidewalk, still in silence. When she turns to the left and I turn to the right, she gives me a tiny wave, and walks away so fast she's practically jogging.

Maybe I really *don't* know how to be friends with her.

59 DAYS AFTER

Sidney

I've started to dread my time in the pool. Whatever it is that's in my head, I just can't seem to shake it. Looking into the glassy water is like staring down into my failure. And my future failure. Today is the official start of the season—our very first meet—and for all of the work I did this summer, all of the time I've put in at the gym, I don't feel like I've improved nearly as much as I should have. I shove my bag into my locker and adjust my suit straps.

"Can someone send Sidney out?" A male voice rings out in the locker room, and several girls gasp or jump before realizing the voice is coming from the doorway that leads out into the pool area.

I don't jump, I freeze. Because it isn't just anyone's voice. It's Asher's. Several girls look at me, but it's not in a curious or suspicious way, as much as a get-out-of-here-before-he-comes-in-for-you way. It feels like everyone should know about the history between us, but why would they? We've hardly spoken at practices—no one has any reason to suspect there's any sort of messy past between us. I'm not sure if I like it that way or not.

I slam my locker door shut and snap a hair tie around my wrist as I grab my swim cap. I bypass the showers, because whatever Asher wants certainly can't take long. I'll be back before I get in the pool. A sudden wave of panic trills through me when it occurs to me that there aren't many reasons for Asher to see me. What if something's happened with my parents, and they couldn't get ahold of me, so they went through him? Do I have my phone on me? I think about turning around to pluck it out of my bag, but I can see him just beyond the door, standing alongside the tiled beige wall.

He's in his suit, his hip leaning against the wall, arms crossed. So much skin. I will never be immune to Asher like this. I can almost smell the lake, hear the waves in my ears.

"What's wrong?"

He turns, his face confused. "Wrong?"

"I just . . . I wasn't sure what you wanted. I thought maybe it was something with my parents or . . ."

His face turns apologetic. "No, it's not anything bad. It's just . . ." He bites his lip and shifts his shoulders, and six summers of studying Asher tells me he's nervous. "Come with me, I'll show you." He has something clutched in his hand—I can see a thin strip of blue peeking through his fingers. The pool area is almost empty. There are a few people milling around, but mostly everyone is still in the locker rooms. We pass another guy from the team as we walk toward the diving blocks, and Asher nods his head in greeting.

Asher sits on the edge of the pool and smacks his hand down on the tiles next to him. I should sit, but I'm in shock. Asher has only spoken to me once since our run together. And even then, it was a few sentences about swimming. He looks up at me impatiently, and I know if I don't sit down he won't stay. I'm on borrowed time. Borrowed patience, probably. I lower myself next to him, leaving half a foot between us. I don't know if it's him or me that can't be trusted to touch, but I'm not risking it either way.

"Are you nervous?" He says it casually, like we're two normal people, and not us. And I know without him saying anything that he's talking about the meet, not us.

"What do you think?" I flutter my feet nervously in the water. "I feel like a tiny bomb, like once I get in the water I'll explode—maybe in a good way, maybe not."

He smiles. "That's what I figured." He opens his hand and reveals a small glass bottle. It's pretty, like something I could see his mom having on a shelf somewhere, and it has a little black rubber stopper. He shakes it in the air in front of him.

"I'm sort of afraid to ask what's in there."

"We're christening the pool. Turning it into your happy place." He pulls the black stopper from the tiny bottle and holds it in front of me.

"Is that . . ." I swallow back the lump forming in my throat and take the bottle. "Why do you have this?"

He shrugs. "Sentimental pack rat, remember?"

I take a quick look around the pool to see if anyone is watching us, and hold the little bottle of lake water in front of my knees. Slowly, I pour it into the pool. "Are there magic words we're supposed to say?"

Asher laughs, and the sound unwinds something I didn't even realize was coiling in my chest. "This is my first pool christening, but just imagine I'm in the boat next to you. You always swam like a beast across the lake."

"That's because you were chasing me. I was sure you were going to hit me with the boat."

"Hm."

I look down at my bare toes under the water, at the dark pink polish I put on last night. "This is really nice." I don't deserve it. I never deserved him—sweet, perfect, hopeful Asher—and I certainly don't now.

"I'm just being a decent human who doesn't want to see another person die." It's exactly what I said to him that night at the lake, when he was drunk.

"How am I going to die?"

"Well, you could drown." His voice is deadpan, his face serious. "You're not that great of a swimmer." He smiles and I poke him in the side with my elbow. We haven't been this close in what feels like centuries. That old feeling is back, the buzzing nervousness of him being close to me, able to touch me at any moment. But he's not going to touch me at any moment, I remind myself. He's trying to be a friend. Because I asked him to.

"I thought I was a beast."

"You could get so nervous that you take the angle all wrong on your dive and crack your head open."

I let out a sharp laugh. "Wow, that's dark. I thought you were supposed to be helping me with my nerves."

He shakes his head like I'm being ridiculous. "You're not scared you're going to crack your head on the bottom of the pool."

Of course I'm not. *Now* all I can think of is the fact that Asher and I are sitting here, talking and teasing, just like we used to. That we're only inches away from touching. That for these few minutes, it's felt—for the first time—like we might make it through this unscathed. He must register our proximity, too, because in one smooth move his arms cross over his chest. He angles away from me and back to the pool.

"Why did you get so drunk that night? Why'd you kiss me?" The words pour out of me like the lake water now in the pool. I've always wanted to know, but was too scared to ask. I don't know what has changed now. I suppose I have nothing left to lose. Except for this race. And this moment with him.

"Sid . . . I'm not doing this."

Asher looks around us nervously, and I remember we're surrounded by our teammates. We both have races to think about. Of course he doesn't want to be bothered with this. "Right. I'm sorry."

"I had the water. I knew you'd be nervous. It was just—when

I decide I'm going to do something, I follow through." He pushes himself up and towers over me. "Good luck." He says it to me the way he would to any other teammate. The same way he'll say it to ten more people before the afternoon is over.

There's already five feet between us when I say, barely over a whisper, "You, too."

60 DAYS AFTER

Asher

On Wednesdays I have classes from eight-fifteen straight through until two o'clock, so by the time I get back to my room I'm ready to eat my World History textbook, and I only have forty-five minutes until I need to be at the pool for practice. I make a quick stop at my room for my practice bag and as many protein bars as I can grab. Ryan usually walks over with me, but when I open my door I don't find my roommate.

I'm not entirely sure what I'm looking at. The first thing I see is the web of string, densely crisscrossing from every wall. Then I see the tiny little hooks secured to the wall . . . the little peel-and-stick kind. And while I really wish I could think this was Ryan, I know it wasn't. Luckily, my practice bag is in my little closet, which is just next to the door. My protein bars, on the other hand, are clear across the room in my desk drawer. Getting to them would mean dismantling this web, and I'm going to leave that to the person who let this happen.

When I get to the locker room, Ryan is standing by the bench, and it's clear he's waiting for me. A giant grin spreads across his face when he sees me.

"So? Tell me what happened."

"You can see when you get to the room." I set my bag on

the bench and pull my shirt over my head. "You're cleaning it all up."

His face drops for just a second. "It can't be that bad."

"It is. And you shouldn't have let her in our room."

Ryan shakes his head at me. "A hot girl wanting into your room seems like an okay deal to me. You're just hangry." He punches me in the shoulder.

"This isn't any hot girl, this is Sidney. And it doesn't mean what you think it does." I don't want to get into this with him in the crowded locker room. For Sidney, pranking me was just getting all of her frustration out. For me, pranks were the only way for me to connect with her after she shut down at the end of that first summer. We didn't prank each other when we were actually together, and I can't go back to that. Maybe I can't let myself admit that pranks wouldn't turn out the same way this time around. "Just don't let her in again, okay?"

Ryan doesn't get it, but he nods anyway. I have to see Sidney at practices and in the dining hall, and around campus, but my room is the one place I'm safe from this new reality.

67 DAYS AFTER

Sidney

I flinch every time I walk into my dorm room. And that should be a bad thing, but actually it feels strangely comforting. Like slipping on an old pair of pajamas. The ratty kind that are ugly and worn, but make you feel nostalgic. In the shower, I wish and pray that I'll be soaked by cherry Kool-Aid. That my slippers will mysteriously be filled with tapioca pudding, or glued to the floor. But day after day, things in my room are uneventful. It's a week before I realize that Asher isn't going to retaliate, and two before I admit to myself that I've gone about this all wrong.

I can't go backward with Asher. There's no re-creating the past with us. We aren't the same people we were when we were freezing each other's underwear and sabotaging shampoo. The only thing I can control right now is swimming, so when Ellie gets home from classes we go on a run before dinner. After dinner, we eat our weight in ice cream, and I tell her all about my summer, and Asher. It feels good to get it off my chest, and the next time I get in the pool, I feel a little bit lighter, and a whole lot more like myself.

72 DAYS AFTER

Sidney

Our third meet is at home on a Friday night in mid-October.
My first meet wasn't horrible, and my second was better, but
I still wasn't where I wanted to be. But as I kneel next to the
starting block, splashing water on my suit, the water doesn't
look as intimidating as it did a few weeks ago. This pool—and
everyone standing around it—*is* starting to feel like home. I
shake out my legs and stretch my arms, swinging them behind
me and in front, letting my shoulders relax. When the whistle
sounds, I take my place on the block, the roughness under my
feet comforting somehow. And when the starting buzzer blares,
everything around me melts away.

I've been in my head a lot since I got to Oakwood. Thinking
about everything my body is doing, making myself crazy. But as
I cut through the water tonight, feel it rush over me as I break
the surface on entry, I just shut it all off. The only thing I think
about is the water and the way I feel moving through it. When
my arms burn I think about the lake, and how much harder it
was swimming against the light chop. I think about that tiny
bottle of *my* lake in this pool. I swim lap after lap, thinking
about nothing but the water and how I'm meant to be in it.

When my palms slam against the touch pad, I don't look at

the scoreboard right away. I look up at my mom and dad, to the spot where I know they're perched in the bleachers. They're both on their feet. Everyone around them is sitting, but my parents are standing, clapping and cheering like absolute lunatics. Mom is pointing to the far corner, to where our times are lit up in lights. To where I shaved three seconds off of her event time. Ellie reaches her hand down to me, helping to hoist me up and throwing her arms around me. *I did it.*

Mom and Dad take me to dinner to celebrate. We sit in a booth at a little Italian restaurant in town, plates of spaghetti in front of us. Swimming makes me ravenously hungry, and I'm practically shoveling noodles into my mouth. My parents have been making small talk about my school year so far, what Ellie is like, how my classes are. Even though we talk at least once a week.

Dad picks his napkin up and then sets it back in his lap. "Sylvie and Greg wanted us to tell you congratulations. We thought about inviting them, but"—Dad glances from me to Mom—"you know." I saw Sylvie and Greg up in the stands by my parents. It was slightly weird seeing them all together. It's how I once imagined things would be: our parents watching us swim together, all of us going to dinner afterward.

I almost apologize that they're not here, but all I can think right now is that Dad and Greg are the whole reason this happened. Greg pushing Asher to fix things with me, my dad deciding he didn't want to do morning swims with me anymore.

"This is *your* fault," I say, matter-of-factly. "If you'd sucked it up and just spotted me across the lake . . ." I wave my fork at him. "Your boredom is what started this whole mess."

I expect Dad to laugh, but he doesn't. Instead, his voice is apologetic and soft when he says, "I'm sorry, Chipmunk."

Guilt immediately wells up in my chest. "I'm just kidding. It's my fault, not yours."

"It's . . . a little mine." Dad runs a hand over his head, the same move as when Mom catches him smuggling vacation jerky out of a grocery bag. He lets out a long sigh that almost whistles. "You're right."

"About?"

"I wasn't actually bored spotting you. I love spotting you, I—"

"Wait, what?"

"It's just . . . this thing with you and Asher has gone on so long, and we all thought, if we could just put the two of you together, out on the water, that maybe—"

"What?" My voice is angry, harder than I mean it to be. "Maybe we'd just fall in love and swim off into the sunset?"

Dad's face softens and his voice is slow and controlled. "We thought you two would finally have it out. That whatever was going on, whatever the issue was between the two of you . . . that you'd have time to hash it out. The two of you falling in love was the farthest thing from my mind." Dad looks up to the ceiling and runs his hand over his head again. "Though I can't say your mother and Sylvie have never considered the possibility."

"At least they never tried to push us together," I mutter. "Not like you and Greg." I wonder if it was a coordinated effort, Dad opting out of morning swims and Greg prodding Asher to fix things between us.

"I *am* sorry, Chipmunk."

I want to stay mad, but it's nearly impossible when my dad is looking at me like he feels absolutely horrible. What did he do wrong, really? I don't regret what happened out on the lake because of him. And as much as I want to, I can't wish away everything that came after it. I don't think I want to.

When I get back to my room, Ellie has music blasting out of her laptop, and there are two glasses and a few bottles sitting on her desk.

"Um, where'd you get that?" I pick up the orange bottle and smell it. Who knew something could smell sweet and also burn your nostrils at the same time?

"Corrie bought it for me. We're meeting up with everyone in an hour to celebrate." She points to my closet and then hands me a glass. "Get ready."

Aside from the juniors—like Corrie—and seniors, everyone on the team is underage. None of the upperclassmen are going to risk getting arrested—and kicked off of the team—for serving minors in their own apartments. And campus security turns a blind eye to anything in the dorms, but there are way too many of us to fit in anyone's room. So instead, we've all been drinking and getting dressed, and now we're converging in the middle of campus for my rite of passage as an Oakwood athlete. I stare at the silver contraption in front of me, and the giant pit of sand below it; this is where big moments are celebrated.

I've heard about this before—I've seen the photo of my mom doing it—but even when I threatened to break her record, I never fully believed it would happen, because I am 100 percent unprepared for this.

"It's tradition," Ellie says, pushing me toward the pit of sand. "Get on it already." She smacks my butt and I jump.

It's not that I'm scared—my head is a little too fuzzy to be scared—I'm just not sure how exactly I'm supposed to mount this . . . thing. In front of me hangs a giant silver ball. It's several feet across, and it dangles like a pendulum over a giant pit of sand. As it moves, the pointed tip below it cuts designs. Miley's song might have made this a hot spot for students, but the Oakwood sports teams made it a tradition way before Miley made wrecking balls cool.

"There's a sign," I say, nodding at the plaques every three feet around the rectangular pit of sand.

"Those don't apply to us," someone shouts from behind me. "We're here to celebrate." In what starts out softly and slowly grows louder, my name rolls off of my drunken teammates' lips in a constant cadence. *Sid-ney. Sid-ney. Sid-ney.*

I stand next to the ball and reach my hands up, but I can barely reach the top, let alone get enough leverage to pull myself up.

Ryan steps forward, lacing his fingers in front of him so I can step up. With a hand on his shoulders I propel myself up, grabbing onto the cord as Ryan continues to push my foot up. Once I'm standing, the ball wavers under me. I wrap one leg around the cord to steady myself, and prepare for what I know is about to happen.

Two more guys join Ryan, and with hands pressed against the silver ball they push forward through the sand. A little squeak escapes me as they step out of the way and I'm flying through the air. Music plays out from someone's phone and cheers erupt. I don't care about the signs anymore. This night is *so* close to perfect—just one person away from perfect, actually—and I could stay up here forever.

I ride the ball standing up, and sitting, and at one point Ellie jumps on with me, before dismounting because it makes her dizzy. I'm standing on the giant silver ball, one leg raised behind me like a ballerina, when a voice cuts through the air. "You could get arrested for that, you know." My foot wobbles a little when I realize whose voice it is. "Or fall and break something." I look to where our team is huddled to one side of me. His hands are shoved in his pockets. "Twist an ankle maybe."

"Maybe I shouldn't jump this time," I say.

Asher climbs over the fence until he's a foot away from the ball. "Jump."

I stare at him, at his arms stretched out for me.

"Do you trust me?"

I don't say anything, just let myself fall off of the giant silver ball, until I'm safely in his arms, my feet barely hitting the sand.

He looks at me like I just fell off of a ten-story building.

"You came."

"First record-break of the season." He smiles and looks at me conspiratorially. "Of course I came."

Maybe it's the way Ellie's drink is making my skin prickle and my head slowly detach from my shoulders like a balloon on a string, but instead of pulling away like I know I should, I wrap my arms around Asher. His body stiffens against me, and he doesn't move for a second, but then his hands rest on my back, and he's squeezing me. Suddenly, this night feels complete. And that's scary, because the one thing I can't guarantee in my life right now is Asher Marin.

73 DAYS AFTER

Asher

The cafeteria food is questionable sometimes. Like just now, I ate a "fried vegetable." As if they couldn't be bothered with identifying which vegetable it was when there are a million out there. Spoiler: it was a pickle. I nearly puked in the middle of the cafeteria, and it's possible that Ryan will never come here with me again. Is a pickle even a vegetable? Is it legal to vaguely label food like that?

On the table my phone buzzes, and my mom's face appears in the middle of the screen.

"Hi, sweetie. Could you do me a favor?"

I'm expecting her to tell me not to go to parties, or to remember to take my laundry out of the machines so no one steals my clothes, but she surprises me when she says, "Can you run up to the lake house?" She lets out a sigh. "There was a big storm last night. Dad's worried one of those limbs could have come down. The trees along the house are in rough shape. We should have had those limbs all cut at the end of the season." I didn't notice anything about the state of the trees this summer, but I wasn't exactly paying attention. I had other things on my mind. "Kris and Tom are out of town and you're closer than us."

"Sure, that's fine."

"Can you go tonight?"

"Tonight?" It's already eight o'clock. "I sort of had plans."

"Please?" Her voice is pleading. "It's only a few hours. You can be back in time to go out. You're all up until two a.m. anyway, right?" She laughs, but it sounds more nervous than amused. "Just take a quick look through all the rooms to make sure the roof didn't leak, and then you're free. I'll mail you a gas card."

"You don't have to do that."

"Okay. I love you."

"Love you, too."

By the time I leave the dorm it's almost nine thirty. I shove a change of clothes, protein bar, and a bottle of water from my mini fridge into my bag, in case I decide to spend the night. I hadn't thought about how close the lake house was to school— maybe I could take friends up there one weekend. Maybe some friends from the team. Would I invite Sidney? Would I have to? I wonder how weird it would be for her to know her teammates were hanging out at her house—*our* house—without her.

It's weird that we have this shared thing. It feels a little like we're a divorced couple, and the house is our kid. She was right about that—how awkward it would be going to the house if things went south between us. Except that she's the one that forced that situation into existence.

Driving to the lake in late fall feels so strange. The grass has lost its brightness, and the trees are all in their deep yellows and oranges, some of them with leaves already shed. It's like going to an entirely different place. All of the signs that usually mark the sidewalks with the announcement of fairs and festivals are gone. Downtown, half of the shops are closed for the season— the little wine tasting room and yogurt shop are dark. I'm not sure if I like seeing it like this. I wonder how different it will feel next summer, without Sidney.

When I pull into the driveway, the first thing I notice is that nothing has changed. There aren't even any leaves on the ground, let alone branches down. Now that I think of it, I didn't see signs of a storm anywhere as I drove here. I pull out my phone to text my mom.

> Asher: No sign of a storm. I think you got bad intel.

Mom: Really? While you're there, will you pop inside and grab a few things from the kitchen for me? I left some of my good baking dishes behind.

I get a list of four different dishes and kitchen utensils to re-trieve, and climb out of my car. Something about this lake is like a magnetic pull. It's always the first thing I have to see—before going into Lake House B, or checking to see where Sidney was, I always went to the dock. And today is no different. The day is cool and the lake is flat. All along the shoreline, docks are empty, the pontoons and fishing boats put away for the winter.

Down the dock, a pop of color against the faded gray boards catches my eye. Fifteen feet down, a cluster of three rocks sits. They're painted—with cresting blue waves, clusters of green ivy, and little purple flowers, like the rocks Sidney makes. Did she leave them down here? I consider leaving them, then scoop them up and take them with me to the house—they won't fare well out here in the snow. I set them on the kitchen table inside, not sure if I'm going to leave them, or take them with me. Show-ing up at her dorm with three random rocks might seem like a giant excuse to see her. And while I wouldn't mind that, I'm also not sure I'm ready to dive headfirst into full-blown friend-ship with Sidney. I thought I could—that maybe, with time, I could look at her differently. But after the way she looked at me at the wrecking ball, I'm not sure my heart can handle it. It's bad enough that eventually I'm going to have to see her at parties, and eventually I'm sure with other guys. I wish I was a better person—the kind of person who could be happy for her happiness. Maybe I will be, someday, but I'm not there yet.

I'm pulling Mom's red baking dish out of a cupboard when I notice another pop of color. At the edge of the kitchen, there's a rock painted with a cluster of little white flowers and a few feet to the right, there's another, leading into the hallway. I pick them up, and see another partway down the hall, just outside of the laundry room. And another, just outside of Sidney's bedroom. The door is open, and inside there are three more rocks in a triangle. If they were breadcrumbs—which is what they feel like—they'd be leading me to the bathroom. That door is closed, but not latched, and when I nudge it open with my toe, I half-expect something to jump out at me. Or to be hit by something. At the very least, I expect something to spray all over me. But the door swings open harmlessly, and the room is empty. No shaving cream covering the floor. Not a single menacing thing. Except that on the mirror, in slashes of red, there are four words:

MEET ME AT MIDNIGHT

I can't decide if it's better or worse than finding the bathroom filled with bees as I'm doused in lemonade. It just feels like two different kinds of torture. So I get into my car, leaving the pile of rocks on Sidney's bed, and I drive back to school.

Sidney

This was a really horrible idea. Maybe one of my worst. Because unlike all of my pranks of the past, I have no control over this. Asher deciding not to show up means it's over. There is no backup plan for him ignoring me. And to add insult to injury, I had to get Sylvie involved to make this happen. Had to tell her the whole sad tale to convince her to lure him up here, even though I knew she had heard at least some of it. And for what?

Now everyone knows all of the sordid details of how I ruined everything. It's bad enough that my mom will probably harass me for the rest of my life—for the next five years at least; probably every time I bring a guy home. *Will I bring guys home?* I think maybe I'm ruined for that. Going back to ten-day relationships doesn't sound that bad. There's three-hundred-sixty-five days in a year, divided by ten—but probably add a three-week buffer between them . . . I'm thinking through how many guys have to be interested in my sarcastic mouth when I hear the footsteps clunking along the dock.

"What's up, Sidney?" The fact that he's here should fill me with hope, but I hate how resigned Asher's voice sounds right now.

"How far did you make it before you turned around?" He's late, which means he wasn't going to come, but he did. And deep down, I know it's because he's too nice to leave a girl sitting alone on a dock at midnight. And that should send a bucket of ice water over my plans, but it doesn't. It's just another reminder of what a good person he is. And how much better I have to be, to even begin to be worthy of spending time with him.

"I drove all the way back to the dorms." He sits down on the dock next to me, huddling his knees up to his chest like I am. It's way too cold to be in the water. "I barely had enough time to make it back here. You lurking again? Tracking my car?"

"No, I just know you." He said it to me once, told me all of the ways he knew me, and I wish everything after those texts had gone differently.

"Hm."

"You know, I've had a lot of time to think since I've been at school." My voice is soft, not nearly as confident as I wish it was. I sound scared. I *am* scared. "I'm still settling in with girls on the team, and getting to know people in my dorm and in my classes. You make friends everywhere you go, but—"

"But you're lonely, and now you want to talk to me?"

I shake my head. "No, it's not that. I mean, yes, I do want to talk to you." God, this is already going badly. And I'm so nervous I'm just rambling. "I'm just saying . . . I've had a lot of time to think the last month or so." I let go of my knees and sit cross-legged on the dock, twisting to face Asher. "I've had a lot of time to think about all of the reasons I knew we wouldn't work, and—"

Asher drops his chin to his hands. "And you've got me out here in the middle of the night . . . *freezing* . . . so you can re-mind me of all of those reasons? Sidney, this isn't—"

I put my hand on his next to me, and he looks up, as if I've electrocuted him. "Just let me finish?" I keep my voice soft and I don't move my hand. "I'm not here to torture you. I swear."

Asher bites his lip and nods.

I don't want to move my hand, but I do, because I'm not sure I can think straight while I'm touching him. Not when his eyes are still burning with something I haven't seen in a long time. "You liked me for so long . . . you showed me." I swallow down the anxiety rising up in my throat, threatening to choke me. "You showed me the rocks, and the picture, and you told me everything. So . . ." I pick up the little box tucked in next to my side. "I've never dated anyone longer than ten days. I've never liked anyone longer than that. And it's always me, not them. Me who gets bored, or annoyed, for the dumbest reasons. I screw it up every time. I've always been good at a lot of things, but I'm not good at this. You thought it was you I didn't trust, but that's not it at all. It's me. *I'm* the one who would ruin us."

"You already did that." His voice is hard but it doesn't feel mean. Maybe because it's so quiet it's practically a whisper.

"I know." I rest my hands on the box in my lap and look out at the water. "I hate failing. And with you, it always seemed safer to just not try. What if you didn't like me the way I liked you? What if I screwed everything up? What if you realized after ten days that you didn't want me?" I look up at the sky and then to him. "I think we were always doomed."

He shakes his head angrily and I charge forward, my voice in a panic. "Because I was never all in." My voice is frantic, like I'm racing something. I think I am. "I give a hundred and ten percent to everything I do, and with you, I just gave up." Asher turns his face toward me, and it's hard to keep going but I do. "You, Asher Marin, are scarier than swinging on a giant wrecking ball of doom, or cracking my head open on the bottom of a pool. And I was so scared of losing you, that I lost you anyway." His eyes are locked with mine, and I can't remember what I was saying. I look back toward the lake to try to clear my head.

"What's in the box?"

I had forgotten the box was on my lap, clasped between my hands now. The lid slides off with a breathy sucking sound, and I place it on the dock between us. "You showed me how much you liked me." I turn to look at him, just for a second. "And now I'm going to show you."

I take a piece of plastic out of the box and hold it up between two fingers. It glows bright in the darkness. "From my ceiling that first summer."

"Your crab."

I nod, and Asher holds his hand out. He smooths a thumb over the glowing surface.

"Your *meet me at midnight* note." I pull the bright white paper out of the box and wave it in the air. "And this is *my* contraband picture of us." I pull it out of the box and hand it to Asher. "Your mom sent it to me."

"Hm." Asher lets out a pleased grunt. It's the same photo he had tacked to his wall.

"Mine was in my locker," I say, my voice a little embarrassed.

I pull out the weathered paperback of Asher's favorite book from a few summers ago. "I've read this four times."

Asher takes it from my hand. "Did you love it?"

"I hated it. But you loved it—you were obsessed with it—and I wanted to know why." I pluck the book out of Asher's hands and put it back in the box.

I pull a concert stub from the box. "I went to a Greta Van Fleet concert last fall." Asher's hands are clenching either side of the dock, so I don't hand it to him, I just let it flutter back into the box. "I told myself I was going because you played that stupid song so many times that it ruined my brain, but I think maybe I hoped you'd be there. That I could see you out in the world, being normal. Not like you are with me—the way you are with your friends."

There are other things in the box but I can't bring myself to pull anything else out. Asher is quiet and motionless beside me, his face still hard. And I think the only thing I've accomplished with my *box of Asher* is to make myself look a tiny bit psychotic.

"What is all this?" Asher's voice is cautious when it finally breaks through the cold silence.

"This"—*How do I even explain this to him?*—"this is proof. Proof to myself, that I had hope at one point. Hope that the second summer, or third, or fourth, I'd finally work up the courage to do something." That lump is back in my throat. "I was braver when I was fourteen, I guess."

Asher looks at me, and his face is unreadable. "You scare me, too."

"I'm still scared. But I've seen the worst-case scenario now, and . . . I'm ready to give a hundred and ten percent. I'm ready for morning swims, and twice-a-day training, and whatever lists and spreadsheets and goal planners it takes to make this work."

"Spreadsheets, huh?" There's amusement in Asher's voice. I really do suck at the romantic stuff.

"Metaphorical spreadsheets," I clarify. "I told you, you're the romantic marshmallow one." I raise my eyebrows at him and muster up a nervous smile.

His hands are still resting on top of his knees, and I put one of mine on top of his. "I like who I am with you. I like who we are *together*. And I'm not scared anymore, because there's nothing worse than this."

Asher

"How long have you been planning this?" When I smile at her, I can see the anxiety drain out of her face. "The rocks, and scamming my mom into getting me here . . . this is the ultimate anti-prank. How many checklists did this take you?"

She scowls at me, but it's the good kind. The kind that tells me she still thinks I'm funny. "One."

We sit in silence, and it's freezing, but I'm afraid to move. If this is all some sort of weird cafeteria-food-induced dream, then I'm not ready for it to be over.

"Hey, Sidney?"

"Yeah?"

"I really *really* don't hate you."

"No?" She leans into me, presses her lips to mine, and pulls away far too quickly. "That's good, because I'm pretty sure I'm in love with you."

Sidney

There are at least five seconds of silence after I say it, and I'm half committed to plunging myself into the icy lake and waiting for unconsciousness, when Asher turns his head to me.

"Finally." The smile he gives me feels like it could stop wars. Maybe it has. "I was running out of pranks. That's the real reason I had to call the truce."

"No more pranks." Even as I say it, I'm not sure if it's true. "Well, only the good kind."

"No Kool-Aid showers?"

"And no lemonade bedsheets." I smile, remembering one of my favorite pranks of all time.

"That's one of the few times I was actually pissed at you. No pun intended. But that was truly twisted."

I smile. "Yeah, but you love how twisted I am."

"I think it's more like I love *you*, and you just happen to be twisted."

I lay my hand in the space between us on the dock. "Cease-fire?"

Asher laces his fingers through mine, and twists toward me, his face so close I know he's going to kiss me. So close I can feel his warm breath on my cheek when he says, "Truce."

EPILOGUE

THE NEXT SUMMER

Sidney

"How much do you hate me right now?"

Asher shakes his head against the blanket, and I don't have to see his face to know he's annoyed. He hates when I ask him that, when I tease him about how horrible we used to be to each other. I poke him in the side with my elbow and then prop myself up on it so I can look at him. He's wearing an OAKWOOD SWIMMING T-shirt and his pajama pants. Even in the middle of summer it's a little chilly at 4 a.m., so the blanket laid out under us also wraps up around our legs. Overhead, the Perseids rain down in tiny bursts of light. This is the most we've ever seen, the latest we've ever been out. It's the peak of the shower and our last count was one hundred and four. Of course, we can never know if we're seeing the same meteor at the same time, so we won't be turning our numbers in to NASA or anything.

"Okay, how much do you like me right now?"

He raises his eyebrows at me and I know what he wants.

I smile, and lean down to his ear, resting my face there when I do. "How much do you *love* me right now?" I don't mean for it to be a whisper, but out in the dark it's hard to do anything but.

He looks at me and smiles. "It's hard to quantify."

"Try."

He turns his face from the sky to me. "More than all of the stars . . ." His lips touch mine, gently and quickly; it's not our first kiss or our hundredth, and it's certainly not our last. "And then some."

ACKNOWLEDGMENTS

This book wouldn't have been possible without the last twenty-some years I spent vacationing on a beautiful lake in Northern Michigan. And for that, I owe my parents a heartfelt thank-you, for giving me so many wonderful summer memories to pull this story from.

A huge thank-you to everyone on my publishing team who has championed not only this book, but my last two as well: my amazing agent, Michelle Wolfson; my awesome editor, Melissa Frain; my cover designer, Daniela Medina; Saraciea Fennell; and the whole team at Tor Teen.

To all of the readers who picked up *Love Songs & Other Lies* or *When Summer Ends* and have come back for more, thank you! Your support means everything. Thank you for giving me space on your bookshelves, saying hello at events, and recommending my books to others. I love hearing from readers, so please don't hesitate to reach out on social media or via my website at jesspennington.com.

Last, but far from least, I'd like to thank all of the bloggers, bookstagrammers, librarians, and voracious readers who have helped me spread the word about *Love Songs & Other Lies* and *When Summer Ends* and have continued to support me with

Meet Me at Midnight. Writing is such a solitary act much of the time, and promoting a book can make you feel a little bit like a one-woman army, but having an amazing group of supporters behind me has truly made this whole experience amazing. Thank you all for using your passion (and free time!) to promote books, including mine. I could never list all of you, but if you've ever blogged about one of my books, posted a gorgeous photo on Instagram, recommended it to a reader at your library, told a friend about it, or tweeted a promo, then THANK YOU! And an extra-special shout-out and virtual hug to all of the amazing bookish folks on my street team:

Belle Ellrich at Belle's Archive, JoAnne Wills at Mahkichi's Not-So-Secret Books, Kayla at Kayla Reads and Reviews, Felicia Mathews at Bookishly Slytherclaw, Melissa Gums at Melandherbooks, Sophie at The Mind of a Book Dragon, Olivia Whetstone at The Candid Cover, Andi at Andi's ABCs, Linda Harr, Melanie Parker @meltotheany, Sarah Longhurst at The Clever Reader, Kristi Housman at Confessions of a YA Reader, Christy Jane and Kelly at BookCrushin, Katherine Paschal at Smada's Book Smack, Lauren Bodiford at Lala's Book Reviews, Auburn at What She Will Read, and Nicole Hoefs at Boundless Bookaholic.

Jordan Bishop at The Heart of a Book Blogger, Melanie at TBR and Beyond, Theresa Snyder, Jaime Arkin at Fiction Fare, Astrid Pizarro at Book Lover's Book Reviews, Victoria at Latte Nights Review, Venessa @reading_past_bedtime, Jill Hart at Radiant Lit, Courtney Kurhayez at Buried In A Bookshelf, Mina at My Fangirl Chronicles, Mir at TBR and Beyond, Justin Turczak at A Court of Coffee and Books, Liv at Liv's Wonderful Escape, Heather Currie, Hallie @bookloaner, Karlita at Tale Out Loud, Laura at librarianlaura.com, and Kathleen P. at Travel, Books, and More . . . Oh MY! You all are amazing!